FIRE OVER ENGLAND

THE NOVELS OF
A. E. W. MASON

They Wouldn't be Chessmen
The Sapphire
The Three Gentlemen
The Dean's Elbow
The Prisoner in the Opal
No Other Tiger
The Broken Road
The Four Feathers
Miranda of the Balcony
Clementina
The Turnstile
The Truants
At the Villa Rose
Running Water
The Courtship of Morrice Buckler
The Philanderers
Lawrence Clavering
The Watchers
A Romance of Wastdale
The Witness for the Defence
The House of the Arrow
The Winding Stair

SHORT STORIES

Ensign Knightley and other Tales
The Four Corners of the World
Dilemmas

FIRE OVER ENGLAND

BY
A. E. W. MASON

LONDON
HODDER & STOUGHTON LIMITED

First Printed	-	-	June,	1936
Reprinted	-	-	July,	1936
Reprinted	-	-	July,	1936
Reprinted	-	-	October,	1936
Reprinted	-	-	November,	1936
Reprinted	-	-	December,	1936
Reprinted	-	-	March,	1937
Reprinted	-	-	August,	1937

*Made and Printed in Great Britain for Hodder & Stoughton Limited
by Wyman & Sons Limited, London, Reading and Fakenham*

CONTENTS

CHAPTER   PAGE

		PAGE
	PREFACE	7
I.	A KNOT OF RIBBONS FOR ROBIN AUBREY	9
II.	THE REHEARSAL	20
III.	THE SECRET VISITOR	33
IV.	THE SIGNET RING	49
V.	NOT FORESEEN IN THE PLAN	56
VI.	ROBIN DINES IN STRANGE COMPANY	71
VII.	METAMORPHOSIS OF CAPTAIN FORTESCUE	82
VIII.	THE BETTER PLAN	94
IX.	THE WINGED MERCURY	103
X.	THE GALLOWS' MARK	113
XI.	THE RENUNCIATION	120
XII.	ROBIN TAKES SERVICE	132
XIII.	THE KNOT OF RIBBON AGAIN AND A SUPPER AT BARN ELMS	139
XIV.	MASTER AND MAN	154
XV.	GUISEPPE THE VALET	161
XVI.	DANGEROUS MOMENTS	167
XVII.	DEATH OF SANTA CRUZ	177
XVIII.	MEANWHILE	183
XIX.	A BRIDPORT DAGGER	189
XX.	PLOTS AND CONSPIRACIES	202
XXI.	ON THE EDGE OF THE GRASS	212
XXII.	THE DEVICE OF THE ITALIAN SINGERS	220
XXIII.	A VAIN PURSUIT	231

CONTENTS

CHAPTER		PAGE
XXIV.	IN THE GARDEN AT ABBOT'S GAP	237
XXV.	GREGORY BECOMES NOTICEABLE	250
XXVI.	AT THE ESCORIAL	256
XXVII.	THE BEGGAR ON THE CHURCH STEPS	264
XXVIII.	GEORGE AUBREY	271
XXIX.	OLD TRICKS AND GOOD TRICKS	283
XXX.	ANTHONY SCARR	293
XXXI.	ROBIN PAYS HIS FARE	303
XXXII.	THURSDAY	311

In his " Life of Napoleon " Monsieur Bainville wrote :
" Each generation believes that the world began with
it, and yet whoever broods over the past sees that
many things were much as they are to-day."

This is particularly true of the Elizabethan age.
The differences between then and now are in the main
superficial—differences of dress, of entertainments, of
transport, of government, of machinery. But in the
deeper circumstances of character and opinion, and
the conduct which springs from them, these two
turbulent epochs have much in common which they
manifest in the same way. Youth takes to the new
element of the air in the same eager and adventurous
spirit in which it then took to the new element of the
sea. Fear of the introduction of papistical practices
rouses Protestant England to the same fervour of
refusal as it did then. The same passion for peace is
accompanied by the same quiet and staunch belief
that if war must come the nation cannot be beaten.
There is the same reluctance to meddle with the entanglements of the Continent. And the freedom of
the Low Countries is still the chief principle of foreign
policy.

Even in minor matters the resemblance stands.
The swift and wide expansion of Walsingham's secret
service and its swift contraction when the need was
past find a parallel in the history of our late war.
At so many other points, such as the love of sport,
the revival of music, and the friendly country life,

the two ages touch so closely that in writing this book I seemed to be writing a book of our own times ; and so have been led to break the reticence of a lifetime and begin it with a preface.

A preface, however, gives me the opportunity of acknowledging a special debt to Mr. Conyers Read for his " Mr. Secretary Walsingham," and to Professor J. E. Neale for his enthralling " Queen Elizabeth."

A. E. W. MASON.

March 16*th,* 1936.

CHAPTER I

A KNOT OF RIBBONS FOR ROBIN AUBREY

THROUGH two drowsy hours of a golden afternoon
the scholars of the Foundation droned their
Latin odes in the Lower School; and the Queen's
Grace sat upright in her high chair and listened. The
door stood open to the disturbing invitations of
summer, an oblong of sunlight on the dark floor, the
clear notes of birds, a rustle of wind in the trees, the
distant cries of labourers in the fields, the scent of
hay. But the Queen had neither eye nor ear for them.
She sat with her great farthingale spread about her,
her bodice of blue and silver with the open throat and
the high collar at the back, all slashed and puffed and
sewn with pearls the size of beans; and she bore with
schoolboys' Alcaics and Sapphics and Dicolons and
Distrophons and Monocolons as though July were her
favourite month for such diversions. A dragon-fly buzzed
into the long room, a noisy, angry flash of green and
gold beat fiercely against the walls and was gone again.

The Queen never so much as turned her head.
This was the year 1581, and Elizabeth's third visit to
the school at Eton, and the Odes to do her honour
were her appointed occupation for the day. So she
gave her whole mind to it. Also she enjoyed it;
which is more than can be said for her Court behind
her, with the exception perhaps of her secretary, Sir
Francis Walsingham, who had a passion for learning.
At one moment the voice of a boy cracked as he

recited his piece and ran up into a squeak. The
Queen caught the eye of another boy in the second
row, and exchanged the glimmer of a smile with him
and so made him her slave for life. This was the last
of the recitations, and when it was finished the Provost
stepped forward in his scarlet gown. He made a little
speech, he, too, using his best Latin, and presented
Her Grace with a printed copy of the odes bound in
covers with ornaments of scarlet and gold. Elizabeth
raised her hand to take the book and her arm caught
upon the carving of her chair. A knot of silk ribbon
with a gold button in the middle of it was half torn
from her sleeve and hung dangling. Anywhere else
she would have sworn a good round trooper's oath,
but to-day she was in her most gracious mood, and
seeing the look of agony on the Provost's face, she
burst out laughing.

" Nay, good Doctor, you shall keep that look for
my funeral. If I leave a bow behind me, you have
twenty-five pretty scholars here who will string it for
me at my need."

Readiness is the better half of wit, and the little
quip served its turn. A full-throated yell of applause
rewarded her. She rose to her feet with the book
still in her hands and addressed the school.

" There was a day when I could have bartered verses
with you and perhaps not had the worst of it. But
the business of Government has so rusted my Latin
and abolished my Greek that you can have nothing
but my mother-tongue from me. Ah, if only I had the
leisure I once enjoyed ! " And she closed her eyes
and fondled the book and sighed.

There had been an occasion when Philip's Ambassador had complained to her that she had stolen all
the wages of his master's troops on their way up the
Channel. She had sighed disconsolately then and

answered that if only she could sit in a nun's cell and tell her beads quietly for the rest of her days she would be happy. The Ambassador had been neither impressed nor amused. He had written off angrily to his master that she was a woman possessed of a hundred thousand devils. However, she had an easier audience in the scholars of Eton. They believed in her yearning for the simple life. Little murmurs of sympathy broke out. Not one but would have given years to ease the load of Government from her shoulders.

"But you will forgive me my lack of scholarship," she continued, "if I ask in plain English for a holiday for you to commemorate the day." And as the cheers burst out again she turned to Dr. Thomas, the school's master, who could do nothing but bow his consent.

"I thought that would commend me to your hearts," she added dryly, and indeed holidays were shining rarities in those days at Eton. "Yet with no less warmth take this old saying of Demosthenes to your bosoms. 'The words of scholars are the books of the unlearned.' So persist in your studies for the good of those less fortunate than you."

And so, having delivered her little necessary tag of erudition, she handed the book to a Maid of Honour and stepped down from her dais.

In the court outside the school a very different scene greeted her eyes. Gone were the frieze gowns and sober habiliments of the scholars. Her coaches, her lackeys, her red halberdiers waited, and slanting outwards from the door like the spokes of a painted wheel, the Oppidans were ranged to speed her on her going. They had no place that day in the Lower School. It was only by a breach in the old charter that they got their education there at all. They lived in appointed houses in the village under the tutelage of dames or hostesses as they were called then. Now, with their private tutors amongst them, they stood gracious in their youth and eagerness and glowing in silks and velvets and the bravery of their best attire. Elizabeth's eyes shone and her heart quickened as she looked at them—the buds, lusty and colourful, on that tree of England whose growth she had tended with such jealous care for three-and-twenty years. It is true that she pruned a bough here and there with a sharp axe when she needs must, but for the most part she watched that it grew, its bark untapped, spaciously and freely and turbulently to its own shape. All the scraping and paring that her people might not be taxed, all her long vigils with her statesmen, all the delicate, perilous corantos she trod, now with the Emperor, now with the Valois in Paris, now with Philip in Madrid—here in the sunlit yard were proved to her well worth the while even if she had not enjoyed every minute of them. These lads, tall and sturdy with the shining eyes, as she was their glory, were her prop and her pride.

She looked along the row to her right, and a movement stayed her eyes. A tutor was thrusting one boy forward into the front of the line and dragging another boy back out of it.

" Stand you back, Robin, behind me," he said in an impatient whisper, which reached the Queen's ears. " And you, Humphrey, in your proper place in front."

A favourite pupil was being set where he might catch the Queen's eye if he was fortunate, and that favourite pupil was smiling contentedly with little doubt that he would be so favoured.

The other lad, Robin, fell back without a struggle and without a sign of resentment. He was used to the second place, but not because he was stupid or dull or inferior or the worse looking of the two. A single glance at his face proved that. But for him humiliation would have lain in making a to-do over an affair so small. He fell back, eager to see rather than to be seen. The great Queen who held their hearts in her hand was to pass them by on her way to her coach. To watch her as she went was contentment enough, and he watched with shining eyes and parted lips, a goddess rather than a woman.

But a woman she was, and very much of a woman. She had no taste for busy and officious people who must be giving orders when they should be standing modestly in their places. A grim little smile tightened her mouth. She would put that forward tutor in his place. Moreover, she liked beauty and straight limbs and the clean look of race ; and all those qualities were plain to see in the young Oppidan now forced back and half hidden behind the tutor. She turned to the master with a smile.

" Call me out that young dorado, good master," she said.

Her voice in ordinary talk was thin, but it reached across the yard to the tutor, and that unhappy man rushed upon his undoing.

" It's you, Humphrey, whom Her Grace calls," he said, pushing his favourite forward from the line. " Be quick ! It's you," he urged excitedly, and the Queen's voice rang out, strong now, and alarming, whilst her black eyes widened and hardened till the tutor drooped his head and quailed before them.

" No, it is not ! " she cried. " What ! You will hold out against me, will you ? And expound my meaning to me like a lawyer ? Know, Mr. Ferret——"
She had a pretty gift for nicknames, and she could have invented none apter than this one. The tutor was a thin, long creature, with small, twinkling, reddish eyes and a little nibbling mouth ridiculous in a man ; and what with a steep sloping forehead and a sharp receding

chin, his face seemed to be drawn to a point at the end of a long nose. " Mr. Ferret "—Elizabeth repeated the name with relish, and a ripple of laughter ran along the ranks of the boys. Even the Provost and the Master smiled. The tutor's face was bent towards the ground, so that no one could see the malignant fury which swept across it. But he was never to forgive her the phrase, and never to forgive one at all events of those boys for the gust of joyous laughter which welcomed it.

—" Know, Mr. Ferret, that in this realm it's I who say which one shall stand forward and which one stand behind. God's wounds, Dr. Provost, there are tutors at Eton who need a stiffer schooling than your pupils, and let Mr. Ferret see to it that I don't take the cane in hand myself."

She could play tricks like a tomboy on her courtiers, she could exchange a jest with any peasant in the fields, but she could be right King Harry when she chose, and she chose now. The tutor cringed before her. His mortification was drowned in a wave of fear. She was terrifying, and there was no one to gainsay her. The sweat gathered upon his forehead ; his knees shook. She had made a public fool of him. She could set him in the stocks like a rogue if she would.

But she was content with the lesson she had given him. She looked again towards the master.

" Call me out that brown lad."

" Robin Aubrey," cried the Master, and the ranks parted and Mr. Ferret, with a gasp of relief, stood aside. But he kept his head still lowered, lest his eyes might be seen even in their fear to hold a threat.

Robin Aubrey himself was hardly in a happier state. A boy of fourteen years, he was made up of one clear purpose and great dreams, and at the heart of those dreams the great Queen was enshrined. Now she had chosen him amongst his companions. She had called him out from them. He would never be able to cross that patch of sunlit ground to her, he felt sure. His heart so clamoured within his breast that he would stifle before he had gone half the way. His tears so blinded him that he would never see her. The most that he could hope for was that he would swoon and die at her feet. Yet by some magic—how he could never explain—he was there on his knees before her. He dared not lift his eyes to her face, but he felt her slim hand upon his shoulder and heard her voice— oh, miracle! just a woman's voice, but very warm and friendly, in his ears.

"Robin Aubrey," she said slowly, relishing the English sound of the name.

"Of Abbot's Gap in the County of Dorset."

Was it really his voice he heard so clear and steady? Someone started as he spoke, a pale, black-bearded, sickly man who stood a couple of paces behind the Queen and at one side.

"What!" she cried gaily. "My good Moor knows you. Were you his page at the Court of the Emperor?"

Her good Moor was her principal secretary, Sir Francis Walsingham; he was more fortunate in his nickname than Sir Christopher Hatton, her Vice-Chamberlain, who was her "mutton," but he did not relish it overmuch. He smiled without any amusement.

"Your Majesty, Mr. Aubrey's father was my friend," he said sedately, and Robin knew who he was.

"Robin Aubrey," Elizabeth repeated. "Mere English, then!"

"And on my knees to England."

Had Robin sat up of nights for a twelvemonth

conning phrases he could have lit upon none which could so delight his Queen as this one spoken in an honest burst of passion. That she was mere English was her pride, and no doubt she owed something of the witch-craft with which she drew so many hearts to her kinship with her people, her liking for their sports, her share in their homely humour.

" These lads, Sir Francis," she said with a sigh of pleasure. " And how old are you, boy Robin ? "

" Fourteen, your Majesty," and then in a hurry : " But I shall be fifteen next month."

" God bless my soul, a man ! " cried she. " And whither go you from Eton ? "

" To Oxford."

Perhaps Elizabeth had had enough of scholarship for one day. Perhaps she saw in Robin a page who would set off her Presence-Chamber pleasantly. He was of the make she liked. Brown waving hair, a white, broad forehead, brown eyes set wide apart, the nostrils fine, the chin firm, the hands and feet long and slim—lady-faced a little, perhaps, but without weakness ; one who had lived amongst dreams, but with spirit and strength enough to make of his dreams a living truth. Something of the dandy, too, in his fine doublet and breeches of cloth of gold, his long stockings of white silk, his cloak of deep blue velvet slung from his shoulders and the flat scarlet cap which he held in his hand. Certainly, as Elizabeth looked down at him, she thought he would make a shapely figure at Whitehall.

" Oxford ! " she said with a little grimace. " To put your eyes out with a book."

" Nay, your Majesty, I shall hope to keep my eye in with a sword and use it in the Queen's service."

" No doubt," she returned dryly. " You'll conquer a world and hand it as a Christmas present to a poor woman who wants nothing but to live in peace and amity with her neighbours. You would do better after all to write me an ode bidding me marry and have a mort of children, like the scholars in the Hall."

" Your Grace," and Robin threw back his head as he knelt and cried, " were I a grown man and a great prince besides, I would have written one already which would have outscholared all the scholars."

Again he marvelled. Was this he, Robin Aubrey, exchanging pleasantries with so bold a face and so free and joyous a voice and exchanging them with the world's wonder and paragon ! And they came to his lips unrehearsed ! He was in that tense mood which duplicates a person so that one self acts and speaks, whilst the other stands at his side, notes each gesture and word and accent and criticises or approves. How would Her Grace take his audacity ? Would she give him a taste of Mr. Ferret ? He held his breath. Her Grace laughed roundly and patted his shoulder.

" A courtier ! " she cried, well pleased. " Monsieur D'Alençon has a rival and must look to himself," and as her hand fondled his shoulder that plaguey knot of ribbon dangling on her sleeve caught her eye. Well, she had made many of the incommodities of life serve her turn in the great matters, now she would use one of them in the small. She snatched the knot quite off her sleeve.

" Boy Robin, if you tire of Oxford and your sword-play there, you shall bring this knot to me at Whitehall, and poor though I am, I shall make shift to find a place for you."

Robin took the knot reverently and kissed the hand which gave it to him.

" Up with you, lad, for on my troth your knees must be growing sore with these pebbles for their cushion, and wait upon me to my coach."

B

She took her leave of the Provost and the Master and mounted into her great litter, with her ladies in attendance. " God bless you, boy Robin," she cried, waving her hand to the lad, and so drove off between cheering throngs up the hill to Windsor Castle. There she spoke a shrewd word or two to her Moor about him, and straightway forgot him for many a day. But she left a boy behind her with his brain in a whirl—and a shameful recognition that the purpose to which his life was dedicated had suddenly grown unsubstantial as a shadow.

Elizabeth was forty-seven years old in this year of 1581, and though she had lived through perils and anxieties intricate enough to age an archangel, she had retained a superb look of youth and strength. She had run neither to angles nor to fat. She was majestical and homely ; a great Prince with her sex at her fingers' ends ; she was more English than she knew. For she was English of our day—English in her distaste for cruelty, English in her inability to nourish rancour against old enemies, English in her creed that poverty needed more than the empty help of kindly words. Enemies enough she had, even amongst those who most pretended their loyalty. But to the honest youth of her times she was the nonpareil. It is no wonder that Robin's thoughts were drawn after her as by a magnet. Service to her would be a song upon the lips ; death for her would be a golden door.

" What said she ? "

" What did you answer ? "

" You'll be for the Court to-morrow."

" Aye, and for the Tower the day after."

Robin found himself the centre of a group of his companions. Questions rained upon him, questions friendly and questions envious. Robin dusted his knees and clapped his scarlet hat on the top of his thick brown hair.

"We had some private talk," he said, with a magnificent indifference, and laughed as he spoke. But he looked about him eagerly and his laughter stopped and a shadow dimmed the brightness of his face.

"Where's Humphrey?" he asked.

But Humphrey Bannet and the Ferret, otherwise Mr. Charles Stafford, of Jesus College, Cambridge, had crept away to their house at the end of the village.

Robin was a little disturbed. Because of him, his friend had been put to a stinging humiliation and in the face of the school.

"I shall have to make my peace with Humphrey at supper," he reflected, and he added ruefully, "though with Mr. Stafford at his elbow, it will not be easy."

Meanwhile he had a little battle to fight with himself. Little perhaps, but still more serious than he had ever imagined that such a tussle could be until this afternoon. However, there it was upon him. It had got to be met, fought through, won and finished with, before he took his place at the supper-table to-night.

CHAPTER II

THE REHEARSAL

HUMPHREY was the only son of the widowed Sir Robert Bannet who lived in great state and magnificence at his big house of Hilbury Melcombe midway between Dorchester and Wareham and a little to the north of both of those towns. He was of an old Catholic family, but in these years suffered little disability on that account. More difficult times were to come. But the wise woman who sat upon the throne of England, looking over Europe torn with wars, was determined that in her realm, at all events, religion should not be the dividing line of politics.

Robin's house of Abbot's Gap was less than twenty miles away from Hilbury Melcombe, and though he was brought up in the Protestant faith, it seemed well to his uncle and guardian who was busy with his own affairs at the western end of the county, as it did to Sir Robert Bannet, that the two boys should share the same tutor at Eton. The tutor however was Mr. Charles Stafford, who was Sir Robert Bannet's secretary. He was chosen by Sir Robert, and the good, easy uncle at the other end of the county acquiesced in the choice, since it saved him a deal of trouble.

The three of them occupied the last house in the long, single street of Eton. It was commodious enough to provide a study and a bedroom apiece, accommodation for their servants and a common room for their meals and recreations.

On this evening Robin slipped quietly into his study and sat down in his window-seat above the meadows to fight his battle out. He had made plans, sacred plans, and had never thought for a moment that he could dream of forswearing them. But he had never dreamed that this glittering temptation of the Queen's favour would be dangled before his eyes as it had been this afternoon. He despised himself, but he was honest. He was tempted. The fame of Elizabeth's Court was high and splendid. There was none like it for gaiety and colour, for amusement and opportunity. It was presided over by a lady, herself of high spirits and gaiety. By a scratch of her pen she dispensed power and wealth. There was the dark side of course to that shining mirror, but how should a boy let it frighten him ? A page at the Queen's Court ! Robin drew up his knees to his chin on the window-seat and clasping his hands about them with a little wriggle of pleasure, saw the world opening like the dawn. There would be the months of progress during the summer, the tournaments, the great houses ringing with laughter.

" I could spare a few years," he argued. " In any case, I must wait till I'm a man."

But when he was a grown man, perhaps with a pleasant, profitable office, wouldn't he put off year after year the thing he had sworn to do ? Wouldn't he gradually cease to feel the shame of a man forsworn, covering it all up under the fat of his indolence ? Until middle-age came and the chance was gone. He saw himself suddenly as in a distorting glass, mean, a fugitive from himself, despicable, and not knowing it.

" No ! " he cried, and he got to his feet ; and, having washed himself vigorously as though with that

clean water he washed the foulness of his thoughts
away, he went in to the common room very late for
his supper. He found Mr. Stafford and Humphrey
nearly at the end of theirs.

"I beg your pardon, sir," he said, with a bow to
Mr. Stafford, "I wasn't noticing the time."

Mr. Stafford raised a protesting hand.

"Not a word, I pray you! Humble people like
Humphrey and myself must not be so foolish as to
expect good manners from a Queen's favourite. It is
condescension enough if he takes his supper with us
at all."

Robin did not answer. He had indeed a sense of
guilt rather than of triumph. He had always taken
the second place without troubling his head about it.
Sir Robert Bannet, of Hilbury Castle, was a much
more important figure in the County of Dorset than
fourteen-year-old Robin Aubrey. Mr. Stafford, too,
was a dependent of that house. It was in the natural
order that Mr. Stafford should set Humphrey forward
and thrust Robin back, and for the humiliating
consequences both to Humphrey and the tutor, Robin
was inclined to reproach himself. He looked un-
happily across the table at Humphrey, a black-haired
lad of Robin's own height, handsome enough in his
doublet of grey velvet, but with such a scowl upon
his face as took all his good looks away. Robin tried
again to make easier a difficult moment.

"I am very sorry," he said. "Not sorry for what
happened to me. There's no boy in the world but
would give a year of his life for so gracious a favour,
but I wish with all my heart that it had happened
without "—and he searched for a phrase which would
not reopen wounds—" causing either of you pain."

Humphrey Bannet worked his shoulders angrily.

"Let's not talk of it," he rapped out, and there the

debate might have ended but for Mr. Stafford. He
could not let a resentment die. He must worry a
grievance until it was once more raw. Smiling and
suave as velvet he interrupted :

"No, but, my dear Humphrey, we must talk of it.
This is Robin's day. Very likely he will never know
such another. It will be his annus Domini. He will
reform his calendar to keep its memory green. It
would be ungenerous to Robin not to make the most
of it, as he will, we may be sure. For even now he
must come back to it with a kindly hope that his
triumph has not given the rest of us poor people pain."

"Sir," Robin stammered miserably, "you go out
of your way to put me in the wrong. If I spoke of—of
this afternoon again——"

"And you did, dear lad, you did ! "

"It was merely to wish that it would make no
difference between Humphrey and me, and that——"

"No, but you may be satisfied it will make none,"
said Mr. Stafford. He seldom let anyone finish a
sentence, and as a rule prefaced his interruption with
a "no, but", even though the interruption was
merely to repeat in other words what had already been
said. "It is not now, Robin, that we listen to you
with impatience. A little bragging and bravado is
more than pardonable. But I pray you to be careful
in after years. We shall have you saying : 'When
Walsingham had his head cut off '—and Mr. Stafford's
face suddenly contracted with such a fury of rage in
his eyes that Robin was startled. It was only for a
second that the hatred showed and Mr. Stafford was
back in his vein of banter. But during that second
a veil was dropped. A ferret indeed ! Robin saw a
man dangerous with the cold hatred of a snake.
"'When did Sir Francis die on the block ? ' you will
ask, Robin. 'Let me think, sir ! A moment, and I

shall tell you.   It was two years after the Queen gave
me a ribbon from her sleeve.' "

Humphrey Bannet laughed stridently, and Robin
shifted his body in his chair.

"Or it will be," continued Mr. Stafford, again
imitating waggishly some prosy old bore stuffed full
of tedious reminiscences, " ' Humphrey Bannet went
first as Ambassador to France—a minute, and I have
it.   It was in the summer just fifteen years after
Her Grace called me forward and was pleased to
approve of my velvet cape and my pretty face.'   And
then our Robin will sigh and pluck at his grey beard
and tell for the thousandth time the story of that
famous moment."

Robin's cheeks flamed.   A schoolboy is as defence-
less against the raillery of his tutor as a private on a
parade ground against the sarcasms of a sergeant-major.
However poor and heavy the wit, Robin was the butt
ready-made.   He was wise enough not to answer, and
the most uncomfortable meal which he could remember
dragged miserably to its end.   Mr. Stafford rose at
the end of it a little disappointed.   He had always
resented Robin's ability to withdraw within a fortress
of dreams and hold his own there against all invaders.
Mr. Stafford looked down at the young head of his
pupil.   The candlelight burnished the brown waves
of hair;   there was an odd contrast between the
gaiety of his shining doublet, his stiffly-starched white
ruff and the lonely brooding look of his face, which
might have touched even an enemy to a gentler mood.
But Mr. Stafford only foresaw another opportunity of
sport.   He smiled suddenly :

"Come !   We are wasting time," he said genially.
" We have work to do."

He moved to the door, called aloud for the table
to be cleared, and set himself to arrange the furniture

at the other end of the long room. For a moment
Robin and Humphrey were alone, and rather timidly
Robin stretched out his hand across the table.

" Humphrey ! " he pleaded in a low voice.

" Well, and what now ? "

Humphrey would not see that outstretched hand.

" I think that if Mr. Stafford had been less busy, it
is very likely you whom Her Grace would have called
out——" Humphrey interrupted him with a bitter
cry.

" Her Grace ! Her Grace ! We hear too much of
Her Grace, I am thinking. There are other names for
her, I think, less polite but more apt. Wait but a
little ! They are only muttered now. We shall hear
them in the street, be sure. ' Mere English '—oh,
no doubt, but born in Babylon, eh——"

Humphrey came to an abrupt stop. At the other
end of the room, behind Robin's back, Mr. Stafford
was flapping his hand up and down in the air in.
consternation. Humphrey was brought to his senses.
He saw Robin staring up at him with startled,
incredulous eyes.

" I was talking like a fool, and meant not a word
of it," he said quickly. " It was lucky no one was
listening but you, Robin. Else that fine appointment
in France which Mr. Stafford there has reserved for
me would go to someone else." He laughed heartily
and clapped his hand into Robin's. " There ! We are
friends again. Envy, Robin, envy ! But not even
Her Grace shall come between us " ; and he held
Robin's hand until he saw that the dismay had faded
out of his face and a smile had made it warm again.

The table was cleared. Mr. Stafford set a chair for
himself in the middle of the room and took up from
a table a book of manuscript.

" That chair on the left-hand side is the garden

door. The Court cupboard at the back represents the exterior of the Prince of Padua's palace. The chest on the right is a garden seat. Lorenzo, son of the Prince of Padua—that's you, Humphrey—is discovered seated."

It was the custom of the school to act a play before the summer holiday began, and this year the Master had adapted, and at the same time duly mitigated, a comedy by Terence. The Greek landowner had become the Prince of Padua, his scapegrace son the Prince's heir, and the crafty slave, whose tricks and rogueries were the Roman poet's stock-in-trade, was now a valet in the Prince's retinue. Mr. Stafford was going to devote this evening to a rehearsal of the scenes which the two boys had together, and he looked forward to a considerable amount of enjoyment.

" Carlo Manucci—that's you, Robin—the valet— cautiously opens the garden door, hisses out ' Sst ! Sst ! ' to attract his young master's attention, and then sneaks in. Now begin ! "

Robin pretended to open the door and thrust his head in. He whispered " Sst ! Sst ! " and then crept on to the stage on tiptoe. No doubt the cunning was exaggerated ; no doubt, on Robin's entrance, the most unobservant of men must have smelt conspiracy a mile away—indeed, why Robin was ever cast for the artful valet no one but Mr. Stafford could have explained. His knavery was so transparent, his shiftiness so explicit, that even a Prince of Padua must have taken a stick to him in the first hour of his service.

Mr. Stafford, however, held the stick.

" No, but, Robin, the secrecy is overdone. Carlo Manucci *sneaks* in. Those are the directions of the Master, writ in his own hand. He sneaks in. No more than that, Robin. If you are natural, that is

all that he wants. Sneak in, Robin! Try it again.
Be natural."

Robin tried it again :

" Hist, my young Lord ! "

Mr. Stafford set his book down on his knee, and
gazed despairingly about the room.

" Well," he said at length, in a hopeless voice, " Go
on ! Lorenzo leaps up in terror."

" My father ? " cried Humphrey in dismay.

" Oh, very good ! " exclaimed Mr. Stafford. At
last he had acting to content him. " My dear
Humphrey, admirable ! The true note of terror !
Carlo Manucci takes him up, playing on his terror.
You, Robin."

The dialogue went on :

Carlo : Home he comes. A Roman father with the
down-turned thumbs.

Lorenzo : I'll hide !

" Bravo ! " came from the mouth of Mr. Stafford.

Carlo : And lose your hide !

Mr. Stafford uttered a groan.

" That'll never do. It's a jest, Robin, a play upon
words ! ' I'll hide,' says he. ' And lose your hide ! '
you answer. The audience should laugh. Try it
again, my boy ! "

And the more he tried, the more self-conscious and
awkward he became. He could not let his arms hang
quietly at his sides. He must do something with them.
He felt that his hands had swollen to the size of
melons and that his feet were as clumsy as an
elephant's.

Mr. Stafford shook his head.

" I am not sure but what you'd do it better on
all-fours. However, let it go ! Now Carlo unfolds
his plan. But cringe, sir, cringe ! The supple back,
the leering, unpleasant face ! Let us see you bend,

my good Robin! We know that you can. We saw
you bending to the ground this afternoon, a proper
lackey!"

Mr. Stafford could not keep his thoughts long away
from the humiliation of that afternoon. Mr. Ferret,
was he? He wanted schooling more than the
scholars, did he? He heard the ripple of laughter
running along the ranks of the boys, and he tingled
with shame so that his feet beat upon the floor.
Robin was to blame for it. If Robin had modestly
effaced himself instead of thrusting forward in his fine,
new clothes—Mr. Ferret indeed! He could get no
redress from the Queen—as yet, at all events. What
was it that good Cardinal Allan at Rheims called her?
"The beast that troubles the world." Mr. Stafford
smiled as he recollected the words. A good phrase
that! Better than Gloriana! Well, they would see
what they would see. Meanwhile her exquisite young
sycophant was not enjoying himself—there was
consolation in that—Mr. Stafford had managed to
break through the boy's armour at last. Robin was
red one moment and white the next. His lips were
trembling. Another turn or two of the levers, and
there might be tears. In fact, there ought to be tears.
And since there ought to be, there should be. What
else was a tutor for except to make sure that what
ought to be should be?

"You would be the gallant, the gentleman cap-à-pie,
would you, Robin? Oh, no, no, no! You're the
varlet, sleek and slippery, and mean. We must strip
you of that pretty shining doublet. A leather jerkin,
sir, and you'll forget the ribbon knot within your shirt,
as Her Grace has forgot it these many hours past."

Mr. Stafford was in full flight. On his rare visits
from Hilbury Melcombe to London he had slipped
away to Paris Garden and discovered a new and acute

enjoyment in the baiting of bull and bear. He had felt himself pinched and tumbled with the mastiffs and yet still found himself upon his feet. He had shaken his ears with big Bruin, imagined his own flesh torn by the dogs and knew that it was not torn. The sharp teeth had crunched on the bone, yet there was never a mark, never a speck of blood. He had revelled in the thrill and not suffered from the pain. To-night he was doing the baiting himself, and the enjoyment was more exquisite than any even to be got at Bankside. He was the mastiff, Robin the bear, chained by his silken leg and muzzled by his duty into the bargain. He could have hallooed himself on, like the rabble—he—Mr. Stafford, the tutor. His little eyes sparkled, the long nose twitched ; and then, when the sport was at its height, the boy who should be bursting into tears was looking over his head with such an expression of relief as filled the tutor with fury.

"What is this ? You pay no heed to me now ! " he cried, and he swung round in his chair.

The door in the corner of the room was open, and in the doorway stood an elderly man in the frieze jacket and cloth hose of a servant.

"Dakcombe ! " said Mr. Stafford angrily. " We have not done here. Off with you ! Robin, you should order your servants better ! "

Dakcombe stood his ground.

"A gentleman wants to see Master Robin."

"Let him come then at a more reputable hour, and if Master Robin's conduct has been seemly, he shall see him."

"Mrs. Parker says that Master Robin must not keep the gentleman waiting."

"Oh, she does, does she ? " he began very sarcastically and came to a dead stop. He had been

set down once that day for taking too much authority
upon himself.   He had no wish that a second humiliation of this same kind should be his lot in the evening.
He was merely the private tutor of the two boys.
His charges were paid by Sir Robert Bannet of Hilbury
Melcombe on the one hand and by Robin Aubrey's
uncle and guardian on the other.   He had no
independent prerogative.   But Mrs. Parker was the
hostess appointed by the school.   In the last resort
she was the real authority.   As Mr. Stafford sat in
doubt, Robin stepped forward from the scene.

" By your leave, sir ? " he asked, and the boy's
movement recalled to him another movement made
by quite another person in the yard before the lower
school that afternoon.

" Oh, yes," he said to himself.

Even in the midst of his resentment and shame
Mr. Stafford's eyes had been alert.   Someone in the
Queen's neighbourhood had moved, had spoken.   In a
twinkling he was all honey and smiles.

" Certainly you must not keep your visitor waiting,"
he said suavely.   " And you will remember, Robin,
that in the edge and stress of rehearsals, sharp things
are said which are of no account afterwards."

" I shall certainly remember, sir, that sharp things
are said," Robin answered gently ;   and he followed
Dakcombe out of the common room and closed the
door behind him.

Mr. Stafford made sure that the door was closed.
Then he went to Humphrey Bannet and said in a low
voice :

" You let your tongue run away, boy.   To talk of
the Queen so—it was madness."

Humphrey nodded his head.

" Robin thought it just the froth of my humiliation.
But I was mad.   I can't always guard my tongue

when I'm talking to Robin," and he added slowly, looking down upon the ground, " I hate him so."

" Why ? "

Humphrey did not answer. He beat gently upon the chest on which he sat, with the palm of his hand, and still looked at the floor.

" Why, Humphrey ? " Mr. Stafford insisted.

The answer came with a quiet malignancy which in a boy's mouth came near to shocking even this partisan of a tutor.

" Because he's always one place ahead of me. At our books, at our games, in our good-looks, in the favour we are received with. Always. Are we together ? Who has a compliment, a smile, a glance for me, until he has had his fill of them ? And what is he after all, Robin Aubrey, compared with me ? Why am I second always ? " With a quick gesture he covered his face with his hands. " I'll never forget this afternoon."

Mr. Stafford laid his hand upon his favourite's shoulder.

" It'll not be always so, Humphrey. Great changes are coming, great reversals. Robin Aubrey will be on his knees to you one of these days." Mr. Stafford grinned like a wolf, but Humphrey was still looking at the floor and got no comfort from his expression.

" One of these days," he repeated impatiently. " The smallest difference made between us bites and stings me until I can't sleep for thinking of it. I hate myself almost as much as I hate Robin."

" Differences ? " Mr. Stafford asked, pressing him.

" Here's a visitor to-night who mustn't be kept waiting," Humphrey explained sullenly. " For whom ? Does any visitor of note ever come to see me ? Who is it ? " he cried, starting up in a fury. " I'm going

to find out.   Let him visit the two of us !   I'm going
to find out."

But Mr. Stafford thrust himself between Humphrey
and the door.

" Not yet, Humphrey," he said.   " Listen ! "

For a moment they stood over against one another,
the tutor and the pupil.   Then they heard a door
close across the corridor.

CHAPTER III

THE SECRET VISITOR

W HEN Robin went out from the common room he saw that the door of his study facing him stood open and that a single candle burned upon the mantelshelf. But he did not at once cross the passage. He leaned back against the wall by the side of the common room door, with the light from the candle on the mantelshelf opposite flickering across his face. It looked so wan and tired that Dakcombe feared he was going to fall and moved to his side to support him. But Robin shook his head. He had been pressed by his tutor's jeers to the limits of his endurance. He stood breathing deeply like a man who had run a mile. His hands fluttered at his sides. Then he raised them and hid his face in them. He wanted mothering at that moment ; but there was no one there but an inarticulate serving-man, no one who could understand the poignancy to a boy of little things. After a second or two, however, he dropped his hands.

" Thank you, Dakcombe," he said gratefully.

He was imagining that Dakcombe who had served his father, before he had served him, had overheard Mr. Stafford and had come to his rescue. He did not believe that any visitor had called upon him at ten o'clock of the night, or that Mrs. Parker would have admitted him if he had.

He went forward into his study, shut the door and

crossed the width of the room to the candle on the
mantelshelf. It was a long room of dark panels and
sombre curtains, and the solitary candle made one small
pool of light in a wide place of shadows. Robin stood
staring into the flame unaware that his eyes were fixed
on it and lost in some other world of his own imagining,
until a quiet voice spoke from the seat in the window.

" I should have sought you out, Mr. Aubrey, at a
more convenient time. But Secretaries are not their
own masters and must seize occasion as it comes."

Robin swung round on his heel and stared towards
the window. His eyes blinded by the candle-flame,
saw nothing but candle-flame for a moment and then
through it, as though pushing a pair of tawny curtains
apart, stepped that white-faced, black-bearded
Italianate man, whom the Queen had called her Moor.

" You were watching me, sir," said Robin very
directly. He almost accused. He certainly asked for
an explanation.

" I was recognising you, Mr. Aubrey," said the
other, advancing to the fireplace.

Robin smiled and the warmth of his smile was not
due to the ready aptness of the reply. He took a
taper and lit the remaining three candles upon the
mantelshelf ; and after a moment's pause he crossed
to the window at the end of the room opposite to that
where his visitor had been seated. By this window
an old prie-dieu stood and with the air of one reverently
celebrating a great event, he lit two other candles
on the top ledge of it, between which an ivory crucifix
of Italian workmanship hung upon two nails. Then
he came back to his visitor, the smile still warm upon
his mouth and a great friendliness in his eyes.

" I light all my candles to thank Sir Francis Walsingham for the kind heart which brought him here."

" You know me then ? "

"I heard you say that you had been my father's friend."

Walsingham's face was naturally cold and grave and harassed, but it lit up now and softened. He became very human, and amusement changed altogether the melancholy of his eyes, the amusement of a man recognising his own defects.

"I owed a great deal to your father, Robin, when I was a Member of Parliament for Lyme and he the great gentleman of Bridport. I make friends with difficulty. It is my fault. I have some barrier of manner, not, I believe, of heart, which stands between me and others. I try to be genial and seem to be false. I make a jest and it has lost its savour before it is told. If I say to a man, 'I like you,' I make him ask, 'Now what aim has he in saying that?' If I tell a story, however short, I am aware long before I have done that I am winding up some dreary dead thing out of a deep well. I see men who jostle each other by chance in a doorway and go on arm in arm for the rest of their days. I envy such men. Only once has that happened to me, and the other man was your father. We had, to be sure, something in common. He was a great traveller; I spent much of my youth abroad. But in other things he was my opposite and complement, bold and free with a great laugh which shook the rafters——"

"Until my mother died," said Robin.

Sir Francis nodded his head.

"At your birth, Robin," he added gently. "After that he left Bridport and built Abbot's Gap in the Purbeck Hills at the other extremity of the county. He became, I am afraid, a restless and unhappy man. You should know better than I. For I saw him but once or twice during those later years. But my love of him has not diminished, and so, since Her Majesty was moved to speak a shrewd word about his son on her return to the castle this afternoon, I pushed my duties aside so that that son might hear what she said from my lips before I return to-morrow to Whitehall."

Robin was moved by the great Secretary's consideration. He had been wincing through the evening under the disparagements of Mr. Stafford, which stung none the less keenly because they were crude. The courtesy of the statesman was by contrast comforting as wine ; and that the statesman was stirred by any reasons but kindness and old memories, did not occur to him. To thrust his papers to one side and pay a visit to a mere schoolboy at ten o'clock of the night ! Kindness and old memories could alone explain it.

The fireplace was set in a shallow recess. Robin set a heavy chair forward.

" No one, sir," he said with a laugh, " shall charge you with disloyalty if you are comfortably seated before you repeat to me what the Queen's Grace said. And my study will be honoured."

Whilst Walsingham seated himself, he stood back against the panels of the recess, the fireplace upon his left hand, the side wall stretching out upon his right. Walsingham so turned the chair that he faced Robin.

" Her Majesty said that when she called you out, dismay was writ so large upon your face and so sharp an ague set you trembling, your colour so violently flamed and faded that she wondered whether you would ever come to her. Yet you were only the better nerved to play your part well, to say the unrehearsed fit word, to bear yourself as a gallant gentleman before his Queen. From such, she was pleased to add, the State and the Prince got always their most fruitful servants."

Robin drew in a breath. Again it is to be borne in mind all that Elizabeth meant to all that was generous and loyal in the youth of that day. She was forty-seven years old, and if you looked closely enough you might see no doubt that she wore a wig, and if your memory for colours was precise you might recognise that it was a trifle redder than the wig she wore a year ago. But youth saw nothing of that. Her figure was young, her eyes bright, her movements stately when she would and swift when she would. She was their inspiration. Years ago she had set herself to win their love. What had once been policy had long since become an impulse from her heart, and therefore a thousand times more puissant and compelling. She was tolerant, she neither taxed nor molested, nor wasted them in foreign entanglements. Louder and louder was growing the confident sound of her people marching behind her. It is no wonder that Robin was moved by her praise, that his face shone and his heart beat faster.

"The Queen said that, sir ? " he asked.

" Mark the words, Robin. The State and the Prince," and Sir Francis spoke, leaning forward in his chair. " To stand gracefully in the Presence Chamber ! To carry a fan or a prayer-book ! To drop prettily on a silken knee and say that Her Majesty is served ! Service to the Prince—lackey's service, but not service to the State. The State and the Prince, Robin."

As he spoke, the Secretary saw the boy's face change. A wariness crept over it. It was not merely then to show a kindness to the son of an old friend that Sir Francis had torn himself from his affairs. Robin was at once upon his guard and the statesman in front of him knew it. But he did not betray his knowledge.

" You learn here the living languages ? " he asked easily, as though he was merely interested in the school's curriculum.

" Yes, sir."

" That is well. Knowledge of the living tongues alone helps one to understand the diversity of men. Your father spoke many. No doubt he grounded you."

" He did."

Robin's face was a mask now, his voice a level monotone. Of hours in the Library gilded with the romance of some old poet of France or Italy, of days in the saddle on the crest of the Purbeck Hills, or in a fishing boat on the sunlit water of Warbarrow Bay when George Aubrey and he, friends of an age rather than tutor and pupil or father and son, had played at being foreigners—of all these memories not a trace showed in him. His father had grounded him, yes, but during the last five solitary years Robin had schooled himself.

" You speak French then ? "

" I can make a shift with it."

" Italian ? "

" Passably well, perhaps."

" And Spanish ? "

" With the accent of Italy."

Sir Francis was silent for a moment. Then:

" That is no great matter."

He stretched out his legs and leaned back in his chair.

" I have no news out of Spain," he said indifferently. " From France, from Italy, all that I need. But from Spain and the Portugals none."

Robin did not answer. The wary look had passed from his face, as the time for wariness had passed. He had discovered his opponent's game.

" The Holy Inquisition has seen to it."

Sir Francis shot the words out suddenly and bitterly with his eyes on the boy's face. Surely now he would see it quiver, its set obstinacy dissolve. The same fury which burned in his eyes would leap into the boy's. One movement Robin made and one alone. His right hand rose to the breast of his doublet and fingered something hidden beneath it. Doubtless, thought Walsingham, that flimsy knot of ribbons which was as like as not to become the lad's undoing. But with the gesture Robin answered calmly and reasonably :

" No doubt, sir, if the need should come, you will find the means under your hand."

Walsingham was a patient man. He had to be with so changeful and elusive a mistress as Elizabeth. But he was almost at the end of his patience. Robin wasn't the idiot his remark made him out to be. Even if the wide-spaced eyes and the sensitive features were unreliable, his conduct this afternoon in the courtyard before the lower school was evidence enough. Robin was holding out against him with a purpose ; very likely a trumpery purpose such as to taste the colour of romance at a Court with a Queen at the head of it ; but nevertheless a purpose sufficiently definite and strong to harass Sir Francis Walsingham. He took another way.

" I have something to tell you which concerns your father. A secret which he and I shared alone, and after to-night you and I will share alone. Nay, I am practising no cheat upon you. Lay your suspicions aside, and listen to me. On a night in May eleven years ago—we cannot be overheard ? There are those in this house who must not overhear us——" and Walsingham drew back in his chair with a gasp. " You think I am play-acting ! I am not."

Was there such another exasperating boy in the world ? Walsingham laughed suddenly and quite humanly at the absurdity of his position. He with his ear against the panel and his eye at the keyhole of all the Council Chambers in Europe except Spain

—he, her Majesty's Principal Secretary, he Burghley's right hand man, to be questioned at every turn and borne down by an obstinate schoolboy! Comic! Maddening but comic.

That laugh, however, served his turn. Robin relaxed and answered with a smile.

" I beg your pardon, sir, we shall not be overheard. Dakcombe will be standing at the door. On a night in May eleven years ago——"

" Mark the date well! On the afternoon of May the twelfth, 1570, a messenger of mine brought a prayer for help to your father, George Aubrey. George Aubrey left Abbot's Gap at nightfall and riding by the great heath and Cerne Abbas he crossed the shoulder of the down to my house at Sydling St. Nicholas. I sent my servants early to their beds. I set open the gates, and went down to the broken cross where the road turns up to my house ; and in the dark of the morning I heard the clatter of his horse."

Sir Francis was leaning forward and speaking in a low voice. He was making his story as romantic and vivid as he could that it might strike with the more lively force upon the imagination of the boy propped against the wall in front of him. But it gained upon him too as he told it so that it rang true.

" We tied up his horse in the big barn at the side of Sydling Court, and I brought your father secretly into the house. There I besought his help. Pope Pius the Fifth, the good man, had excommunicated Her Majesty in February of that year. The Bull freed all Catholic subjects of Her Majesty from their allegiance. But it did more, Mr. Aubrey. It made her assassination a godly act, a deed which conferred money in this world and Paradise in the next. But the assassination of a Prince is not to other Princes a politic proceeding. Elizabeth gone that way, it would be ' whose turn next ? '   The Valois, Philip of Spain, the Emperor Charles would have none of it. The Bull was not published. But I, Mr. Aubrey, wanted it published."

" You, sir ? "

" Yes, I. The Queen walks unguarded. Through her palace of Whitehall runs a public road. Her garden at Richmond is free to whoso wills to wander there. Never lived a woman so careless of her safety as Her Grace."

" But if the Bull was not published ? "

" It was none the less known to every traitor in the realm, the reward and the sure place amongst the Saints. Well, I wanted it known to the honest people, too, so that in her own despite Her Majesty should be saved. A dagger in the dark is more dangerous than a dagger in the daylight. And I was right. For when the Bull was published, there broke out such a cry of wrath in this country as rang a tocsin at every corner of Europe. I talked to your father that night."

" How was he concerned ? " Robin asked.

" I had a copy of the *Bull*. George Aubrey was a loyal Protestant, a country gentleman never seen at Court, a man of a high spirit. He rode away that night with my copy of the *Bull* in his pocket, and he rode towards London. He reached London on the morning of the fifteenth, and at six o'clock that morning the *Bull* was posted on the door of the Bishop of London's Palace. It was posted there by a Catholic, who suffered the extreme penalty ; but if it had not been, your father would have nailed it the next night on St. Paul's Cross itself."

He spoke with a rising voice, sitting erect, his eyes burning and a gloomy passion in his face.   He repeated his words, making of them a challenge to the son :

" Your father would have nailed it the next night on St. Paul's Cross himself."

" And suffered the extreme penalty, too," said Robin.

Walsingham did not flinch from that rejoinder.

" Very like," he said quietly. " It had the look of treachery. We should have been hard put to it to prove it loyalty. He did the great service to the realm, the service which earns no honours—nay, which may stain a name with ignominy until that name be borne by no one on the earth."

Walsingham's spiritual home was Geneva. A kindly father, a domesticated householder, a munificent patron of letters, a scholar with the new Italian taste for clipped and geometrical gardens, all these characters he was, but they did not make his strength. He got that from his faith. He was of the creed of Calvin. He would have poured out the money of the realm for it. He would have drawn his sword for it any time these last ten years since he had been Her Majesty's principal secretary. He would have forced Elizabeth to draw hers and ruined England, but for her nimbler mind, which would not have her people taxed and delighted in windings and twistings which left her secretary dizzy. He sat with the fire of a fanatic burning in his deep and gloomy eyes, watching the boy against the wall. George Aubrey was his best friend. But he had reckoned up his qualities, and used them without a qualm, even though they might have brought him to the hazard of shame and the executioner's bowelling knife.

" Why, sir, do you tell me this secret ? " Robin asked, and again the answer came :

" I have no news out of Spain, and in a few years must have."

Robin shook his head. By chance or by design—and which it was Robin never knew—Walsingham had pressed him into this corner between the fireplace and the side-wall of the recess. He could not escape without the appearance of flight. He was held at a disadvantage which confused him. Yet he must stand firm, using clear words, but keeping his purpose still hidden within his heart, his own secret treasure.

" What ! " cried the secretary, torn betwixt anger and scorn. " You will hold out against me, will you ? I must keep my vigil night and day at a grip with great matters of the realm, and I am to be baffled by a schoolboy ! What thought burns in you ? "

" My father died in Spain," Robin answered simply.

An excuse ? Or a reason ? Or a fear that the like fate should happen to him ? Walsingham could not tell. There was not the quiver of a muscle in the boy's face, not a break in his voice. The voice was pitched in a higher note, but that was all.

" I heard so."

" But you know."

Walsingham shook his head.

" I had then, as I have now no good news out of Spain. I never saw your father after that night when he came to Sydling House. I heard that he had travelled to Italy and thence into Spain."

" Where he was arrested."

" Yes. People might come and go. I speak of seven years ago. They came and went at their own risks."

" My father was arrested because he had with him in his luggage a book, a little book, a copy of the ' Precepts of Cato.' "

" But translated by Erasmus," said Sir Francis Walsingham, and bit his lip. He was showing too much knowledge for a man who had no news out of

Spain. " I heard that too.   A translation by Erasmus, the arch-heretic.   That was cause enough."

" Cause enough for the rack and the stake," said Robin ; and still his face was a mask, and still his voice was steady, more shrill perhaps than even a moment ago, but steady and quiet as that of one speaking of exciting things which had no personal touch.

" At the stake ?   You are sure of that ? " cried the Secretary, leaning forward.

" There was a famine in Spain.   Ships which carried wheat from England were given a safe conduct.   The *Catherine* out of Lyme was one."

" It brought back the gossip of the ports ? "

" No ! " cried Robin.   " It brought back its master, Richard Brymer, a man of Lyme.   On a summer night he sailed in his ship's pinnace with the tide round Portland Bill.   He drew in by the Mupe Rocks and beached his pinnace in Warbarrow Bay in the morning. He found me there.   I had been swimming ; I was drying in the sun on the sand——"

Suddenly that even voice stopped altogether, and so abruptly that Walsingham doubted for a moment his estimate of Robin.   There was, however, no other sign of distress visible in his manner.   He stood up erect against the wall, speaking steadily in a shrill sing-song, and then came silence sharp upon speech, as a shutter upon sunlight.   It was a schoolboy re-citing his piece on a prize-day and suddenly forgetting the word which came next and his mind going blank. And yet if it was only that, why did the secretary, not an imaginative man, see shaping itself in front of him with extraordinary precision the picture of a brown curving beach, a summer morning, a circle of high cliffs, a boy of ten stretched out brown as the beach on which he lay, digging in his feet and letting the sand run between his toes, and over the shining water a ship's pinnace sailing in a light wind with a man at the helm, bringing such news as might well make in an instant a man out of a boy—and a secret iron man, however much the slim elegance of his looks belied him.

"What did this Richard Brymer tell you?" the Secretary asked intently.

"That whilst his ship was unloading at Vigo he had gone to Madrid—that on a Sunday he had been caught up by a great crowd all in holiday dress—that he had gone with it to the Square of San Bernardo. Richard Brymer had a smattering of Spanish. The place they were bound for was called the Quemadero. There was to be an *auto-da-Fe* and amongst the heretics to suffer was an English traveller."

"And he saw your father?"

"Yes. Brymer was on the outskirts of the crowd. But the procession passed at his elbow. My father walked in it wearing the yellow sack and the high conical hat. . . . He dragged his legs, his face was wasted with pain. . . . Richard Brymer saw the smoke of the faggots curling up into the air. . . . He was crying like a child as he told me."

The picture of the beach was still before Sir Francis Walsingham's eyes. He saw the sun cross the sky and drop behind the cliffs to the west—and the boy still lying on the sand, but the pinnace gone and the place empty. He watched the boy rise with a shiver and dress himself in his clothes and go up alone through the gap to an empty house.

But a movement of the real boy in front of him tore this picture into wisps as a wind shreds a mist. Robin again raised his hand to his breast and fingered it, feeling for something which lay hidden beneath his doublet. The Queen's knot of ribbons! So that was the talisman which kept the voice equable, the face unravaged. A knot of ribbons, a hope of the Queen's favour, the promise of life at a brilliant Court. Walsingham beat upon the arms of his chair. Then he stretched out an accusing finger which pointed at the boy's hand.

" And it means no more to you than a cloud across the moon ! The Quemadero, the yellow sack, the dragging limbs ! Even Richard Brymer was more moved. For you have the Queen's ribbons against your heart ! "

And in the midst of his anger the Secretary was flung back amongst perplexities. For Robin's arms shot out from his sides, straight to their full reach at the level of the shoulders. He stood erect with his feet together, the gold of his dress gleaming against the dark panels, his eyes closed, his face at last quivering and tormented. He stood as if crucified. Then slowly his head dropped on to his breast.

" Sir, you press me too hard," he said in a whisper.

Shame ? Or the breaking of a great control under the torture of his questioning ? Walsingham could not answer. One thing alone was clear to him. The boy had reached the limits of his strength. Walsingham rose from his chair.

" Very like ! " he said in an easier voice. " I must go. Your bedtime is past, Robin, and my hour of leisure."

He set his cloak about his shoulders and drew it up to muffle his face.

" Of my visit to you, of what I told you about the Pope's Bull, of Richard Brymer's story it will be better to breathe no word. Your friend, young Bannet, is of a Catholic family, the tutor, Mr. Ferret "—and a smile of enjoyment lit up for a moment the Secretary's pale face—" of the same faith, no doubt. Be wary of them, Robin, even in your sleep."

Robin walked towards the door, but Walsingham stopped him.

" Nay. I'll take my leave of you here. I want no ceremonies."

He gave his hand to Robin and then let it fall to his side.

" Well, we shall see what we shall see. Fare you well ! "

Outside the door of the room Dakcombe was standing sentinel. Across the passage a thread of light showed that the door of the common room was ajar. Walsingham took a step and closed it softly, and holding the handle gave his other hand to Dakcombe. Dakcombe would have raised it to his lips, but the Secretary stopped him.

" You owe me no such reverence." He clapped George Aubrey's old servant gently on the shoulder. " We grow old, my old friend, each keeping his ward in his own way. Look well to yours, and God prosper you."

He drew his hat down over his brows. Like all men of mysteries, he had grown to practise mystery when there was not a shadow of need for it. If he paid a call upon the young son of his greatest friend no one must know it. If he had wanted a feather for his hat—though it is difficult to imagine Sir Francis aware of such a want—he would have bought three bits of a feather at three different shops and sewn them together in the dark. At the door of Mrs. Parker's house his litter awaited him. He was forty-seven years old then, but grievously aged with the stone. Warbarrow Bay and a boy changed into a man in the course of a summer's day by the story of a sea captain with the tears running down his face. The dark panels of a room and a pretty young waterfly of a lad clutching a knot of ribbons to his breast and dreaming of soft luxurious days in the pageantry of a Court. Which was the true picture ? Her Majesty's Principal Secretary went back to his papers in Windsor Castle and that problem was still unresolved.

CHAPTER IV

THE SIGNET RING

THE answer was in the long dark room from which he had just departed. Robin stood for a moment or two on the spot where Walsingham had left him. He then walked with the dragging steps of his father at the Quemadero to the fireplace and one by one extinguished the candles which he had lit in honour of the Secretary's visit. He did it very slowly, his thoughts far away and his body very tired. He left alight only that candle which had been burning when he entered the room an hour before, and the candles on each side of the crucifix. He looked uneasily about that shadowed room, not quite sure that he was alone. But being now sure, he unbuttoned his doublet and drew out from against the white lawn of his shirt, not a crumpled bow of ribbon but a signet ring hung upon a fine gold chain. The stone set in the ring was an emerald in the shape of a shield, and deep into it were cut two initials, G. A. He smiled rather wistfully as he looked upon the emerald shield. Then he moved as though drawn by a magnet to the *prie-Dieu*. And when he stood in front of the *prie-Dieu* with the ring in his fingers and the ivory crucifix before his eyes, his loneliness had its way with him. He had held his own against the Queen's Secretary. Words had been spoken to him which had cut like knives and he had concealed the wounds they made, had kept his voice steady, his eyes impenetrable. Now

D

the defences were down. He dropped upon his knees in front of the crucifix and bowed his young head upon his arms. A passion of grief shook him. His father with the great heart and the great laugh and the high spirit rode with him again on the Purbeck Hills, the river winding like a band of silver through the water-meadows to Poole Harbour on the one side, the sea and the crescent of Warbarrow Bay on the other. He sailed again out to St. Alban's Head, he holding the tiller, his father the sheet of the sail. They talked of foreign cities in foreign tongues. They would visit them all together. A storm of tears burst from the boy's eyes. The sound of his sobbing filled the room. He sank down at the foot of the *prie-Dieu* and crouched there, his legs drawn up beneath him. The yellow sack, the face wasted with torment and the black of dungeons, the dragging limbs, the smoke curling up from the Quemadero—the boy, crouched in his gay bright dress on the floor of the room, cried with a breaking heart, even as Richard Brymer of Lyme had cried by the side of his pinnace, the rugged old sailor with the brown of the sea upon his face, and the horror of what he had seen burning in his eyes.

Sir Francis was about this time being carried in his litter through the Castle Gate, still in something of a fret over a fruitless visit. He would have been at a greater ease if he could have looked into the long, shadowy room of Mrs. Parker's house. But another did. The door was opened with great care that not a hinge should creak. It opened into the room and at first hid Robin altogether from the eyes of the watchers. But it was slowly pushed back and back until the *prie-Dieu* was disclosed and the unhappy boy sobbing on the floor at the foot of it, with his hands to his face and the tears running out between his fingers. There were two who looked on, Mr. Stafford and

Humphrey Bannet. Humphrey made a movement, shrugged his shoulders and was on the point of speaking. But the tutor set a finger to his lips, and as secretly as he had opened it he shut the door again. He drew Humphrey back into the common-room across the passage.

" Cry-baby ! " said Humphrey.

" Aye, you can laugh now. But if you had laughed in his hearing, if you had spoken, if he had seen you even, he would never have forgiven you. He would have felt shame at the sight of you to the end of his days."

" Would that have been so great a matter ? " said Humphrey scornfully.

" Who shall say ? "

Humphrey Bannet looked at his tutor in surprise.

" An hour ago you were not so careful how you offended him."

" An hour may bring great changes, Humphrey, even in times less changeful than these. One may make a friend."

Humphrey Bannet laughed.

" If Robin Aubrey made a friend to-night, he seems to have got little joy of it."

They were standing face to face in the common-room, and Mr. Stafford spoke in an uneasy voice.

" Here's a good rule, Humphrey. Before you do the thing which won't be forgiven, make sure that it's worth while. Weigh it well, however small a thing it seems."

The tutor was disquieted. Who was this late visitor ? Stafford had remarked the little movement of Francis Walsingham in the courtyard that afternoon when the boy had knelt at the Queen's feet. He knew of the friendship between the statesman and Robin's father. He suspected that Walsingham was the visitor. And they had talked for a long while. What had Walsingham—if Walsingham it was—sought from Robin Aubrey ? He was a subtle searcher ; he had his spies everywhere, he kept them unaware of each other, so that he could check what one said by the statement of a second; he neglected no opportunity of knowledge, he could be secret and slow till the last necessary fact was collected, and then he could be swift—appallingly swift—as Tyburn certified. Mr. Stafford shivered a little. The great house of Hilbury Melcombe had its own concealments and mysteries. It was natural that Mr. Stafford's fears should run to them and should imagine that what he dreaded should be disclosed was already known or in the way of being known to this crafty fox amongst the Queen's servants.

"Wait ! " he said.

He might after all be torturing himself without reason. Robin's visitor might be some harmless gentleman from Dorsetshire who had talked of old days to an impressionable boy. He went out into the passage and listened at Robin's door. All was quiet now within the room, though a line of light showed still upon the boards. Mr. Stafford returned to the common-room.

"Call to him ! " he said to Humphrey. "But wait till he answers."

Humphrey Bannet went out into the corridor.

"Robin," he called. "Are you alone ? "

There was no answer, and he called again, more gently :

"Robin ! Robin ! "

In a little while Robin's voice answered muffled and low.

"A moment, Humphrey ! "

And there followed a sound of hurried movement

inside the study. Robin had been still sitting crouched upon the floor when the summons reached his ears. He rose to his feet quickly, dried his cheeks and eyes with his handkerchief and then blew out the candles on the *prie-Dieu*. He had a wish that no signs of his abasement should be visible even to Humphrey his friend. He buttoned the signet ring away within his doublet, and crossing to the door, threw it open.

" I am alone," he said, and seeing that Mr. Stafford was at Humphrey's elbow, he stepped backwards to the mantelshelf so that he should have the light of the one candle behind him and his face still remain in shadow.

" So your visitor has gone ! " said Mr. Stafford.

" He has gone," Robin answered, and thereupon he astonished Mr. Stafford. In those days boys stood until they were bidden to be seated, and when they sat, they sat tidily. George Aubrey had schooled his son in good behaviour as well as in the living languages. Never, to the knowledge of the tutor, had Robin behaved as he behaved now. He tumbled into the great chair in which Sir Francis Walsingham had been sitting, without so much as a " By your leave," and sprawled there, his legs stretched out, his ankles crossed, his arms hanging down, just like a captain at an inn.

" And taken your manners with him," said Mr. Stafford sourly.

Robin did not rise at the rebuke, he did not change his attitude by an inch. His knees had given under him. He had come so utterly to the end of his strength that he dared not trust himself to stand upon his feet.

" I do think so, sir, in very truth," he answered in a voice which was faint with fatigue. " There are old stories of ancient people who sap the vigour of younger ones to replenish their own. I think such an one visited me to-night."

"An old man, then?" cried Mr. Stafford, and a little eagerly. An old man? Why, then, it would not be Walsingham. But Robin dashed his hopes.

"Not so old if you count by years."

"Youngish-old, then?" said Mr. Stafford despondently.

"Or oldish-young," answered Robin. "Have it, sir, as you will."

"Should I be right in saying a strong Puritan?" Mr. Stafford asked slyly.

"We didn't talk religion," said Robin.

Humphrey laughed impatiently.

"It must have been a Jesuit, who though he took your manners, Robin, left his quibbles."

"Or a Puritan-Jesuit," said Robin, and at once Mr. Stafford took him up.

"In that case, Sir Francis Walsingham. The phrase fits him like a glove. We need look no further."

And indeed the description was not inapt—a Puritan in the austerity of his belief, a Jesuit in his devices. But Robin was on his feet the next moment and looking up into the face of Mr. Stafford, his bearing very respectful, his eyes quiet but very intent.

"Was it he, sir?" Robin asked slowly.

The tutor could not interpret the boy's look. There was no threat in it. It was calm as a pool. Yet for a moment Mr. Stafford was seized with a panic and startled enough to betray it.

"And if it was he who came muffled up in a cloak to avoid recognition, why should you, sir, be at so much pains to publish his name?"

Mr. Stafford stammered some foolish excuses about his care for his pupils and the heavy charge it laid upon him, whilst a black rage filled his heart. Why, he might be the pupil and this grave-eyed lad looking up into his face—yes, actually looking up—the tutor calling him to account.

Robin heard him out until he stopped ; and then with a bow he went to the mantelshelf and took up the one lit candle.

" With your leave, sir, I shall to my bed," he said.

At the door leading into his bedroom he turned with a smile upon his face.

" At this moment, sir, I could play Carlo Manucci to your complete satisfaction," he said. " For I can hardly stand upright."

With a nod to Humphrey he went into his bedroom and closed the door.

CHAPTER V

NOT FORESEEN IN THE PLAN

FOUR years afterwards and in the same month
Robin rode to Hilbury Melcombe. He had
been for the last two years his own master, but there
was little change at Abbot's Gap to show for it. The
house still slept behind its shutters, a desolate and
inhospitable place. Robin was for most of the time
at Oxford and for the rest of it where nobody knew.
When he came to Abbot's Gap it was suddenly and
after nightfall, so that few knew of his coming. He
would pass a few days there, ordering his estate and
his revenues strictly with his steward, sailing his
boat in Warbarrow Bay and sitting late into the
night over his books in the library where he had been
wont to study the living languages with his father.
Then as silently as he had come he would be off again.
He refused the companionship of his neighbours and
so fell into disuse with the house.

It was surprising, therefore, that he was bidden to
Hilbury, and no less surprising that he accepted.
But he had accepted gladly. A halting time had come.
He had a week between what he reckoned to be the
two momentous periods of his life. It was to be a
week of holiday and enjoyment, in which he would
renew his old friendship with Humphrey and recapture,
if only for seven poor days, something of the sparkle
and the laughter which belong to youth.

He left Abbot's Gap an hour after his dinner with

a servant riding behind him and leading a third horse with his luggage packed upon its back. He was starved of pleasure, and with the great beeches in full leaf, the hills baking themselves brown in the sunlight like any modern maiden, the ferns and wild flowers fresh in any patch of shade, and the song of the thrush and lark overhead, he threw off yet another wrapping of deliberation with every step he took. He strewed the bridle-path with his cares and trampled his plans under the hooves of his horse.

His way led over the Purbeck Hills and down across the water-meadows. He left Wareham and the great heath away on his right ; and as he rode he made his plans. Plans the poor lad had to have, he had so schooled himself to weighing the this against the that from his boyhood. So plans he made now to cram each waking minute of a week full to the brim with pleasure. He would start with a match at tennis after breakfast, say, at seven-fifteen or so, or tilt at the ring in the courtyard, or have a bout with the foils or shoot at the butts. Then he would hunt one day—Hilbury was famous for its stags—course the next day, go wild-fowling on the third with that fine new caliver which was on the pack-saddle of the led horse. On the fourth day there would be hawking. After dinner he would play any game that was forward, from keelpins to quoits, and after supper a galliard or a coranto in the great hall, with a game of primero in between would carry him happily to bedtime. It was to be a week which should bubble with all the unenjoyed enjoyment of his past years, and all the rounded enchantments of full manhood on which, the week once ended, he must turn his back. A week to hold the pith of years. He would sleep of nights, and as for clothes no dandy in England should outshine him.

Thus he planned as he rode through the park where the beeches and oaks dotted the sweep of turf, and here a shrubbery, there a little wood broke the great expanse. But in all his reckoning he had forgotten the one pastime which was the most likely to capture and enchain a youth who had starved himself of pleasure and disciplined himself like a monk. The first hour of his visit, however, was to open his eyes to his omission.

The great house built of red brick and glowing in the sunlight of the afternoon was strangely silent, and strangely empty. The house party, he was told, had gone hawking and was holding an assembly or, as we should say, a picnic, in a glade some miles away. Supper was therefore put off until six o'clock. Robin was conducted to his bedroom on the second floor and his bags were carried up to him. He changed his dress at his leisure and descended into the hall. It was four o'clock, but the hawking-party had not yet returned. He was suddenly aware, however, that he had not the house to himself. For in a room upon his right hand behind the big staircase, someone was diligently practising the scales upon a virginal.

" Some poor little girl with a governess at her elbow," he assumed. On such an afternoon ! Robin shook his head over her hard fate. Up and down the unseen hands were flying over the keyboard. Not very correctly, that had to be admitted. For every now and then one note stumbled into another note, or two notes would be struck together. Then a silence would follow and all begin over again. Sad work for a little girl on a summer afternoon ! Robin felt a great pity for her. Probably her tears were dropping on the keys, as she thought of the house-party eating good things in a glade whilst she was pinned upon her music-stool, like Andromeda on her rock, with a dragon of a governess no doubt to rap her knuckles when she made mistakes. Of course, a little girl must learn the virginal for her own comfort and consolation in her after-life. But on a summer afternoon, was it fair ? Robin settled his ruff before a mirror. It was a smart new ruff of fine cambric, delicately embroidered with silver, and starched just stiffly enough to hold its pleats in order and not to spoil its look of fragility. Robin turned his head to the right and to the left. It was a very good ruff.

And suddenly the scales tinkled evenly and true. The little girl had mastered them. Robin was delighted with her. She deserved a treat.

" Ah ! "

An idea occurred to him. He turned again to the mirror and smoothed his doublet down. It was a fine new doublet, pointed in the latest fashion and of dark crimson velvet with tight sleeves and a puffing of white satin at the shoulders. It was a good doublet, and the jewelled pomander which swung on a golden chain set about his shoulders set it off well. The breeches matched it. They were quite new-fangled affairs and very satisfactory—padded and closed tight round the thighs with golden garters, and short enough to show off properly the long straight legs in brown silk stockings. A cape of Venetian brown swung from his shoulders and was tied with a silver cord upon his breast. Robin swung this way and that on his heels. The little girl at the virginal ought to have a treat. Well, she should have one. He waved a perfumed handkerchief at the smiling young coxcomb who confronted him in the mirror, marched to the door behind which the scales were played, flung it open, stepped proudly in, bowed low till his body made a right angle with his legs, clapped a hand upon his heart, cried in a fervid voice :

" Good Mistress Andromeda, Perseus is here——"
and felt that he had made such a fool of himself as
he had never done in all the eighteen years of his life.

For there was no dragon of a governess ; there was
no little Andromeda. There was only a grown-up
young lady seated at the virginal, whose slender hands
arrested on the board made the keys yellow as jealousy
itself. Her back was towards him, she was dressed
in a pink satin gown with a high, fanlike collar of
lace which showed him only a wealth of pale gold
curls on a small head. And in a voice which was
startled, but low and more excellent than music, she
answered :

" Mr. Perseus, there are scales upon my virginal,
as there were no doubt scales upon the dragon, but
you are, I am afraid, rescuing your ears from them
rather than rescuing me."

In another mirror hung upon the wall above the
virginal their eyes met and moved no more. There
was never anything so convenient as that mirror. Its
fellow in the hall was a thing of no value. It merely
reflected a coxcomb admiring his clothes to a coxcomb
admiring his clothes. It was hardly to be considered
a mirror at all. This one above the virginal was, on
the other hand, magical. It showed to Robin at the
door a small oval face with a firm, little, rounded chin,
a red mouth opened in laughter and disclosing the
prettiest white teeth, dark eyebrows below a white
forehead, and a pair of big eyes of so dark a blue
that surely no sea could match them, and with a
sparkle in their depths such as gleams in the heart
of jewels. Lovely ? Robin was struck with the
poverty of words. A paragon ? The world's wonder ?
The envy of the planets ? Fie, she was warm as earth.
When did a planet laugh ? Nay, when did any other
girl laugh so that each note struck upon the heart

and made it breathe the melody of birds ? She was the incomparable maid.

The incomparable maid was gazing into that bewitching mirror, too. She saw a brown-haired boy's face over a big white ruff, a face flushing in confusion, with lips parted in wonder, and brown eyes which held hers as his were held by hers. Messages passed between them which neither the one who sent them nor the one who received them could yet interpret. But they were of enormous significance. Both knew that. They changed the world. She dropped her eyes first, the long, dark, curling lashes eclipsing the universe. He spoke first, his voice trembling a little. Was this all, these threadbare foolish words that so overwhelming a moment put into his mouth to speak ?

" I broke in upon your playing."

The maid nodded gravely at the mirror.

" You did."

And the ground crumbled beneath him.

" Oh ! "

Remorse so deep, disappointment so sharp, never sounded so loudly in an " Oh ! " before. At least, so his ears told him. The maid was quick to comfort him.

" But I am glad that you did."

She smiled again and he breathed again. The blood rose into her cheeks, her brow. What lunatic had thought the universe eclipsed ?

She rose hastily from her seat and faced him. She was middling tall now that she stood up. Her doublet was cut low in the front, as was the way with maidens. She showed him a white slender throat on which the small head was poised most daintily.

" You, Sir, wait upon Sir Robert. He has not yet returned from hawking. I am only a visitor at the house. Cynthia Norris at your pleasure."

"Cynthia Norris," Robin repeated, lingering on each syllable and nodding his head foolishly. He was still a little dazed. "There is music in the name."

"More than in my fingers," said Cynthia ruefully. Certainly she did not play the virginal well. It looked as though even the angels had their limitations. Robin's wits were astray, and he had no comforting words for her.

"You are from Winterborne Hyde," he said.

"Yes," she agreed. She looked at him inquiringly, repeated her name with a trifle of emphasis and then, holding wide her skirt, sank in a curtsy before him. A lovely movement. He could have watched its repetition for a twelvemonth. But that she should pay so much respect to him shocked him.

"You must not, Mistress Cynthia, sink by an inch of your stature to me," he protested.

"And how should I know that?" she asked demurely. "You may be the great Cham of Tartary."

Robin flushed to his forehead.

"My manners have gone with my wits." He bowed as low before her as he had done to her back. "I am Robin Aubrey."

For a moment Cynthia Norris was utterly startled. Then as he stood erect again she looked him up slowly from his feet to his head. Robin smiled vaguely, and felt as uncomfortable under her scrutiny as a young man could. He had promised himself to give a little girl a treat in the spectacle of a fine young gentleman dressed up for a killing. But in the fact he had given a big girl a surprise and apparently no pleasure with it. She was perplexed, and he had been at pains to cut a dash. Poor fool, he was just a clotted pudding of vanity, a homely kitchen thing served up in a porcelain porringer. No wonder she disapproved.

Besides, his stockings were wrinkling down his legs like a pantaloon's. He felt absolutely sure of it, though for the life of him he dared not look.

" Indeed ? " said she.

" Of a truth," he answered.

And suddenly she comprehended, though what she comprehended he could no more tell than a cat could tell the time by the clock. Her face lightened. The perplexity vanished from her face. She began to laugh, and merrily, at some excellent jest.

" To be sure," she cried, mocking him. " So spruce and trim ! You must be Robin Aubrey. Give you good day, fair Robin. We are well met, Master Aubrey. When last Wednesday comes again, you will indeed be he."

And her eyes lighted on a small diamond earring which sparkled in the lobe of his left ear. She might have seen just such an ornament in the ear of any young exquisite, but in Robin's it entranced her. She clapped her hands delightedly, her laughter bubbling, her dancing eyes bidding him share it with her.

" Mr. Robin Aubrey ! " she cried. " Indeed, you do very well to tell me you are Robin Aubrey," and once more she dipped in a derisive reverence to the floor. " I know you from your diamond earring and your jewelled pomander." She looked at his modish, pointed shoes of brown velvet pinked with red to match his doublet. " None but misers foot it so daintily."

His voice broke through her laughter, loud as the bellow of an animal in pain. " Miser ! " he cried ; and looking at his face her laughter ceased on the instant, and she put her hand to her heart as if the whiteness of his cheeks and the distress in his eyes checked its beating.

" Miser," he repeated in a lower tone, nodding his

head to the syllables. So that was what was said of him wherever his name was known. And reasons for the name could be put forward. The belief could be argued. And there was no defence. Worse, there could be no defence, unless he was false to every dream that he was trying to dream true.

" Miser."

The word hurt horribly. It had never occurred to Robin that in that word lay the quite natural explanation of his secret life and the closed shutters of Abbot's Gap. Someone had been the first to use it, to be sure—some enemy. Someone had composed this detestable picture of a young skinflint gloating over his money bags in the corner of a locked and guarded house ; and the picture was there to be composed by anyone who was in the mind to belittle him. Very likely he would not have been so seriously distressed had another, even another girl, thrown the name at him. But it was this girl, Cynthia Norris, who lived at Winterborne Hyde. If ever his name had been mentioned in her presence, this was the epithet and portrait she had of him. Oh, horrible ! " Robin Aubrey, Miser."

The words were painted in front of him. Her laughter had set them forward in relief. They marched with him, a canopy, a banner of disgrace.

" What can I say to you ? " he stammered.

Still Cynthia had not got the truth.

" We share the blame," she said gently. " You set the jest on foot. I followed but overshot you. I beg your pardon—Robin Aubrey is a kinsman of yours."

" He is myself," said Robin.

" Oh ! " she cried in a whisper. The blood rushed into her face. Her hands flew up to it and hid it. " I am ashamed. My dear, I would not have so hurt you for the world."

The gentleness of her words moved Robin. He went to her side.

" You must not trouble yourself for so little," he said. " The blame is mine, if blame there is." He was sorely tempted to blurt out to Cynthia all the hopes and dark passions which had held him from his boyhood in so strict a thrall. He had kept his heart shut against the charges of Sir Francis Walsingham more easily than he was now able to against the contrition of Cynthia's voice.

" I did not know you. Else I should never have endured such foolish gossip. You have a very good cause, I am sure, for everything you do," she said, nodding her head wisely. " And if you keep your house locked and your windows dark, there is an excellent reason for it. Oh, I don't ask for it." Her eyes belied her lips. There was so tender a confidence in them, so eager an appeal to share his secret. " But if you could tell me ! It's pleasant to be sure that, whatever the rest may think, there's one friend who knows."

For a moment her hand rested on his arm. He was tempted as he never had been. She drew him down beside her on the long music stool. He felt the skirt of her dress against his leg. But he had lived with his secret too many years, nursing it with a fierce jealousy. No, not even to her—yet. He strengthened himself with that " yet."

" It is too heavy a tale for a summer afternoon," he returned, trying to speak lightly. But he did not dare to look at her lest he should see the appeal of her eyes waver into doubt and doubt again into utter disbelief. But if he had looked he would have seen only disappointment.

" Tell me rather why I find you practising your scales alone whilst all the rest of the house is at play."

E

" Why, sir, if I didn't," and she made an effort, though with as little success as he, to take up a careless tone, " I must put the company to the torment of hearing me.   And that my good nature would not have.   We are to act a Masque in the long gallery on Saturday night and there must be music to it.   Sir Robert's musician, Nicholas Bools, will play the lute, my cousin Olivia the pandora, and I, poor wretch, the virginal.   Yet more wretched than I the company which shall hear me."

She heaved a great sigh and played a scale upon her knees.

" I shall need Perseus on Saturday night," she exclaimed with the glimmer of a smile.

" At the first complaint, Perseus' sword will be out of its scabbard."

" Alas no !   For Perseus will be singing to my false notes as best he can without any scabbard to draw a sword from."

Robin sat up on the stool.

" There is to be a Masque."

" On Saturday night."

" And I am to sing in it ? "

" You are to do more than that.   Everybody in the party is to write some lines of it.   To-morrow there will be nothing but sighing poets from the garrets to the cellars.   By nightfall all must be done."

" Very well," said Robin.   " I shall write a madrigal to Cynthia."

" There is no Cynthia in the Masque," Cynthia returned severely.   " You will write exactly to the fraction of a sentiment what Mr. Stafford bids you write."

" The Ferret ! " cried Robin, and Cynthia broke into a laugh and cried " Hush."

" The name has stuck then," said Robin grimly

"Like other names, my friend Robin, but with greater justice," said Cynthia gently. Then she looked at him curiously. "You are that boy with the knot of ribbons," she said suddenly.

"I was that boy," Robin returned, drawing himself up majestically ; and Cynthia laughed again.

"Boy Robin," she said mischievously. "That we were told was Her Grace's word. Well, well, never lose heart. One day you shall swear big oaths and wear a little brown beard at the end of your chin. Bless your soul, sir, rubbing will not bring it on," and Robin dropped his hand quickly. "But all things will come if God pleases, even little brown beards."

Robin smiled absently. In the midst of her raillery Cynthia had been warning him that he must expect to find that others believed him to be a miserable lick-penny. Since Mr. Stafford was still of Sir Robert Bannet's household, it was very likely he who had spread the story, and seen that it lost nothing of its bitterness as he spread it.

"I might go," he said slowly. "I might trump up some fable of a message and go before they returned from hawking."

"Would that be very brave ? " Cynthia asked in a meek small voice.

Robin threw back his head.

"It would be comfortable."

"No doubt," she answered. "But must you be comfortable ? "

Robin swung round to her.

"Do you believe this slander ? "

"No."

"Then I shall stay," said he.

"It is a matter entirely for you to decide," Cynthia replied sedately.

" It is and I have decided," said Robin firmly.

He needed no advice from anyone, thank you, on a subject so personal. He would outface the winks and nudges of the whole county. Was he a coward that he should run away from them ? Not he ! But let them beware how they spoke—good Mr. Ferret above all.

" So it is Mr. Stafford who is composing this Masque," he said.

" With your good help," said she.

Suddenly he turned to her.

" And I am to play a part in it ? "

" Most important. You lead all in to the great hall."

" A herald ? "

" Well," Cynthia drawled out the word. " A kind of herald. A herald in a manner of speaking."

" A servant then ! "

" Yes."

" I knew it."

Robin rose to his feet petulantly and sat down again.

" I wear a leather jerkin and linen galligaskins," he exclaimed indignantly.

Cynthia's lips twitched. " Boy Robin," she murmured under her breath. Aloud she said :

" If they can be made in time."

" Carlo Manucci," said Robin.

" Carlo Manucci ? " and Cynthia repeated the name This queer little scene was to live in Cynthia's memories, so that each word that was spoken from the moment when Robin broke into the room stood out, each movement which the pair of them made fell into its place. She was laughing at the boy now and at his woeful face because for an evening his fine clothes must be laid aside. She was to remember it with a wistful amusement and with it that name of Carlo

Manucci; so that great harm was done and great
perils incurred. She would have given very much to
have let the name pass without a question and slip
altogether from her recollections. But she dwelled
upon it.

"Carlo Manucci? Who is he?"

"A servant in another play. I played him and
Mr. Stafford arranged that I should. I played him
abominably."

"In a leather jerkin and linen galligaskins?"
Cynthia asked demurely.

Robin nodded his head gloomily.

"And Humphrey is to be the Prince of Padua, no
doubt."

"Oh, no, no," Cynthia returned. "This is a
Masque. There are the Virtues in it, and allegories.
Humphrey is the God in a Cloud."

"Better still!"

"He comes down to earth and marries the Golden
Nymph."

Robin swung round towards the girl impetuously.

"If Stafford thinks that the servant——"

"In his leather jerkin and linen galligaskins," said
Cynthia.

"Is going to stand humbly aside whilst—No!"
He clenched his fist and then he checked himself.
"I get hot for nothing. You are playing the virginal."

At this point Cynthia should no doubt have rated
Robin for his impudence or sailed majestically from
the room. But in truth there was no impudence at
all in Robin's outburst. Sincerity and passion rang
in his voice, and Cynthia, hearing them, feeling the
chords of her own heart vibrating to them, sat still
and silent, now pale, now red. She had adored it
when Robin broke in upon her scales with his look of
romance and his debonair humour. But—but—would

not the passage of this week have been easier and
smoother if he had stayed outside that door ?   Not
even in the pretence and imagery of a Masque was
Humphrey Bannet to marry her.   So the young hot-
head at her side.   Not five minutes ago he had been
speculating whether he should stay or leave some
excuse and rush off before the party returned from
the day's hawking.   A word from her and he would
have gone.

" But it would have been a false word," she reflected,
" and I stopped him from going."

She stole a glance at him as he sat at her side, his
face thrust forward mutinous and sulky above his
ruff.   But even so she must smile.   " Boy Robin,"
she said to herself and knew that even now she would
stop him again, if word of hers could and he threatened
again to go.

" Humphrey shall be the God in the Cloud.   It is
very well.   And I shall be the servant.   That is very
well too.   But to quote Sir Francis Walsingham, we
shall see what we shall see," he said portentously.

What they did see was the God in the Cloud.
Humphrey Bannet burst into the room, his long
riding-boots bespattered and the dust upon his clothes.

" Cynthia ! " he cried and saw the pair of them
sitting side by side.   He paused for a second.

" Ah, Robin ! " as Robin got up without any haste.
" You are very welcome.   My father is changing his
dress, but he will be coming down in a few minutes."

He took Robin's hand.   It was coldly said and
coldly done.   It was not known by Robin that in
the Norris family and the Bannet, though the one was
Protestant and the other Catholic, there was serious
talk of a marriage between Humphrey and Cynthia.

CHAPTER VI

SIR ROBERT BANNET greeted Robin warmly in the Hall as the party assembled there before supper.

"I am very glad to see you in my house, Mr. Aubrey," he said, and taking his young guest by the arm he made him known to a group of people here and there.

Sir Robert was a soft white wily man between fifty and sixty years of age who so far had walked carefully and safely in times which were not too easy for men of his belief. He was a declared schismatic, willing to pay his fine for absenting himself on Sundays from the parish church when called upon to do so. And this was seldom until later in this very year 1586. Elizabeth was no crusader. Tolerant by nature and tolerant by policy, she could wink her eyes even at treason, if to wink would help the common wealth and do even a little to obliterate the cursed line of creed which split the kingdom like a deep fissure in a fair surface. Sir Robert was left to walk his wary path untroubled. A traveller caught by the night might haply looking down into the valley see the old chapel of Hilbury Melcombe brightly lit by many candles and hear the organ rolling out upon the darkness the solemn music of a mass. But if on arriving at Dorchester or Ware-ham he laid an information, he would be sharply told to mind his business and not meddle in matter which needed better brains than his. Sir Robert, sleek and smiling, made friends with all, and Robin noticed that a fair proportion of the forty guests assembled in the hall was like himself of the Protestant faith.

He noticed too that the story about himself was widely known. He was received with something of the same incredulity which had been shown by Cynthia Norris. No one expected the miser of Abbot's Gap to wear the look of this young court gallant. Nudges and winks there were too, and when Sir Robert was called to other civilities Robin found himself alone, his cheeks burning with shame. A voice behind him said clearly :

" Well, well, it is quite in nature. The prettiest butterflies were once grubs, though to be sure I never believed it of robins."

Robin did not turn round, but he had a hope that he would remember that voice. Mr. Stafford slipped up to his side and trusted that his old pupil had not forgotten his tutor.

" I have the liveliest recollections of Mr. Stafford," said Robin.

" There is to be a masque," said Mr. Stafford. " A simple foolish affair which we shall eke out with country songs. A few words each of us will write. The God of the Cloud, which is of course rain, marries the Golden Nymph, which is of course the earth, and prosperity comes of it. You are to act in it, Mr. Aubrey, if you will be so obliging."

Robin nodded his head.

" I am to be the servant who brings all in."

" Yes, most important. We shall make our own dresses," said Mr. Stafford.

" You need not trouble about mine," said Robin.

" I have one which will do very well. I wear it on my thrifty days, so you may be confident that it suits my mean condition and is sufficiently threadbare."

Robin spoke loudly so that as many as stood near might hear, and in a voice of extreme friendliness. For the first time since he had entered the hall Robin heard one or two laugh with him instead of at him. Mr. Stafford stepped back a pace at a loss how to take the words, and with a look of fear in his eyes. A pretty girl to whom Sir Robert had presented him but whose name he had not caught stepped to his side.

" That was well said, Mr. Aubrey," she cried, in a clear and pleasant voice, and as the others fell away she continued in a lower key, whilst a smile dimpled her face, " I am Cynthia's cousin, Olivia Cheveril."

" You are to be the Golden Nymph," said Robin.

" For the moment I am bidden—but I shall not tell you by whom—to be a shepherdess. But on my faith," and her smile broadened into a laugh, " I never saw a lamb which stood in such little need of shepherding."

At that moment the doors of the Great Chamber were thrown open and supper was announced. The meal was served at three tables set in the form of a cross-beam and two uprights laid upon its side on the ground. Robin found himself with Olivia Cheveril at his side at one of the side tables. He looked eagerly about him for Cynthia and found her at the chief table with Humphrey Bannet at her elbow. Humphrey Bannet was talking to her, but her eyes were wandering a trifle anxiously over the guests. They found Robin after a while and so sweet a smile lit up her face that it set his heart throbbing, and the colour reddening and paling in his face. It needed his companion's voice to call him down to the earth.

"And now that we have trod down the stars," said Olivia dryly, "shall we nibble?"

Course succeeded course. Fish, plaice, conger and whiting with cunning sauces of saffron and ambergris; pasties of fallow deer, wild-fowl and capons, garnished with green peas, and salads and sweet potatoes and artichokes; great joints of beef and mutton were served upon Sir Robert's silver plate. Sir Robert Bannet kept abreast of the times in his great house. The guests ate with the new-fangled silver forks and drank beer and muscadine and Rhenish wine from the new Venice glasses, and finished the meal with sugarmeats and apricots and bumpers of charneco. Robin hardly knew what he ate and hardly was aware of his neighbours, though from time to time he regarded them vaguely with kindness and a great pity. Olivia talked of the Masque and wondered how in the world they were going to present it.

"We have but the six days to write, learn and rehearse it, to make the dresses and paint the scenery. There are to be clouds solid enough to support Gods and virtues, and therefore solid enough to break the heads of us poor humans below."

At that a soldierly youth with a frank and open face leaned over the table from a place a little lower down.

"Nay, Mistress Olivia, never fear for the clouds. I shall hang them up and fix the ropes. Trust to John Savage. I have fought in the Low Countries where we were put to such shifts that nothing comes amiss now. Your clouds shall stand firm as earth itself and then swing to the floor as lightly as a feather."

"We shall be much beholden to you," said Olivia.

"Put your faith in John Savage," said the other, and he turned back to his corner of the table.

"Faith, John," said a pale, contemplative young

man who sat next to Savage, " is of two kinds. It may be a private, independent judgment, or a compulsion of religion. Now which is yours ? "

The soldier turned eyes of reverence upon the speaker.

" You shall tell me, Anthony," he said, and he listened with the humility due to an oracle whilst Anthony with divisions and sub-divisions expounded these high themes.

" I love to hear you talk," John Savage exclaimed in admiration, " though when you've done, I don't know whether I am standing on my head or my heels ! "

Anthony, whose family name Robin was in a moment to hear, smiled in a faded sort of way, and a third man, older than the other two, broke in upon them noisily :

" My good Babington, was this the sort of talk which occupied my Lady Shrewsbury's table when you were a page in her household ? I remember my dear friend, the Count of Aremberg, saying to me over a posset : ' I love you, Captain Fortescue, for you never mix your wine with philosophy.' The Duke d'Alençon made a third at our little gathering, and he patted me on the shoulder and agreed."

The three names of Babington, Savage and Fortescue were to be known all over England within the month. Robin knew nothing of them at this time but he was amazed to see three men so dissimilar brought together in so close a conjunction. The plain soldier, a man of his hands, the dilettante philosopher with his meticulous arguments, and the flamboyant Captain Fortescue. The last indeed was the oddest of the three, and Robin wondered how in the world he came to find himself a guest at Hilbury Melcombe. Never had he heard so many great names dragged into the conversation

and flung together with Captain Fortescue as bosom
friend of them all. He was as fleering and boastful a
talker as a Captain of Fortune on Hounslow Heath.
He was dressed to match his words, in a slashed satin
honey-coloured doublet, a grey cloak plastered with
gold lace, and breeches of blue velvet.

"We are to have a Masque here, are we?" he
cried. "When I dined with His Grace the Duke of
Guise in Paris we had the players from the King's
Theatre to entertain us. I never saw such company.
Bernardino de Mendoza was amongst the least of 'em."

Mr. Babington jogged Captain Fortescue's elbow.
The name of Mendoza had rung out in Captain
Fortescue's high, feverish voice, and it had reached
to the head table. It was not a lucky name to be
heard in an English house. For not one of those
present but knew that Bernardino de Mendoza,
Spanish Ambassador, had been drummed incontinently
out of the kingdom two years before for complicity
in Throckmorton's conspiracy. Sir Robert himself
caught the name and glanced indignantly at the
offender. Captain Fortescue, however, was not
abashed.

"As I say," he continued, "the fellow was of no
account. He's the Spanish Ambassador to France
nowadays and therefore one can't but meet him, if
you live hand-in-glove with the gentility. An alarming fellow, Mr. Babington! He said things—I'll
warrant there's no truth in them"—and he lowered
his voice—but Robin heard a whisper of "sixty
thousand men, sir, with Parma at their head."

He heard no more, however, for Sir Robert, whether
from fear of the indiscretions of Captain Fortescue, or
because the meal had come to its end rose from his
chair in the centre of the long table. He said a word
or two to his neighbours, and was making a circuit of

the tables when his musician, Mr. Nicholas Bools, a small, round, consequential man, went up to Robin.

" There will be singing to-morrow, Mr. Aubrey, in preparation for the Masque. We shall meet after supper in the long gallery. You sing a part at first sight, of course ? "

Robin agreed. It was the ordinary accomplishment of a gentleman and he had not neglected it.

" As well as another, I hope. I have not the gamut of a blackbird but I have more notes than a cuckoo."

" And all crotchets, Mr. Aubrey, I'll be bound."

Captain Fortescue was standing opposite to Robin and bending forward with both his hands upon the table amongst the silver plates and the shining glass. His eyes, hostile and cunning, gloated ; his round, fattish face was flushed. He was laughing a little to himself with a sort of Watch-me leer towards Savage and Anthony Babington. It would have been obvious a mile away that he was going to be very sharp and witty at Robin's expense. Olivia Cheveril gasped at Robin's side.

" Very crotchety singing, Mr. Aubrey, and a great economy of music, I'll be bound. Music's a golden thing so we may be sure you'll not squander it. A few crotchets no doubt——"

" But no quavers, Captain Fortescue," Robin answered quietly ; and he laughed easily and naturally. " I will sing you point and counterpoint, the two of us alone, in a quiet corner of the park, to-morrow before breakfast, and we'll find out if your singing is less clumsy than your wit."

Captain Fortescue drew back, astonished and disturbed. He had thought to put this boy down, to see him shrink in confusion and himself to sail off with a flirt of his embroidered cape. And here the boy was quietly bidding him to a duel. But before he could think of an answer John Savage drew him back.

" I am the man to do the singing for you, Captain Fortescue.   At five in the morning, good Mr. Fire-eater," he said hotly to Robin Aubrey.   " I know the prettiest place for a singing-match——"

" No, no ! "

A smooth voice spoke and Sir Robert thrust himself smoothly between Savage and Captain Fortescue.

" Mr. Savage is ready for everything, from clouds in the great hall to a singing-match in the park.   But we shall only sing after supper in the long gallery, each one taking up his part in great amity.   To-night the ladies bid us dance there and that too in great amity and friendship."

White and soft and smiling Sir Robert led off Captain Fortescue and John Savage, and Robin noticed with surprise that he seemed to pay a special deference to the ridiculous Captain.   What in the world could Sir Robert Bannet of Hilbury Melcombe have in common with so flighty a person ?   He turned round to put the question to Olivia and discovered that she had gone from his side.   In her place stood a man of middle-age and middle-height plainly dressed in a suit of a mulberry colour, with the most unnoticeable face.   The nose was a nose, the mouth a mouth, the eyes a dull grey or a dull green, whichever you choose, the complexion neither tanned by the weather nor pale with an indoor life but just leaden, and even his voice had no individual tone by which it could be remembered.

" I sat upon your other side at the table, Mr. Aubrey," said this man.   " You were not aware of it. No, I beg you not to excuse yourself.   I am not conspicuous and I prefer it so.   I ask you to observe the arrangement of these tables."

They were alone now in the great chamber. Robin looked at the tables. He could see nothing odd in the way they were set, but his companion was looking at him with a sharp birdlike glance as though he should.

" Do you see nothing in it ? "

" No," Robin answered, with a shake of the head. " I see one long table and one at each end supporting it. It all seems very usual in a great house."

Robin was rather inclined to look towards the door. There was to be dancing in the long gallery, and there was a maid up there perhaps—he dared to hope it—wondering with some indignation why he tarried.

" Yet it is a pattern to be remembered, Mr. Aubrey, even though you see no mystery in it now," the other observed. " One of these days I think you will find it used for a different purpose than the convenience of a meal."

There was no special emphasis laid upon any word, but the words were strange in themselves, and a curious discomfort began to steal over Robin. It could not come from this insignificant person nor from the ambiguity of his speech, nor from the actual arrangement of the tables, he assured himself. Yet he was troubled, so that for the moment he forgot the long gallery, and his feet ceased to tingle to be off. He hated mysteries, for they seemed to threaten the secret aim of his life. It seemed to him that the candles burned suddenly dim, and the air grew suddenly cold—so cold that he did actually shiver.

" My name is Gregory," the stranger continued. " I am Arthur Gregory, of Lyme, and I had the honour of knowing both your father and your mother. It is curious that we should meet in this house, being both of us Protestants. But Sir Robert Bannet is a wise man and believes in boiling Protestant and Catholic in the same pot."

There was a kind of a sneer in Mr. Gregory's voice and Robin answered quickly :

" Well, he has excellent warrant for that, since so Her Majesty has been doing ever since she began to reign." And with that remark Robin got himself out of the room.

He hurried up the stairs to the long gallery and watched with a cloudy brow Cynthia Norris dancing a pavane with Humphrey Bannet. But she was his partner afterwards in a lavolta, and the touch of her hand in his and the throbbing of her heart against his as he swung her round in the leap lifted him again to the stars. There is a pause in that dance when partner stands opposite to partner with the feet together. During one of these pauses Cynthia chided him, though with a smile in her eyes and a quivering of her lips which denied her anger.

" Will you quarrel with everyone, sir ? "

" Nay, I quarrel with none, Andromeda. A fine Captain thought to put me down. But that is done with."

" I am glad. I met you but to-day, and I should grieve to drop rosemary into your grave before the week's out. We take two steps to the right."

Robin took two steps to the right, protesting that nobody under a General should ever kill him, so long as he held a place in a corner of her thoughts. At the next pause she said :

" You looked at Humphrey with the moodiest eyes that ever I saw," and this with a quick glance at him and away again.

" He danced with you."

" And should he not ? This is his father's house and I am a guest in it. I have learnt something of natural history to-day."

" Share your knowledge with me ! "

' There are brown bears in the Purbeck Hills."

Robin stepped forward to gather her for the leap, but she recoiled in a mock terror.

" God a' mercy, would you eat me, sir ? "

" Yes, indeed ! " said he, as his arms went about her. " Bears eat honey twice a day. It benefits their health."

He swung around, and their feet flew.

F

CHAPTER VII

METAMORPHOSIS OF CAPTAIN FORTESCUE

FOR these two a week of enchantment followed. They lived within a golden mist, each minute bringing its amazement—a chance-meeting in the rose garden, a pair of horses which would lag side by side and very close, a discovery that each shared the same miraculous thoughts. After dinner when the elders smoked in the arbours, there were the rehearsals of the Masque in the long gallery. True, Cynthia sat at the virginal and Robin declaimed his part upon the stage, but their eyes met and she would miss a note and he a cue, and in a sweet confusion all must be done again. These unspoken messages which neither had been able to interpret on the afternoon when Perseus broke in upon Andromeda were now as easy to read as the alphabet. Robin had long since explained to her how he had thought to find a little girl practising her scales with a dragon of a governess at her side. There had been destiny in that—and kindness. The household might hoot at him for a miser if it chose and he would meet it with a smiling face. He had an armour against it—a new sort of armour which had nothing in common with the watchful secrecy of his boyhood. And though odd things were happening during that week at Hilbury Melcombe, they hardly disturbed the dreams of these two infatuates.

But odd things were happening. On the Wednesday, for instance, at dinner-time, Dakcombe, greyer by five more years than when he waited upon the boy at Eton, brought over a dozen letters which had been delivered at Abbot's Gap by the carrier. Robin ran upstairs with them and arranged them unopened on a little table by his window. They were letters of great importance to him and would need thought and a very careful perusal. There was no time for that now with dinner smoking upon the table, and it was more prudent to leave them with their seals unbroken against the time when he would have leisure. But dinner was followed by a rehearsal and it was not until four o'clock of the afternoon that Robin was free. He went up to his room, but as he reached out his hand to take up the letters, he dropped it again at his side. He looked round the room uneasily. Nothing so far as he remembered had been disturbed. He opened a coffer and pulled out one or two drawers. Nothing had been touched. Yet the order of the letters had been changed. The one on the top—he recollected the handwriting quite clearly—was no longer on the top.

He sat down in a chair and for a moment was troubled. Someone had come into the room and handled those letters whilst he was held by the rehearsal in the gallery on the floor below. He turned them over one by one. He carried them to the window. Not a seal had been tampered with, and they were all sealed. But someone had been curious. Who ?

Mr. Stafford, Sir Robert's secretary, had been directing the rehearsal. Robin was certain that he had never left the gallery while it continued. Robin ran anxiously over the names of his fellow-guests. There was only one whom he could reasonably suspect.

" Captain Fortescue," he decided.

Fortescue, a braggart, an adventurer, with his loud talk and his flaunting clothes, was a little out of his place in this company. He had boasted of

an acquaintance with the Duc de Guise, the hottest
of Elizabeth's enemies in France—aye, and with
Bernardino de Mendoza too.   Robin, as he recalled
Fortescue's boastings at supper on the first night of
his visit, grew more certain and more and more
alarmed.   After all, this was a Catholic house.
Messengers were always travelling backwards and
forwards between England and the Continent, plotting
the liberation of Mary Queen of Scots and a revolution
which would dethrone Elizabeth.   Robin remembered
that when Sir Robert had led Captain Fortescue away
from the supper-table, he had shown to him a deference
rather difficult to understand.   Robin examined the
seals upon the letters again and with an intense care.
They had not been broken—that was certain—and
without breaking them no one could have read a word
of what the letters held.

Robin read them all now with the door of his room
locked.   It was well that no Captain Fortescue had
read them, he reflected, with a gasp of relief, and he
burned them all then and there upon his hearth,
beating out the flakes until nothing was left but a pile
of minute and indecipherable ashes.   At supper he
watched Captain Fortescue but not by a glance or a
question did the Captain betray the slightest interest
in Robin's correspondence.

On the following night the second of these strange
events occurred.   Robin was waked from his sleep by
the clatter of a horse ridden at a gallop.   It was
Robin's habit to sleep with his windows flung wide to
the air and the curtains open ; and out of the quiet
of the night the noise broke with a startling urgency.
It grew nearer, louder.   Someone was coming to
Hilbury Melcombe in a desperate haste.

Robin flung back his bed-clothes.   His room looked
out from the front of the house to the left of the great

Porch. He ran to the window, his heart sinking and fluttering within his breast. All the careful secret plans were ripe now. The ashes in his hearth proved it. Within the next week the dreams would begin to crystallise into actual facts and deeds—unless he was stopped at the last moment as others had been—many others.

The moon was at the full and the Park slept so peacefully in the bright silver light that Robin could hear the fallow deer cropping the grass a hundred yards away ; and above that sound the horse's hooves. A second later he saw the messenger, at the corner of a small coppice. He was swaying in the saddle like a drunkard. Yet when he came in sight of the house he plied his whip—as though some strict order that he carried must be delivered out of hand.

" It is for me," Robin said to himself in despair.

During how many years had he striven and spent and lived to make one dream true ? And he was caught now in a trap. A minute and he would hear the messenger's riding-boots ring on the floor outside his door and the order to open which could not be disobeyed.

The rider drew up at the door, flung himself to the ground, passed his arm through the reins, and hammered upon the panels like a man out of his wits. Robin drew back a step lest he should be seen. He could hear the man breathing in sobbing gasps and Robin's fears were lightened. There was too much of panic in the sound for the bearer of a message. Here was someone with a private trouble, a private terror. Robin approached the window again. He was on the point of crying out that he would come down when the door was opened. He saw Anthony Babington, and heard his cry of alarm.

" It's Barnewell ! "

Babington was joined on the drive by John Savage, and a moment later by Captain Fortescue. They had slipped dressing gowns over their night-clothes and they clustered about the new-comer. Robin was not the only man to lie that night at Hilbury Melcombe with a quaking heart.

"She spoke to me," cried the rider whom they called Barnewell. "I was in the garden by the river —choosing a place—when she appeared. Oh, my God! she came straight to me. She knows everything. She said: 'You see I am unarmed.' Her eyes beat me down. It's the death of all of us"; and his voice ran up into a shrill scream.

A little silence followed and then Babington said:

"All must be put off. I have doubted, as you know, whether we had the right, or whether we should wait until some other did the work for us——"

John Savage broke in upon him petulantly.

"Oh, debate and philosophy—I'm sick to death of them. The work's for me to do. I was chosen."

And just behind Robin's shoulder someone breathed sharply.

Robin swung round as if he had been struck. Mr. Gregory of Lyme was standing in the room with his finger to his lips. He was fully dressed.

"I sleep in the next room," he whispered. "I was writing a letter when I heard the noise. Was there ever such mad talk? I never did hear the like of it," and he uttered a low and contemptuous laugh. "The good Barnewell spoke one word of truth, however. Can you guess which it was, Mr. Aubrey?" and he laughed again this time with a passionless cruelty which made Robin's blood run cold.

Under the window the horse's hooves rasped on the gravel. Gregory and Robin looked cautiously down. John Savage was leading Barnewell's horse to the stables and the others had gone into the house.

"A handful of Zanies thinking they'll convulse the

world ! Well, wise men draw together by some affinity of nature. Why not addlepates, too ? " said Mr. Gregory.

Below them a step sounded and the house door was gently closed.

" That's the God of the Clouds, no doubt, Mr. Aubrey, but we have no proof of it, alas ! " Gregory resumed rather bitterly. " No Bannet will show his nose to-night where an honest man could see him. The God in the cloud is a very appropriate character, Mr. Aubrey. You are to play a servant, I understand. Shall we see to it that character is appropriate too ? "

This time Mr. Gregory spoke on a kindlier note. He was standing opposite to Robin in the moon-lit room, swaying backwards on his heels and his toes. " It's evident why such as you and I were bidden to this week of entertainment, Mr. Aubrey. We are the screen and curtain. It wouldn't be likely there'd be plotting and conspiracy with the house half full of Protestants."

" Plotting ? " Robin exclaimed. " Come, Mr Gregory. Nobody's going to plot with a feather-head like Captain Fortescue, and he was out with the others in the porch."

" Captain Fortescue ! " said Mr. Gregory, laughing again. " Aye, there's a Captain for you. He didn't seem over passionate to sing point and counterpoint with you, Mr. Aubrey, the other night."

He broke off abruptly and again his finger went to his lips. Outside the door the stairs creaked, a foot stumbled and then all was silent again.

" It's all at an end. We may to our beds ourselves."

" As if nothing had happened ? " exclaimed Robin, and Gregory turned back from the door and stood close by him.

" Just that, Mr. Aubrey. As if nothing had happened. Indeed nothing has happened—no, nor will. Put to-night altogether out of your head. It will be wisdom to-morrow if you have slept the sleep of a tired boy through all this clatter.''

Robin was very willing. He did not understand the talk upon the drive, or Barnewell's terror. Mr. Gregory's exclamations were a riddle to him. There were other matters with which he was concerned. Indeed the most perplexing element in the night's adventure was the inconspicuous Mr. Gregory of Lyme. Why was he still up and dressed ? How had he crept so silently into the room ? Whence did he get the authority with which he had spoken ? Was there not, too, a problem about three tables which Mr. Gregory had set to him ? The problem to be worked out before six o'clock, or there would be two hours' detention and a hundred lines of Virgil. . . . Robin fell asleep at that point, and when he woke again the sun was up and the birds noisy in the trees.

But the enigma of Mr. Gregory remained with him. The unnoticeable man who suddenly spoke with the command of the Centurion : '' I say unto one Go and he goeth, and to another Come and he cometh, and to my servant Do this and he doeth it.'' Thus had Mr. Gregory of Lyme spoken to Robin the night before, and Robin had obeyed him wondering. He was to wonder more, however. The day was Friday, and the house Catholic, and though no constraint was put upon the guests, a certain sedateness was observed in the entertainment. No field sports were arranged for the morning and no one danced in the long gallery after supper. For once the household went early to bed. Robin was sound asleep when a hand twitched at his shoulder. He awoke reluctantly to see Mr. Gregory at his bedside with a candle in his hand.

'' What ! Must you be here again ? '' Robin asked sullenly. '' Do you never go to bed ? ''

"I shall sleep for a fortnight when I am back in my house at Lyme," said Mr. Gregory.

"Well, I wish you were there now," said Robin, and he turned over in the bed, so that the light might not fall upon his eyes. But Mr. Gregory of Lyme was not satisfied.

He shook Robin again, laughing softly.

"These boys! They are like dogs. They must run here and there, eat their food, and play games, and then in an instant they're asleep and damn the fellow who wakes them! I have something to show you."

"I don't want to see it," said Robin.

"You will regret it all your life if you don't, Mr. Aubrey."

"Life is full of regrets, Mr. Gregory. Who am I that I should not have my proper share of them? Oh!"

For Mr. Gregory had pinched the wick of his candle and the smell which arose from it made Robin sit upright in his bed.

"That's better," said Gregory with a grin. "I reckoned that your senses would be delicate. If you will dress, I will show you why Captain Fortescue was unwilling to sing point and counterpoint with you in a quiet corner of the garden."

"Oh, very well. I shall never rid myself of you unless I do."

Robin rubbed the sleep out of his eyes and smoothed the rumpled waves of brown hair upon his head. What with points to be tied and doublets to be buttoned, dressing was a complicated business in those days.

"Some light shoes, if you please, Mr. Aubrey."

"Well, I am not putting on my riding-boots and spurs, am I, Mr. Gregory?"

"You are very well now, Mr. Aubrey."

"God be praised," said Robin.

Willy nilly, he was thoroughly awake, but mutinous.

" The night is for sleep, Mr. Gregory," he grumbled.

" So you tell me, but you must widen your knowledge, Mr. Aubrey. As I see it, it's for plots and treasons, Mr. Aubrey, for black hearts and bloody assassinations, Mr. Aubrey. And so you shall say before you get into your bed again."

Gregory spoke quite equably, as one speaking of every day affairs, priming his candle the while with his forefinger and his thumb. But for the second time he awakened in Robin an eerie kind of uneasiness.

" You are the most uncomfortable man I have ever come across."

" I hope that others in this house will shortly say the same," said Gregory. He smiled pleasantly but he raised his eyes from the candle flame and Robin was shocked by the cruelty which gleamed in them. Gregory opened the door to the width of an inch, peered and listened and then taking Robin by the sleeve, he blew out the candle he was carrying.

" You will follow me without a sound."

Outside the door the big house stretched dark and silent. Mr. Gregory flitted ahead, Robin trod upon his heels. At times the corridors were so black that it was only Gregory's touch upon his sleeve which told Robin that he was there in front of him. At times a shaft of moonlight from a tall window threw a slant of silver across the floor and lit them up for a second as they passed. Robin fancied that they were moving towards the east wing, but he could not be sure. His guide, however, never faltered in his direction of the way. He turned and twisted and went on, as though every corner of the house was known to him. At one of these corners Gregory stopped and laid a hand upon the lad's shoulder. Robin could not see his face, but he felt the grip of the hand tighten.

" Listen ! "

Gregory hardly breathed the word.

Robin wondered whether he would hear a thunderstorm, so wildly his heart was throbbing in his ears. But after a little while a sound reached him from very far away—not the kind of sound which he had expected, the creak of a stair, a stumble against a coffer or a stool—but a curious hum like the drone of bees about a hive which swelled suddenly and diminished and continued in a monotone with every now and then for a brief minute a complete intermittence. The buzzing grew louder as they advanced, grew loudest as Gregory carefully turned the handle of a door and opened it. Robin was led into a room as black as pitch. The sounds rose from below them.

"Take care," Gregory whispered. "And not a sound."

He knelt down upon the floor and in a wall which their faces almost touched, there appeared a thread of light. The wall was nothing but a pair of stout doors. Gregory drew one of them towards him. The chink widened. Robin looked straight down into the big chapel of the house. The little room was a private loft. The doors opened from the roof to the floor of it. A step forward and Robin would have pitched down on to the stone pavement of the chapel forty feet below. The chapel was lit, candles burned upon the altar and a small company of people were on their knees. At the altar with his back towards them a priest in his vestments was intoning a mass, and every now and then the worshippers joined together in a response. Anthony Babington was present, Barnewell who had ridden to Hilbury in such desperate hurry the night before, some others of the guests, and kneeling alone on the first of the altar steps was the young soldier, John Savage.

Robin looked for Sir Robert and Humphrey, but

neither of them was anywhere to be seen. Then the priest lifted something from the altar, rose from his knees and turned towards his congregation. It was well that Gregory had gripped tight Robin's shoulder, otherwise a cry would have burst from the boy's lips. For the man in the priests vestments was Captain Fortescue, of the gold embroidery and the braggart voice.

" Watch !   Watch ! " whispered Mr. Gregory.

The priest raised before them a flashing poniard. He held it aloft for a few moments. Then he descended the steps to John Savage and bent over him. He said, using the Latin tongue :

" Take this consecrated weapon ! Let it serve God ! "

No more than that and Robin realised that Captain Fortescue in the priest's vestments was a different being from Captain Fortescue in the embroidered cloak.

John Savage took the poniard reverently, kissed it and slipped it into a scabbard at his side. As the priest reached out his hand and began to pronounce a blessing, Mr. Gregory of Lyme shut the door.

" Let us be quick ! " he said.

They hurried along the corridors as quickly and silently as they had come. When they were again in Robin's bedroom neither spoke for a little while. Robin dropped into a chair and buried his face in his hands.

" So behind this fine entertainment," he said at last, " Protestants and Catholics boiling in the same pot, there has been rank treachery ? "

" Yes," said Mr. Gregory.

" Then she ?   The she of whom Barnewell spoke last night ? "

" Yes," said Mr. Gregory. " The Queen. Barnewell went to the Palace gardens by the river at Richmond. All the world may walk there with her Grace's goodwill. He went to see behind which bush a murderer should stand."

" And she approached him ? "

" She said, ' See, I am unarmed.' She has no fear. She will not go guarded."

" And to-night ? " cried Robin in a low voice. " The dagger ? "

" Consecrated by Mr. Ballard, the Jesuit priest fresh from that fine Englishman Cardinal Allan at Rheims," said Mr. Gregory contemptuously. " But have no fear, Mr. Aubrey ! That dagger will not find its way to the Queen's heart." He dropped his hand upon Robin's shoulder. " Her servants will see to it."

There came upon Robin an overwhelming sense of his own insufficiency. Others watched for her, toiled for her, spent their fortunes and their lives for her, subduing themselves to their work, masking their faces—that was his trouble. He could not mask his face. He had that art still to learn.

" How shall I meet them to-morrow with an open face ? " he cried.

" I think few of them will be here to-morrow," Gregory answered. " You will meet Sir Robert and Mr. Humphrey and your good friend the Ferret, no doubt—all no doubt very innocent people. You must school your features, Mr. Aubrey. But the rest will have gone Londonwards, the priest with them."

Mr. Gregory of Lyme was right. When Robin went down the stairs to breakfast, he discovered that the house-party was the smaller by the absence of Babington, Barnewell, John Savage and Captain Fortescue, and a good many others amongst Sir Robert's guests. Affairs had called them all to London.

CHAPTER VIII

THE BETTER PLAN

A T noon on the Saturday Cynthia Norris and Robin Aubrey were standing side by side on the gravel walk at the back of Hilbury Melcombe. They had been busy with their rehearsal all through the morning and waited now for Sir Robert's trumpeter to call them in to dinner. At their feet the garden fell away in a steep succession of terraces to a stream in the bed of the valley; and the noise of the water tumbling over its tiny lashers rose in a clear small music to their ears. The floor of each terrace was a mown, well-watered emerald lawn, in the midst of which an oblong lily pond was set in stone. A stone wall backed it overhung with clematis as white as stars, red roses and eglantine. On each side of the terraces winding steps in stone led down between tall urns, and in the ponds fountains played. Over all the sun flamed in a pale-blue sky.

" This is our last day together," said Cynthia, and she did not try to hide the wistful appeal of her voice.

" For a little while only," Robin answered.

Though no word of love had yet been spoken by either of them to the other, they were grave with the great gravity of lovers.

" You go early to-morrow ? " Robin asked.

Cynthia told him of the arrangements for her departure. A cart would start at daybreak, carrying the baggage of her cousin and herself.

" Olivia and I will ride off after breakfast. I shall dine at Olivia's house and go on alone afterwards."

" I have a better plan," said Robin, staring down into the valley, and Cynthia's lips twitched suddenly.

" Had you not a plan in your cradle, sir ? For a new kind of rockers, I think. And when you cut your teeth—yesterday, was it ?—did you not have a plan for drawing them down with a poultice ? Well, well, let me hear how you improve upon mine ! "

But alas ! before she could hear, the trumpeter blew his summons.

" We have not the time now," Robin exclaimed. " Why must we be always having meals ? "

" Because pasties made of air are only satisfying to——"

Before she could utter the word Robin turned quickly round upon her. " To whom ? "

Cynthia gasped and got red and sought to cover her confusion with a laugh.

" It is not for me to say," she said in a hurry, and so was more confused than ever.

She looked about her for help and through the windows saw that the great hall was filling up with people and now she wanted them away.

" What of this better plan ? " she asked in a still greater hurry. " When shall I hear of it ? "

" To-night, if you will."

" I will," said she.

Robin looked down the garden slope.

" The third terrace," he said.

" I cannot see it from here," she replied.

" Nor from any of the windows. That's why," said Robin, nodding his head wisely, and again the blood mantled Cynthia's cheeks.

" When the Masque is ended——" he began.

" There will be congratulations and more eating and drinking——"

" And such a hubbub and confusion, that no one's absence would be noted."

" And out here there will be moonlight and silence," said Cynthia.

" On the third terrace," Robin resumed, " there is a setting of yew hedges like a theatre and a bench placed ready——"

" Yes, and at the far end of the lily pond, a Mercury poised ready for flight." Cynthia took him up. " A warning ! "

" A pretence. For he never flies," Robin answered. " I shall be there on the bench."

Cynthia laughed suddenly. But there was a little break in her voice as she asked :

" In your leather jerkin and your linen galligaskins? "

Robin laughed in reply with a great enjoyment.

" Mr. Stafford wrote my part, and I have studied it with great care. There are only ten lines in it, but I have sounded the character better than he who wrote it. The servant I play is no Carlo Manucci. No ! I have the truth of him. He is the sort of servant who goes courting in his master's clothes."

Cynthia's laughter bubbled from her lips.

" On the third terrace, Carlo. I shall be there to hear your plan."

" And three words only, my dear," said Robin softly. " But three words as long as life—longer if God wills."

And once more the gravity of lovers drove the laughter from their faces and delayed their feet.

The afternoon was given to the last touches, a scratch meal was taken by the performers, and they retired to dress. No girl ever prinked herself before her mirror with a greater care to look her best than

did Robin that evening. There was to be an hour
in the garden when he would plead for a great prize.
He was not worthy of it, to be sure, but he meant to
look as worthy of it as he could. He put on a rose-
coloured velvet doublet and breeches of the same hue
fitting close. His stockings were of a lighter shade,
his small ruff was piped with gold, the roses on his
shoes matched his doublet and were spangled with
silver. He carried a pair of embroidered gloves to
give his hands something to do when he was standing
on the stage, and went down to the long gallery where
the players were assembled. All there was bustle and
disarray. It seemed as though the Masque would
not be ready for a month. But even in the midst of
the confusion Mr. Stafford found time to fling up his
hands in indignation at the sight of Robin. For a
moment he was the tutor again at Mrs. Parker's house
at the end of the lane.

" But you are a servant, sirrah ! Odd's life, but
this is rank contumacy ! The Masque is ruined. You
are the first to be seen. You lead all in. You Jack
Doodle, the buttery servant. By God, sir, the
Masque's ruined."

Robin shook his head gravely.

" I go by the lines, Mr. Stafford. They are of your
composing. I rush into the great chamber, followed
by Torches—these are the stage directions—when Sir
Robert and his guests are finishing their supper."

" Jack Doodle rushes in, sir."

" And Jack Doodle speaks at once your admirable
lines, Mr. Stafford. The very spirit of poetry is in
them.

> 'Hold, gentles all ! Be patient whilst I prate
> In fairer mien than fits my mean estate.'

In other words, Jack Doodle is wearing his master's
clothes. There's no doubt of it."

G

Mr. Stafford exclaimed upon the stupidity of his pupil.

"Nay, sir, the words refer to the civility of your address. Besides, mien and mean represent a play upon words." But Mr. Stafford was called off to where a corner of the cloud had got loose. Robin looked at Cynthia, who, seated already at her virginal, was abubble with delight, and gathered the torch-bearers behind him. At the right moment he rushed into the Great Chamber. Sir Robert and his guests were duly amazed and prettily counterfeited their alarm at the irruption. However, after debate, they agreed to be led in and hear "a rustical foolish allegory designed for their delight."

It went very well. Mr. Stafford's doggerel was interspersed with country songs. There were dances, heyes and caprioles, and even a dump. The cloud descended very properly to earth—John Savage was a better carpenter than he was like to be a bravo. Humphrey Bannet made a fine descending figure as the god, and an entertainment which would not have been found tolerable in a later age was received with enthusiasm. In the midst of the congratulations and applause Robin slipped out of the gallery. There was no one on the staircase. The hall was empty. Outside the garden slept in the moonlight, its flowers closed.

At the west end of the third terrace yew hedges a yard thick and more than Robin's height made a small amphitheatre about a bench. There Robin waited. In front of him the oblong pond lay still and shining as a strip of silver, and beyond it the bronze Mercury on a pedestal stood holding his cloak up behind his head, poised for flight. Whither? Robin asked himself. Nowhither. There he stood, week after week, month after month, year after year, on moonlit nights and summer days, through storms, through mists, always poised and never flying. A message to deliver which never was delivered, someone to serve and the service never done.

A little cry brought Robin to his feet. Cynthia, holding up her farthingale so that it could not catch her feet, came running down the winding steps, now out of sight, now some jewel in her hair flashing in the moonlight, now plain to see from head to foot. She ran with such light, swift steps she might have been flying on the errand which the Mercury shirked. She came to Robin, her eyes like stars, her white throat and bosom rising and falling. He had thought out some fine speeches to make to her, but alas! he had wasted his time. His arms were out and she within them before a word of them could be uttered.

" Cynthia ! " he whispered.

" Boy Robin," she answered with her cheek against his heart.

Robin spoke his three words.

" I love you."

He lifted up her chin with his hand and kissed her upon the lips.

" Oh, if you had not come to Hilbury ! " she moaned.

Robin comforted her. It wasn't possible that he shouldn't have come. In the dawn of time it was ordered that one night of late July in this scented garden Cynthia Norris and Robin Aubrey should plight their troth. Cynthia, however, must still torture herself.

" There was so much persuasion. The two families, neighbours, two estates would have become one."

Robin held her off, gazed at her as though she had been striken to death and then gathered her again to his heart.

" Humphrey ? "

" Yes. And I might have yielded."

" Never ! "

But Cynthia insisted.

" But I might ! No one had caused me a single added heartbeat. So why not Humphrey as well as another ?   When you broke into the little music-room —oh ! "—she had to pause as she looked back on the miracle of that afternoon, to draw a deep breath, to make sure by running her hand over his shoulder, that he was here in flesh and blood—" I was miserable. I think that was why I played so many wrong notes."

" I am sure of it," said Robin stoutly.

" I was thinking that I was set apart from other girls, that I couldn't love. And then I looked up, and there were you staring at me in the mirror as if I were the earth's only jewel. Oh, I adored it—and the next day I adored you—and to this pass am I come, oh shameless ! " but she ended the words with a quick laugh which was full of pride and delight in her shamelessness.

The quiet and the peace of the night lapped them about. It was the girl who remembered, the first of the pair, where they were.

" We must go back. They will all be sitting down to supper."

Robin held her fast.

" Dearest, you hold my heart."

" It shall be wrapped in rose leaves."

" You must hold my secrets too."

Cynthia smiled.

" What a lad it is for secrets and he not full-grown yet."

" I shall never be taller than I am to-night," said Robin.

" God be praised," she returned. " Else I should never reach your lips ; " and her hands tightened about his neck.   " I shall buy a gold casket for your secrets."

" You shall have them to-morrow.   I shall ride with you when you go."

" Then Olivia will have them too," said Cynthia disconsolately.

But Robin had his better plan.   On the way to Wareham the road forked.   The road to the south climbed the Purbeck Hills, and thence a track wound down to Abbot's Gap.

" I want you to come down with me to my house. I have that to tell you which I have told to none. You will hold everything of me then, heart, secrets— honour."

He spoke gravely and simply, and Cynthia answered him at once.

" I will arrange it with Olivia."

They went together up the steps, and the house, with its lighted windows, rose storey by storey within their view.   " We'll keep our secret for to-night," said Cynthia.   Separately they slipped into the hall and separately they sat at supper.   Early in the morning Robin sent off his servant with the led horse.   Olivia, Cynthia and he rode away at seven.   At the corner where the road forks by Bindon Abbey, Cynthia and Robin said good-bye to Olivia.   At eleven o'clock they looked down from the sun-browned ridge to Abbot's Gap in its cluster of trees and the sea shimmering away beyond Warbarrow Bay.   To the west the great crouching lion of Portland Rock stretched into the Channel with the bloom of the hills of Egypt upon its flanks.   Cynthia reined in her horse and gazed down and out.

" Our home, my dear," she said in a low voice, and she reached out a hand to him.   But Robin's eyes were looking out beyond Portland.   The lovely coast-line had vanished altogether from his view.   He seemed to be listening to a voice from beyond the edge of the sea, to be watching some strange procession draw up from out its depths. He turned to her and took her hand gently. There was a look upon his face which she had never seen till now.

"Even then, sweetheart, you were in my thoughts," he said. "I wanted all done and to be hasting home."

She was to remember that saying through many a day and to cherish it. Now she answered not a word, having at her command a great gift of silence.

"It is steep here and the track bad," said Robin as he led the way down a winding track as hard as iron. But before noon they had come to Abbot's Gap.

CHAPTER IX

THE WINGED MERCURY

THEY stopped in front of a gatehouse which had been built of grey stone, but was now weathered to the warm brown colour of all that corner of England. Its walls were buttressed and without a single ornament, and in the middle of it was set a great door strong enough to outstand a battering ram. Robin as a boy used to imagine that it meant by its plainness to surprise you with the beauty of the house behind, like an ugly face masking a gracious mind. A high wall of red brick stretched away on its left hand. On the right the home farm and the stables stood back. Robin jumped down from his horse, rang the loud bell at the door and held Cynthia's bridle whilst she swung herself to the ground. Dakcombe opened the door and stood gaping. Never had Robin before brought so fair a visitor. With a yell he rang the bell again for the groom, and forgetting all his manners he dashed back through the gatehouse. The groom with Robin's baggage had already arrived, and he came forward now and led off the horses to the stables.

Robin and Cynthia walked through the passage into the court behind, and as she saw the house in front of her the girl uttered a little cry of delight which seemed to Robin the sweetest sound he had ever heard.

" Oh ! Lovely ! " she cried, clasping her hands.

They were standing on a pavement of flat stones. In front of them a little wall of small grey bricks was

almost hidden by roses of white and red, purple phlox
and little ferns and oxlips which bloomed from the
interstices.   On each side of this little wall broad stone
steps rose to a stone terrace, itself a wealth of flowers,
on which the house stood, a house of gables, with an
exquisite oriel thrown out from the hall like a wing.
It had high mullioned windows, fluted columns topped
by great eagles and such fine chiselling of stone as
made it fit rather to rank with jewels than with
buildings.   Cynthia was still lost in admiration when
an oldish woman came out on the terrace and curtsied
low to Cynthia.   Robin presented her to Cynthia.

" This was my nurse and is now my housekeeper.
Kate, Mistress Norris honours my house by dining here,
so the cook must roll up her sleeves and set to work."

Kate, the housekeeper, hurried off to the kitchen,
and coming back to the hall, carried off Cynthia up
to the best bedroom.   Cynthia was dressed for riding
like a boy in a doublet and short breeches and long
brown boots fitting close to the legs and reaching up
to her thighs.   Kate brushed her and waited upon
her whilst she washed with a wistful appeal in her
manner which quite went to Cynthia's heart.

" It is all clean swept, mistress," she said, " and the
furniture polished, so that you could see your face
in it.   And Bedfordshire mats on the floor."

" It's beautiful, Kate," said Cynthia.

" But, lack-a-day, it's empty, mistress, and that
spoils all.   May I show you the house ? " this
cunningly.

" You could show me nothing which I more desire
to see," said Cynthia eagerly.

Where Robin lived, where she was going to live—
oh, wonder of wonders, and hardly yet possible to be
believed—there was not a corner which she overlooked.   She was taken to the long drawing-room with

one window upon the gatehouse and the court, and the other upon the rose garden behind a big round stone dovecot with a thatched roof, and white doves fluttering and walking stately on the red brick paths.

" The kitchen garden is all set away behind, mistress," said Kate. " Oh, we keep up with the times. Not a cabbage or an onion to be seen or smelt, although they are here within the reach of our hands."

She led Cynthia down five steps into a pretty powder closet at the side of the drawing-room. That gave a view to the side of the court where gabled rooms joined the main building in an odd, pleasing, jumbled fashion to the gatehouse.

" There are guest-rooms there," said Kate, pushing back every curtain so that the light shone brightly where they stood. " And other guest-rooms in the gatehouse. Oh, of course, Abbot's Gap is a small house," she added with a show of deprecation, but even more clearly declaring that there was not a manor in the county to compare with it.

" It's a treasure of a small house," cried Cynthia, and the two looked at one another and some understanding passed between them on the instant.

" But alack-a-day, it's empty," Kate repeated, but now in a quite different tone, and Cynthia smiled deliciously and blushed so that even her forehead was rosy.

" And Mr. Robin ? " she asked, dropping her voice as if she had suddenly joined in a conspiracy.

" He sleeps over the other side with his windows on the sea," said Kate, and her face suddenly became careworn and old. " It's here, Mistress, that he should sleep, looking out upon honest land. The sea calls men to death, and when they've heard it in their sleep they can hear nothing else by day."

Cynthia went down the stairs with a chill at her

heart. The sound of her boots upon the oak stairs rang hollow. The house itself seemed to ache from its emptiness.

Robin was waiting for her in the oriel, a small square room with linenfold panels on the walls and the Aubrey arms painted in dark blue and gold on the upper panes of the great window. He started eagerly forward.

" I heard you go from room to room," he said.

" I loved it."

" Ha ! " said he in a great contentment. " I knew you must and yet I feared you wouldn't. Let us dine ! "

The dining-room had its windows upon a wide bowling-green smooth as velvet. It was guarded upon the one side by the high red-brick wall and upon the other by a great yew hedge which for height and breadth had not its equal in the county. The cook had roasted a fat chicken and served it up with a salad and green peas. They drank claret and for a second course ate gingerbread, figs and apples. When they had done Robin took Cynthia by the hand.

" Come ! " he said, and crossing the hall, he led her up the stairs to the library, where two great windows overlooked the valley and the stream which danced down it and the coloured cliffs and yellow beach of Warbarrow Bay. For a little while Cynthia gazed out, the memory of Kate's words in her thoughts and a mist gathering in her eyes. Then she sat down upon a bench in the window and said :

" Yes, tell me, Robin."

He told her of his father quietly and simply, yet he made a picture of him stand out vividly before his mistress's eyes. She heard George Aubrey's great laugh ring out, saw him bending over his foreign books with his boy, and understood the restlessness which had entered his blood after his wife's death and drove him from time to time about the world to prevent his companionship with his son becoming sour to him and a burden. "We are not of an age, Robin, pretend as we may. I must go for a while," he would say, and the next day he would have gone.

"The Precepts of Cato translated by Erasmus! A little harmless book in his baggage. That was all! But the rack came of it and months in the dark of a dungeon and a broken man dressed up like a clown tottering to a stake in the Quemadero."

Cynthia watched the colour ebb from her lover's cheeks, his brown eyes harden, his mouth set, and the youth vanish from him altogether; and she shivered. He was at her side in the window the next moment, his voice all gentleness.

"But it couldn't end like that, sweetheart! With such cruel shame unpunished. What! I to live contentedly in this house which he built, on the land he planted, ride on the hills where we rode together— I should have a ghost at my side driving me down from littleness to littleness until, craven in the big thing, I become craven in all. A mate for you? No, nor for a drab in the stews of a city."

Cynthia's heart stood still. The garden of Hilbury, the scented air, the trees whispering to the moon, all of ecstasy and promise which last night had held were dissolving into the torn gossamer of a foolish dream. But she did not argue or dissuade. She laid a hand upon his and claimed her share in his secrets.

"What will you do, Robin?" she asked gently, and in gratitude for her reticence Robin kissed her lips and got back a full half of his youth.

"This is what I have dreamed of ever since Richard Brymer of the *Bonaventure* told me of what he had seen in the square of San Bernardo, told me down there on the sand of Warbarrow Bay. See!"

He opened a drawer in a great bureau and drew out some scrolls of parchment. He carried them back to the window, and one by one unrolled them on her knees.

"The *Expedition*, built at Poole, the *Admiral*, five hundred tons, a tall ship, a hundred and eight feet of keel and over thirty of beam. She carries culverins and demi-culverins for her big guns, and a dozen quick-firing minions and falcons in the waist. She's finished and ready with her stores and ammunition on board. She'll carry two hundred and fifty men all told and no Gentlemen Adventurers to make trouble.

"Then there's the *Sea Flower*, three hundred and fifty tons, she and the *Grace of God*, her sister ship, were built at Weymouth.

"The *Golden Real*, one hundred and twenty tons, was built at Falmouth, and the *Lyon*, my pinnace of sixty-two tons, at Fowey. I had them built privately in little harbours, so that not a whisper of my purpose might get out."

"And what is your purpose, Robin ? "

Cynthia had raised her hand to her head, the hand on Robin's side, as she bent forward to examine the plans of his ships. But indeed she saw nothing at all, so thick a mist of tears blinded her eyes.

"I mean to celebrate an *auto-da-fé* of my own," Robin answered grimly.

He was seeing just as little of the plans as she was at this moment. The very room had fallen away. He was watching a round sea, in shape perfect and bright as one of Sir Robert's silver platters, but red from sky's rim to sky's rim with the red of burning ships.

"Each ship will drop down its river with the tide at night, and make for the Scillies. There we shall meet. We shall sail out into the Atlantic and a thousand miles west of the Azores we shall wait for the Gold Fleet. Philip's Gold Fleet."

" And all's ready ? "

" To the last rope. Sir John Hawkins has helped. Drake, too. Both of them secretly. Burghley and Walsingham would stop me if they knew. Oh, I've lived in a fever lest a breath of it should reach their ears. But all's ready. Dakcombe brought to me at Hilbury on Wednesday a letter from each of my captains. I sail from Poole on the *Expedition* on Saturday. Now you know why they call me miser. All my fortune's in these ships. But I'll come back rich as a Genoa banker, and the crime punished."

" Hasting home."

Cynthia repeated the words he had spoken on the high brown hill above the house, but her voice broke as she repeated it ; and as he reached forward to gather up the plans of the ships spread out upon her knees, a great tear splashed upon his hand.

" Cynthia ! "

He took her in his arms and she clung to him. But again she did not try to dissuade him. It was a time when men breathed adventure. It inspired the words they spoke and wrote. It made their dreams turbulent, their hearts high. They went forth from their homes, boys and men, to the White Sea, to the Indies and Cathay, to the Guinea Coast and the Spanish Main. They went for the greater glory of God and the honour of the Queen and the filling of their pockets. But so many never came back ? It was that thought which filled Cynthia's heart and overflowed from her eyes. She could not prevent her lover. She would not have him eating out his heart with shame. No, he must go. Since thus throughout his boyhood he had planned, thus he must do.

" You would not have me stay ?   Like the Mercury
in the garden, sandalled and winged, with its service
to do and its service never done ? " Robin cried.
" Bid me go, sweetheart !   If I were false to my father,
how could I be true to you ? "

Cynthia nodded her head and spoke through her tears.

" It is so.   My tears are traitors, my dear love,
and slander me.   You must go though my heart
break.   But oh, come back to me !   Else I am a
widow before I'm a wife."

She freed herself from his arms and stood looking
out down the little valley to the sea.   She tried to see
the work all done and him hasting home on a battered
ship loaded to the water's edge with Philip's gold, but
what she did see was a youth white and beautiful as
a god washing hither and thither in the green depths
of the Atlantic.   Robin rose and stood by her side,
the edge of his pride quite blunted by the misery of
her face.

Cynthia passed her arm under his and pressed it
to her side.   In a whisper she asked :

" How long, Robin ? "

" A year.   In a year I shall ride up to your house
of Winterborne Hyde with my heart upon a golden
plate and cry your name to the skies."

He tried to make his voice sound very hearty and
his words very jaunty and Cynthia tried to laugh
very merrily.   But it was too hollow a performance
and both suddenly ceased.

" I should have waited," Robin said bitterly.   " I
should have held my fool's tongue till I returned——"
and Cynthia turned on him with all her heart in her
face.

" My dear, you couldn't, and I thank you because
you couldn't.   This one day is ours.   More than the
day.   For last night we were in the garden at Hilbury."

Again as she spoke Robin saw the bronze Mercury across the pool, his winged sandals on his feet, his cloak raised behind his head, poised for the flight which was never to be taken.

" Never," she said, " no, not when your heart most fails you, if ever it should, never say to yourself again ' I should not have told her.'   That would be treason."

She moved away from him and about the room, touching a quadrant, an astrolabe, a cross-staff, as though each instrument held part of him, and she wanted to add to it part of her.

" I want something which belongs to you, Robin," she said softly.   " Something quite small which I can take into the palm of my hand and so call you back to me."

Robin took a gold sovereign from his purse and a pair of shears from the table and cut the coin in half. One half he kissed and gave to her, the other he put away again in his purse.   Then he turned to a *prie-dieu* against the wall which had once stood in his study at Eton.   Above it an ivory crucifix hung upon two nails on a little stand flanked by candles.

" This was my father's," he said.

He lifted the crucifix from the nails and, handing it to her, he dropped upon his knees before her.

" Through life and through death I am yours," he said.

Cynthia took the cross and held it against her heart. With the hand which was free she stroked his hair as he knelt.

" And so God be with us, my dear love," she said.

He had hardly risen to his feet when the great bell at the gatehouse was loudly rung and rung again. Over Robin's face there spread a look of anxiety. Few visitors came down from the hill to the young recluse at Abbot's Gap ; and this one came in urgency.

Now that his little fleet, in which all his wealth was sunk, waited for nothing but the high spring tides to put to sea, he saw in every strange occurrence a threat to upset all.

" Wait here, Cynthia !   I'll send the fellow away."

He went quickly from the room.   He left Cynthia standing with the ivory cross in her hand, and trying to beat down a hope which would clamour at her heart, even while she hated herself for her treachery.

CHAPTER X

THE GALLOWS' MARK

OUTSIDE the gatehouse Mr. Gregory of Lyme sat upon a horse whose flanks were white with sweat. As Robin came to his side, he took from a pouch at his girdle a letter folded and sealed but with the seals broken.

" This reached me, Mr. Aubrey, at Hilbury some three hours after you had started. You see the mark of the gallows upon it."

He handed the letter to Robin, who saw the sign marked so ⌐‾‾‾⌐ in black ink upon the outside.

" You will remember that I called your attention to Sir Robert's arrangement of his tables in the great Chamber. The gallows way, Mr. Aubrey," and Mr. Gregory of Lyme laughed—not very pleasantly to Robin's ears.

Robin's heart sank a little. It was true no doubt that the severe statesmen of Her Grace looked with disfavour on the private expeditions against Spain, and called them piracies. But men were not hanged for them. They made their peace by giving Her Grace the lion's share. Still, men were hanged and Robin had not got so far in his adventure as to be able to offer Her Grace a share. He turned the letter over and his heart rose again. The superscription showed that the letter was for Mr. Gregory at Hilbury Melcombe. So, if anyone was going to be hanged, it was Mr. Gregory of Lyme, and what with his ill-timed visit to-day, and his general interference, and a sort of superior know-all air which he had, Robin was sufficiently prepared to see him hanged without too much sorrow.

" The letter is addressed to you, Mr. Gregory."

" And bears the gallows' mark," Arthur Gregory continued quite comfortably. " I'll not say that Sir Francis Walsingham's wit is of the rapier kind. There are moments indeed when I doubt whether he has any sense of humour at all. If he has it's of a crude bludgeoning make. As thus "—and he pointed to the letter. " When Sir Francis is in a great pother and must have his business attended to instanter, he sets the gallows' mark upon the outside, just as Sir Robert Bannet arranged his dining tables in the great Chamber. Now the letter contains an enclosure for you, Mr. Aubrey, as you will see if you unfold it. And though I prefer to amble rather than to gallop, the gallows' mark advised me to make what haste I could after you."

Robin opened the letter. Within was another and smaller superscribed by the same hand and sealed with the same seal. For a moment he hesitated.

Mr. Gregory was watching the boy with a dry smile.

" Needs must read, Mr. Aubrey, when the Queen's Secretary writes."

Robin thought.

" Well, I outfaced him once and went my own way, and I a schoolboy ! "

He tore open the letter and read.

The Lady who gave you a knot of ribbons bids you bring it back to her, and without delay. I shall look for you to-night at Sydling Court. There is need of heave and ho.

Robin stood frowning at the handwriting. There is need of heave and ho—there was a curious phrase. Did Sir Francis know of his purpose? Did Her Grace mean to give her blessing on condition that she got the lion's share? Or was it all excuse and delay and the sea-road forbidden?

"There is an answer needed," said Robin. "Will you dismount, Mr. Gregory. Dakcombe will take your horse and——"

But Mr. Gregory broke in upon him, wagging his head :

"No, no, no, Mr. Aubrey. I'll not sit in your parlour whilst you contrive some answerless answer which will let you out. There's the gallows' mark, I notice, upon your letter as upon mine. I wish you joy of it, Mr. Aubrey. For myself I am out of my road by a dozen miles."

Mr. Gregory of Lyme gathered up his reins with a grin and rode away by the way he had come, down towards the Bay for a hundred yards or so then to the right hand through a gateway and so past the church and up the hill. Robin watched him with a sullen look until he had disappeared. An inconspicuous, interfering, little busybody, Mr. Gregory of Lyme ! Very useful no doubt to Sir Francis Walsingham at the Parliament elections, and to carry letters and to point out gallows' marks, and to explain nothing of his errand, Just the servant for the Queen's secretary with his finger always at his lips.

Robin took the letter up to the library and even at this moment of anxiety Cynthia could not but smile. With his hair all rumpled and his eyes glowering he had so completely the air of a sulky schoolboy resentful of the injustice of his master. She took the letter from his hand, and bent her brows over the queer mark on the outside of it.

" The gallows," Robin said gruffly, and the girl uttered a cry and lost all the colour from her cheeks.

" Nay, it's no more than a hint that obedience should be swift. Sir Francis has an ingenious humour."

" Sir Francis ! Oh ! "

She sat down upon a couch and read the letter quickly whilst Robin stood in front of her.

" The Lady of the Ribbons."

Robin nodded gloomily.

" The Queen."

" You must go, Robin," and again she looked at the gallows' mark and she shivered.

" This is his doing ! " Robin cried. " God's death, the Queen with murders and Leagues and Emperors watching for her eyes to close just for a minute in sheer weariness—how should she remember a snuffling schoolboy she tossed a knot of ribbons to four years ago ! "

" Yet, Robin, you must go to Sydling St. Nicholas."

" He practises with me, that dark rogue ! " and dropping down by her side he seized her hands. " O love of mine, I am put to it ! I am afraid of him. That's the truth ! He came to see me once. When he had gone I felt as boneless as a fish."

Cynthia looked at him shrewdly :

" Yet you held out against him ? "

" Did I ? "

Robin stared in front of him, picturing the long room, the candles burning upon the mantelshelf, and the pale Italian man with the sombre eyes holding him penned against the wall. " I thought I had ! But I wonder now whether he wished to press me no further. Oh ! " and Robin covered his face with his hands. " He sapped me of all my strength. When he went, he left a baby behind him."

There was such a look of discouragement upon his

face, so evident a fear that all his plans and dreams were come to nothing, that Cynthia must take his side with all her loyalty. Their separation, for a time certainly, for life perhaps, suddenly became to her a little thing. The one great need for them both was clear as glass to her. He must dream his dreams true. He must keep his tryst with Philip's gold fleet. Else there would be disappointment, self-contempt, a cramped and bitter life worse than no life at all.

"If you go now, Robin, there needn't be any delay," she said. "We go together, dearest. You leave me at my gate. You go on to Sydling Court. On Tuesday you will reach London. You can still sail out from Poole with the spring tide. Let us go!"

She sprang up and gathered her gloves from the table. Robin took his courage from her and they rode again up the steep brown hill. At the top just for a second Cynthia reined in her horse. It was she now who looked out over the sea.

"All done with and hasting home!" she said, drawing a deep breath, and yearning for that distant day.

She looked downwards to Abbot's Gap glowing amongst its beeches like a ruby in a bed of moss, and so turned her back upon it.

The sun was sinking when they came to the gate of Winterborne Hyde. Her hand rested in his for a little while, and a word or two passed between them.

"You will send me a word if ever you can—how you are, where you are—and oh, come back to me!"

"If I can, at the first moment that I can."

Brave faces and sorrowing hearts, voices which broke ever so little and words which were the poorest currency of their thoughts. There was no issue from their trouble but that he should take his risks and she suffer for them.

"God be with us, my dear," said Cynthia, as he

held the gate open for her; and he rode on alone towards that high down between Cerne Abbas and Sydling St. Nicholas.

He was strung to a high note of passion which he had never reached before. It sharpened all his senses so that he saw the country through which he rode with an amazing clarity. A pond by the roadside in which the reflection of the sun shone red, a cluster of trees upon a green knoll, a tiny church set back in a meadow. Such ordinary aspects of a journey became to him so distinct that ever afterwards he was able to close his eyes and ride again every foot of the way. And a curious illusion crept over him. This way George Aubrey had ridden on a summer night to the same house whither he was now travelling. He had a conviction that he and his father were one, were riding now with the same unknown order to be laid upon them at the end of it, and to be accepted as George Aubrey had accepted it before. An order which might end in ignominy and a shameful death. Robin tried to shake the fancy out of his thoughts. His father had been despatched on a particular and hazardous errand—to nail the Bull of the Queen's excommunication upon the door of St. Paul's Church. There could be no repetition of that errand, no need of the secrecy, no possibility of the like disgrace, or the like appearance of treason. Yet the illusion stayed with him. Here his father had turned from the road on to the rough grass track across the shoulder of the down. Night had fallen then. It was falling now. When he reached the top of the ridge, it had fallen and the moon was bright. Far below him a few lights gleamed in the windows of the long village street, and the moonlight made of the thatched cottages a pattern of black and silver. Thus George Aubrey had looked down; thus he was looking down,

Robin Aubrey. They were one being, bound upon one errand with the disgrace and the death of a felon at the end of it.

The shoes of his horse rang loudly between the cottages. Here was the shaft of the broken cross where the road turned up to Sydling Court. But there was no man waiting at the cross to guide him. The absence of that expected figure—for Robin only understood now with what a sure foreboding he had expected it—lifted him from his obsession. He came up out of ocean depths into clean air. He was sane again with youth's horizons melting cloudlessly in front of him. He would outstand Sir Francis Walsingham, gallows' mark and all, as he had outstood him once before. He would celebrate his *auto-da-fé* in the Atlantic; and then, his piety satisfied and his fortune replaced, it would be heave and ho for home. Mr. Gregory of Lyme—puff! Robin blew him away. Sir Francis? Robin would remember his years, and his friendship with his father, and his high position in the realm. Robin would be very circumspect and use his gentlest manners. But he would not be fobbed off by any pretence that the Queen remembered him. Robin turned to the right just beyond the broken cross. At the top of a short hill two gateposts glimmered white but the gate itself was open. Nowadays a shrubbery screens the house, but then a flat grass plot within the circle of the drive stretched from the gateway to the door, with no obstruction but a stone sun-dial in the centre. The house which Walsingham held on a lease from Winchester College was open to the view with its great tithe barn and its church behind a wall upon the left, and the garden sloping down to a spinney on the right. The windows were lit. Robin was expected, but without secrecy. He rode up to the door.

CHAPTER XI

THE RENUNCIATION

ROBIN gave his horse into the charge of a groom and his hat and whip to a footman. He was led into a small dark room at the side of the house, where a man sat at a round table, his head bent over a litter of papers. A pair of wax candles burned in a high branched candlestick of silver on the table between the door and the man who wrote. But upon Robin's entrance he got up, and over the twin flames Robin saw again the white, black-bearded face which during the last four years had caused him so much disquiet. The lines were deeper, the expression more haggard, the black beard and hair were flecked with white, but it was the unforgettable face of pain and passion—actual pain and slumbering passion—which had daunted Robin in his study at Eton. There was now, however, a gentleness in the dark eyes and a kindly smile upon the lips which Robin felt to be more alarming than a frank hostility.

" I should have known you again, Robin, amongst a thousand," said Sir Francis, and of all questions he put the most unexpected. " And is Dakcombe still with you ? "

Robin had to lay a tight hold upon himself. What was it that was said of Walsingham ? " He outdoes the Jesuits in their bow and outreaches them with his equivocations." Was it mere friendliness in the great man which prompted that question ?

" Yes, sir. He is still at Abbot's Gap."

" Ageing, no doubt, like the rest of us. But it's better to grow old, since we must, serving, than to grow old prattling."

He walked round the table, and taking Robin by the elbow, led him towards a chair ; and Robin recoiled. No doubt he was tired by the long day and its agitations. Moreover, he was not yet quite free from that mood of exaltation which made him attribute to small accidents of time and place a particular warning and intention. The candles threw the shadows of Walsingham and himself in a grotesque distortion upon the walls of the room ; and confusedly he began to wonder whether these nightmare figures swelling and dwindling on the walls were not true likenesses and characters. By a chance as Walsingham led Robin towards a great oak chair, the statesman's shadow grew enormous and quite outdid his own. It only wanted colour to make a picture of the Last Judgment for the painted window of a church ; a scene where a monstrous bloated hobgoblin with a pointed beard leads some helpless panic-stricken boy to an infernal punishment.

Something of Robin's confusion became evident to Walsingham.

" You need food," he said.

" No, sir, I thank you," Robin answered.

" Wine, then," and Walsingham struck a bell and, looking at Robin's white face, he said to the footman " Charneco."

The man brought a jug of Venice glass filled with a dark wine of the colour and character of port, and smaller glasses wherefrom to drink.

Walsingham poured the charneco into one glass until it was brimming full, and put it into Robin's hand.

"Drink," he said gently. "I have news for you which it will tax your strength to hear."

Robin drank the wine slowly. He needed time for his vigour to return to him, and he must have all of it if he was to hold his own. But he was at an age when between exhaustion and energy the difference is one of minutes. He set the glass down and turned to Walsingham. Walsingham had twisted his chair round so that they were sitting face to face, with the candles upon one side and half-way between them, so that neither had any advantage of the light.

"You have news for me, Sir Francis?"

"And need of you. The hour has come," said the Secretary very gravely.

Robin was quick to interrupt.

"I ask your pardon, Sir Francis, you will have under your hand servants more fit than I."

Walsingham shook his head.

"It is for me to judge. As I once said to you four years ago I have no news out of Spain, and I know no one more likely to bring it me."

Robin was more at his ease now. It was the old argument, but he had a better reason for resistance than he had had four years ago. There were only dreams then. All was in train now, the wings were buckled on the heels.

"I have plans, sir, which may be perhaps of some service to the realm."

He was aware that the words had a sort of boyish arrogance in the sound of them, deferentially though he spoke. But Sir Francis did not laugh, nor did he flash out in scorn.

"I know very well," he answered quietly. "Those five fine ships——" and Robin lifted himself half out of his chair. He checked, however, the cry which was on his lips and sank back again.

" The *Expedition*, of five hundred tons, now lying in the roads at Poole ; a great ship, Mr. Aubrey, and well provisioned for its work. The *Sea Flower* and the *Grace of God* at Weymouth, the *Golden Real* at Falmouth, the *Lyon* pinnace at Fowey—all manned, their cannon at the ports, the powder and shot below the hatches."

There were admiration and a warm sympathy in the tone of the older man, but they were unnoticed by Robin. Had they been they would not have diminished by an ounce the bitterness of his disappointment. Powder and shot, indeed ! This man had more of it in his body than all the arsenals of Plymouth.

" So you knew what I was doing ! " he stammered with a voice of awe. He had been so secret, so cleverly secret, so pleased with the cleverness of his secrecy. He had dissembled so warily, built his ships in different ports, used different agents, attributed to their owner different names. In the great new burst of trade which sent merchants trafficking to the White Sea, to China, to the Levant and the Indies, he had found an excuse and a purpose for their building. Yet Walsingham, with his head buried in his papers at Whitehall, might have been looking over his shoulder whilst he studied his prints, or borne him company when he walked the decks. No wonder the shadows on the wall had shown him a monstrous, bearded jailer with a hapless puppet of a lad in his grasp. " So all the time you knew."

Sir Francis was not proof against the flattery of Robin's reverence.

" I have no news out of Spain, but I have very good news out of England," he said dryly.

Robin beat upon the arms of his chair.

" I have sunk all my fortune in those ships," he cried despairingly, " dreaming of one thing."

" Her Majesty will need those ships, make no doubt of it. Already she is feeling the pinch. Five good ships of war, Robin. Hawkins shall treat with you. You will not suffer."

" Suffer ? " cried Robin, and he rose to his feet. " In my purse ? That is the smallest part of it. You know of my ships. Do you know, Sir Francis, of the mission on which they were bound ? "

Sir Francis took the ordinary view. He had dabbled himself in the ventures of those days. To raid this or that possession of Spain, to pillage a fleet of Spain in mid-ocean, to come home loaded down to the gunwale with the treasure of great monasteries and the ingots of the mines—they were all at the work, from the big Companies of the City of London to the squires of Western England. Sir Francis, although, as we say, he dabbled in such expeditions himself, was too much of a Puritan to rate their morality very high. Philip of Spain ! By all means snatch your profit from him when you could, but there were times of peril when the realm must cry halt. And one of these times was now.

" I can guess," he said, leaning back easily in his chair, the master of other men's secrets and the door-keeper of his own. " But you shall tell me, Robin."

Then followed five humbling minutes for the great Secretary, during which he learned how easily the subtlest mind may go astray in its judgment of men— of boys, too. He had thought Robin at Eton a boy swollen with the favour of the Queen, a dreamer, to be sure, but of victories in a lady's drawing-room.

For a profit, he would send out a fleet of fine ships, like a merchant, the risk for others the gain for him, whilst he dallied snug and warm in his fine clothes at the Court. Indeed, Walsingham had charged him with a cowardly indifference to his father's death. Sir Francis went hot and cold as he remembered his injustice. For now here was that boy, standing slim and straight with a passionate white face, telling him of a day when in mid-Atlantic such a funeral pyre was to be fired in remembrance of his father that the roar of its flames would be heard even by Philip at his prayers in the gallery of the Escorial.

" My thoughts, Robin, have done you a great wrong," he said remorsefully when Robin had finished. " I beg you to pardon me."

Robin was used to people thinking ill of him. But he was young and by nature generous, and apologies from a great man busy with great affairs were uncomfortable things.

He shook his head with the ghost of a smile upon his lips.

" I wanted you to think ill of me, Sir Francis. Thus I should slip through your fingers the more easily. But, alas, it was not to be."

There was so great an admiration in Robin's eyes that Walsingham's vanity could not but be tickled.

" No, my boy," he said, complacently stroking his beard, " that could not be. What ! Do I doze over my task like a dunce ? Or like a good physician do I keep my fingers on the pulse of the times ? And count each fluttering of the blood and trace it to its cause ? God's wounds, but you took me for a goly-pragmion," and he laughed with more than a little satisfaction. Robin laughed in unison. Oh, Robin, who was practising now ?

" There was never a hope I should deceive you," he cried.

" Never, Robin. We may say that, I think. You and I, we may say that. Never a hope ! "

" Then you'll let me go ! " Robin implored eagerly.

" You have watched me build my ships, buy my powder in Holland——" and suddenly Walsingham rose to his feet, all his amusement gone. " You will not hinder me ? " Robin prayed, his hands stretched out, the eagerness upon his face itself a prayer.

" Wait ! "

Sir Francis turned to a cabinet against the wall. He unlocked a drawer and took from it a closely-written letter yellow with age.

" Yourself shall hinder you, Robin."

With the letter in his hand he resumed his seat. He took the jug of wine and replenished Robin's glass.

" Drink ! "

There was a solemnity in his manner which daunted the boy. He sat down slowly, his eyes upon Walsingham. He took up the glass without looking at it, so that some of the wine was spilled. He drank, and over the rim of the glass his eyes still watched the Secretary. Walsingham waited until he had finished.

" I have no news out of Spain," he repeated. " Yet every now and then a letter comes to me from a foreign friend. For what it is worth, I make my use of it. Here is one. It comes from a Genoese banker who travelled to Madrid to discuss with King Philip a loan. I have found him trustworthy." He wound the letter about his fingers as though he could not bear to part with it, then he suddenly thrust it forward.

" Read ! If you believe what you read, why, Richard Brymer, captain of the *Catherine* out of Lyme, who with the tears dropping down his face told a naked schoolboy on a beach the story of an *auto-da-fé* in the square of San Bernardo, made too much of his story."

With hands which now trembled instead of implored,

Robin took the letter and read. The Genoa banker
had watched the *auto-da-fé* from a better vantage
than Richard Brymer of the *Catherine*. He gave a
horrible description of the screams of agony, the
wasting of the bodies of living people in the flames,
the dreadful stench of burning flesh, so that Robin
could hardly keep from vomiting whilst he read it.
But his father, crippled with torture and clothed in
the San Benito, walked in the procession as a reprieved
penitent. He had been tossed out afterwards to beg
for his bread on the steps of the church of the Virgin
of Almudena.

" Why ? " Robin asked in a strangled voice. " Why
show him even this rag of mercy ? "

" Neither you nor I can sound the black minds of
these children of the Devil," Walsingham returned ;
and Robin caught at another detail.

" A penitent ! "

A picture of George Aubrey, with his great laugh,
and his gallant heart and all the clean freshness of the
country-side in his face and his voice, rose up in
front of him to deny it. So near to release ? Half an
hour—perhaps an hour more—perhaps to a man so
weakened mercifully much less—of torment to be
endured and then peace ! Oh no, George Aubrey
would not have yielded.

" I don't believe it," Robin cried fervently. He
threw back his head, mutinous against the slander.
His voice rang claiming Walsingham's agreement as
his right.

But Walsingham did not agree. He sat and brooded
looking down at the floor.

" Who shall say to what pain may bring a man ? "
he asked, and he looked at Robin and looked away
again. " You, in your youth and your beauty and
your health, can't imagine how the strongest may

become under pain a babe babbling for mercy. I know. We are shaped in the likeness of God, but we have pain, pain which made our Lord Jesus man instead of God ! Read on ! "

Robin dropped his eyes again to the letter. When all was said, Walsingham knew George Aubrey better than Robin, his son, had known him. George Aubrey was Walsingham's great friend. " I make friends with difficulty. . . . There is some barrier stops me," Walsingham had told Robin, but in this solitary instance the barrier had been broken down. Yet he believed this letter told the truth. Robin read on.

The Genoa banker, a few days afterwards, had seen the penitent in a ragged cloak crouched upon the steps of the church. Being a timorous man and the negotiations for the loan having failed, since Philip had no good security to offer, he had approached this beggar on the steps in a roundabout, secret fashion. He had dropped a few pence into the beggar's lap. In return, the beggar had asked for his name that he might remember it in his prayers. But the banker, the loan having failed, and he in no good odour, and timorous by nature besides, had refused it, and got himself away from such dangerous company as quickly as he could.

The whole letter was so circumstantial and precise that Robin was staggered by it. His father ! Brought to that pass, a beggar in rags on the steps of a church, and he, Robin, wearing the fine clothes and living in the fine house above Warbarrow Bay ! Robin covered his face with his hands, dropping the letter upon his knees.

" That's horrible," he whispered. Then he turned to Walsingham. " And you believe it, sir ? "

Walsingham raised his shoulders.

" How shall I say whether I believe it or no. I

have no news out of Spain." Once more he thrust
that need of his under Robin's eyes. " See when that
letter was written. There it is, the month, the year."

Robin uttered a cry.

" Four years ago you received this ? "

" More than four."

" Then, when you came to me that night at
Eton——"

" I had it in my pocket. I had a thought to show
it you. I came to your lodging to show it you. But
we were not of a mind, Robin. I held my tongue.
Nay, never blame yourself or me ! What could you
do then ? Or I ? No ships can any longer put into
Spanish ports. No English but traitors dare walk
the streets. Spain's a closed book, Robin. Rumours
—to be sure, blowing sharp and blowing soft. But
since that letter came to my hand, nothing of account."

Robin hardly heard. He was watching. He stood
in a straight, long, narrow street between houses so
tall that even at this hour of noon it was dark as
night. Beyond the mouth of it lay an open square
in a blistering sunlight. From the spot where he
stood he could see the corner of a great church with
tall doors of green copper up to which led a long
flight of shallow steps. Men and women passed up
and down, the women for the most part dressed in
black, the men in bright colours with the sun sparkling
on a jewelled chain or the hilt of a sword. Was there
a cripple crouched upon those steps, beseeching alms ?
Robin could not see so far. He bent his ears. He
could hear the whine and sing-song of every beggar
that ever lived. His father !

" Oh ! " he cried. And he heard Walsingham
speaking.

" Answer me this, Robin ! If I let you go, if you
light this proud funeral pyre in the Atlantic and the

roar of its flames reaches to Madrid carrying the
name of Robin Aubrey with it, what happens to
George Aubrey on the steps of the Church of the
Virgin of Almudena ? "

There was no answer but the one. Robin might
twist and turn as he liked.

" If he lives," he said.

" If he lives," Sir Francis repeated.

He was not going to argue for or against. He
would but weaken his own implacable question.
What will happen to George Aubrey on the steps of
the Church of the Virgin of Almudena ?

It was only for a moment now that Robin tarried,
and that moment was spent not in speculating upon
the chances of life and death for a man of crippled
body and broken spirit, but in shredding away
altogether the fond dreams which he had so nearly
dreamed true. Then he rose to his feet.

" Once, sir, you thought that I was fondling beneath
my doublet Her Grace's knot of ribbons," he said with
a smile.

Sir Francis almost said " Yes," but he checked
himself in time. God's death, but he was Sir Francis
Walsingham, Principal Secretary to the Great Queen
who kept all Europe thinking. He was not going to
fall into traps set for him by a lady-faced, long-legged
undergraduate.

" I forget small things so that I may remember
great ones," he replied tartly.

Robin inclined his head.

" But it was not a small thing to me. For it hurt."

" Hurt ! " cried Walsingham in a pet. " Why
shouldn't you be hurt ? Am I not hurt ? I have
heard Her Majesty tell me before the whole Court that
she'd set me in the stocks, and I dumb as a rated
schoolboy ! Was that enjoyable, d'you think ? Hurt,

'odd's wounds ! Are you so tender a piece of flesh ? "
And so, with a laugh : " Well, what is it you hide
against your heart, Robin ? "

Robin unbuttoned his doublet and drew out the
emerald signet ring slung upon its gold chain.
Walsingham started forward.

" Let me see ! "

He took the ring in his hand and his face softened,
as he turned it over.

" George Aubrey's," he said softly. " I remember
it very well. Your mother gave it to him on her
betrothal." He dropped the ring so that it dangled
on its chain, and clapped Robin gently on the shoulder.

" You do well to carry it. You do very well," he
said, thinking of the great friendship which had bound
George Aubrey and himself together and of the
disparity of their fates.

" If God so wills, you shall have your news out of
Spain and I George Aubrey," said Robin.

CHAPTER XII

ROBIN TAKES SERVICE

" YOU have not supped? Neither have I,"
said Sir Francis. " Her Majesty's servants,
amongst whom you are now one, take their meals
when they can."

It was perhaps a meal a little too delicate to content
most of the gentry of that day. A dish of whiting
fresh from the sea served with a saffron sauce, a wild
duck and a lettuce salad with a bottle of claret to
bear them company, a cake of marchpane with
cherries and purple grapes fitly waited on by a glass
of alicant, eased them both a little of their anxieties.
They ate in a light and cheerful room in the front of
the house, and Walsingham talked of the surface of
things, dipping in only now and again some request or
instruction.

" There are those who despise our English cooking,
Robin. But they are chiefly these fine new ladies
who have never seen the outside of London Wall, yet
cannot speak without mangling a French phrase.
They are wrong as you will find when you are in
Italy."

" Italy ? " said Robin.

" You will go by way of Italy," Walsingham
returned, " you who speak Spanish with the accent of
Italy." And Robin wondered whether there was one
word ever spoken in his hearing which this man forgot.
" But we will talk of all this anon—in London. I

should have ordered a hare for you perhaps? It is the fashionable dish."

" Your wild duck, Sir Francis, was for me the happier choice."

" I am glad. I do not allow hares at my table. It is said they breed melancholy, and God knows, I have enough melancholy in my nature to be unwilling to risk an addition! You will travel to London to-morrow, Robin, and bring that knot of ribbons with you, or as like as not you'll get your ears boxed."

" To-morrow!" Robin exclaimed, with a thought that he must somehow first arrange a meeting with Cynthia to explain this sudden overthrow of his plans.

" To-morrow," Walsingham repeated slowly. " There is so much to be done. I must have authority from you to deal for your ships with Sir John Hawkins to your best advantage," and Walsingham chuckled. " Old Jack—he's a fox."

" Then it was he who betrayed me. I have been wondering," Robin cried.

But Walsingham shook his head.

" You have been wandering, Robin. There was never a hint from old Jack. But I know now why Her Majesty's frugality so little discomposed him. We could have one new ship. No doubt a small ship was opportune. Two? Well, at long last, two if needs must, with many sighs. Three? Did we all want to ruin her? God's death, was she made of gold like an idol in India? We could all go to the devil. And there were we biting our fingers and old Jack as easy as a gentleman with a pipe of tobacco after his dinner. Were there not five good ships, including an Admiral, of five hundred tons building for Mr. Robin Aubrey on which he could close his fingers at any moment? I doubt but what every one of them would have been fetched back before it had reached the Sleeve whether you willed it or no."

" He would have been false to me ? "

" And true to the realm. The hour's at hand. This is the year 1586. 1588 has long been prophesied as the year of great trial and disaster. Only three years ago there was so notable a conjunction of the planets Jupiter and Saturn that no wise man dare neglect its warning. A year and a half, Robin," and the shadows darkened on his face and fear shone in his eyes.

One may call it coincidence or what one will, but spread wide over all England was the belief that the year of 1588 would be the year of destiny for the realm. Laws and empires were ruled by the planets. Perhaps 1588 would see the destruction of the world and the second coming of Christ ; or plagues and famines, or a new deluge, or treasons and conspiracies and a horrible alteration of kingdoms. Ever since 1583 books of prophecy and warning had been issued, so that the belief was loud in the mouths of common men and beggars and a secret fear at the hearts of men with possessions. Each man, of course, interpreted the message according to the run of his thoughts. To Sir Francis Walsingham it meant Philip of Spain, the assassination of Elizabeth, Mary Queen of Scots on the Throne of England, and Papacy re-established over all the land.

" You have had a foretaste, Robin, during this last week," he said sombrely. " Ballard, Anthony Babington, John Savage ! The three elements of treason. A priest to consecrate, a philosopher to balance the yes against the no, and a man-at-arms to strike the blow. Oh, those three will do no harm. They'll be taken during this week and pay the penalty. But what if stronger brains and sharper minds take up the task ? A priest less talkative and gaudy, a philosopher more sure of his philosophy, a man-at-arms less simple ! The Queen will not be guarded. You heard Barnewell at your window. ' I am unarmed,' she said, coming boldly towards him."

And Robin cried aloud :

" Glorious ! "

" Aye, and foolish," returned Sir Francis. " The great woman ! And you clap your hands, on your knees to her high spirit and her courage. The great *Queen* to me on whose life hangs the peace and contentment of the world. You shall see for yourself the risks she runs. The Bannets will go scot-free to plot her murder again. You'll see it. Neither father nor son was in the chapel that night when you and Gregory watched. Neither father nor son met Barnewell at the door. She'll hold them innocent from policy. She works for Catholics as well as Protestants to gather behind her. She thinks it's happening. She'll not upset it. You'll see ! And Guise is gathering sixty thousand men for an invasion and Philip is gathering his Armada ! The enterprise of England."

He sat moody and silent.

" I must have news of that Armada, Robin, the number of the ships, the men they carry—sure news. Once on a night like this your father came to Sydling Court and went away on an errand which could bring no reward and might mean ignominy and death. In the name of the Queen, I claim the like service from you."

He rose as he finished, and Robin stood up in front of him. The boy was troubled by the charge which was laid on him. His five ships, his private *auto-de-fé* on the sea—these were far away now, vanities, imaginings fit for a children's fable. He had never doubted his capacity to carry out that enterprise. But this great need ! Could he discharge it ?

" What I can do, Sir, is done," he said, " but——"
And the Secretary took him up with a smile.

" What you can't do will be done."   And he clapped
Robin on the shoulder.   " Come ! Let me choose
my men, Robin ! I have the name for choosing
well."

He rang a bell upon the table and ordered Robin's
horse to be brought to the door.

" We shall settle the particulars in London.   You
have a lodging in the Strand."

Robin laughed.

" You know that, too ? "

" To be sure."

Walsingham reflected for a moment or two.

" It will be better that you stayed at your lodging.
If you stayed with me at Barn Elms, your visit would
be noticed, and though we know nothing of Spain,
Spain knows all it wants to know of us.   You will
post to London to-morrow, and I will send a messenger
to your lodging on Tuesday."

As he led the way out into the hall, he said softly :

" And you will breathe not a word of your departure
or your new plans to anyone."

Robin stopped.   No, Sir Francis asked too much.
Something must be said, to one person.   It was
impossible that he should keep silent.   Walsingham
looked into the boy's troubled face.

" It is a hard saying but a wise one.   I shall con-
vince you in London."

There would still be time, Robin thought, for him
to see Cynthia before he went away.   Since possibly
he would be able to meet her but the once, it would
even be better if he waited until all the details of his
charge were fixed.

" I shall wait until I have heard you in London,"
Robin agreed.   But he felt that this service laid upon

him was already clutching at all that he had, demanding the surrender of all, love, friendship, life too.

They went out of the house. The garden slept in a lovely silver light. Away to the left, a long, high wall at the bottom of the slope threw a coal-black shadow across the ground like a huge ditch. On the lawn here the sparkling dew was as the lamps of elves. There was no sound in all the world. Walsingham stood as though amazed by the beauty of the familiar scene.

" Shall Spain foul this land ? " he cried in a low voice. " Her soldiers trample its gardens ? Put to the fire its honest, friendly people ? Fire over England ? No ! "

Robin left him standing there, his sombre face lit with his passionate love. He himself rode homewards in a sober mood. Youth though he was, there was no joy of adventure in his blood as he thought upon the service to which he was committed. He grew into man's estate on that long and lonely moonlit ride. Over the shoulder of the down, past quiet sleeping villages and fields where he heard the cows cropping the grass, he rode. Fire over England—no ! What tiny thing he could do, at the expanse of strength and courage and brain and life, to hinder that catastrophe, he would, however menial and lowly. But Cynthia must know. That of course was settled.

Before he left England Cynthia must know.

And that, having been settled, Robin turned to a question which throughout the evening had greatly perplexed him.

How long had Walsingham known of the ships which Robin had been building ? Yes, and by what channel had the knowledge reached him ? He was a subtle searcher of secrets but here was one which should have been safe from him. He was a man of

many curiosities, but Robin had never heard that
things of the sea engaged him. Sir John Hawkins
had not told him. How then had he known ? And
as Robin put to himself the question for the twentieth
time, he suddenly reined in his horse.

" Of course ! "

There had been an evening at Hilbury Melcombe
when his letters had been handled. And Mr. Gregory,
of Lyme, had occupied the next room. Mr. Gregory,
of Lyme, was the rock on which his five ships had
foundered. For those letters told all. There was one
from each shipyard.

Robin rode on again, and stopped again. For the
seals of those letters had not been broken. He had
examined them. No, not one had been defaced in
any way. He gave up the problem. It was a futile
one in any case, since Walsingham did know.

But what was mystery to Robin Aubrey riding back
under the moon from Sydling Court to Abbot's Gap
was made plain at a later day.

The Reverend Dr. Fuller made a Collection of the
Worthies of England, almost a century later, and found
a place amongst them for Arthur Gregory, of Lyme.
" He had the admirable art of forcing the seal of a
letter ; yet so invisibly that it still appeared a virgin
to the exactest beholder. Secretary Walsingham made
great use of him about the packets which passed from
foreign parts to Mary Queen of Scotland," and
apparently some use of him about the shipbuilders'
letters which were brought over by Dakcombe to Mr.
Robin Aubrey at Hilbury Melcombe.

CHAPTER XIII

THE KNOT OF RIBBON AGAIN AND A
SUPPER AT BARN ELMS

" WAIT here ! "
Walsingham left Robin standing in the
garden and walked by an alley-way of limes towards
the Palace. It was nine o'clock in the morning and
the river was astir with rowing-boats and wherries.
Across the water on the Surrey side the Queen's
barge lay at its moorings. Robin was hardly less
nervous to-day than he had been when he had been
called out from amongst the Oppidans at Eton, but
he made as brave a show of indifference as his quickly-
beating heart allowed him to do. For though this
was the private garden of Whitehall there were citizens
of London enjoying the sunlight and the air as though
the place was their own demesne. Robin understood
now how easy of accomplishment a crime such as
Babington had planned really was. The road from
Westminster passed under an open archway opposite
to the door of Westminster Hall and wound past the
tilt yard and the cockpit amongst the many buildings
of the Palace. The garden, with its lawns, its alleys,
its flower-beds edged with box and marjoram lay
open to all comers. And here the Queen walked with
her latest favourite or one of her ladies-in-waiting.
Robin saw her now coming towards him from a great
hedge of rosemary, with one of her maids behind her.

He advanced to her, his hat in his hand, and dropped
on a knee in front of her.

" It's boy Robin," she said, and she gave him her
hand to kiss. " You have brought me back my knot
of ribbon ! "

Robin had had a little gold case made for it, with
the lid richly chased and set with rubies. He opened
the lid and offered it to Elizabeth.

" I would lose a knot every day if I thought it would
be so daintily restored to me." She took the case in
her hands and the knot from the case and held it
against her sleeve. " It is clean out of fashion now,"
she said. She was wearing a gown of white silk with
an embroidery of pearls, and certainly that faded bow
of blue was altogether amiss. " Yet I shall keep it to
remind me of a very loyal servant, until in his good
time he claims it again."

She snapped the lid of the box down and, beckoning
to her maid, bade her set it apart in the rose cabinet
in her chamber.

" You shall walk with me, boy Robin," she said,
and when they were out of hearing, " you are set upon
a dangerous and thankless mission. I cannot protect
you whilst the work is forward and no trumpet will
sound for you when it is done."

There was a note of compunction and a great
gentleness in her voice, and with them a smile as if
she were pleased to walk with him.

" Yet, Your Majesty, no service could be more
felicitous to me. For I serve Your Grace first in some
special need, and thereafter myself."

" Aye, I heard something of that from my Moor,
else I'd have sent him to the devil and bidden him
seek someone from the greedy crowd besieging me."
She drew a great sigh, half of it genuine, half of it
heaved up to persuade this good-looking stripling what

a forlorn and lonely woman it was that he walked with. " If you knew how I am plagued by the cupidity of men. They must have money and titles and God knows what if they but hold a stirrup for me when I mount ! But for love of me, where shall I look, Robin ? " And she heaved another great " heigh and a ho " which set Robin's heart swelling with pity.

" To ten thousand like to me, Your Grace, who have but once seen your face and to thousands more who have never been so blessed," cried Robin eagerly.

" Is it so, good Robin ? " she asked wistfully. " In sooth I hope it is." She walked on with him for another step or two. " I had thought to keep you nearer to me, but the good of the realm overrides us all. So fare you well and when in God's time you come back you shall find in your Queen a very grateful and loving woman."

She had assumed in a second her royal dignity. Robin dropped upon his knee and she gave him her hand again to kiss. Then she smoothed his cheek and tapped it once or twice with a smile.

"These boys who give everything and ask for nothing," and now she sighed with no pretence whatever, " and, alas ! we must take them at their word. I should give you some favour by which you should bear me in your remembrance, but I should be adding peril upon peril. So go your ways ! "

Robin returned to his lodging and changing his dress for one of a more sober hue, waited upon Walsingham at his town house by London Wall, and there, meeting Sir John Hawkins and two conveyancing lawyers, signed the papers which gave the Secretary authority to deal for his ships with the Queen's navy.

"So all is clear and your affairs in order," said Walsingham. " If you will sup with me to-morrow at Barn Elms, we shall arrange the particulars of your mission."

It was a pleasant family party where grave matters and grave manners were laid aside. The Principal Secretary warmed to a reticent sort of gaiety; his daughter Frances who was married to Sir Philip Sidney then fighting in the Low Countries put a sprightly face upon her anxieties. They were at pains to make Robin at home, but they sent his thoughts winging away to Abbot's Gap and making pictures for him of some such household where Cynthia moved and sat making everything beautiful by the daintiness and glamour of her presence.

" Oh, I have got to come back ! " he said suddenly, and Frances Sidney looked at him across the table with so kindly an understanding in her eyes that it quite revived his courage.

" Of course you will—as my dear man will," she answered with a little gasp of fear in the middle of the sentence, and a smile of courage at the end of it. " Take it from an old married woman "—she was nineteen and Robin's age—" women would rather have a call upon their bravery than no reason to be brave."

She gave him a little nod of reassurance and rode away to a lighter topic. So she knew of Cynthia, else she would never have used those words. Robin flushed red and was comforted. He turned to Sir Francis.

" Mr. Gregory of Lyme is a very observant person," he said.

Sir Francis did not blush like Robin, but a faint tinge of red crept over his face.

" There is a gift of observation," he returned. " I think Mr. Gregory has it."

" It enables him to read letters from their super·scription," continued Robin.

Sir Francis swallowed, though he had nothing in his mouth to swallow.

" They call it second sight," he said gruffly.

Robin smiled and said with deference :

" I am glad to know, sir. For otherwise I should have called it first sight, since he seems to know the contents of the letters even before those do to whom they are addressed."

Frances laughed delightedly, Walsingham himself with an amusement which was not so genuine. Lady Ursula, his wife, had not an idea of what they were talking about. Walsingham rose and said to his wife :

" My dear, I shall carry our guest away with me to my room. We shall sit late, I expect."

Robin took his leave of Lady Ursula. He lifted Frances Sidney's hand to his lips and she returned his courtesy with a warm pressure of the fingers and a gleam of tears in her eyes. But she said nothing, for words were of no use in her case or in his. She lived in terror of the dark day which was to come in two months' time and rob Elizabeth of the choicest jewel of her Court. He was to go forth on a desperate mission without profits or honour, but with such cruel privacy that even his true love must never know till all was done in what corner of the world he wandered or what he did.

Robin followed Sir Francis Walsingham into his library at the side of the great hall.

" To our affairs."

He drew out a chair from a big square table with a smile and a gesture. Whilst Robin seated himself he turned to a bureau in a corner of the room, and unlocking a drawer fetched out some official papers and a little notebook. With these in his hands he set himself down on the side of the table opposite to Robin.

" Here is your licence to travel abroad," he said

unfolding a parchment with a great seal and the signature of Lord Burghley at the bottom.

" You will see that you may travel with five horses and two servants." He handed the parchment across the table.

" Two for my baggage," said Robin.

" You are a young gentleman of style and fortune making the grand tour for the improvement of your mind."

" But my fortune is gone," said Robin ruefully.

" It is on the way to its restoration," replied Walsingham. " Meanwhile, here is a letter of credit upon the Paris branch of the house of Fugger in Frankfurt and another upon Rospoli the banker at Genoa."

Robin looked at them and made sure they were in order.

" And here is an order upon Sir Thomas Gresham in Old Change for one hundred pounds in gold, which you will draw before you leave London."

Robin folded the order and the letters of credit and set them upon the licence to travel.

Sir Francis was sitting with a paper in front of him. He read it diligently and affixed his signature and then extended it across the table.

" This is of so much importance that were you to lose it before you could deliver it you might as well start homewards the next day."

Robin read the letter.

" It commends me to Giovanni Figliazzi at the Palazzo Negro at Florence."

" Giovanni Figliazzi," Walsingham explained, " is the ambassador of the Duke of Tuscany to the Court of Spain."

Robin frowned.

" He is then a friend of King Philip."

" And in very high favour," Walsingham returned imperturbably. " But he is a better friend to me."

Robin bowed.

" I shall deliver it as quickly as I can."

" To be sure," said Walsingham, reaching out his hand. " You will say in France that you are reserving the glorious treasures of French art and learning for your homeward journey."

He took the letter to Figliazzi, folded it and lighting a taper on the table at his side, sealed it with his signet ring. He held it out again, but Robin drew back.

" You have forgotten something."

" I ? "

" Yes."

Walsingham turned the letter over. The super-scription was correct.

" And what have I forgotten ? "

" The gallows' mark," said Robin.

The Secretary laughed in a very good humour.

" I reserve that note of distinction for my friends in England. The gentle hint might not be understood in Italy."

Robin packed away the letter of introduction with his letters of credit and his order upon Sir Thomas Gresham and his licence to travel in the pouch at his belt.

" Figliazzi expects you," said Walsingham.

" I shall use all haste."

" The more the better. There are five galleons which Philip has hired from the free city of Genoa, manned with Italian soldiers and sailors. Figliazzi will have the charge of those ships ; he will sail with them to Lisbon."

" Lisbon ? " cried Robin recoiling.

" It's your only road to Madrid. There are many

K

Italian galleons and galleasses assembling in Spanish ports. Those from the free cities and from Leghorn go straight to Lisbon. Sr. Figliazzi must go there and see all ordered properly, before he goes to Madrid."

" They are assembling at Lisbon ? "

" Others from Philip's own kingdon of Naples and the Papal States are to make their rendezvous at Cadiz, where I think, another Sir Francis of a more active body than mine may haply lead a lively pavane," he said with a dry smile. But the smile broadened in a moment. " And I think it likely, Robin, that a sound, swift ship lately built at Poole and named *The Expedition* may set prettily to its partner in that dance."

For a second there flashed through Robin a wild hope that he himself might sail on *The Expedition*. There would be landing parties. The battle over he might make his way to Madrid.

Walsingham read the hope in the boy's face, and shook his head.

" It will go out and the port burnt and so home again. Besides Lisbon is the very hub of the Enterprise of England, as they call it. That I know. From every harbour on the continent where ships are built, the best workmen are being hired. Wherever cannon are being cast, cannon are ordered. And all for Lisbon. But that's all I know. What I must know is this : the name of every ship, whether it be galleon or rowed galleasse, or small frigate, its tonnage, the number and the calibre of its guns, the trained soldiers that it carries, its captain, yes, every ship, a complete list of the Invincible Armada as they call it," and a note of ridicule crept into his voice, " that we may give them a true and hearty welcome."

A curious glow had spread over his pale face. The long years of doubt and hanging off and step-toeing on, of prevarications and shifts, of skies clouding and clearing were coming at last to their end. The disclosure of the Babington conspiracy would certainly bring treachery into so plain a light that even Elizabeth could no longer save the head of Mary of Scotland. With her removed, there was England, a new province for Spain, a saving addition with its wealth and commerce to bankrupt Philip's Empire. The stage was all set. Walsingham had never a doubt to what end and climax the play would go—neither he nor any other loyal Englishman. God would be with them for one thing. But they must be ready, and to be ready they must know to a demi-culverin what strength they had to meet.

"Lisbon first!" he cried. "You will travel in Figliazzi's train, a young Italian gentleman, speaking Spanish, as we know, with the accent of Italy."

Was there nothing which this man ever forgot, Robin wondered.

"In a few months Figliazzi will proceed from Lisbon to Madrid. Again you will go in his train, your work for the realm done, and yourself free for your pious task."

"I shall do what I can," said Robin.

"You will want an Italian name."

Robin looked up with a start.

"You will leave your own behind you on the borders of Italy," continued Walsingham.

"Yes."

"It must be a name which will escape attention."

Robin laughed.

"I have it, sir."

"Let me hear," said Walsingham.

"Carlo Manucci," said Robin.

It was the name of a character in a play. He had acted it once. Well, here was another character to be acted with something of the same trickery and diplomacies. He must act this part better than the earlier one to be sure, for in this case the stake was the stake not a flogging. But the same name would be suitable.

"Carlo Manucci," Walsingham repeated, and he wrote the name in his little book, and looked at it straight and looked at it sideways.

"Carlo Manucci. It will do as well as another."

Sir Francis Walsingham made a good many mistakes in his career. He was wrong when he wanted to pour out Elizabeth's small Treasury to the arrogant deputation from the Low Countries. He was wrong when he urged her to squander money on the grasping and needy Earls of Scotland. But perhaps he was never so wrong as when in his ignorance he told Robin that as a name Carlo Manucci would do as well as another. However Carlo Manucci was agreed upon.

"But you must not sign your letters by that name," he added.

"No!"

"You will send them in the Ambassador's bag to Florence, and they will be addressed to Mr. Arthur Gregory at my house on London Wall."

"I shall remember," said Robin.

"And you will sign them D.1." ·

"D.1." Robin repeated.

Sir Francis shifted in his chair, and hummed and ha'ed for a moment.

"I do not as a rule let one of my agents know of another. It is for their own security that they should work in an independence which is complete." Walsingham did not give his reason. But it was plain enough. Under the question, a prisoner could reveal no more than he knew. "But there will be one in Cadiz with Medina-Sidonia in a like case with you. Figliazzi

knows of him and if there be need he will make you
acquainted."

Upon that he shut up his little book and replaced
it in the drawer of the bureau.   Robin rose to his feet.
The interview was over.

" You have no other instructions, sir ? "

" None," said Walsingham as he locked the drawer.
" Yet, wait a little !   There is one, of course, so plain
that it hardly needs utterance."   His back was turned
towards Robin.   He was still very busy with his
bureau.   The order hardly worth utterance was thrown
backwards over his shoulder in an off-hand and
indifferent way.

" You will say not one word about your mission to
anyone in the world, man or woman, boy or——"
there was a pause for perhaps the space of a second
as he withdrew his key from the lock—" girl."

Certainly he was very easy and confident, but no
answer was given to him.   It was obvious nevertheless that he waited for one.   His back was still turned
to Robin and his hands still pretended to be busy
with his bureau, but he was waiting.   Every line of
his figure proved it.   He got an answer in the end,
very quietly given, and very likely the answer he
expected, though the last one which he desired.

" That, sir, cannot be.   There is one who must
know."

Sir Francis heaved a sigh.   Love affairs were the
very devil.

" I heard something of this," he said, turning about
ruefully.

Youth he wanted and must have for this service,
youth with its courage, its inspiration, its indifference
to the for and against when there was work at its
hand.   The plague of it was that he couldn't have
youth without what goes with youth—passion, a girl

like any other girl with just a different tilt to her chin
set upon a throne as the world's nonpareil ; by
whose Heaven-sent wisdom every plan must be tested ;
to whose bosom every dangerous secret must be con-
fided. Else there's treachery to love, and that's not
to be thought upon. If only Cynthia Norris, of whom
he had an account from Mr. Gregory of Lyme, had had
some small setback in her health at the time when her
visit to Hilbury Melcombe was due, what a deal of
argument would have been saved. However, argument
must be used, and the Secretary settled down to it.

" This young lady—she is a neighbour of the
Bannets."

" No doubt."

" And the two families are friends."

" It is so."

" And would have if the young lady favoured it, a
closer link than friendship."

" I believe so," said Robin sullenly.

" Well, then ! The Bannets are traitors and none
the less because Her Majesty in her clemency winks
at their treasons. Also perhaps I wink a little too, since
certain letters come from time to time out of France
to Sir Robert Bannet, which, thanks to your friend
Gregory, I get a glimpse of first. But let Miss Cynthia
in a moment when she's off her guard, drop a hint of
your mission, and Carlo Manucci goes to the stake."

" She never would."

" And with him that old beggar man on the steps
of the Church of Almudena—my friend, your father,
whose house stands waiting for him with its comforts
and its luxuries by the sea," said Walsingham relent-
lessly.

" She will hold her peace," Robin cried in a voice
of anguish, " however much they go about with
her."

" Every second she must guard her tongue, her eyes. Why put her to such a torment ? "

" It would be a worse torment if I left her without a word, to think that I had played with her heart and fled, a trifler."

"Would she think that?" Walsingham asked quickly.

There was the trap open in front of Robin. If she held him of so little worth, was he right to put her so high ? If at the first moment her judgment went so wide astray, could he trust her as the keeper of his secrets ? If she mistook him for a traitor, would she not mistake traitors for friends ? But Robin was honest even to the discomfiture of his own argument.

" No, she would not," he answered.

" Well, then ! This young lady—a Mistress Cynthia Norris, I think——"

" And know," Robin added.

Walsingham smiled and acknowledged the thrust.

" Mr. Gregory writes of her in superlatives."

" Mr. Gregory is a little too meddlesome for my taste," Robin exclaimed in a rage. " I think he would look very well with the gallows mark on his neck instead of on his letters."

Sir Francis allowed himself to laugh.

" Gregory has, as you may have noticed, no sense of humour, Robin. Yet I should like to repeat your remark to him for the pleasure of seeing his face when I repeated it. But he is too valuable a servant for me to practise with."

" So you practise with me instead, sir," said Robin.

" If I do it's for the good of this realm," cried Walsingham all at once in a great heat. " I set that above all and such feeble steps as I can take for your security I take because I set it above all." His anger fell from him after he had spoken, and he added in a gentle and compassionate voice.

" Also I am not without care for you, Robin.   Had
I another agent of the same strong purpose and the
same discretion, I should choose him in your place
and give you your chance of banners and trumpets
and a splendid name.   But the grave need of these
times overrides us all.   Come !   This young lady knows
of your plan against the gold fleet ? "

" Yes."

" Let her think you have set out upon it ! "

" And what of Drake's attack upon Cadiz with *The
Expedition* as one of his ships ? "

" We can change her name."

" But not her crew.   She was built in Poole.   She
is manned by Poole men.   How could Cynthia not
know ?   She will know that it has sailed without me.
What will she think of me ?   A braggart, a coward who
runs at a hint of danger——" and again Waslingham
broke sharply in upon his words.

" Will she ? "

And again honesty and his clear faith in the loving
spirit of his mistress defeated Robin's argument.

" No, she will not," he answered gently, whilst a
tender smile softened the set of his lips.   " But if I
leave her without a word, though against all seeming
she will keep her trust in me—she will suffer—oh,
a martyrdom."

Walsingham did not contradict him by a word or a
gesture.   With a very pretty dignity he spoke of
himself and his own home.

" My family, like all families that ever I heard of,
has had its share of joy and sorrow.   But never until
these last few months did I fully learn or admire the
fine strength of women's hearts, their endurance, the
brave face they show the world.   You saw my daughter
Frances to-night.   Her lively spirit and tender friendliness make this house of mine fragrant.   She was

married but a few years ago to that young knight who is the very flower of England. They are a fair and lovely couple. But at any moment a messenger may come galloping to the door with the news that Philip Sidney lies stricken to death upon a battlefield. Yet only by some look of pain which we surprise in her eyes, by some little trembling word which in spite of herself she lets fall, can we guess at the martyrdom in which she lives. But would she have it otherwise, do you think ? Would she have him clinging to her skirt rather than fulfilling his life, be the end what it may ? Would she prefer him to be a stranger of whose glory she might carelessly read ? No ! Well, then, will your Cynthia fall below her ? I who don't know her will still dare to make answer. No ! For I know you, Robin, and your heart will not have chosen at random."

· The argument was not perhaps very fair, but it was sincere, and it had its way. Robin's thoughts leaped forward to a day when he would be standing in the hall of Abbot's Gap, his father upon one side, his torments quite forgotten, Cynthia on the other, her eyes shining, her lips parted, her anxious imaginings repaid.

"It shall be as you wish," he said. "But if it should be God's will that I do not come back, someone must tell her how it was that I left her without a word, with what pain and with what trust."

"That I promise on my hope of salvation," said Walsingham, "and Frances herself shall be your messenger."

CHAPTER XIV

MASTER AND MAN

OVER a smooth sea of sapphire the great galleasse *Regazzona* swept past the brown hill-sides of Spain. A favouring light wind just filled the square sails upon her three masts and her bowsprit, and on the lowest deck below the broadside guns thirty long oars a side churned the dark water into a glistening froth. It was growing towards noon, and though the season was late September the sun rode high in a cloudless sky of summer. Two hundred feet the ship measured between her uprights and at her stern two great castles towered into the air, the topmost projecting farther over the sea than the lower and beginning later, so that they gave to a sailor below in the waist the appearance of two huge broad steps. At the stem the bowsprit was slanted high, and below it her long stout ram sheathed in bright steel cast a shadow over the water as though some enormous pike swam ahead and directed the ship. The wooded Cabo de Gata, where now the lighthouse stands, stretched out towards the ship on the starboard side, then fell behind and opened out the deep bay of Almeria.

The Admiral's cabin, with a gallery over the water, was in the lower of the two stern castles, and at the closed door a sentinel with a musket was placed to make sure that no one entered. Within the cabin an odd scene was occurring which would assuredly have mystified any intruder. In an armchair a slight Italian man of middle age with a crest of light hair on the crown of his head and a bald lane on each side of it, sat with a bare leg and foot lifted on to a cushioned stool in front of him. There did not seem to be anything very amiss with the leg and foot. They were shapely enough to satisfy even Queen Elizabeth, but the poor man was groaning, as though he was afflicted by the worst torments of the gout.

"Ouch!" he cried, and "Madre de Dios," and if the youth who knelt in front of the stool with a bowl of hot liniment at his side reached out a hand he broke into the most violent threats and curses.

"Touch me, pig of a fellow, if you dare! I'll have you skinned, you rogue! I'll feed you limb by limb to the fishes! Oh! oh!" and he leaned back in his chair with his eyes closed, an exhausted man, near to his end.

"Well, you must, I suppose," he groaned feebly. "These vile pretentious doctors and their trumpery prescriptions!"

The youth dipped a sponge into the hot lotion and took the outstretched foot with the other hand as gingerly as if he handled a quite priceless porringer of porcelain.

"What! Would you, would you?" cried the sufferer, seizing up a stick propped against a chair.

"But, Señor Marques," the youth answered appealingly, speaking Spanish with a marked Italian accent, "the lotion will relieve the pain and do you a world of good! My poor mother suffered in the same way."

"What!" exclaimed the Señor Marques in a rage. "Your poor mother dared to suffer as I do? You're a liar, Guiseppe. It requires my delicate blood to suffer as I do! Oh! Tortures and executions! It's demasiado hot, your cursed loción——"

So he went on mixing bad Spanish with excellent Italian, until with a sigh of relief his anger and his anguish passed.

" That is better, Guiseppe ! You shall have a silver piece to reward you for your gentleness. Undoubtedly that is better. Now the bandage, but not too tight, you rascal, or I'll set you at one of those long oars with the galley slaves."

Guiseppe said soothingly :

" Molto cuidado, Señor Marques," and he bandaged the foot with a gossamer touch.

There was yet another servant in the cabin, a young, small black-haired Italian at whom the Señor Marques directed a glance whilst Guiseppe was busy with his bandage. At once the Italian looked out of the stern window over the empty sea and cried out in a sort of English :

" There's the strangest ship that ever I saw. Oh, look ! Look quickly ! "

Guiseppe, however, continued his bandaging without as much as lifting his head. Then a slipper was fitted on and the Señor Marques said :

" You shall give me your arm, Guiseppe ! I shall walk a few yards. So ! "

He shot another glance at the Italian. " You can go, Andrea Ferranti, and get ready my almuerzo."

Andrea Ferranti disappeared into the private galley at the side of the cabin. Guiseppe lifted the Señor Marques and propped him up and supported him up and down the cabin. Suddenly Ferranti threw open the door of the galley and shouted urgently :

" The Signor Carlo Manucci is wanted at once."

Guiseppe's entire attention was occupied by the Señor Marques, who was certainly very difficult to please that morning. He leaned his full weight upon Guiseppe's arm—he made himself heavier than he was

—and each time that he put his bandaged foot to the ground he yelped in a spasm of pain.

"The almuerzo, Andrea, you dog! And you, Guiseppe, let me fall and I'll have you keel-hauled, I will. God bless me, was there ever such a clumsy rogue?"

Then in quite a different voice he exclaimed:

"Good! We progress. We do not turn our head when the English is spoken. No! And if Carlo Manucci is summoned, that means nothing to us. That is excellent."

He moved with agility back to his chair, whipped the bandage off his foot, drew on his stocking and gartered it, stepped into his shoe, and as Andrea Ferranti brought the luncheon into the cabin he said:

"Since we are private here and there is a watch upon the door, and the lesson has been well learnt, you shall lunch with me, Carlo. Lay the table for two, Andrea!"

The Señor Marques became, in fact, the Signor Conde Giovanni Figliazzi, who was enjoying himself enormously as he acted or rather overacted the part of the gout-ridden old admiral of the Spanish fleet, Santa Cruz.

Robin had travelled to Florence as Carlo Manucci, and at the Court of Tuscany had quickly made a friend of Figliazzi.

"Andrea Ferranti, my body servant, may be trusted, He comes from my lands and has been in my household since he was a boy. He has a brother in the service of the Marquis of Santa Cruz, who is the best admiral that Spain ever had and the very brain of the Armada. You will do well, I think to make your account with him."

It was Figliazzi's bold notion that, with Ferranti's help, a place might be secured for Robin in the household of Santa Cruz."

" I must not appear in it," he said, " for my master's sake and my own duty, but secretly I shall do what I can. I promised that to my old friend Sir Francis on account of the friendship which we had when he was the English Ambassador in Paris. I renew that promise to you on account of the friendship which I have now for you."

Robin had made his account with Andrea Ferranti, as Figliazzi had advised him. He gave him a hundred crowns and added :

" There will be as much for your brother if I am hired, and again as much for you when the work is all done."

Andrea had taken the money and had looked askance at the plan.

" We shall see, at Lisbon. There is so great a compulsion upon men for the ships that places on shore go abegging. But can your Excellency hold a plate and not spill it on a lady's lap ? Can your Excellency lacquer a pair of boots ? Can your Excellency cook a *pollo con arroz* and get just that saffron look and taste in the rice which turns it from food into a dish ? "

" I will go to school, Andrea, with you for a master," said Robin.

Andrea was not disposed to make light of the capacities required by a good valet.

" And when the rudiments are learnt there are more delicate duties. Can your Excellency starch and crimp a ruff ? "

At that Robin looked glum.

" Can your Excellency open a letter ? " Ferranti asked slyly.

" That is an art which, above all others, I wish to learn," Robin cried eagerly.

" And your Excellency is right. For how shall a

valet serve his master well unless he knows more of his master's affairs than his master is willing to tell him ? " said Andrea sententiously.

Robin carried his difficulties to Figliazzi, who again came to his assistance. He would send his secretaries and his staff on in the first of the ships to leave Genoa so that his lodging might be prepared in Lisbon against the time of his arrival. He himself, with two servants, Andrea and Robin, should leave on the last of the ships and Robin would have the long voyage in which to learn his new trade. Thus all along the Spanish coast, through the Straits with the Moorish hills upon one side and the great rock of Gibraltar upon the other, and out round Cape St. Vincent, Figliazzi and Robin played the game of master and man. A game which filled the time for Giovanni Figliazzi with a prodigious amusement. He made a character in a play out of the harsh old gout-ridden admiral, invented each day new incommodities of temper and new duties for the servant to fulfil. Robin on his side studied his part as never actor did. A game, yes, but lives hung upon his playing of it properly—his own, that most likely of a ragged cripple crouched upon the steps of a church in Madrid, and perhaps a third life, too. Robin thought as he gazed one moonlit night upon the rock of Gibraltar which moved him by its rough likeness to the great head of Portland, yes, a third life, too, might depend upon his acting, since away beyond Portland and inland from Warbarrow Bay a girl with her eyes strained towards the sea waited and wondered with a bursting heart.

In due time the *Regazzona* came to Cascaes and, after standing by at the anchorage for the night, crossed the bar of the Tagus in the morning between the Tower of St. Bugio and St. Julian's Castle.

No visitor entering Lisbon harbour to-day will see

what Robin saw, so entirely has the face of the city,
changed.   The dark wooded heights above the sandy
cliffs on the southern bank of the river rise not much
more built upon than they were.   But on the northern
side the land itself has changed.   The Tower of Belem
now stands upon the shore, but then it crowned an
islet in the channel and the water lapped the walls
of the Monastery of San Jeronimo ; and of St. Julian's
castle, but the one storey remains with its Indian
turrets at the four corners to recall that strong place
which Philip built to guard Spain's new kingdom.   A
few peasants live amongst its arches, the outer wall
about its platform is gashed and broken and exposes
its layers of red tiles beneath the stone.

But when Robin sailed past it on this autumn
morning it towered high and sheer from the river's
edge, its dark surface broken only by the orifices of
its cannon and the balconies and windows at the top.
It commanded the deepest of the two channels and a
great banner waved high above the roof.   Robin gave
less heed to that formidable hold than he was to give
to it in the months which lay ahead of him.   For his
eyes turned to the harbour now widening out in front
of him, and for a moment his heart stood still.   The
galleasse passed into such a forest of tall masts that
the land itself was hidden ; and so deafening a din of
cries, such a pounding of hammers, such a creaking
of carts upon the quays, such a clashing of iron filled
the air that he must shout even to a man with his ear
close to his mouth before a word that he said could be
understood.   It seemed that the doom of England
was being fashioned here before his eyes.   But his
spirits revived as he watched.   The work was but
begun and everywhere was visible Philip's leaden foot.

CHAPTER XV

GUISEPPE THE VALET

" THIS is the young person, your Grace," said the major-domo, and with a gesture to Robin Aubrey: "Stand forward, Guiseppe!"

The old collossus who was bending his bald head over columns and columns of figures spread upon the table turned his chair and fixed his eyes upon the lad. They were remarkable eyes, big and black, very steady and searching, and quietly alarming. But the Marquis of Santa Cruz was an alarming man. Amongst the commanders of great fleets he had in that day the greatest name of all. And though he was now in his seventy-third year, his belly fallen, and his health gone, he had still the readiness and resource which had enabled him in earlier days to sail his ships into the gap in the line and save the day at Lepanto ; and still the ruthlessness which made him put to the sword every prisoner taken in the rout of Strozzi's fleet at the Azores. Robin had as much ado to keep his knees from shaking as he had had long ago when his Queen called him out from among the Oppidans at Eton. It seemed to him that Santa Cruz was never going to take his eyes off him. "He is looking into my soul." Robin was sure of it. How could he hope to outface this old conqueror with all his experience of men ? And Santa Cruz still looked at him. "He is stripping every rag of my disguise off me," Robin cried to himself; and then Santa Cruz spoke. He asked a bewildering question.

"And did you move forward?"

Robin could make neither head nor tail of it.

"When Diego announced you?" Santa Cruz continued impatiently.

"I moved forward three paces."

"Move again! Stand in front of me!"

Robin's heart turned to water. But he moved forward, none the less, and stood respectfully before the Marquis.

"He's trying to frighten me," Robin reflected, and added, "Yes, but he's succeeding."

Santa Cruz growled in his throat, and Robin thought: "Another minute of this and I shall be on my knees confessing all. He can see that I've stained my skin."

But again Santa Cruz surprised him.

"Get my shoes! Take off my boots!"

A pair of light shoes was lying by the hearth. Robin fetched them. The Marquis was wearing brown boots of untanned leather which reached above his knees. Robin knelt in front of him, drew off the boots carefully and tenderly and slipped on the shoes. Then he stood up again.

"Guiseppe Marino?" the Marquis asked.

"Your Excellency, that is my name."

"An Italian?"

"Of Leghorn."

It was going to come now, Robin said to himself—the accusing finger, the one word "liar," and the dungeon at the bottom of the Tower afterwards. But a third surprise awaited him.

"Diego, you will explain to this boy his duties," and so the old man turned back to his figures, and Robin got himself out of the room as quickly as he could.

On the stair outside Diego turned Robin over to Giacomo Ferranti, who was waiting with a white face to hear how the interview had gone.

" I am hired," Robin explained, " and with few words. But what persuaded his Excellency, heaven knows."

Nor could Giacomo Ferranti help him to a better knowledge—nor anyone indeed except Santa Cruz himself had he been so minded. For none but Santa Cruz knew in how desperate a sickness Santa Cruz was caught. The enterprise of England—if he could live to sail up the Channel and burn Elizabeth at St. Paul's Cross ! That was all he asked. If he died now, would the enterprise ever be brought to its proper godly result ? Medina-Sidonia, now in the south at Cadiz, was an ass, a reluctant, plodding, uninspired ass. Recalde, a good wary sailor of the puritanical kind, and a veteran like Santa Cruz himself was not the man for so vast an authority. Alonzo de Leyva, his own second-in-command here at Lisbon, was a cavalry officer and a hot-head. Miguel de Oquendo, who was fitting out the Guipuscoan squadron up at Passages, he Spain's Philip Sidney, was the only man with the spirit and the wisdom for so tremendous an undertaking : and his youth and a joyousness he found in living were not the qualities which would commend him to Philip. He himself, therefore, must live and hide his maladies as best he could from as many as he could, but most of all from himself.

There was the rub. He had to play the old man's game of pretending that he was young, else would Philip never be master of the world. But it was a difficult business and Guiseppe Marino was likely to help him.

" I who could sleep like the dead with sailors scouring the deck a foot above my head, am tormented if a heavy foot shakes the floor," he acknowledged in a rare moment of confession. "The jar of a rough hand, and I'm in pain. Mother of God, a vibration of the air and I'm jangled like an ill-tuned fiddle ! "

Thus the light-footed Guiseppe, who could remove a boot so deftly that a swollen leg was not aware of it and yet lend the support of a shoulder of steel, became with every day more and more of a necessity to the old Admiral. Guiseppe got the rough edge of his tongue often enough, but so did everyone else. The old man lived at the top of the Torre Sao Juliao and it was his banner which Robin had seen floating on the high flagstaff when the *Ragazzona* sailed over the bar of the Tagus.

The expedition was to sail in the summer of 1587, but nothing was ready at its time. Medina-Sidonia tarried at Cadiz with the squadron of Andalucia, there were no tidings of the galleons from the Levant and Naples, the *San Felipe*, King Philip's own East India-man, had not yet come to harbour with its treasure, the gold fleet from the west was behind its time. And then in March Drake struck Cadiz, anchored a few weeks later off Cascaes, flaunting his English flag in the sight of Santa Cruz's windows, and, realising that the harbour was not to be forced, was off again to the west.

"Look at that man ! " cried Santa Cruz. "And there's my good Master in his Oratory making out a list of rations for me between prayer and prayer. So many aves for San Lorenzo, so much dried fish for each soldier, and more aves than dried fish ! Drake'll have the gold fleet next."

He pushed out with what ships he had ready in pursuit, and coming to the Azores found that Drake had picked up the *San Felipe* with a hundred thousand pounds' worth of treasure on board and was out of reach bound homewards for Plymouth.

Robin sailed on that wild goose chase with Santa Cruz, and by the month of July when he returned, the year was too late for the Enterprise of England.

"The astrologers were right," thought Robin. "It will be 1588, after the conjunction of the planets, when the great ordeal of the world will come."

Through the rest of the year the work went faster at Lisbon and out of the confusion a sort of order began to emerge. The gold fleet came safely to port, Oquendo brought his fleet from Passages into the Tagus, the galleons from Naples joined the Armada, and Santa Cruz's great bureau grew fuller and fuller with lists of ships and their captains, their armament and their complements of men, their barrels of water, their stocks of powder.

Robin used to slip out of the Tower when he had a few hours free and make his way to the eastern quarter of the town. By the side of the Church of Nossa Senhora da Graça a steep narrow flight of steps led up into a network of small streets where little houses painted a dark red and roofed with green tiles climbed one upon the shoulders of the other as though each hoped to get a clearer view of the harbour. In the midst of them a tavern was kept by a kinsman of the Ferrantis. There Robin met Andrea and after drinking a bottle of wine, the two men would move away into the darkness and Robin would pass to him a letter which Andrea would take away with him to Figliazzi's house.

They were bulky letters now and Figliazzi began to wonder about them. He weighed one of them in his hand, thoughtfully.

"How does Guiseppe get these details?" he asked.

" Your Excellency," Andrea replied, " it might be that he had a key."

Figliazzi remembered that he had had some keys made for some new boxes of his own. A duplicate key from an impression upon wax might have been cut at the same time. It was on the whole better not to inquire.

" He runs a great risk," Figliazzi continued as he locked the letter away.

" He is in a great hurry," said Andrea. " He gave me news for your ear. The Marquis de Santa Cruz will never sail with the Armada."

It was now the month of January, 1588, the preparations far advanced and the whole navy assembled except the Andalusian fleet, or rather that part which Drake had left of it. That still loitered at Cadiz. Figliazzi was startled. Here was news indeed to rejoice the heart of his good friend Walsingham.

" Guiseppe is sure of that ? "

Andrea bowed solemnly.

" His Excellency is dying. He is seventy-three, he was stricken to death by the burning of Cadiz and Drake's flag waving within sight of St. Julian's Castle. His legs are swollen. His blood beats in his veins till it seems they must burst. He rages, sparing neither God, nor Man, nor Drake."

And in this classification Andrea was only echoing the general opinion. There were four species of existences recognisable ; God, the Devil, Man, Drake. Giovanni Figliazzi sent Robin's letter on with all the speed at his disposal and day by day the fleet of England grew.

CHAPTER XVI

DANGEROUS MOMENTS

THE worst days to Robin of all that long ordeal occurred in the first week of February of the year 1588, the year of prophecy. The accumulation of the months brought a certain habit and ease in the performance of his task, but counterbalanced that with a fear that with habit might come carelessness. The fear was all the more real because he wanted youth's large share of sleep. He found himself falling asleep upon his feet as he waited at a door ; for a fraction of a second he would lose his senses whilst he bent over his master's gouty leg and get a cut across the shoulders for his indifference. It is right to say that the menial character of his duties no more troubled him than it troubled in later days a good soldier in the trenches. The fastidious are bad servants when great causes are at stake. But under the stress of the long dangerous days and the yet more dangerous nights, the steps of the great Church in Madrid were growing dim, his own country with its honest friendly people, as Walsingham had described it, was becoming a fabulous island set in seas which never were, and even the face of the maid he loved was receding amongst the stars. So far he had plodded on, care at his elbow, in his eyes, in his steps But how long would it be before in some moment of fatigue he would cease to care what happened to him, to the Queen in her garden at Whitehall, even to Cynthia and Abbot's Gap, so long as oblivion came and sleep ?

The first of these worst days was Tuesday the fourth day of the month. All that morning Santa Cruz, tormented by his pain, was rating his commanders. First it was Medina-Sidonia's turn, a poor dull man of middle-age who loved to idle away his days in his orange groves at St. Mary Port and found himself tossed by the favour of his King into great duties for which he had neither capacity nor will. He had travelled overland from Cadiz and climbed the stairs to the high lodging in St. Julian's tower where Santa Cruz sat over his papers at his big table. Robin showed him in and closed the door, but the old man's voice roared out with so much violence that hardly a word was lost to the valet on guard outside.

" Look ! " he cried. " We are to carry a hundred and eighty long-frocked priests, and eighty-five surgeons ! Eighty-five surgeons to twenty thousand men and the English to fight ! God save us but we've tasted of those men ! "

Medina-Sidonia smiled complacently.

" There'll be little fight in them when they behold the Armada."

" They'll go down on their bellies, I suppose, at the wind of our coming, as Drake did when he ran under your guns at Cadiz and burnt your ships to give him an appetite for his dinner. And you command the Andalusian squadron ! Mother of God, but for His Majesty's most remarkable good will you'd command no ship at all in my fleet. I wouldn't buy my bedpans from you if you were a tinker, nor a pair of galligaskins if you were a tailor. Well—what are you short of besides seamanship ? "

Medina-Sidonia was short of five guns for each ship.

" And you've powder for a day. What are we going to England for ? The fireworks ? "

" We shall grapple and board," said Medina-Sidonia.

" Ho ! ho ! " cried the Marquis in a fury of derision. " They'll come into your parlour, will they ? Just simple tarry sailor-men, the English ! And Elizabeth ? She'll crumble like the walls of Jericho, I suppose, when you blow your penny trumpet ! Ouch ! "

For he had stamped with his swollen foot. Medina-Sidonia left the note of his requirements on the table and got himself away out of the range of the old man's voice. But Miguel de Oquendo went next into that high room and met with a different reception. The bellowing voice sank to a murmur, and an hour passed before Santa Cruz struck his gong. Robin entered the room. Santa Cruz was writing. Oquendo was standing in front of the hearth with his back to a log fire. His fame stood next to the Grand Admiral's in all but Philip's esteem. He was then a young man in the early thirties, of a high courage and a cool mind, a good sailor, a great gentleman and with such good looks as few are blessed with. Robin was careful not to look towards him.

" You will fetch some papers from His Excellency's ship, the *Senora de la Rosa*, Guiseppe. Here is an order."

Robin took the paper, and turning so that he showed his back to Oquendo, walked towards the door. But he had not taken more than two steps before a strong hand was laid upon his shoulder and swung him round.

" Stop ! You ! "

For the first time Robin stood face to face with Oquendo, and his heart sank. Very slowly the Spaniard looked him over from his feet to his face. They were of a size and it seemed to Robin that he had never seen eyes so piercing. His heart went down into his shoes, would have sunk lower if it could, so watchfully did those keen eyes survey him.

Worse than his glance, however, was Oquendo's silence. He twisted the ends of his moustache. Then he lifted himself once or twice upon his toes. But still he said not a word. And turning about in his chair, old Santa Cruz looked on with a grin.

Robin knew that the Marquis had a tenderness for Oquendo, he recognised in him a mate, a man of his own quality, and allowed him a liberty which he vouchsafed to no one else. But Robin was strung to such a tension of his nerves that he saw disaster in the smallest anomaly. He was in the condition of Santa Cruz himself, a sharp sound and he was tormented, a vibration and he shook.

" Guiseppe ? " said Oquendo, twirling his moustaches.

" Marino," added Robin.

" You're of the seaboard ? "

" Of Leghorn."

Oquendo's eyes brightened.

" Can you handle a rope ? "

Robin's heart began to climb again into its proper place.

" Your Excellency, I sailed in my father's fishing boat when I was a boy."

" And yet you can spend your life between the pantry and the parlour when there's the ocean at your feet and riches to be gained."

Oquendo laughed contemptuously and Santa Cruz broke in.

" Miguel, leave that boy alone. Mother of God, am I to have my servants filched from me ? Go and pick up a galley slave, Miguel. If Guiseppe sails with the Armada, he sails on my flagship and nowhere else. Off with you, Guiseppe, upon your business."

Robin ran out of the range of Oquendo's keen eyes as quickly as he could. He made haste to the *Lady of the Rose,* which was lying against the easternmost quay, delivered his order and was given the packet of forms and requisitions and made off homewards. But he had not reached the Tower when he saw Oquendo coming towards him. That would not have troubled him, but Oquendo saw him, and hailed him.

" Guiseppe ! Guiseppe Marino ! "

Robin perforce stopped.

" Your Excellency, I have the papers."

Oquendo waved them aside.

" Have you no wish to make your fortune, lad ? There's treasure in England. A man might take that trip with me and go back to Italy with his pockets lined with gold, and his soul saved into the bargain. What say you ? "

Robin murmured a few words of his duty to his master. Oquendo stroked his moustache and laughed.

" You can keep that pap for the old man, when you put him to bed. A tall lad like you nursed on the sea should be thrusting a boarding pike not holding up a cripple. The *Lady of the Rose*—remember that name ! I'll hide you on board where the old curmudgeon'll never find you."

And with a nod he sauntered on along the clanging quays. The great Admiral's day was done. Out with him ! Brutal days wanted brutal ways. Not that Oquendo bothered his head about his brutality. He was in the pride of his strength and old men are for the dust-heap as all the world knows. He left behind, however, a very troubled Guiseppe. Not troubled about the vanity of past triumphs or the disconsolate tragedies of age—such speculations could be left to the philosophers—but about his own affairs. The odd apathy which had been creeping over him was dissolved.

" Santa Cruz won't let me go. Oquendo wants

me. All very flattering but most damnably incon-
venient," he reflected. " Figliazzi's off to Madrid in
a month. His work here is done, mine almost done.
One night more and every detail of every ship down
to the last barrel of water will be written down for
Mr. Gregory of Lyme. But then ? How am I to
get away ? "

He could find no answer to that question, but the
night of Thursday answered it for him. It was a
dark clear night. From the guard-room in the foot
of St. Julian's Castle a few lights shone out upon the
water, but above it the great Tower was lost in darkness. Not a lamp shone at any window. There was no
sound of any movement. Yet in the blackness of a
corridor something did move. There was a vibration in
the air, swift and faint as though someone far away unlatched a window silently and as silently closed it. But
no window was opened and closed ; someone had
passed. That was all. And in a little while at the end
of the corridor a pale glimmer modified the darkness.
Someone had opened a door upon a slatted shutter.
Almost at once the door closed again, the corridor was
once more black. Inside the office of Santa Cruz,
however, Robin Aubrey was standing. From his feet
to his chin he was sheathed in black and a black visor
masked the whiteness of his face. Only his breathing
showed that he was there.

He stood like an image until the shape of the room,
the bulk of the table, the massive bureau, the frame
of the long window swam into his vision. The floor
was covered with thick matting. Mats, too, were laid
at the foot of the door and of the window, for on days
of gale the wind stormed at every cranny of this high
lodging like a fierce enemy. Robin lifted the edge of
the mat at the door and covered the crack between
the door and the floor. He had no shoes upon his

feet and he moved silently as a wraith. He glided
from the door to the window. He was wearing long
black hose and a doublet of black velvet fastened with
black buttons, and without a tag or a point to catch
upon the edge of a table or the back of a chair. He
set the doors of the window open upon the room, and
unlatched the shutters. Outside the shutters a
balcony of carved and ornamental stone overhung the
rocks a hundred and fifty feet below He looked out
towards Cascaes and that open sea where he had
dreamed once to light a funeral pyre which should
redden the water with its glow and confuse the heavens
with its smoke. A boy's dream, but even now after
this long year lived under the outspread hand of
death, he could not smile at it except wistfully. He
shut the vision of it from his eyes. His work lay here
in the room behind him. His last night's work. He
stepped back into the room, closed the shutters but
left them unlatched and left the doors wide open.
Then he crossed to the table. From the pocket of
his doublet he took a candle, and placing it on the
table, struck a light and lit it, and the room became
a den peopled with huge distorted shadows. Two
thick wax candles stood in heavy candlesticks of silver
upon the table. Robin removed one of the candles
and set his own in its place. Robin's candle was of
wax too, with a cotton wick so that it should give
out no smell.

About his waist a strong cord was wound and a
dagger hung in the cord. He laid the dagger on the
table. Then he took a key from his pocket and
inserted it into the lock of the escritoire. He let
down the flap. The pigeon-holes were stuffed with
papers bound together by tape. Other papers lay
upon the ledge beneath the pigeon-holes—the last
details of the equipment of the last ships to be mobilised

for the Enterprise of England. Robin took them over to the table. There was paper enough and to spare littered upon the table. Robin gathered some sheets and set them ready at one end. He had a pen with him and a small bottle of ink slung on a black cord about his shoulders. He drew a wooden stool up to the table and sitting down upon it began to copy the documents which he had taken from the bureau.

" Italy with the Levant Islands, under Martine de Vertendona, ten Galeons eight hundred mariners, two thousand soldiers, three hundred and ten great pieces," he began to write, and so followed on with the particulars of each ship. What store of biscuit each ship carried, so that each man might have a quintal a month for six months, how many pipes of wine, how many quintals of bacon, how many of cheese and fish, of oil and vinegar, of peas and rice. How many barrels of fresh water, what number of spades and lanterns, of spare sails and ropes, of ox hides and lead plates to mend the damage done by the cannon of the enemy. Then came the number of bullets and quintals of powder for each gun, of the muskets and calivers for the fighting tops, the partisans and the halberts for the boarders. Robin wrote the particulars down with the name of each ship against them, whether great ship or caravel. And the night waned as he wrote. Each of the official documents he set back on the ledge of the bureau in its original place as soon as he had copied it. And at four o'clock in the morning, when one more hour would have seen his year's work done with, his head nodded on his shoulders, his eyes willy-nilly closed and re-opened and closed again and as he sprawled forward on the table, his elbows slid out. One of them touched his dagger and pushed it to the table's edge. Robin drew a long breath, his head was on his hands, his whole body relaxed in a delicious irresistible relief. His arms spread just a fraction farther apart, and the dagger clattered upon the oaken elbow of Santa Cruz's great chair and tumbled with a thud upon the floor.

For a moment Robin wondered whether the clatter was a noise in a dream. But he saw the dagger on the floor. As he picked it up he heard a great thump on the ceiling above his head, and his blood stood still in his veins.

Santa Cruz had heard it too. The catastrophe, foreseen and guarded against through so many nights had caught him at the last.

A feeling of despair descended like a cloak upon Robin's shoulders, muffling for a moment his every sense, so that he remained on his stool in a paralysis. And over his head he heard Santa Cruz dragging himself about his room.

During the first moments when activity returned to him, Robin acted like an automaton, but he acted quickly ; so carefully had he rehearsed each successive thing which he must do, if this mischance befell. He put back the requisition which he was copying into the bureau and locked the flap and slipped the key into his pocket. He folded and placed within the bosom of his shirt the copies which he had been making. He set the stool against the wall and he heard the thump of the old sailor's stick upon the floor and a door whine upon its hinges. He thrust the pen between the buttons of his doublet, and fixed the stopper in the ink bottle about his neck. Santa Cruz would be upon the stairs now, but he could only move slowly and with great care lest with his huge weight he should fall. Robin could hear him shaking the house.

Robin replaced the big candle in its socket, blew

out his own and thrust it into his pocket. Was it his own voice which he heard coming and going in sobbing breaths ? He had come so near to the end of his service, and now disaster and death !

But he was wide awake now. He placed the dagger between his teeth. He slipped across the room and drew down the mat at the door until his fingers told him that it lay flat. He went out by the window, setting the latch at an angle and closed the glass doors behind him. With the thin edge of his dagger inserted between the doors he dropped the latch into its socket. He went out on to the balcony and closed the shutters, just as he had closed the windows. He was on the balcony now, but there was neither safety nor conceal-ment yet ; and through the lattices he heard the door of the room flung open and saw the flicker of a candle held in an unsteady hand.

CHAPTER XVII

DEATH OF SANTA CRUZ

JUST within the doorway of the room old Santa Cruz was standing, his swollen leg criss-crossed with bandages, his great bulk muffled in a crimson robe. He leaned upon a thick oak stick and in his left hand he held above the level of his eyes a candlestick with a lighted candle. Under his left armpit was tucked a naked sword. It was not fear which made his hand shake, though the grease from his candle bespattered the floor. For he looked as dangerous and angry as a bull, a bull with his strength sapped by the banderilleros. His eyes travelled about the room warily, truculently. Something had clattered in this room, bounced and clattered again and then fallen with a soft thump. By the mercy of God he had been awake. For the first time he thanked Him that old men can't sleep. For not one of his mouldy lack-linen scullions would have heard it ; or done aught if he had heard it but bury his craven head under his blanket. No, not even the soft-footed smooth-faced lackey who could nurse him like a woman and sustain him like a man. Dastards, sheep, quicksilver at the sight of a cut finger !

The old man dragged himself across the room to the table. He dropped rather than laid his candlestick upon it. He lifted his oak stick on to it and clung to the back of his arm-chair, breathing in great difficult gusts which wrenched his body and made a

horrible loud sound in that empty room. When he
had recovered a little he bent over the chair and felt
the cushions on the seat. No, no one had sat there.
He reached forward and felt the big round candles.
The wax of both of them was hard and cold. No one
had lighted them. Yet something had fallen in this
room, something had struck and clattered.

" What ? . . . Who ? . . . Answer me ! " he bullied
and he thumped the table with his fist.

All this time he had been holding the sword under
his arm, and it shone in the wavering candle-light
from its great basket-hilt to the point, now bright and
blinding like sunlight on a mirror and now blood-red.
He lurched along the table and over the matting to
the glass-doors of the window. The latch fitted into
its socket, fitted home ; and the day of finger-prints
had not yet come. He raised the latch and let it fall
back again into its place.

It might be—yes. Fingers which were not heavy
with age or crippled with rheumatics, fingers which
were cunning and deft, fingers which he would cut off
at the knuckles, there on that table with this sword
he carried under his arm, might have shot that latch
down into its socket. He should have bidden Guiseppe
change that latch for a bolt. No, Guiseppe should
have changed it without any bidding at all. Mother
of God, what were servants for ! . . .

Unless—yes, unless Guiseppe's fingers were the
fingers he was going to mutilate. The rascal was on
the balcony. Good ! Well, he must be deft and
cunning himself. He wanted to see those hands
stretched on the table flat on their palms, yes, and
above them a rogue's white face and frightened eyes,
and a foolish chattering mouth slobbering for mercy.
But he must be cunning and quick and—just for a
minute—God vouchsafe that miracle if ever for his

master he had done good work !—just for a minute move with the nimbleness of youth—the nimbleness of Guiseppe Marino.

Very quietly he unlatched the glass doors. At a touch they swung noiselessly into the room. Santa Cruz listened. He could hear nothing. The rogue was outside those shutters holding his breath, cowering in a corner of the balcony ! Santa Cruz took his sword now by the hilt into his right hand. Good ! He felt twice the man he had been a minute ago. Now for that moment of youth ! He gathered his great frame together, he drew a long breath like a diver before he dives. And the miracle happened. He sprang. Heavy and awkward and grotesque, he sprang with all his force and all his weight against the shutters. They splintered and burst like so much tissue paper. Old Santa Cruz was carried forward by his weight and flung against the balustrade of the balcony, and his sword rattled against the stone. He could turn no quicker than a charging rhinoceros. " The rogue has me," he gasped.

He was at the mercy of anyone upon that balcony with a dagger in his hand whether he cowered in a corner or not. But nothing happened. No steel blade slid cold and sharp into the fat of his back. He turned himself about—even that movement was difficult now—and stood amazed. There was no one on the balcony.

Then Santa Cruz swayed like a drunkard. His head swam, the stars in the dark sky whirled in a mad dance before his eyes.

" Mother of God, what's happening to me ? " he wailed, suddenly pitiful and afraid like a child. Something was happening to him, something quite new, something quite stupendous, but what it was, he couldn't think. He was too dizzy to think at all.

A sharp touch in the night air gradually brought him round. He drew it into his lungs and the stars having had their fling settled themselves again in their orderly pattern. Santa Cruz took a hold upon himself.

" This won't do . . . I can't afford it. No, Spain can't afford it either. . . . There's my sword on the floor of the balcony—I'll not leave it there ! No, I'll not leave it there to shame me."

But some instinct of prudence warned him not to stoop. Or rather, not to try to stoop. Try as he might, he knew that he could never reach that sword with his hand. His crimson night-robe was gathered about his body in a girdle of twisted silk. He un-wound the girdle and turning about so that his buttocks rested against the balustrade, doubled it and with the loop angled for the hilt of his sword. Once he had caught it, but only by an ornament, and he had not raised it more than a few inches from the ground when it slipped and clanged once more against the stone. But the old man was obstinate. He would not leave it. It had been too good a friend to be thus disrespectfully treated. Left to rust in the dews of the morning, the sword which had seen Lepanto and Terceira and was to catch and cast back the sunlight from the white cliffs of England at the Narrows ? No, indeed. Never did a schoolboy angle for a trout in a brook with a greater seriousness than this old gentle-man of Spain for his sword on his balcony over the Tagus. But he succeeded in the end. The loop caught the weapon below the basket hilt and a moment afterwards Santa Cruz was fondling and pinching the blade as though he was a boy again and the hilt the soft palm of his mistress.

But he was cold now. There was a dampness in the air which crept into the marrow of his bones. He was shivering and with such sharp spasms that the blade of his sword beat a tattoo against the stone balustrade. And he had still something to do before he could make sure whether or no his secrets had been stolen. Clutching at the window frame, he drew the shutters close behind him, then stared downwards at his left foot rather stupidly. "There's something woundily odd," he said aloud.

There was no feeling in his left leg at all. It wouldn't hold him up. It wouldn't do anything. It wouldn't even hurt him any more. Somehow he managed to lumber into the room on one leg; and, now clinging to a chair, now to the edge of the table, he dragged himself laboriously and painfully to his bureau. He had the key in the pocket of his dressing-gown and he unlocked it and let down the lid. The papers on the top? Yes, they recorded the equipment of the *Santa Ana*, galleon from the Levant. She was short of her big culverins. Yes, there was the note which he had written in the margin that very night. Nothing had been disturbed.

Santa Cruz locked up his bureau again and coming to his table dropped heavily into his great chair. Was it possible, he wondered, that his senses were playing him false? He had imagined that clatter and thump upon the floor? But if he heard amiss, why to-morrow he might see amiss, and from that what catastrophes might come? If over there, in the mists of the Channel, he was to see ships where there were no ships, hear the roar of cannon where there were no cannons and set his battle array accordingly? What then of Spain? He threw out his arms wide and so dropped his hand palm downwards on the table; and he felt the palm of his right hand grow wet.

Wet?

He lifted it and looked. There was a black smudge upon the skin. He bent sidewards and stared at the table. There it was, the proof that his senses had not played him false, the sure sign that his bureau had been rifled, a smear of ink which had not yet dried. With a bellow the old man rose to his feet and fell back again, and so sat stiff and upright with horror glazing his eyes.

For the stupendous sensation which had frightened him on the balcony was coming back upon him, and this second time it was even more real, more appalling. All the great joys except one had passed away from him, the joy of women, the joy of a great ship rolling down the seas before a strong wind, the joy of choice food delicately cooked, the joy of hunting days in the marshes by the side of the Guadalquivir. But one joy remained and swamped even the memory of the others—the joy of the Enterprise of England. He railed at Philip his master, cursed his penny-wisdom, and his slow meticulous brooding over details and particulars which were the proper concern of underlings. But he served him with a ferocious loyalty.

The Enterprise of England was to set so rich a crown upon his head as not even Imperial Rome had dreamed of. And he Santa Cruz alone could have done it, for he alone amongst the Admirals knew what great stuff the English were made of, what hard fighters they were, what great leaders sprang from nowhere to command them, and how from the Scotch Border to the Channel Ports a passion for liberty and faith was ringing like one deep note of a gong.

The joy of that vast Enterprise was forsaking Santa Cruz now. It was fading away. Even the anguish that he who should have led would have no share in it at all, was fading away behind a red mist which every instant grew denser and redder and was flecked with fire like the discharge of cannon. Santa Cruz could not move and in his wide-opened eyes the awful look of horror stayed long after his heart was still.

CHAPTER XVIII

MEANWHILE

AND meanwhile what of Robin? The balcony on which he had taken refuge was supported upon two strong brackets of fretted stone which ended in straight columns with projecting feet carved to resemble the heads of dolphins. These columns descended into the air just below the two exterior corners of the balcony. Robin had looked down upon them from the balcony many a time with a shrinking heart. The columns were about five feet in height and below the dolphins' heads at the end of them he could see the waves breaking upon the rocks a hundred and fifty feet beneath. On one of those heads he would have to balance himself if need befell. And need had befallen.

He uncoiled the rope from about his waist leaving, the last loop securely tied about his middle. The coping of the balcony was stretched upon stone columns separated one from the other by a space of six inches. Robin dared not yet make fast the loose end of his rope to one of these columns, since, if he did so, the rope must pass over the top of the ledge and betray him. He bestrode the ledge and bending down doubled the rope round one of the columns from the outside. Then commending his soul to God, he swung down upon the doubled rope, and with his feet felt for and found the dolphin's head. There he stood clinging desperately to the rope and dizzy as a drunkard. He dared not look down, he closed his eyes. If he slipped on the smooth stone beneath his feet! If his hands loosened their grip. Almost they did, almost the desire to loose his hold and have done with it mastered him. But there was too much at stake for cowardice long to have its way with him. There was England, his uncompleted work, Walsingham's faith in him, and Cynthia—the Cynthia he had seen in his Library, dominating her fears and her full heart, her lovely face alive with courage. Robin renewed his spirit from the strong image of her in his thoughts.

He reached up, he opened his eyes wide, and balancing himself upon his tiny perch, he tied the loose end of the rope with a clove-hitch round a column. After a second or two he looked down below the tiny pedestal on which he stood.

But he was not safe from detection even now. Santa Cruz had but to bend his head over the balcony and he would be seen. He would be caught in as helpless a position as could be imagined. A blow from Santa Cruz's great stick, a cut from Santa Cruz's long sword and he would go hurtling down through the void on to the rocks below.

Behind the foot of the pillar on which he stood a tiny ledge ran along the inner side of the latticed bracket underneath the balcony to the wall. Only on that ledge would he be screened from the eyes of anyone upon the balcony. But to reach that hiding-place, he must step round the pillar from the dolphin's head, he must get a hand grip on one of the holes cut through the stone, and this on a dark night when all must be done by feel and touch and the least slip meant a cry and a broken body to make a plaything for the waves. Robin, clinging still with his left hand to the rope, groped with his right round the pillar along the great bracket until it reached a diamond-shaped cut in the stone. Through this he passed his hand and gripped hard and tight. Then he passed round his right foot, and felt for the tiny ledge. It was some inches below the level of the dolphin's head, and Robin's toes went tapping and stretching as he lowered them. He touched it at last. It was not wide enough, but it must serve. He drew himself under the balcony, shifted his left foot from the dolphin's head to the ledge, found another cutting for his left hand and so clung there to the bracket like a bat.

The end of his rope he must leave knotted about the foot of the balustrade else he would never be able to climb up again on to the balcony. It was not likely to be seen even by one who searched on a night like this.

" The old man must stub his toe on the knot before he discovers it," Robin said to himself, and he heard the shutters above his head splinter and crash back against the wall and the old man lurch against the balustrade. His sword rattled on the floor.

Thereafter a silence followed, all the more alarming because Robin could not account for it. Santa Cruz was standing without a movement just over his head. Robin could hear him breathing, so still was the night. Why, then, he must hold his breath himself and he, too, must not move, must not ease his muscles by the slightest change of pose, lest the breast of his doublet or his sleeve should rustle against the stone.

A sharp fear made Robin's heart jump into his throat.

" He has seen the rope knotted round the baluster. He is standing up there playing cat and mouse, waiting for a cramp to knot up my tendons and snatch me from my hold ! "

He saw himself swinging out on the rope into the

air and then the flash of Santa Cruz's sword and the rope severed.

A movement was made upon the balcony at last, but it only added vividness to his horrid vision. The sword dragged on the stone, fell down again and rang and was lifted at the last.

"He'll use it now," Robin thought. "Trust him to use it." He looked down between his feet to the white of the breakers flashing in the darkness a hundred and fifty feet below and wrenched his eyes quickly away. The old man's heavy step sounded and Robin clung even more desperately to his buttress.

"Now!" he thought. "Now!"

And whilst he was expecting to hear the whistle of the sword and feel the rope drop loose the shutters were slammed to again.

Such was his relief that he was in greater danger of falling from his hold than he had yet been that night. The sweat poured down his face, his legs trembled, a weakness was stealing over him. He hooked an arm through the lattice work of the great bracket and then loosening his grasp of the rope he took a coil of it round his upper arm and seized it again and so stood the more secure.

Santa Cruz was satisfied then! But Robin must give him time to drag back to his room; and he had now no sounds to guide him. He could only guess how much longer he must wait. He counted a hundred very slowly. He had to move now if ever he was to take that long upward step round the pillar on to the Dolphin's head. He drew in a deep breath, raised his left foot, found the head under the sole of his foot, shifted his weight and hauled himself round and up. For a few moments he swayed dangerously—once more on the smooth curving stone. Then he pulled himself up by the rope, secured a hold upon the coping with one

hand and the next instant stood again upon the
balcony. He cut the rope away from the baluster
and wound it again about his waist. Then he turned
to the shutters and consternation seized him. For
through the lattices of the shutters a light still shone.

There was no going back for him on to that dolphin's
head. Nothing could have made him face the ordeal
again. He would wait where he was, and if Santa
Cruz came out again on to that balcony—well, it was
the Admiral's great share in Spain in the one scale and
his little share in England in the other. Robin drew
his dagger from his belt—and waited and—waited.
The night grew chill, there was a freshness in the air,
in a little while the dawn would come. He glided to
the shutters and opened them. He could see into the
room, but the table where Santa Cruz sat was to the
left and outside the range of his eyes.

He could hear no sound.

" The old man has fallen asleep or gone to his room
and left his candle burning."

Robin stole on tip-toe into the room. Asleep?
There was something in the Admiral's attitude, some
vague suggestion of collapse which spoke of a repose
deeper than sleep. Robin with his dagger ready in
his right hand crept to his side. The old man's mouth
had fallen, his eyes were staring, his breast quite still.
Death not sleep.

The bureau was open. Robin took the two papers
still left to be transcribed, he drew up the oak stool
again to the table and by the light of Santa Cruz's
candle, with Santa Cruz's dead body sagging at his
side, he sat himself to complete his work. He must
be quick, yet must omit nothing and put no wrong
figures down through haste—guns, culverins, minions,
baseliscos, soldiers, mariners, barrels of cheese, of
salted meat, of water.

He was getting towards the end of his work when an appalling thing happened in that room. The dead man moved at Robin's side, his arm which had been lying on the table struck Robin and slipping down, dangled. Robin sprang to his feet, his dagger was raised to strike, and sheer horror checked his hand in time. The muscles of the old man stiffened by death, were relaxing. As Robin watched him, he sank lower in his chair, he became smaller, he shrank, as if only now the undaunted spirit had left reluctantly its outworn shell.

Robin sat down again to his work. When he had finished, he left the bureau open, the papers which he had copied in front of Santa Cruz, and the candle still burning. As he crept to his room, the dawn was breaking.

CHAPTER XIX

A BRIDPORT DAGGER

IT seemed incredible to Robin that a man could have as many relations as the late Marquis of Santa Cruz. They descended from all the hills of Portugal, aunts, nieces, nephews, cousins to the faintest degree of consanguinity, and his dead wife's sisters and brothers and nieces and cousins, all swathed in black, all wailing and weeping and making such a din of lamentation that a stranger must have thought that the last tender blossom of the family had been nipped by an untimely frost. Yet the old rough sailor could never abide any of them. His ships were his family. On them he lavished all the affection that he had. Of his relations in the flesh, there wasn't one fit to command a jolly boat. Lawyers came, too, and, Robin fancied, all those hundred and eighty priests whom Philip, to Santa Cruz's disgust, had appointed to the fleet. In the midst of this confusion, Robin, his wages paid and service terminated, slipped away as quickly as he could, lest Oquendo should get hold of him.

He took refuge in the little posada behind the Church of Nossa Senhora de la Graça in the old Moorish town where he was wont to meet Andrea Ferranti. There he wrote out his last despatch to Sir Francis Walsingham, and being at once elated that his work was ended, and so worn with fatigue that he could hardly keep his eyes open, he included in it a foolish flamboyant phrase, which was to bring him to an hour of such stark horror and peril as left a scar upon his soul for the rest of his life.

He wrote :

This completes the list of the ships and their complements which will sail in the first of the summer on the Enterprise of England ; with the exception of the Andalusian squadron which your Excellency has an account of from another source. May Her Majesty be well prepared for the danger is great. Yet there is this comfort. Santa Cruz is dead, and there is no man here with the bold stroke and the long vision fit to take his place. Your Excellency then will have no more news out of Spain from me. D.1 is dead and buried with Santa Cruz. It is now the hour of one Carlo Manucci, a young gentleman speaking Spanish with the accent of Italy, for whom I beg your prayers.

Having given this letter to Andrea, he betook himself to bed and slept for twenty-four hours ; and woke with an uneasy sense of duties neglected, and was filled the next moment with such an inordinate relief and so soaring an elation that for the first time he realised the strain under which for more than fifteen months he had been labouring. His plans were set. He must lie close in this refuge till he had washed the dark stain from his skin and the black dye from his hair. His clothes were at Figliazzi's fine house in the broad avenue behind the offices of the Inquisition. With Giacomo Ferranti as his servant, he would cross the Tagus and take horses to Setubal ; and one evening when Figliazzi and his train arrived at that first stage on the road to Madrid, Carlo Manucci would humbly ask permission for himself and his servant to ride with him, and so escape the marauders and cut-purses on the road.

*   *   *   *   *

Robin was not yet clean from his disguise, when a certain Mr. Christopher Vode, coming from Paris, landed at Rye. Now licenses to travel in foreign countries were sparsely granted to Englishmen, and a strict surveillance was maintained at the ports ; yet Christopher Vode slipped through with hardly a question ; an achievement the more remarkable, since he carried a letter written by Lord Paget, the most important of the Catholic refugees in Paris and one of Elizabeth's bitterest enemies. But instead of delivering the letter to the person to whom it was addressed, Mr. Vode rode post to London and carried it to Sir Francis Walsingham's house of Barn Elms. There the letter was opened by the artist in opening letters, Mr. Gregory of Lyme, and duly copied. Then it was refolded and the original seal, which had been removed unspoilt by means of a knife with an astonishingly thin sharp blade heated in the flame of a candle, was delicately moulded and worked into new hot wax. Christopher Vode watched the dexterous fingers of Gregory with a cringing admiration.

" Oh, if I had your gift, Master Gregory," he cried. " What a profit I could make of it for the safety of Her Majesty and the advantage of the realm ! "

Mr. Gregory had no taste for rhapsodies, even when he believed them to spring from the heart, and in this case he did not. He shrugged his shoulders and answered in a dry tone :

" Even if you had the gift, you would have to cure that shaking hand before you could use it."

He cast a look at a face lined and disfigured by years of ill-living and added :

" And I have a fear that the time for that cure is past."

Christopher Vode took no offence at the words. He became reproachful, penitently and obsequiously reproachful.

" A few months ago you might have justly said so. But now that I have seen the better side——"

His eyes were uplifted, the sleek smile of the saved wreathed his face without improving it, and Gregory of Lyme broke in testily.

" Oh, yes, yes. The better side being that on which the butter is spread."

He turned his chair so that he looked Vode straight in the face.

" A few months ago, you said. It is, I think, seven months since you offered to Sir Francis to spy upon your friends, to work for us, pretending to work for them."

" Seven months ago I saw my error, the error of my birth in its true light."

" Very like, very like," said Mr. Gregory, cutting him short. He handed the letter back to Vode. " Well, go your ways, and watch well how the letter is received."

Mr. Gregory was a philosopher. Those who used the double cross must expect the double cross to be used upon them. He was not dogmatic about it. He could divide the for and the against as impartially as the late Anthony Babington. Research might discover exceptions to the rule, but he doubted much that Sir Francis Walsingham was one of them. Walsingham had his ear to too many panels and his eye to too many key-holes of the Council Chambers of Europe, to escape being sold by one of the agents he had bought :

" And Christopher Vode would sell his own mother for a pint of canary," Gregory thus concluded his argument. " So why not, Sir Francis. God make me a talkative parrot, if I'd trust him out of my sight ! "

He reached for a copybook in which he kept the

records of Walsingham's agents and the missions on which they were employed. Christopher Vode was not, however, a rarity in an age when conspiracy set the table for politics and treachery seasoned its dishes. He was the second son of a loyal Lancashire Catholic family, but was born with some vice in his blood which made him a gamester, a cheat and a profligate. Disowned by his family and ruined in his fortune, he had coined his religion by becoming a secret agent of the traitors in England, and the refugee traitors in France. Having sold himself to the one side, he then sought Francis Walsingham and sold himself to the other. He had the craft to disclose to his Catholic employers in France and the North of England that he had secured a place in the household of the Principal Secretary, and persuaded them that they had thus a staunch friend in the very heart of the enemy's camp.

"Not a very valuable friend," Gregory said dryly, as he consulted his book.

Nobody trusted him with deep secrets or critical negotiations either on one side or the other. He was a carrier of letters, a mere valet and post-boy in the service of treason, and got but a poor pittance and much fatigue as his reward.

He set off from Barn Elms with the letter in his pouch and on the second day came, after nightfall, to Hilbury Melcombe. It was part of his trade to make a great show of secrecy. Ride with him and his head was always turning back over his shoulder to discover whether he was pursued. Sit with him in a room when a sudden clamour arose in the street, and he would swallow and say, facing courageously his fate :

"They have come for me. Well, I know how to die."

It was six o'clock when he led his horse to the stables, walking it over the grass. He crept on foot to

N

the front door and knocked with so urgent and yet so cautious a touch, that one might have thought that a justice of the peace was lurking behind every bush. And when the door was opened, he plunged into the hall, locked it behind him, and stood listening, and panting.

"Sir Robert is within?" he asked in a quick, low voice.

"Yes, sir," said the servant.

"I must see him on the instant." He leaned his ear against the door, and stood up, his own man again. "All's safe. Tell Sir Robert it is Mr. Vode."

He was shown into that very room where Cynthia Norris had once fumbled the notes of her virginal, and a modish young gentleman had thought to give a little girl a treat. Sir Robert came to him anxiously.

"You are from France?"

"I bring a letter."

"Let me have it."

Sir Robert tore the seal, read the letter and re-read it.

"You know what it says?" he asked.

"I know only that Lord Paget was in the blithest mood when he gave it to me."

Sir Robert nodded his head once or twice.

"He might well be. He might very well be," he said softly. "How did you travel?"

"To Southampton. I landed early this morning," said Christopher Vode, pressing his hands to his eyes, as though he had hard work to keep them open.

"You shall have the softest bed and the best entertainment my house can give," said Sir Robert warmly, rising up from his chair.

But beds of down were not for him that night, Christopher Vode replied sorrowfully. Sir Francis Walsingham, God rot him, was a bitter task master

and a suspicious one. He had letters from the British
Ambassador in Paris which he must deliver.

" I have come far out of my way, Sir Robert, and
must make up my time by the loss of yet another
night's sleep. But I am starved, too, and a cut from
a pasty and a cup of wine, I must needs have, if I am
not to fall from my horse."

Sir Robert had him served in that small room, and
while he ate questioned him how the Duke of Guise
stood with Henri Valois and what headway the Prince
of Bearn was making in his penniless kingdom. Mr.
Vode answered at random, for he had a cause very
much closer at heart which needed some delicacy of
approach.

" Sir Robert," he said when he had finished his meal.
" There come from time to time to Walsingham's
house on London Wall, documents, informations—
I know not what—which it behoves the honest patriots
and those who look with sad longing eyes for the
re-establishment of the true faith to know."

It was a misfortune for Mr. Vode that he must
always over-colour his phrases, so that when most he
desired to produce a sure impression of fervid sincerity
then most he inspired repugnance and suspicion. Sir
Robert was treading almost as perilous a measure as
the Great Queen was wont to tread and with something of her wariness. He was not to be limed by this
poor trickster.

" No doubt," he said stroking his beard, " there are
informations. It would not be Sir Francis Walsingham, unless there were informations."

" They come from one quarter, Florence."

Robert Bannet was surprised.

" Florence ? "

What in the world had the little Duchy of Florence
to do in these great affairs which were convulsing the

world ? Rome, Madrid, Holland, Paris, Vienna—
Yes. In the kaleidoscope of policies and combinations
and alliances, news from any of these towns might
be of urgent importance. But what should the Grand
Duke have to say that concerned the state of England ?

" I do not think, Mr. Vode, that we need keep
awake o' nights over informations from Florence."

Mr. Vode however persisted.

" Sir, the Duke of Tuscany's Ambassador is in high
favour with King Philip."

" He is the less likely to send informations to Sir
Francis Walsingham," said Sir Robert.

Christopher Vode smiled.

" I wonder."

Did he not himself bowl with one side and bat with
the other ?

Like half the noblemen of Scotland ! And not a
few of them in England.

Sir Robert took his meaning.

" It may be so. There is little honesty in public
affairs to-day," he said sententiously.

" Very true, Sir Robert. I had, moreover, a word
with my Lord Paget from which I learned that the
Tuscan Ambassador is at Lisbon."

Sir Robert Bannet sat up in his chair.

" Indeed, and is it so ? Informations from Lisbon
might be of value."

" These, I must think, are of special value."

" Why do you think that, Mr. Vode ? "

" They are received with special precautions."

Sir Robert rapped the table impatiently.

" Come, come, Mr. Vode ! There are too many
wrappers round your meaning. A big nut doesn't
always mean a large kernel."

Mr. Christopher Vode, however, was not the man
to undervalue his wares. People took you at your

own value and estimated your merchandise by the advertisement you gave to it. Mr. Vode drank a mouthful of his wine before he replied.

" In the first there is an effort to pass them through unnoticed. They are not addressed to Sir Francis at all."

" To whom then ? "

" To Gregory."

" Gregory of Lyme ? " Sir Robert asked with a tightening of his lips. He looked at Vode with a closer scrutiny.

It was, indeed, through Vode that knowledge of Mr. Gregory's activities had come to the ears of the Popish party in the realm. Robert Bannet could never hear his name now without bethinking him of the fool conspiracy of Ballard and Babington, which had been nursed and sanctified in this very house, when Gregory of Lyme was a guest. He had kept himself and Humphrey out of any open connivance of the plot, but he was aghast at the recollection of the risks he had run.

" I do not meddle with Gregory of Lyme," he said, stroking his beard.

" Nor is there need to, sir."

" But these communications are addressed to him."

" Addressed, yes. But not delivered."

" How so ? "

" They are carried at once to Mr. Phelippes."

And at the mention of that name, an extraordinary change came over Sir Robert Bannet. He was shaken altogether out of his calm. A black look of rage convulsed his face, his eyes blazed, his voice trembled with passion.

" That villain ! How is it God lets him live ! So many years he's overdue in Hell ! " and his fingers tore the lace at his wrists.

It was Phelippes who had de-cyphered the fatal letter of Mary Queen of Scots, which commended the assassination of Elizabeth. That was now known to the world. The trial of Mary had brought it to light. Without Phelippes, the tragedy of Fotheringay would never have taken place. Without Phelippes, Mary of Scotland would still be alive, perhaps already seated on her throne. There was no name, except perhaps Walsingham's, which roused such wild hatred amongst the enemies of Elizabeth. It took Bannet some minutes to regain his self-control, and bring his mind back to the subject in hand. Then he nodded his head once or twice.

"These letters are carried to Phelippes?   Proceed!"

"Yes, and at once."

"They are written in cypher, then."

Vode raised his hands.

"I suppose so."

"You have not seen them."

"No more than the superscription."

Sir Robert Bannet had the letter from Paris in his hand. Oh, no doubt the great crisis was at hand. Elizabeth's shifts and evasions, her promises of marriage which were never fulfilled, her offers of loans which were never paid—they had held off her doom for thirty years, but she had come to the end of them. The beast that troubles the world. Yes, but the beast could double and twist no more. She was in her corner with her back to the wall. It was honest tooth and nail now.

"It would be well to have the contents of those letters," he agreed.

"But how?" asked Vode in a despairing voice. Yet his eyes were fixed cunningly upon his host.

"Let us consider," said Sir Robert. "When that

false scoundrel—his name burns my tongue—has
finished his de-cyphering, what happens to it ? "

" It goes at once to Sir Francis."

" Wherever he may be ? "

" If he is in the house, Phelippes takes it to him
with his own hands. If he is at Court, a tried servant
rides with it."

" And if he is at Sydling St. Nicholas ? "

Mr. Vode was quick to understand all the suggestion
which lay behind that simple question.

" No doubt something might be done that way. A
horse may stumble, a rider's head may strike a stone.
But Walsingham has gone no farther afield than Barn
Elms this many a month. There are so many meetings
of the Privy Council, so much hobnobbing with Burleigh
and Hawkins, and agents of my Lord Leicester, that
the poor man has not had a moment of leisure."

" What of the tried servant, then ? Is he—amen-
able ? "

Bannet had come to the point which was Mr. Vode's
concern. Mr. Vode lifted his eyebrows and spread
out his hands in protest.

" How should I know ? I have not a real wherewith
to try the tried servant."

" Many reals could be found," said Sir Robert
cautiously, " if the prize were worth the price."

" But that cannot be known until the money's
spent," Vode argued very reasonably.

" No," Sir Robert agreed, and,

" No," Mr. Vode repeated,

and there it seemed the matter would be left. But
Sir Robert looked again at his letter from Paris.
No opportunity must be lost now. It was so certain
that the long-delayed enterprise was to be undertaken.
What should he do ? Hold a middle course ? Lie
soft and avoid risk ? Yes and see every honour

snatched, and vast estates granted to those who had struck for the Church and for Philip, before Philip and the Church had won.

He leaned forward and tapped Christopher Vode on the knee.

" Bring me these informations and you shall ask your price for them. But I know nothing of them until they are here, on the table, in front of me. I am no party to any attempt to obtain them. I will not appear as the rich man who tried to seduce a faithful servant from his duty, as I might well be made to look. I will not say to you, you shall have money if you do this or that. No, Mr. Vode. We have a phrase in this county. A Bridport Dagger. Do you know what that is, Mr. Vode ? "

Mr. Vode was a little put out of countenance by Bannet's evident distrust of him.

" No, sir. I never heard of it."

" It is a hempen rope, Mr. Vode. And ' ifs ' have brought too many good men to suffer the thrust of it, for me to feel worthy of their company."

Sir Robert rose to his feet as he ended, and smiled.

" But you will be wishing to go, lest you set Sir Francis wondering why you dawdled on the way."

Bannet accompanied him to the stables, and saw him ride away on the grass at the edge of the drive, so that no sound might be caused by the hooves of his horse. Vode was using the same precautions as he had used on his arrival. He did not indeed hope to impress his host by the exhibition. But such displays had from long habit become part of his very nature and he could no more avoid them than change his skin.

" A mountebank," said Sir Robert sardonically, " but he has his uses."

Once clear of the Park gates, Vode set his horse

to a brisk trot, and coming to Poole, went comfortably to bed at the best inn, untroubled by any fear of Walsingham's suspicions. Nevertheless he did not sleep, tired though he was. In this country with the threat of war so close and so many great families still dabbling in treason and conspiracy, there were surely great fortunes to be made by a clever man who played his cards well. But he must hold good cards to begin with. He must have a good secret to sell, and Mr. Christopher Vode thought that he was on the scent of one. He would have liked, of course, to have secured some conditional promise from Sir Robert written down on a sheet of paper, which, even if he could not lay his hands upon the secret, might have got him some greater favour with Sir Francis Walsingham than he enjoyed at present. But the secret was his great opportunity. He had been looking for it for years, and here it was, under Phelippes' nose. But how to bring his own nose into the exact position of Phelippes' nose was a problem he had not yet solved. Chance might help him—chance which solved so many great problems if a man was alert to seize it when for a second it flashed within his sight. The letters addressed to Mr. Gregory of Lyme and carried straight to Phelippes and from Phelippes straight to Walsingham ! Suddenly Mr. Christopher Vode saw Sir Francis hand them to him on a salver, and to his amazement heard him say, " Make your profit of them, my good fellow. For your merits have never received their proper meed." But by this time Mr. Vode was asleep and dreaming.

CHAPTER XX

PLOTS AND CONSPIRACIES

SIR ROBERT BANNET went back to the room in which he had entertained Christopher Vode and sat alone sunk in a deep speculation. He put altogether aside Vode's story of a great secret. That might be true or not. But whether true or not, it could not hold his thoughts at this moment. Sir Robert Bannet was a man of clear, cold, calculating mind. If he came into the open it would be at the last moment when there was no longer safety in the shadows. And that last moment was very near. He never had come into the open. To break cover was not in his nature. He was certain that he would feel naked in the open.

There was so much circumstance in the letter from Paris that he could not disbelieve it. Then he must stand on the one side or stand on the other ; and if he chose his side ill, he would not stand for long ; neither he, nor his son, nor his house. It would be the Bridport dagger for the lot of them and his house a reward to strangers. But after an hour of doubt and conflicting argument he hit upon a scheme which would push off the last moment of decision to so convenient a date that there would be no risk when it was made.

He struck a gong and to the servant who answered it he said :

" You will ask Mr. Humphrey and Mr. Stafford to

join me in the Library, and we must not be
interrupted."

Mr. Humphrey was playing a game of billiards with
Mr. Stafford. He was more than a little flushed with
wine, and he was losing and he did not like to lose.
He was very glad, therefore, to break off the match.
No less glad was Mr. Stafford, for he was winning and
he thought it impolitic to win. But he was in that
rare state when the very billiard balls made themselves
his sycophants. Let him deliberately miscue, he made
a cannon. Let him strike his opponent's ball with so
much deliberate ferocity that both must jump off the
table and he lose his point. No, they both rebounded
and rebounded from cushion to cushion, until in disgust
at so much useless labour, they glided into pockets
at opposite ends of the table.

In the Library, Sir Robert bade his son and Stafford
be seated, and before them he laid the letter from
Lord Paget in Paris.

" The hesitations and the doubts are at an end.
Pope Sextus puts his hand into his pocket. A million
pounds when the Armada puts to sea, a million when
its soldiers are landed on our shores. It was for that
Philip waited. The fleet is assembled at Lisbon. In
July from Creech Beacon we shall see it in the Channel."

Sir Robert was no doubt encouraging himself by
making the ultimate best of Lord Paget's letter. But
his exposition of it reacted upon him and for once
in a way there was a thrill in his voice and a gleam in
his eyes as he announced his good news.

" No but," said Mr. Stafford with a snigger, " here
is the most excellent news that ever we have heard."

He seized upon the letter and read it with little
exclamations of delight.

" No, but they will land at Southampton."

Humphrey Bannet looked up quickly.

" And is that so ? " he said eagerly, and in his turn he snatched the letter out of Mr. Stafford's hand. He was wearied with the monotony of his country life. He longed for the coloured parade of Courts, the pleasures of a great city, the lively gallantries of his time. But here he was penned in a rustic corner, aye and must so remain, quiet and unnoticed, so long as Elizabeth and her counsellors ruled the roost. There were no fine appointments for the schismatics of these days.

" It's down dog with us now," he said bitterly. " It is high time it should be up gentlemen."

But he had something of his father's caution in his blood. And as he read he remarked :

" It does not say that they will land at Southampton. It says only that they may."

" It is left to Medina Sidonia their General," Sir Robert agreed. " That is clear. He may go on to Calais and join with Parma's army and Parma's flat-bottomed boats. The one certain thing is that after all these delays, and doubts, the die is cast."

" And the English ships will be caught guarding Chatham Church," cried Mr. Stafford.

Nothing could chill his enthusiasm. One day the Queen would put her ships into commission. The next she would dismantle them. Always she was torn between her parsimony and her fears. God would see to it that she was caught napping !

" No, but the blow must fall and between the head and the shoulders." Mr. Stafford rubbed the palms together in his glee. " We shall hear the church bells rung backwards and Mr. Ferret will pull on the ropes. Oh yes, my gracious lady, Mr. Ferret will be there. The beast that troubles the world—the murderess ! Blood for blood, a head for a head, Tower Hill for Fotheringay. Mr. Ferret will be near enough upon

that day to fling his cap in your harlot's face, as they
force you on your knees at the block."

Mr. Stafford's mouth slobbered.   He gobbled his
words in the fury of his hatred.

Even to young Humphrey the exhibition was horrible
in its meanness and ferocity.   To the old man it was
simply disgusting.

" We have to decide our own action," he said
coldly, and at that Humphrey's face took on a look
of concern.

" Yes, what we shall do here, in this corner of Dorsetshire when the banner of Spain rides above the
Channel."

" I heard in the market at Wareham two days ago
that five hundred Dorset men were offering themselves
to the Queen as her bodyguard," said Humphrey
anxiously.

" Then the fewer to defend her in Dorsetshire,"
cried Mr. Stafford.

" I was thinking of the temper of the county,"
replied Humphrey, and he turned to his father.   " But
you, sir, have, I think, some policy in your mind."

Sir Robert smiled and laid a hand upon his son's arm.

" We must not be carried away.   It will be time for
us to get out caps ready to throw in the Queen's face
when for a second time she has passed through Traitor's
Gate.   Let us walk gently, we shall be the better
breathed for running hard when we near the winning
post."

He laughed a little and stroked his beard, and
added pleasantly :

" And let us not forget that this is the thirtieth
year of Her Majesty's reign, when it is right and proper
that we should commemorate it."

" We ? " exclaimed Mr. Stafford.

" Above all we who have so much to thank her for

—the permission to stay away from the parish church
so long as we pay a fine, her kindly tolerance of pirates
and the like, so long as they rob and murder those of
our Faith and share with her their profits afterwards,
her persecution and cruelties practised upon priests
and those who harbour them. Oh, we have a mort
of favours to be grateful for ! So I think that in July
we should gather our friends together in this house
to do honour to this great reign."

Humphrey drew in a breath, Mr. Stafford stared.
The old gentleman was to buckle on his breastplate at last.

" We shall ask our friends," he continued, " to come
in some state, since the occasion is so remarkable,
to bring their servants and retainers—armed, of course,
against the mischances of the road. We shall set up
tents in the Park and fill the cottages ; and for a
week or two, three weeks may be, we shall give ourselves to their entertainment. There will be tilting
and jousting for the gentry, football and games for
attendants, and I think a good deal of practise at the
butts for all, with some excellent prizes."

Mr. Stafford had grasped the ingenious plan.

" No but," he began with a snigger, thumping his
fist upon the table.

" You contradict me, I think," said Sir Robert,
polite and acid.

Mr. Stafford sat back in his chair bewildered. The
last word he meant to speak was one of contradiction.

" I meant only to second your remark, Sir Robert."

" I see," returned Sir Robert. " It is a habit which
I have happened to notice and misinterpret before.
It is always ' No but ' with you, and then when we
hang upon your lips for your objection, our remarks
repeated in other and no doubt choicer words. I am
glad to know that my plan meets with your approval.
And Humphrey, what of you ? "

" Why, sir, if Medina-Sidonia lands at Southampton we shall be very well placed. If on the other hand he goes to the Narrow seas, every Protestant will be rushing eastwards to repel him, and still we shall be very well placed where we are."

" And if by one of those calamities with which God has seen fit to afflict us these thirty years, again our hopes are frustrate, why we are celebrating Her Grace's beneficent reign and so disperse each to his home," and then for once the old man was carried away. A wave of passion broke through the reticence of thirty years. He raised his clenched hands in front of him.

" But I don't believe the mischance will come. How will Drake and his fellow pirates stand against the soldiers of Spain ? The humiliations of the Faith will be paid for to the uttermost drop of blood, this year, the year the stars have foretold—the year of wonder. Throw her down !—That was the order and the painted Jezebel was thrown down and the dogs licked her blood. We shall help in that throwing down."

He got up from his chair and struck a gong. He ordered champagne to be brought and in silence they drank to the day when the Invincible fleet would be streaming with its banners flying and its sails bulging, into the conduit between Hampshire and the Needles.

" To-morrow we will begin to prepare our lists," he said, " and this time we will omit from amongst our guests the name of Mr. Gregory of Lyme."

" But some Protestants we must have," objected Humphrey.

" The simpletons," said Sir Robert with a smile.

They began the work of selection the next day, pricking off slowly after much discussion their co-religionists in Dorsetshire and Wiltshire, Gloucester-shire and Shropshire. These again were subjected to a searching revision. There were loyal Catholics who had always been loyal. There were others who, seeing how dissension had been appeased, and religion made seemly by tolerance and a bankrupt nation allowed to grow to prosperity on its own feet, so that it was courted and coveted, and at its word all other nations paused, had become loyal. And there were families on the side of Philip and the Pope, who had even suffered in their members and their fortunes for their faith, yet would put their race above all and, called to the Standard of England, would spend their blood in a glowing scorn to repel, not the Papist, but the foreigner.

They came to the Protestants.

"The Norris family," Mr. Stafford suggested with his pen poised in the air.

Humphrey's face darkened. Sir Robert sat pinching his lips between his forefinger and his thumb with a sly glance at his son.

"We can certainly class the parents as honest simpletons," he said. "Colonel Norris was wounded in the Low Countries, and that, I think, was his sole distinction. Since then, a country squire who does not look beyond the edge of his estate and takes his politics from the parish pulpit. His wife—as long as she can chide and doctor and help the village of Winterborne Hyde and keep her house spotless, she asks no more. Upon my soul, I believe we could fly the banner of Spain from our flagstaff and they'd never notice it."

"Cynthia would," Humphrey returned sullenly, "aye, and be off with the news to the sheriffs within the hour."

"It is true," said Sir Robert sleekly, "that Cynthia has a certain fire and a quicker humour than her parents. Indeed they are aware of it themselves. For I have seen them gaze at her with some bewilderment as though they asked themselves—How did this chick come out of our nest? But we can hardly ask the good Colonel and his housewife and leave the maid at home."

Humphrey's face grew still more sullen.

"She said 'No' to me twice," he blurted out angrily. "I should get nothing but discomfort from her presence."

"Some drowning men have three chances, Humphrey," his father replied, "and if you take your third, the circumstances will be more propitious."

Humphrey looked up eagerly with a light in his eyes, but it faded out in an instant, and he shook his head.

"I took no pleasure in being twice refused in a quarter where it seemed to me I was conferring a benefit," he answered haughtily, and broke out into a sudden violence. "And it would happen again. For I know why I was gainsaid."

"We all perhaps have some suspicion," said Sir Robert. "But it would be a good match. Colonel Norris is a warm man, Humphrey. His pockets are full."

"I think of the girl," Humphrey interrupted.

"And the girl, I was going to add, is admirable," said Sir Robert, smooth as ever. "Therefore since the cause of her refusal is near to its extinction, the third attempt would be worth while, even at the risk of a little shame."

"I don't understand you, sir," said Humphrey obstinately.

"Then let us use a name and make all clear. Robin Aubrey is away with his ships. Our good Mr. Gregory of Lyme for once let a secret escape him."

"Yes!" said Humphrey.

Mr. Gregory had, indeed, let that secret slip and very deliberately. If Robin was thought to be roaming

O

the Atlantic in search of Philip's gold fleet, there would be the less risk of his detection in the household of Santa Cruz.

"Well, then, if the Enterprise of England goes as we wish, his life is forfeit, and after all few maidens die of love. Take heart, Humphrey! Besides"—and now Sir Robert's smile had a less pleasant look— "Mistress Cynthia would be in our safe-keeping. We would keep her very securely, and when Philip is King, her good parents might stand in some peril. She would, being dutiful, wish to purchase their freedom; and we, being then of more importance than we are to-day, might fix the price of it!"

"No, but——" Mr. Stafford began enthusiastically, and seeing Sir Robert's eyes turn coldly upon him, he broke off hurriedly. "I mean, of course, that this is the most subtle wisdom."

Humphrey himself was lifted to a more hopeful view.

"After a little while she might turn to me. I am not so ill-favoured. . . . I can hold my own, I think, when the odds are even . . . and on my soul I want her. . . ."

Sir Robert was for striking whilst the iron was hot.

"That is well, Humphrey, very well. And since it is well, let us make well better! Let us take our good friends of Winterborne Hyde into our council for the drawing up of our programme. It must be all gaiety and entertainment, sports and singing and music on the outside. Underneath it will be the forming into companies, the appointment of officers, the disposition of our troops. But these matters we shall keep very easily from our good thickheads."

Mr. Stafford shook his head.

"And from Mistress Cynthia?" he asked.

Sir Robert raised his shoulders.

"We must take some risk and Humphrey must see to it that the risk is small. On the other hand, there is a great advantage. We are not altogether free from suspicion. We are thought in some quarters to be lukewarm in our loyalty. The object of our gathering might be eyed with distrust. But if we are joined in our plans for this celebration by a family of such known honesty as the family of Norris, we shall be thought people who have been grievously misjudged."

Thus then it was decided. A list was drawn up, the invitations were sent out and Sir Robert and Humphrey themselves rode far afield to commend them. In the end they calculated that they would have a muster of five hundred armed men camped about Hilbury Melcombe in the middle of July—apart from the simpletons ; and the Norris family was asked upon a visit so that nothing might be lacking to make the entertainment worthy of so illustrious an occasion.

"That is a noble thought," said Colonel Norris. "The thirtieth year of her reign ! God bless my soul ! Let me hear no aspersions on the Bannets ! "

"And we are not so far but what I can come back if I am needed," said Mrs. Norris.

"Might I stay quietly at home ? " Cynthia asked gently.

But neither of her parents would hear of it. What ? Stay moping at home when so much splendour was afoot ? Why, it would be rank disloyalty at the best. There would be questions asked.

"Oh, well, if there would be questions asked," said Cynthia with a sigh. The one question which she really dreaded was the question which Humphrey Bannet had already put to her twice.

CHAPTER XXI

ON THE EDGE OF THE GRASS

THE first and indeed the last of these conferences took place at Hilbury Melcombe half-way through March. Sir Robert, his son, Colonel Norris, with his wife and daughter and Charles Stafford were sitting at the high table in the great chamber and the supper was at its last course.

"On the fourth day there should, I think, be some little joustings and tiltings," said Sir Robert, "and on the fifth——"

Sir Robert had got so far when a trifling disturbance amongst the servants behind him interrupted him.

"What is this?" he cried in amazement. The servants talking at their service? Such indecorum had never been seen before at Hilbury Melcombe. There would be some little joustings and tiltings amongst them next.

"There is a traveller at the door, sir, in a great fret and hurry," said the butler.

"He must come at a more seemly time," said Sir Robert. "Has he no name?"

"He would give none. He bade me tell you that he had come on the business you wot of."

And Sir Robert rose quickly to his feet.

"A new steward," said he with a smile. "I shall teach him better manners later on. Meanwhile I beg you my guests to excuse me. He may have some business of importance."

Sir Robert hardly waited to hear the reassurance of his guests before he was in the hall. There, just within the door, Christopher Vode stood, muffled to the eyes in his cloak.

" The mountebank ! " Sir Robert thought scornfully. " I'll wager he rode up on the edge of the grass. Well, come you in ! " he added aloud, and he led the way into his library and lit a couple of candles on his table. As Vode dropped his cloak and removed his hat, Bannet recognised that this time the spy was not play-acting at all. Vode was white with excitement, and such terror was at odds with his excitement, that his face twitched and his teeth chattered in his head.

" I am on the most dangerous business in the world," ne said, directing his eyes into corner after corner of the ill-lit room. " I am on my way from Sydling Court to France. A boat waits for me at Poole. If it were known that I had stepped out of my way—— "

" We should be like to suffer for it no less than you. So to the point ! "

" I have that secret."

Sir Robert's eyes narrowed. The secret Vode was to put his own price upon. Well, perhaps he had ! Nay, the very look of the man was warrant that he had.

" The price, then ? "

" Three hundred pounds."

Three hundred pounds was near to three thousand of our day. Sir Robert lifted his eyebrows.

" I have no such sum in the house."

" And I dared not take it if you had. I will take an order on your bank in Paris."

Sir Robert shot a swift glance at the man's disordered face and frightened eyes. Then he sat down at a writing table and wrote.

" You go to Paris—when ? "

" This very night. I have to carry false news—

yes, deliberately false—that we live in a fool's security
here, that the old harlot thinks of nothing but raddling
her cheeks and languishing on her favourites like a
lovesick girl, and that Sir Francis Walsingham is
banished to his house of Sydling St. Nicholas, as a
wanton stirrer up of trouble."

And Sir Robert interrupted him.

" And is Sir Francis at Sydling St. Nicholas now ? "

" Yes."

" At this time ?   Why ? "

" He is travelling secretly to Plymouth. "

" Plymouth ? "

" He starts at daybreak to-morrow."

Sir Robert Bannet sprang up.   Here certainly was
a circumstance full of menace.   For Drake was at
Plymouth.   If Drake and Walsingham, the two men
who wanted to bring these perils of England to the
open arbitrament of war, were putting their heads
together in Plymouth, the crafty statesman and the
devil-spawned marauder, why, Sir Robert Bannet had
better think twice of his fine celebration at Hilbury
Melcombe of the thirtieth year of Her Gracious
Majesty's reign.   Bannet sat down again, sanded the
paper and handed it to Vode, who put it away inside
his doublet with relief.

" I tell you frankly, sir, I shall not come back from
Paris," he said.   " I saw Babington at Tyburn.   I heard
Ballard's screams and prayers under the disembowel-
ling knife.   God send me a fair passage to France and
this cursed country shall go its own way to hell ! "

He shivered like a man in an ague.   There was
nothing of the mountebank about Mr. Vode now.   He
was a wretch in the very extremity of terror.   After
another glance at him Sir Robert struck his gong.

" You shall tell your news to the three of us, my
son Humphrey, Mr. Stafford and myself.

" No ! " cried Vode. " To you alone."

" They are all as deep in it as I," Bannet returned. " They must in any case hear your story afterwards, but it will be all the more convincing if it comes straight from your lips."

He bade the footman who answered the bell to tell his son and his secretary to ask for the forbearance of Mrs. Norris and join him at once. Whilst he waited for them he crossed the room to a buffet and poured out a brimming glass of his strong Charneco.

" Drink this ! "

Mr. Vode's teeth clacked against the glass, but he drank the wine as if it was so much water. Humphrey and Stafford hurried into the room.

" Sit you down," said Sir Robert. " You, too, Mr. Vode."

They gathered about the table.

" Now speak ! "

And with the candles lighting their anxious faces in the middle of the shadowy room Vode spoke. His story held his audience so that no one interrupted him. No one even made a movement, and they kept their eyes on him from first to last.

The opportunity for which he had been waiting had come by chance, and only in that way could it have come at all. Vode was summoned into Walsingham's presence at Sydling Court.

" It is desirable, Mr. Vode," Walsingham had said, " that our enemies in Paris should have encouraging news. Let them think we sit guarding Chatham Church ! The sooner we shall come to the great trial ! Therefore you will carry this false news all properly cyphered in a special cypher and addressed to Her Majesty's Ambassador. You will see my Lord Paget at once upon your arrival. You will tell him that you carry a dispatch sealed to the Ambassador. You will then take it to the Ambassador, who will drop it into his paper basket, and we need have no fear but that it will find its way shortly to my Lord Paget. Nor need we fear that my Lord Paget will have any difficulty in decyphering it. For I have taken care that the key to this fine new secret cypher is already in my Lord Paget's hands."

Speaking thus, Sir Francis struck his gong and called for Mr. Phelippes that he might put his name to the cyphered message and add the pointing finger in the margin which called attention to the important particulars.

" If you will wait in Phelippes's room," said Sir Francis, " he shall bring the dispatch back to you and seal it."

Christopher Vode had accordingly left Walsingham's office, and in the corridor ran against Phelippes.

" I went on," Vode related to his audience of three, " constraining my steps until I reached Phelippes's room. It was the first time that I had stood there alone. On the table lay a sheet of paper in the minutest handwriting you ever saw. There was a distribution of letters in groups and figures besides. I wondered whether the figures were to be taken at their value and the groups of letters were the cyphered message—and I saw in Phelippes's handwriting the decyphering of that sheet of paper. The figures represented the soldiers and sailors, the number of priests and the calibre of the guns on some ships of the Invincible Fleet. ' You have all the details now,' the letter went on, ' except Medina Sidonia's squadron from Cadiz, which, I understand, you have from another's hand. My work is done.' "

Sir Robert stared at Vode aghast, and for the first time interrupted him.

" That is true ? Up there in London they know even to the equipment ? " he cried.

Vode nodded his head gloomily.

" It must be so. Sir John Hawkins, Mr. Borough, the Paymaster—they have been again and again to the House on London Wall. There is such work at Chatham as has never been seen there. Powder is being bought in Holland, sailors are being requisitioned. All is heave and ho under Chatham Church."

" And Sir Francis is on his way to Plymouth," said Sir Robert. " Humphrey, we shall have to consider of this. This may alter our plans. We may have to make our celebration in a less noticeable way."

Mr. Ferret uttered a groan, but rather at the caution of Sir Robert Bannet than in despair of the great invasion.

" They may be as busy as you will at Chatham," he argued, " but still they will be after the day. See how long it has taken to fit out the Armada ! Besides, before July the Queen will have bethought her of her dwindling purse again. Even if she does not, the Queen's fleet will stand and guard the narrow seas. Drake will do what he can with his Plymouth privateers, but the Armada will catch the fleets divided and over-throw them by one one."

With eager looks he plied Sir Robert and Humphrey, wringing his hands.

" Let us not lose hope, sir, at this crisis of our fortunes. Walsingham knows what deadly enemy he must meet. Very well ! Is he the better for that ? The wiser, yes, but the better ? He must meet it. In that lies all. Oh, there is much still to be said," and he looked at Christopher Vode for encouragement and support.

" There is one thing still to be said," said Vode, " though it does little to help your argument, Sir."

" Let me hear it ! " said Sir Robert.

" I know the name of the man who sent all these particulars to Sir Francis Walsingham, who set the dockyards at Chatham teeming like a hive, who now sends Walsingham secretly to Plymouth, the man who is arming England. That, sir, is the secret you have paid for."

" His name," cried Humphrey, beating upon the table with his fist.

" Let us hear it, so that we may remember it in our prayers," said Sir Robert, " and call down God's vengeance upon him."

" Aye, and man's, too," said Mr. Stafford. " That name must be spread until there's no corner in all Spain which can hide him."

" Speak," said Sir Robert, and Christopher Vode spoke.

" The letter was signed D.1, but in the body of the letter was this phrase : ' D.1 is dead and buried with Santa Cruz. In his place stands now and hereafter till other work of his is done, one Carlo Manucci, a gentleman of Italy, who speaks Spanish with the accent of Italy.' "

" Carlo Manucci," said Humphrey. " You will remember that name when you speak to Lord Paget in Paris."

Mr. Vode smiled.

" I shall remember it very well. I shall remember it still more clearly at the Jesuit College at Rheims. I shall remember it to the Papal Legate in Paris. I shall bear other news than Sir Francis Walsingham entrusts me with, and this news will not be false."

Mr. Vode made his bow and slipped out of the room. He rode his horse away on the grass edge of the drive. He had better reason so to do that night than he knew. There was no comfortable bed for him in the best inn of Poole. He went aboard his ship and only breathed easily when he had sighted the coast of France.

But inside the house Mr. Stafford sat with his brows gathered in a frown. Carlo Manucci—somewhere he had heard that name—surely. An Italian. Mr. Stafford began to count over the Italians he had met. An Italian who was in some close touch with Walsingham. There were many such, no doubt, but how should he, Stafford, have come across one of them ? Yet the name had a familiar sound. Mr. Stafford must put it out of his thoughts, then one day, and soon, he would remember. The more he belaboured his memory, the less likely it would be to serve him. Carlo Manucci ? No ! He must put it quite out of his mind.

CHAPTER XXII

THE DEVICE OF THE ITALIAN
SINGERS

BUT Charles Stafford couldn't put the name out of his head. He saw Sir Robert carefully debating whether or no he should break off his plans, and Humphrey with his face buried in his hands. Carlo Manucci ! And then in an unfortunate moment there came stealing into the room the sound of a wistful melody played upon a virginal. Mr. Stafford caught his breath like a man on the brink of some momentous discovery. If he only waited, without trying to unravel the intricate hidden process of his mind which connected the name with the music, the truth would become clear to him. So he waited, but the secret still eluded him. He had to ask himself questions. Was it the melody which was vaguely associated with the name ? Was it the player ? Was it the instrument ? His inability to answer was altogether too exasperating.

But Mr. Stafford was a man of some ingenuity. He might, perhaps, get his questions answered by someone else. He would be shooting an arrow at a venture, but such arrows pierced a heart at times. The more he thought upon it, the more his little scheme appealed to him. It would be amusing to execute it—and no harm would come of it.

Mr. Stafford drew a sheet of paper towards him and wrote down upon it some half a dozen names.

Humphrey Bannet looked up.

" What are you doing ? " he asked.

" I am preparing to asperse the reputation of **Mr.** Nicholas Bools, your musician."

Stafford sanded the paper and shook the sand off.

" I beg you to wait."

He slipped out of the room, and crossing the great hall, opened the door of the small music-room. Colonel Norris was dozing in a chair ; his wife had a basket at her side and was working at a sampler whilst she nodded her head to the music. It was a homely scene, but rather dull for a girl, and Stafford did not wonder at the wistfulness of the music which was dropping like sweet tears from the fingers of Cynthia at the virginal.

But the music stopped. Cynthia had raised her eyes from the keys. She was watching in the mirror above her head Mr. Stafford as she had once watched Robin. The tears rose suddenly into her eyes as her thoughts went back to the gay smiling youth who had snatched her heart away and given to her his in that memorable second. She turned quickly on the stool.

" Mistress Cynthia, we need your help ! " said Mr. Stafford, bowing low, and Cynthia shut her eyes suddenly as though she was hurt. Perseus on that self-same spot had made a bow—a proper bow, a bow with all the graces in it. Alas ! where was he now ? This was the mere caricature of a bow.

" How can I help ? " she asked.

" We must have music and singing worthy of our festival. Sir Robert is set on it. This is the land of sweet singers. Yet it may be that we have still something to learn from Italy."

Cynthia laughed.

" That is very likely. But though I am flattered by Sir Robert's estimation of my knowledge, you will get, I must confess, a truer comparison between the English polyphonic and the Italian system from Sir Robert's musician than from me." Cynthia answered.

"But that is what Sir Robert doubts," said Mr. Stafford. "Mr. Nicholas Bools has perhaps too long made his home in this nook of the country to be abreast with the new fashions."

"What of me, then?" cried Cynthia, with a laugh.

"You, Mistress, are not quite so sunk in a good opinion of your own mastery of the art. I have had sent to me from a friend in London the names of some singers and musicians from Italy who have made a stir amongst the critical."

Cynthia reflected.

"I have heard of one certainly—Wait, sir! I have the name—Signor Ercole Tolentino."

Mr. Stafford looked down at his list. He uttered a little cry of pleasure.

"Ah! He is here, to be sure," and he marked off a name. It was not the name Ercole Tolentino. That was not written on the paper at all. No, nor any name faintly resembling it. But then Mr. Stafford did not mean this paper to leave his hands; the more especially since it was written in his own handwriting.

"But I remember no others," said Cynthia.

"The names I have here might quicken your memory."

"You might hear them, darling," said Mrs. Norris, without looking up from her sampler.

"Very well, mother."

Cynthia resigned herself to listen. Mr. Stafford fixed his eyes upon his paper. For nothing in the world would he look up. A curious excitement was growing upon him. He could not trust his eyes and his face to conceal it. But he was all ears for a sound, a quick rustle of a dress, a half-checked sigh. All, however, that he heard for the moment was a wheezy cough from Colonel Norris, who had been awakened by the cessation of the music.

" Luigi Savona," Mr. Stafford read.

" Ah ! A foreigner," said the colonel, giving information, and he promptly went to sleep again.

" I never heard of him," said Cynthia.

" He is not a singer, but a lutenist of repute."

" He may very well be," said Cynthia, " but for all I know of him, he may be the parish organ-blower."

" Tomaso Visentini."

" A fine name, Mr. Stafford, but I cannot promise you a voice to match."

Then in the same even voice with just a lift at the end to make the name a question, Stafford read :

" Carlo Manucci ? "

And beyond all his expectations the trick succeeded. Cynthia was taken unawares. She cried out in surprise.

" Carlo Manucci is a servant in a play. Some wit has been practising on Sir Robert. He is not a man at all——" And her voice faltered, and on a low despairing note she breathed : " Oh ! What have I done ! "

Some wit had been practising upon her. She lifted her eyes to the mirror above her head, and could put a name to the wit if she could not put a name to a singer of Italy. Mr. Stafford was standing with such a savage exultation on his face that she had never seen the like of it. It would haunt her, she thought, until she died. His tongue slid out and licked his lips. Had any face ever betrayed so much vindictiveness gratified, or so horrible an anticipation of cruelty ?

" Gino Muratori," Stafford read on, but he could not keep the excitement out of his voice.

In some mysterious way she had betrayed her lover. Somewhere in the world he was masquerading as Carlo Manucci. His enemies knew where, but they had needed her to tell them who Carlo Manucci was. And she had told them—fool that she was—traitress that she was.

" Gino Muratori ? " Stafford repeated.

Cynthia shook her head, and in a vain hope that she would so cover her confusion, she struck a chord and then another.

" Well, we have one name at all events—Ercole Tolentino—whom we must do our best to secure. I thank you," said Mr. Stafford, and with another bow he escaped from the room. He had drawn his bow at the venture and he had pierced a heart.

He hurried across the hall and burst into the library, with so amazed and eager a look upon his face that both the men there turned to him with a cry.

" What is it now ? " cried the father.

" Speak," said Humphrey.

But Mr. Stafford sank down into a chair, his eyes straying wildly from one to the other of his companions.

" To think we never guessed. Guessed ! You and I, Mr. Humphrey, we knew. Carlo Manucci. Mistress Cynthia had the answer pat. Aye, she would give her tongue, I doubt not, to have it back. Carlo Manucci. I read her a list of names, sweet singers from Italy to grace our festival. Did she know aught of them. Ercole Tolentino, Luigi Savona, Carlo Manucci ? ' It is not a singer,' says she. ' It's the name of a servant in a play.' Carry your mind back, Mr. Humphrey, to a day when we rehearsed a play at Eton and Francis Walsingham came to interrupt our rehearsal."

Humphrey had been staring at the secretary as at a man demented.

" Carlo Manucci ? " Stafford repeated, driving the name home. " Who is Carlo Manucci ? Who must he be ? "

At last Humphrey Bannet understood.

" Robin Aubrey ! God's death ! " he cried. He was drawn up on to his feet, his face white with passion. " Must he be ever in our way ? May he burn in hell ! "

A dreadful smile contorted Stafford's features. Never had he looked so viperish.

" We have seen to it at all events that he shall burn on earth. Like father, like son. They will find him. The Inquisition's arm is long, and if it looks sideways from beneath a hood, the sight is the quicker. Like father, like son ! "

The phrase gave the secretary infinite pleasure, so that he rolled it on his tongue and licked it about his lips.

" Mr. Ferret has ferreted to some purpose this evening. Mr. Ferret thanks Her Grace for the name," and he sat mowing and grinning, and rubbing the palms of his hands together in a grotesque and horrible glee which was enough to make a man shiver. And as the vision of that distant afternoon at Eton, when he was put to so much contumely, rose before his eyes, he said :

" Oh, he shall be on his knees again, but with less sprightly an air I think, and not so pretty a dress, and we shall not present him with a knot of ribbons. No, not to-day. A fool's cap and a lighted candle and the high plaza in Madrid, and the lovely country of fields and forest stretching away before the tortured eyes to the snow on Guadarama."

" What is this you are talking of ? " cried the

P

father, incredulously. " Carlo Manucci—the informer
who has ruined our hopes and made every dockyard
in England an anthill for activity is——"

" Robin Aubrey. Yes, sir."

" A boy ! "

Mr. Stafford nodded his head. He had always been
at a loss to understand Robin Aubrey. Something
in the lad had eluded him. But he was clearer in his
estimate now.

" A boy with a dream—a dream that made him a
man whilst he was a boy and kept him a boy after
he was a man. So that things impossible have been
done."

Bannet turned to his son.

" And you say so, Humphrey ? "

Humphrey, who was now staring at the table,
nodded his head.

" I should have known without this proof, if I had
had half the wits of a tadpole. He was always in
front of me—just in front of me, so that what I wanted
fell to him in small things and great things. If we
had hopes of a fuller life, of power, of the triumph
of our Faith, of another Prince—it is he who must
spoil them. Why, even Cynthia "—and he nodded
violently to the door—" even Cynthia Norris he takes
from me."

" You believe that ? "

" How else should she remember what we had
forgot ? Carlo Manucci—that was Aubrey's part in
the Eton play—the servant's part—and we, you and I,
Stafford, chuckling fools that we were, thought it so
suitable. We had rehearsed it evening after evening
—we had forgotten, but she remembers. Pat, you
said, the answer comes pat, without thinking. Had
she thought, she would never had spoken it. A
servant in a play ! Carlo Manucci. Of course, she

remembers, as she remembers every word he spoke to her, every glance of his eyes, every paddling touch if his hand ! Cunning, too, to keep her secret so well."

Oh, yes, Cynthia must come under his lash, too. Humphrey stood, his hands opening and clenching, his face contorted with malevolence.

" He taught her his cunning," said Mr. Ferret. " Oh, he had enough of it. This fine romantical story which has gradually crept out—a little fleet of ships to avenge his father. Oh, bravery ! Oh, worthy example of ancient piety ! Oh, noble son ! And all the while he sneaks about Philip's quays, an Italian gentleman."

Humphrey swore aloud.

" A grocer's clerk, rather, adding barrel to barrel."

" And culverin to culverin and soldier to soldier till the list's complete," Mr. Ferret added in a voice which had lost something of its glee. " Aye, until the list's complete, and Chatham's bustling with shipwrights and Walsingham's on his way to Plymouth."

" God ! that we should split on so puny a rock ! " cried Humphrey. " Why, he has made fools of us all with his lies. A second Drake he was to be—and, God help us, we believed him."

" Ah ! But there's one word of truth in his story," said Stafford, his spirits rising a little, " and one little thought of comfort for us. There was to be an *auto-da-fé*, I think. Wasn't that his word ? Well, with Christopher Vode's help, there will be an *auto-da-fé*. But it will not be held in the Atlantic. No, no ! In the Quemadero at Madrid."

Mr. Stafford found such great consolation in the picture of Robin burning that he must ever be painting it again.

And then Sir Robert Bannet rapped upon the table.

" You talk like children."

For some little time he had been giving only the faintest heed to what his counsellors were saying. They were talking—that was all. Words of fury, words of spite, gloating anticipations which might never be fulfilled, and all the while danger was pressing nearer upon this house in which they sat, danger most swift and sudden, which would need the coolest heads to conjure, if conjured it could be.

" A boy's passion, a man's hurt vanity will not help us in our straits," said the old man, and his two companions looked at him with surprise. There was so much consternation in his face, so wild and hunted a glance in his eyes.

" You did a clever thing, Stafford, when you went into the small drawing-room with your list of sweet singers and lutenists in your hand, eh ? Oh, such a clever, subtle thing ! ' Carlo Manucci,' says you. ' And that's a character in a play.' says she. She says it pat, without thinking, and there you are. Carlo Manucci is Robin Aubrey. Good ! We have him ! Yes, but what is she thinking now in the small drawing-room ? "

This, certainly, was a question which had not occurred either to Stafford in his glee or Humphrey in his anger.

" Do you think she doesn't know now that your list of singers was a trap. Oh, she fell into it, I grant you. But haven't you trapped us, too, with your subtle cleverness ? She's aware now that you know that Carlo Manucci is Robin Aubrey. But why did you want to know it ? Will she put it down to your kindness of heart ? And how did you come to hear of that name Carlo Manucci ? Where did you learn that there was a Carlo Manucci whose activities were important ? Eh, eh, eh, there's a question for you,

Mr. Stafford. And if Cynthia Norris loves this boy, Robin Aubrey, what will she do, Mr. Stafford ? She'll smell danger for her lover in every nook in the house. What will she do to save him ? "

" She can't save him," said Mr. Stafford stubbornly. " Vode will be in Poole before he can be stopped ; he will be in France before he can be stopped. There'll be no saving of Robin Aubrey, Sir Robert."

" And what saving will there be for us ? Robin Aubrey's Walsingham's agent in Spain. Doesn't she know that ? Hasn't she known that all this last year ? A secret between her and Phelippes and Walsingham ? "

Mr. Stafford was quick to defend himself.

" No, sir, she doesn't know it. It's notorious that Walsingham keeps his secrets to himself."

" She knows at all events that Walsingham is the boy's friend, as he was his father's friend. There's not one in the county who's unaware of it. And she knows, thanks to you, that the boy's in danger. What will she do but seek Walsingham out and tell him of your clever play with your singers and your lutenists ? "

Humphrey looked up quickly. That last bitter question did something to revive his confidence.

" But she can't," he cried.

" And why not ? "

" Because Walsingham rides to Plymouth at daybreak and Cynthia Norris is here at Hilbury Melcombe."

But as he spoke, old Bannet lifted his hand for silence, and so sharply that all obeyed him. They listened as if bound by a spell. Suddenly Sir Robert with an oath sprang up and flung open a window. The night was very still. There was not a whisper in the boughs of the trees ; overhead the stars streamed in a clear sky of ebony ; one would have said that but for these three troubled men all the earth was asleep.

" But I heard," said the old man in a low and frightened voice.

" What, sir ? " asked Humphrey in a whisper.

" There is nothing to hear," said Stafford.

And there was nothing to hear while Stafford spoke. But a second later, clear and sharp as the sound of a bell, all of them heard the beat of a horse galloping. The strokes of its feet upon the gravel were loud to them as the strokes of doom. No one moved until they had died away in the distance. Then Robert Bannet flung the window to in a rage.

" She rode on the grass at the edge of the drive, like Vode," and he began to laugh. Both Humphrey and Stafford were appalled by the look of him. He, the cool, careful head, was distraught.

" Treachery taught the one ; love teaches the other."

He bent over the table and snatched up the papers with the plans for the camps and the entertainments.

" Well, we are saved this much trouble," he cried, tearing them up like a man demented. " We shall entertain no guests to celebrate the thirtieth year of Gloriana'a reign. And why, Mr. Stafford ; why, Humphrey, my son ? Because there'll be no house standing in which to entertain them."

CHAPTER XXIII

A VAIN PURSUIT

IN this crisis of their fortunes, it seemed that Sir Robert and his son changed places. The old man drooped in his chair, his eyes dull and tired, his face haggard and twice his age. Even his anger against his secretary was spent. He sat with his eyes set upon the ruin of his house, the ghost of a man who a few hours back had been blithely trimming his sails so that no swift change of wind should catch him unprepared. Such lead as it was possible to take, Humphrey took.

"We must make sure that it was she who rode away," he said. He opened the door into the great hall. The household had gone to bed. The candles were all extinguished in the sconces on the walls. The only light came over his shoulder from the room behind him. He returned into the library and lit a taper.

"Tread softly," he said in a low voice, giving an order now with the authority of a captain. And carrying his taper into the hall he held it above his head, listening. Stafford crept through the doorway, and behind Stafford, after a little while, Sir Robert Bannet appeared, supporting himself against the side of it with an outstretched arm. Humphrey raised a hand to ensure silence, and crept on tiptoe to the door of the small drawing-room. Very carefully he turned the handle so that not a click of the latch was heard, and set the door slowly an inch or two

ajar.   Then he pushed it, and it swung, with a creak
of its hinges, wide open.   The room was in darkness,
but the log fire still glowed red upon the hearth.

" They have gone to bed," Stafford whispered,
creeping up to Humphrey's shoulder.

" The Colonel and Mrs. Norris, no doubt," returned
Humphrey.

" All of them," said Stafford stubbornly.

" Then who rode away from the house ?   And on
the grass verge till there was no need of secrecy ? "

" One of the grooms.   To keep a tryst.   Our
maidens are not so shy that a stranger would mistake
the village for a nunnery."

Humphrey looked at the secretary by the light of
the taper above his head.   Its flame wavered over
their white faces, the secretary trying to counterfeit
a smile, Humphrey gazing at him sombrely.

" We must make sure," he said again.

A massive candelabrum of silver gleamed on a
round table in the middle of the hall.   Humphrey
crossed to it, a shadow rather than a man—so lightly
he moved, and lit the two wax candles which it held.
He blew out the taper and dropped it on the polished
wood of the table.   He lifted the candelabrum and,
passing through the hall to the big doors eased the
bolts out of their sockets and turned the key back
in the lock.   He drew the door open and slipped out
on the gravel round in front of the house.   The
secretary followed close upon his heels, and Sir Robert,
with a little whimpering cry, made a tottering run
after them like a child afraid of being left alone in
the dark   Humphrey turned to him with an un-
pected gentleness.

" Nay, sir, there's no need for you to come."

" I'll not be left behind," the old man answered,
with a quavering voice.

" It shall be as you will."

Humphrey took his father by the arm. All three were wearing light shoes upon their feet, and though the old man's shuffled as he walked, the sound was muffled and would not have waked the lightest sleeper in the house.

The stables were beyond the right wing of the main building and behind it in echelon. The gates of the courtyard stood open. Humphrey pointed to them.

" They were shut at nightfall."

A dog bayed loudly and a kennel chain rattled.

" Down, Morgan," said Humphrey in a low voice. He crossed the yard and rapping on a window, roused a groom.

" Come out quickly," he said, and when the groom had joined them, " Show me the stall of Mistress Cynthia's horse."

The groom led them to the third door in the row of stables. The stall was empty.

" Where does her groom sleep ? "

" Above, sir," and he pointed to a small window over their heads. He cupped his hand about his mouth, but before he could shout Humphrey laid a hand quickly upon the groom's arm.

" No ! " he said. " Shut the door quietly. So ! "

He led the small group away from beneath the window and, still speaking in the same low voice :

" Saddle my roan Victor, and White Arrow for yourself." They were the two fastest horses in the stable. " I shall need you to-night. Be very quiet, I want no one disturbed."

He turned again to his father and Stafford.

" She was in the blue room, I think."

" Yes," said Sir Robert.

" She may have left a letter."

" To her father ? "

" To whomsoever you will," Humphrey returned. " We must have it."

If any notions of ancient hospitality remained in Sir Robert's mind, they must yield to the necessities of the moment. Humphrey led the way back to the house. Once he stopped and listened whilst the flames of his candles burned straight up into the air like the heads of spears. It seemed that a sound would have reached to their ears across all the hills and heaths of Dorset.

" If she left a letter, we must have it," said Humphrey.

The door of the house stood open. He placed the candelabrum on the hall table and lighting the taper went quickly and silently up the stairs. In a little while he came down again carrying his riding-boots in his hand.

" There was nothing in her room," he said, " not a scrap of a letter to her mother or to you, sir, her host. She fled in a panic at the harm she had done. That's the truth."

He looked at Mr. Stafford and nodded his head, but without any menace or anger in his looks. They were all too close upon disaster for the futilities of anger.

" Carlo Manucci—she had betrayed him, her lover." He sat down and, taking off his shoes, drew on his heavy riding-boots. " Carlo Manucci—how should we know that was the name Robin Aubrey was using ? How many knew it ? She, Robin Aubrey, Walsing-ham, and now the three of us. But the three of us, knowing that name, know more than honest men could or should."

He rose to his feet.

" Lock the door after me ! " he said. " But you, Mr. Stafford, will sit up till I return."

" You'll bring her back with you ? " Sir Robert urged.

" I must if we are to keep our heads upon our shoulders," returned Humphrey bluntly.

" But she will be near to her home by this time," Mr. Stafford argued and Humphrey turned upon him with a grin distorting his white face.

" You think she has gone to her home ? " he asked.

" Where else ? " Mr. Stafford asked in surprise.

" To Sydling Court, Mr. Stafford, where to-night Sir Francis Walsingham lies on his way to Plymouth."

Humphrey left his father and the secretary to make the best of his conjecture and, riding with his groom, followed the road to Cerne Abbas and over the shoulder of the down, as long ago George Aubrey had done and in a later year his son Robin. But though Humphrey rode at the risk of his neck that night, he never came up with Cynthia Norris. From the shoulder of the hill he looked down into the hollow where the village stood. There all was black and still. But above the village at the far end lights shone out barred across by the branches of trees. Sir Francis was keeping late hours that night at Sydling Court. Humphrey Bannet imagined Cynthia Norris, travel-stained and tortured by an agony of fear, pouring out her story to Francis Walsingham.

" They know that Carlo Manucci is Robin doing your work in Spain. You must stop them hurting him. Like father, like son—that mustn't be true. On my knees, sir, on my knees."

Humphrey Bannet turned his horse's head. There was no more that he could do than to lie quiet in the house until the blow should fall—betwixt the head and the shoulders as Stafford had said. Humphrey raised his hand and felt the back of his neck. Aye, between the head and the shoulders—he felt the axe cutting through skin and muscle and spine.

A little later he felt the breath of the morning and saw overhead the spangled canopy of sky fading into grey. It might be after all that Cynthia, exasperated by Stafford's trick, had flung herself from the house and ridden home. It might be that Sir Francis Walsingham was not keeping late hours but was early astir. It might be, too, that something might be thought of which would save his house.

CHAPTER XXIV

IN THE GARDEN OF ABBOT'S GAP

CYNTHIA indeed was not at Sydling Court, for she knew nothing whatever of Sir Francis Walsingham's journey to Plymouth. She had fled in a panic, as Humphrey had guessed, a panic of self-reproach. She had never faltered from her faith in Robin—not even when the *Expedition* had sailed back into Poole last year and its sailors had made the very air a braggart with stories of galleons burning at Cadiz and Johnny Spaniard cowering behind his walls.

She had ridden into Poole on the very day when the great ship, sailing full and bye between Brownsea Island and the sandbanks, swept up the narrow channel beribboned like a lady.

"That's Robin hasting home," her heart cried to her tumultuously. The *Expedition* was alone. Of course it was alone. Once in the Channel Robin had crammed on all sail and left the rest of the fleet, deep laden with its treasure, to follow with what speed it could. She heard the heavy anchor drop with a splash which sent all the seabirds screaming and flickering over that quiet haven. "It's Robin," she had cried aloud to them, as she set her horse to a canter. And she reached the quay in time to see the sailors tumbling out of the long boat and no Robin anywhere at all.

With a breaking heart she had listened to them

chattering and shouting to their wives and sweet-
hearts. They had been to Cadiz, not the far Atlantic.
Drake had been their admiral, not Robin.

" Peau d'Espagne, that's the scent for me, duckie,"
roared one of the men, delighted with his wit, and the
man's words and his burnt excited face and the look
of the girl clinging to his arm remained in her memory.

It was the bitterest day which Cynthia could
remember, but in spite of it she had kept her lips closed
and her heart high and her faith in her lover un-
tarnished. And now somehow she had betrayed him,
by a foolish cry extorted from her by Stafford's
cunning trick.

" He wanted to know who Carlo Manucci was,"
she argued, " and I told him."

What she must now do to repair her folly she could
not guess, but she would know. That conviction had
come to her before Mr. Stafford slipped out of the
room. It strengthened in her as her hands wandered
over the keys of her virginal after he had gone. She
would surely know at Abbot's Gap. If she could sit
for an hour in that room looking over Warbarrow Bay
where she and Robin had spoken their last words
and exchanged their last embrace. If she could walk
for an hour in the rose-garden with the doves fluttering
about the big octagonal dovecot and preening themselves on the brick walks ! If she could sit for an hour
on the bench on the bowling green with the famous
yew-hedge upon the one side and the high red wall
on the other. In one of these places the answer
would be vouchsafed to her. She did not argue or
reason about it. To Abbot's Gap she must go and
all would be made plain to her.

She slipped from the room where her father dozed
in his chair and her mother bent placidly over her
needlework. She ran silently and quickly up to her

room. For a minute as she changed into her riding-dress she hesitated whether she should write a message to them or no. But she dared not. There was a voice calling to her, faint as from far away, but very clear and imperative as the voice of God. The morning must dawn for her in the garden of Abbot's Gap. She must not be prevented.

She crept down by a back staircase to a side door, unlocked it and escaped. In the stable yard she gathered a handful of gravel and, flinging it up at the window, woke her groom. He saddled her horse for her quickly.

"I'll come with you, Mistress Cynthia," he said.

"No," she answered. "I know the road I must travel. There's no danger for me on this night, and I must go alone."

Some note in her voice of quiet certainty stopped his protestations. He led the horse quietly across the gravel on to the grass and held the stirrup whilst Cynthia mounted.

"Have no fear for me, William," she said gently. "I thank you," and she gathered up the reins in her gloved hand.

"You are going home, mistress?" he asked.

He heard her draw in her breath and for a moment she sat very still. Then she said gently but with the same odd note of quiet certainty which she had used before:

"Yes. Hasting home."

She cantered for a little way upon the grass and turned on to the hard gravel of the drive. It was then that Sir Robert Bannet first was sure that she had gone.

Cynthia rode warily that night. An accident now, a stumble, a careless loosening of the rein and her great fears might never be resolved. At times she stopped and listened for a sound of pursuit, but none reached her ears. Once past the division of the ways where the road to her home branched off to the left, she lost the fear of being followed ; but the night being the darker for the great forest of beeches which she skirted, she went still more carefully. She must win to Abbot's Gap. She reached the long slope at the back of the Purbeck Hills and mounted into a bitter air. Below her all was hidden, the winding river through the water-meadows, the little grass-walled town of Wareham and distant Poole—not a light gleamed in any window, not a star drew a trembling golden finger across a stream. There was, she remembered, a heavy white gate at the top of the hill whence the steep crumbling track twisted down on the farther side to Abbot's Gap. It took her some little time to find that gate, but to her good fortune, when she found it, it was open. For a yard or two her horse's hooves brushed through grass. Somewhere close the great signal beacon which was to warn all Dorsetshire of the coming of the Armada towered at the head of the track. Cynthia made it out as it stood high and black between herself and the starlit sky. Here she paused, recollecting how Robin had paused when to this spot together they had come. Here she looked out towards Portland in the west, remembering with what strange and ardent eyes Robin had looked into distances not visible and watched imagined scenes as in the magic of a crystal. Some great necessity had changed his purpose, some seal had been laid upon his lips, so that even she must walk in ignorance of what he did, of where he laid his head, of even whether he still lived. The tears rose to her eyes ; a sob, a quavering moan broke from her mouth. For a moment she felt that there could be no one more lonely than she on this cold black night in all the width of the world. And then round the Bill of Portland there came into view the dancing lanterns of a ship floating eastward with the tide ; and she drew enough comfort from that trifle to chide herself for a faintheart and a craven. Why, who knew but what Robin himself was aboard that ship straining his eyes towards the land as she towards the sea ?

A little lower down she dismounted and led her horse, so many loose stones there were, so many holes and ruts and so abruptly the steep path turned upon itself ; and a long while after she had dismounted she rang the great bell at the gatehouse of Abbot's Gap.

It was answered with a quickness which surprised her. The clapper was hardly still, the bell was still vibrating and ringing in the air above the house, when someone came running. The bolts were loosed, the door pulled open by a man in a fever of impatience —Dakcombe. He held a big lantern high.

" Master Robin ! Master Robin ! " he cried. " Aye, you would be coming at an unseemly hour when men of sense are in their beds "—this between a chuckle and a sob. " But come you in, I'll mind the horse——"

He suddenly stopped. Cynthia was dressed like a man in her doublet and breeches and her boots to her thighs, and she was tall for a girl. But she was not tall enough to be Robin Aubrey. Dakcombe lowered his lantern with a gesture of utter disappointment. He raised it again and stepped forward.

"It's you, Mistress Cynthia."

His distress left no room in his mind for any surprise that she had come at this unseemly hour. It was not Master Robin. It was someone else, and his voice was dead. Yet in the light of that lantern her slight figure in the bespattered clothes and her tired face might have moved anyone to pity.

Q

" Yes, myself, Dakcombe," she said in a small voice.
There was a question which he hardly dared to ask.

" You bring news, mistress ? "

" No, I come seeking it."

Some look of forlornness in her drooping shoulders,
some note of it in her voice did at last reach Dakcombe's consciousness.

" Take you the lantern, mistress, and go right
forward into the house. 'Tis all open and a great fire
blazing in the hall," he said, broadening out his vowels
in a warmer voice. And he took her horse by the
bridle and led it round the corner of the gatehouse to
the stables.

Cynthia carried the lantern through the gatehouse
into the court behind. The sky was lightening in the
east and the high oriel with its mullioned windows
and its carved pinnacles swung up out of the darkness
against the paling stars. Dakcombe's discouragement had not passed over to her. She indeed was
conscious of a thrill of excitement as the morning
broadened. Through the windows of the oriel and the
hall a big flare of light flashed out and sank and
flashed again from the logs in the hall chimney, like
a harbour light. A harbour light lit to cheer Robin,
since it was Robin whose coming was expected. She
left the lantern on the parapet by the steps and,
going into the hall, stood, her face lit and her chilled
hands thawed in the glow of the fire. But she had
tramped these last difficult miles and only her hands
were cold. Though she had passed through the
house but once, the housekeeper—and she remembered
it with a smile—had been insistent that she should
admire, nay love, every nook of it.

" The rose garden at the back on this March morning
will be black," she said to herself. " I shall wake
the doves in the big dovecot some minutes before

their time. But in the dining-room—that door upon
my left as I stand facing the fire leads to it—a glass
door leads on to the bowling green between the high
red wall and the still higher yew hedge."

She went through the dining-room and out. The
day was breaking clear and still with a pale blue sky
overhead and a promise of gold in the east. The
grass was shaven and tended and grey with the
morning dew like the leaves of an olive tree ; and
under the wall and by the side of the hedge, crocuses
and daffodils were lifting their heads. There Dakcombe found her, and hurrying up behind him came
Kate the housekeeper in a fluster of welcome and
concern. Cynthia must come into the house.

" You're all peaked with your travelling. The
cook—the lazy good-for-nothing slut she is too—is
cooking your breakfast. There's one in the house we
can wake whilst you are eating and he may tell you
more than he tells us, the hard-hearted curmudgeon.
But you'll be better for a few hours in bed first."

" There's someone in the house ? " Cynthia asked,
giving heed to nothing else in the spate of words.

Dakcombe nodded.

" A little square man you wouldn't notice in a
desert. I mind me he came here by a chance the
day you rode here with Robin."

" Gregory ! " cried Cynthia.

" 'Twas a name like that."

Cynthia was staring from one to the other, open-
mouthed.

" Aye, it does seem odd," said Dakcombe, nodding
his head gloomily. " And here you be both together
again. No good came of that other day, though we
hoped much from it. Master Robin off God knows
where and you, Mistress we were all reconciled to,
vanished over the hills."

" So Mr. Gregory is here, and Mr. Robin is expected,"
said Cynthia, with a sudden throb of the heart. " Oh,
more good will come of it this time."

" He came in the middle of the night, Mistress
Cynthia," the housekeeper added. " Shall I wake
him for you now ? Sore tired the poor thing was. He
could scarcely keep his eyes open, so heavy were his
eyelids. He was like a sailor, mistress, he could sleep
standing."

The good housekeeper did not in fact care twopence
whether Mr. Gregory needed a good night's rest, or
whether he did not. She had overpainted his fatigue
with a hope that since Cynthia gave no heed to her
own, she would take pity on Gregory's. " Shall I
wake him for you now, or will you rest awhile ? "

" Wake him now ! " cried Cynthia. She was seized
with no remorse. Let the lazy fellow get up at
once ! If she could be waking, why not he ? Robin's
life, for all she knew, was in the balance. " Wake him
up, good Kate. He has slept too long as it is."

" Very well, miss, and there's that lazy slut of a
cook bringing your breakfast, so come you in."

She had ordered the breakfast to be laid in the hall,
close to the big fire, and Cynthia, throwing off her
cloak, sat down to it. And with that nature began to
get the better of her will. She was not discouraged.
On the contrary. Had she not come straight from
Hilbury Melcombe she would never have found Mr.
Gregory here, and Mr. Gregory was in Walsingham's
confidence. To Mr. Gregory she could tell her story
and from him she could seek knowledge of what
danger threatened Robin, and of how it might best
be averted. She had done very well to come. . . .
She had done—very—and with a jerk she sat up
straight and saw Kate standing in front of her.

" I wasn't asleep," said Cynthia indignantly.

" Oh, no, Mistress Cynthia—oh, no way near it.
Many a person nods like that when they're thinking
deeply."

" Yes," said Cynthia, " I was thinking deeply, Kate,
that you had promised to wake Mr. Gregory for me."

" And is there a thing in this house—may the gentleman pardon me for calling him a thing—that I wouldn't
get for you, Mistress Cynthia ? " said Kate, and Mr.
Gregory came down the stairs as she spoke.

He was gentle and kindly as she had always found
him and plied her with no questions. He let her tell
her story as she would, sitting in front of the fire
beside her. Cynthia was awake now, and watched his
face as she spoke and learnt nothing from it whatever.

" At what hour did this rogue Stafford come to you
with his list of names ? " he asked when she had done.

" It was late."

" Midnight ? "

" Before. At ten, I fancy."

" Now think ! Did any visitor come to Hilbury
Melcombe last night ? "

Cynthia started.

" Yes ! We were at supper. The butler told Sir
Robert that a man had come in a great fret and would
not give his name, but he had come once to the house
before."

" And then ? " asked Gregory.

" Sir Robert got up and excusing himself went out
of the room. He was, I think, flustered."

" And he sent for Stafford and his son ? "

" Yes."

" And they were closeted together until Stafford
came to you with his questions ? "

" Yes. We thought that they were busy with their
arrangements for the festival."

Mr. Gregory laughed savagely.

"A little jousting and tilting! Look to it, good
Sir Robert," he cried, "or you shall do a little jousting
on a hurdle and the executioner shall do the tilting."
He turned again to Cynthia.

"When did this visitor go away?"

Cynthia shook her head.

"I don't know."

For a moment Gregory was silent. Then he said:

"There were three only who were thought to know
that Robin was Carlo Manucci—Sir Francis, Phelippes
and myself. But there was a fourth, Sir Robert's
visitor."

"He knew it—honestly?" Cynthia asked
anxiously.

"'No, my dear, no!'"

"A traitor, then?"

"Yes. Vode."

The name meant nothing to Cynthia. It was
enough for her that there was a traitor free with this
knowledge.

"He must be arrested before he talks of Carlo
Manucci to others," she cried. "We waste time, Mr.
Gregory."

"It is too late," said Gregory gently. "Vode took
ship to France last night."

"Oh!"

It was a moan of pain which broke from Cynthia's
lips. There was no stopping the traitor, no catching
him up. He had the start of them by a day. There
were no telegrams in those days, no cables, no wireless,
no telephones. The semaphore was not yet invented.
By one way alone could the ship or the mounted
courier be outpaced—the beacon, its black column of
smoke by day, its tongue of flame by night. But
if Mr. Gregory had climbed to the great pile of wood
and tar on the top of the hill and set it blazing, all

loyal England would have rushed to arms. Christopher Vode had the start of them by a day. At Paris he would pass on his news and make a second profit from it. From Paris it would pass to Spain—there were a hundred who would speed it on its way, refugees, Jesuits of the College, officers of the Inquisition. Carlo Manucci! From mouth to mouth the name would pass. Spain would be winnowed, the cell made ready, the stake planted.

"I have betrayed him," Cynthia cried in despair.

"No. If anyone is to blame," said Mr. Gregory, throwing out his chest like a man making a great determination, "it is not you. It is my master, who kept you in the dark. But it is the way of men who deal in secrecies. They say 'Hush! Hush!' always, and five times out of ten are put to it to find a reason for their hushes afterwards. No, you were not to be told. No, you would be unable to hide your grief and fears. No, you must be swaddled and nursed. No, you must think of the Plate Fleet and the *Auto-da-fé* in the waste of the Atlantic. You must not know of the dangerous, delicate work on which all these months Robin Aubrey has been engaged. Would that he had sent me to tell you!"

"Dangerous," cried Cynthia, with a hand at her heart. "I knew here!"

"But accomplished," Gregory added hastily. "Accomplished with a skill and a tact beyond his years. Vode is too late, Cynthia. Why am I here, do you think?" and as Cynthia shook her head, Mr. Gregory made a great resolution. He would throw over his secretive master. Cynthia should have the story of her lover's prowess complete.

"But not here," Cynthia cried suddenly.

The sun was up now and pouring in gold through the big mullioned windows of the oriel. She wanted to hear Gregory's story on the bowling green between the yew hedge and the red wall. They went out through the dining room. The air had the warmth of summer. At the border of the yew hedge the grass was speckled with daffodils and snowdrops. Mr. Gregory led Cynthia to the garden seat and told her of Walsingham's discovery that George Aubrey was still alive, an outcast on the steps of a great church in Madrid; of the inevitable change in Robin's plans and the requisition of his ships; of his secret departure to Lisbon in Count Figliazzi's train; and of his year and more of service as the valet of Santa Cruz. He told the story in the glowing imageful language of his day, which was as natural to the rough sea-captain writing up his log as to the poet in his study. And whilst Cynthia listened, she caught her breath and clasped her hands till the knuckles were white; her lovely face grew pale and red by turns, she shivered now and a moment later cried out in relief, and all the while such a passion of pride and love shone in her eyes that had Robin but been there, he would have felt himself paid for all his toil and peril twenty times over. And with her pride came a great humility— and a deep gratitude that she had ridden through the night to this garden, drawn to it as a pigeon to its cot.

"The work is done," said Mr. Gregory, "greatly done. And when the Armada crosses the Sleeve, we shall show them such a play with the iron bowls as will lower their proud stomachs till the end of time. Invincible shall bite the dust of England and find its savour taste of the bitterness of death. Therefore, you find me here. A letter reached Sir Francis four days ago; Robin was travelling to Madrid once more in the Tuscan Ambassador's retinue. But the letter was written five weeks ago. Robin may be upon its heels. He may have been a month upon the journey.

We shall hear no more of him except by word of mouth. Sir Francis sent me to Abbot's Gap post haste to prepare it against his coming, and if God wills it so, his father's, too."

Cynthia's hand went to the pouch at the waist of her doublet. She took from it the half of a gold sovereign, and laying it in the palm of her small hand, gazed at it, and shut her fingers over it and opened them again. Robin was safe now she thought, and Gregory would not for the world gainsay her. For so it might be. It was well for the peace of mind of both of them that they had no inkling of the fantastic horrors which at this hour awaited Robin at Madrid.

CHAPTER XXV

GREGORY BECOMES NOTICEABLE

" I THANK you, Mr. Gregory," and Cynthia rose
from the seat. " I never expected to find you
here. I thought that if I sat for a little while here in
Robin's garden, I might hit upon some way to lessen
the harm that I had done. But that such joy and
pride should come of it, I could never have dreamed."

Kate, the housekeeper, must have been watching
the pair of them through the glass-door of the dining-
room. For as Cynthia rose she came bustling towards
them.

Cynthia clung for a moment to the back of the seat.
Now that she imagined her anxieties at an end, she
was seized again by such weariness of body, that she
could hardly stand.

" There was God's hand in it, I think," she said
faintly.

" I pray that it may be so," said Gregory, and
though there was none of her assurance in his tone,
Cynthia was too tired to take note of the difference.
She was chilled through and through, and shivered.

" I must go," she said, and as she turned, she
staggered.

But Kate was close beside her now, and held her up.

" Nay, Mistress Cynthia, you can't go till you are
rested. You would topple off your horse and lie on
the down with a broken neck. And what would
Master Robin say to us ? "

" But there's my father and mother. They'll be anxious," said Cynthia. " I must go," and her eyes were closing as she spoke.

" There's no need," said Gregory. " For I must be on my way. I have slept, Cynthia. I shall ride round by Winterbourne Hyde and set their anxieties at rest. Dakcombe will ride home with you in the afternoon."

" But they may still be at Hilbury Melcombe," said she.

Mr. Gregory laughed grimly.

" I have a word to say at Hilbury Melcombe myself," he remarked.

And whilst Cynthia still was undecided, Kate added :

" At this moment, mistress, there's a bright fire burning in a bedroom and you chilled to the bone. There are the finest sheets of Holland linen spread that ever you slept in, and the bed turned down, and so it has been all the night since Mr. Gregory came— just waiting for someone to sleep in it."

Cynthia looked up swiftly and as swiftly down again.

" Not waiting for me," she said softly.

" But since he's not come——"

A little smile dimpled the corners of Cynthia's mouth. She was tempted. Her young limbs cried for sleep—sleep with a bright fire in the hearth and in Robin's room, in Robin's bed. Oh, adorable !

" He might come whilst I slept," she tried to object rather than objected. The colour was bright again in her cheeks and it was not the sunlight which set it there, or brought the light into her eyes or the little sigh of delight to her lips.

" And would he be grieved do you think, mistress, if he did ? " said the housekeeper, and Cynthia looked at her, and she looked so roguishly at Cynthia, that both of them and the staid Mr. Gregory broke into a laugh. " Would he leap into oaths and capers, do you think, if I ran down to the gate-house and said to him as he got off his horse. ' There's Mistress Cynthia in your bed, and unless you've brought Parson along wi' you, I don't see how you can get into it yourself.' "

Cynthia laughed and blushed and laughed again.

" I'll stay, Kate," and she held out her hand to Mr. Gregory. " What will you say to my father ? "

" I shall say that Robin is on his way home to England and that you will be on your way to Winterborne Hyde this afternoon. I shall tell him that he is a very lucky man to have such a daughter and such a son-to-be. I shall not mention the name of Carlo Manucci nor will you. But I shall certainly say that Robin is a servant—the servant of Elizabeth."

With something of a flourish Mr. Gregory made his bow and went off to the gate-house. Cynthia walked with Kate into the hall, her feet dragging as she walked, and her head nodding between her shoulders.

" Ah, but we want Master Robin back," said Kate with a sigh as she looked about the hall.

" Robin—and the Parson," said Cynthia with a smile, and then she, too, breathed a sigh.

She was asleep before Kate had gathered up her clothes to take them away and clean.

It was twelve o'clock before Cynthia awoke, and wondered at the strange room in which she found herself. When she remembered, with a blush and a laugh, she smoothed and fingered those fine sheets of which Kate was so proud. She liked them, she liked the thought that Robin, too, was delicate and particular in these niceties of life. She loved him for his sheets, but " for what don't I love him ? " she cried, stretching out her arms. And with that her dreams faded away, and the scene of last night rose stark and clear in her thoughts—Stafford reading out his names —Luigi Savona, Thomaso Visentini, Carlo Manucci— with his eyes on the paper in his hands, and she blurting out like the fool she was, " It's a man, it's a character in a play ! "

She rang the bell over her head and Kate bustled in, prepared for her a hot bath, and arranged the clothes which she had dried and brushed.   Whilst she dressed, Cynthia suggested diffidently :

" Kate, it may be to-morrow that Mr. Robin will come.   It may be in a month.   I should like to come over one day in each week, so that if he is delayed the garden may look its best.   I have charge of the garden at Winterborne Hyde, and know each season's flowers."

It was the merest excuse for returning to Abbot's Gap and wandering about the house and amongst the roses, as Kate very well understood.

" It'll be a blessing, Mistress Cynthia, if you will," she exclaimed eagerly, and proceeded to asperse a very good gardener without a qualm of self-reproach.

" We have the idlest old rogue of a gardener that ever you saw.   It's taken him a day and more pints of ale than you'd drink in a year, to plant a geranium. Aye, he wants a lady with a sharp tongue at his heels. You come, mistress, and very welcome you'll be."

" I'll come each Thursday, Kate," said Cynthia.

So it was arranged, and after dinner, with Dakcombe mounted on one of Robin's horses, she rode home to Winterborne Hyde.

*   *   *   *   *

Mr. Gregory rode thither in the morning, and finding the Colonel and his wife in a great distress and anxiety, set them again at their ease.   They listened open-mouthed to his story of the Bannets' treachery, and were a little hurt at Cynthia's secrecy. " She might have told us," said Mrs. Norris, lifting up her hand. " But in this age of excitements and strange doings, the young people are so masterful that we hardly dare to ask them where they are going," and she sighed for the quiet, old-fashioned times, when girls were obedient and didn't ride astride.

" I knew that something had happened to Cynthia," said Colonel Norris sagely.

The good man had never noticed any change in his daughter at all, but he was not going to pass for a numbskull. " But a certain delicacy kept me silent."

" And the necessities of the realm kept your daughter silent," said Mr. Gregory.

The necessities of the realm made a good high-sounding, impressive phrase, and under the cover of it, Mr. Gregory got himself away. He rode on to Hilbury Melcombe with a good deal more enjoyment than he had felt on the earlier part of his journey. Here, at all events, no diplomacies were going to be practised. He threw his reins to a groom, strode into the great hall, and called loudly for Sir Robert Bannet.

Mr. Stafford came through a doorway, fluttering with anxiety, and wreathed in deprecatory smiles.

" Sir Robert will see you in the library, Mr. Gregory," he said, waving towards the door.

Mr. Gregory did not budge.`

" He will not," he said loudly. " He will see me here."

Mr. Stafford was pained. With a gesture, he dismissed the footman.

" I don't understand," he began.`

" Stand you there and you will," said Mr. Gregory.

From the doorway of the library Sir Robert Bannet emerged. He had aged during this night, so that he seemed physically to have shrunk to a lesser height and a smaller compass.

"Yes," he said in a quavering sort of voice, and behind him showed the sullen dogged, features of Humphrey. "In what can I serve you, Mr. Gregory?"

"In nothing. It may be that you can serve yourselves, but God knows you'll be hard put to it."

Humphrey Bannet pushed himself forward with a hand upon his hip.

"Oh?" he said with a laugh, which not unsuccessfully, counterfeited some disdain. "And is it so?"

"It is so," said Mr. Gregory, very stubbornly.

"And how, if you please, may we serve ourselves, Mr. Gregory?"

"By praying God night and day that Robin Aubrey may return to Abbot's Gap as whole and sound as when he left it," said Mr. Gregory. "For if he does not, it would be better for all of you in this house that you had never been born."

With that he clapped his hat on his head and rode away, leaving behind him on this one occasion, the impression that he was a very noticeable man.

CHAPTER XXVI

AT THE ESCORIAL

MR. GREGORY OF LYME was far out in his reckoning. For it was only upon the day when he sat with Cynthia in Robin's garden that Count Giovanni Figliazzi, having concluded the transfer of the Italian ships to the contentment of his Duke and of the free city of Genoa, set off from Lisbon on the still more difficult errand of negotiating a loan to Philip from the bankers of Lombardy. He crossed the Tagus by the ferry and slept that night at Setubal, where in accordance with his plan, an Italian gentleman, making the grand tour, asked for permission to join him. The Count Figliazzi travelled with a large retinue of gentlemen and pages and servants and a heavy train of baggage as befitted his high condition. In the medley and confusion of their journey, Robin was quickly submerged and the difficulty of finding lodgings for so large a company left little inclination or leisure for inquisitive questions when progress was interrupted by the coming of night.

They rode through a country of reddish earth made pleasant by the green of young wheat, the fruit on the orange trees, the cork forests and the shade of giant eucalyptus trees overarching the road. They traversed clean white villages made gay with bands of bright blue paint, and halted for a meal and a stoup of wine at inns which were nothing but long, dark, low-arched tunnels. Spring was warm in the air and

bright on the country-side ; the company was lively,
the gallantries of the evening numerous. But Robin
was hardly aware of the vivacious life which bubbled
about him, or of the beauties of the land through
which he passed. He went forward in a dream where
hope and fear alternated. Now he climbed the treads
of a staircase which never ended and was always empty ;
now he picked his way through a silent, muffled crowd
of outcasts and beggars, peering into their faces but
never into the face he longed to see ; and now again
recognition was instant and escape smooth. Lisbon,
Santa Cruz dragging himself along the corridor, the
night when dizzy and numbed he clung to the lattice
work of the balcony with the water breaking on
the rocks a hundred and fifty feet below him,
the Armada itself—all drifted away from him
and became unreal as the images of a dream. If he
thought of them at all it was with astonishment that
they had printed so faint a page in his book of life.

The company slept at Estremoz, a little white town
on the top of a hill, and riding amidst olive trees in a
torrent of rain came to Badajoz.   Thence their way ran
through an open, bare country on the edge of the
Sierras, the villages lost the spick and span coquetry
of Portugal, the road was a morass when it was not
a network of ruts.

They halted for the night at Toledo, and the next
morning, when they were clear of the town, Figliazzi
sent for Robin and rode on with him a little ahead
of the troop.

" I had a word some time since," he said, " from
our good friend whom we need not name, that you had
some private business at Madrid of a delicate kind."

" Yes," answered Robin.

" And that it was important that you should despatch
it as quickly as possible."

R

"It is for me of the gravest importance."

"I don't wish to pry into your affairs, my young friend," the Count continued. "Indeed the less I know of them the better. But I have a suspicion which our nameless friend shared with me, that as much secrecy as possible is desired."

"Otherwise I can look forward to a stake on the Quemadero," said Robin grimly.

"I did not catch that remark," Figliazzi answered dryly, "and if I did I should not understand it. You know, of course, that statesmen are proverbially ignorant of geography. So then despatch and secrecy are needed and in both those needs a full purse is of great assistance. We shall halt for the night at Illescas and my treasurer shall advance to you what you require."

Robin was in truth reaching the end of his resources, and though a credit had been arranged for him at Madrid by his banker at Florence, he was loth to waste a day by applying for it.

"I am very grateful, sir—you have shown me such kindness as I had no right to hope for," he said warmly.

"Gratitude in the young, Carlo, is a very pretty quality and rather rare," said Figliazzi with a smile. "I shall not disclaim it, therefore, although I am only fulfilling the wishes of our friend."

But neither he nor Robin was aware of the immense obligation under which that act of thoughtfulness laid the youth. It would have been an ill day for Carlo Manucci had he sent in his name to his banker at Madrid. But thoughtfulness was not to end its offices even at this point.

"In another way I can serve you, at no great loss of time. You are impatient no doubt to have done with your hard travail and to be getting you home," and he saw and smiled at the great wave of longing

which swept over Robin, parting his lips and
flooding his face with colour, and shining in the
eagerness of his eyes. " Yet after all these months,
a day more of anxiety and doubt will not add so
much to the burden that it's worth while risking all
to save it."

Robin cast a quick and rather startled look at his
companion. The Ambassador might disclaim all
knowledge of Robin's private affairs, but he seemed
none the less to have a shrewd suspicion of them.

" Well, then, I do not enter Madrid to-day, no nor
the next day. No, I sleep four miles away at Getafe.
You can, it is true, ride on with your own baggage
and your servant since your papers are in order. But
you will be wise to stay with me. I go from Getafe
to Escorial, where King Philip is at his devotions.
It would be wise, I think, for Signor Manucci to journey
on with me. For from Escorial, since I may be delayed
there, I shall send forward my baggage and my household to my lodging in Madrid, and the young Guiseppe
Marino might go along with the two Ferrantis. You
would pass in without inquiry.

And again neither of them had a suspicion how far
reaching an effect this small change in Robin's plans
was to have upon the lives and fortunes of all those
dear to him. He thanked Figliazzi again.

" So ! Will you fall back now, we should not be
seen in too long and earnest a conversation. You
have only to speak to Giacomo Ferranti and he will
charge himself with your baggage to-morrow and
wait upon you at Escorial."

Late at night the next day Count Figliazzi arrived at
Escorial and in the morning with Robin in his train
attended the High Mass in the lower choir. He was on
the left hand side of the great church just behind the
gallery in which the gilt figures of Charles the Fifth and

his wife kneel for ever with their faces towards the altar. In front of him the broad steps, carpeted in a dull red, rose to the High Altar with its gilded bronze and slabs of rare marble, and across and above those steps Robin could see the small, humble glass door at which Philip was wont to listen to the offices. The door was closed now, but he could not keep his eyes from it. The thunder of the organ, the sweet voices in the alto choro above his head, the gorgeous vest ments of the priests, the candles flaming in their jewelled candlesticks, and this little mean door by the side of the altar seized upon Robin's imagination ; and out of the contrast there grew in his thoughts a strange unsettling shadow of an idea, a confusion of all that he had accepted as beyond question true.

He had come hoping to behold the arch-enemy of his country, of his faith, of himself, the master of half the width of the known world, whose cruel rule had condemned to misery if not to the stake, a harmless traveller because he carried the precepts of Cato in his baggage, and had filled the boyhood of that traveller's son with bitterness. Robin had expected a figure of arrogance, a flamboyant monarch. All he saw was a little mean glass door which might be the entrance to a hermit's cell, and indeed that door led to a tiny alcove and a small bedroom which were little better. No curtains draped it. No guard stood beside it. What manner of man hid behind it ?

In a little while the door slowly opened inwards and Philip of Spain stood in the doorway. No majestic conqueror, but a plain man of middle age, dressed simply in black velvet with an uninspired and sickly face. The heavy outthrust underlip gave to him a brooding, melancholy look. If he was master of half the world, it was clear that he got no joy of his master- ship, and looking at him Robin understood the complaints which Santa Cruz in his bad moods hurled at him. A conscientious plodder, a narrow annotator of minutes, wearing brain and soul away over the proper work of underlings.

As he stood in the doorway, a little withdrawn so that he could see the High Altar and hardly be seen himself, he peeped—the word was Robin's, for there was no dignity in Philip's movements—round the side of the door at the alto choro filled with the chanting monks. There was an old story current that Philip had been sitting, as was his custom, in the last row of stalls at the corner of that choir, when a messenger, still booted and spurred, had pushed through a panelled door at his side and brought him the news of the victory of Lepanto and the overthrow of the Turks. The story had reached Robin's ears and he wondered now whether the memory of that afternoon was in Philip's thoughts and whether he was brooding over another victory which should establish his faith in the Channel, as surely as Lepanto had in the Mediterranean. For more than a moment Philip's dark eyes lingered on that corner in the high choir, and then clumsily, for he was crippled in a leg, he sank upon his knees.

And with that a change came over Robin. The fire of his hatred burned lower than it ever had since Richard Brymer, the sea captain, poured out his tale with the tears rolling down his face on the beach of Warbarrow Bay. Robin had come to imagine Philip as a primitive savage, finding a sensual joy in the infliction of pain and covering a limitless ambition with the pretence that he served his God. But there was no joy in this sombre creature kneeling in the doorway of his alcove, and there was no pretence in his humble devotions.

The unexpected scene following upon the drawn-out

tension of the long months at Lisbon and the curbed excitement which had grown upon him each day as he neared Madrid, threw Robin into a curious trance, of which only long afterwards he understood the meaning. A mist gathered before his eyes, dimming the magnificence of the altar, the red colour of the carpeted steps and the shining vestments of the officiating priests. White and red, gold and purple blended in a screen behind which the actual ceremony of the Mass seemed to move farther and farther away into the distance. At the same time the music of voice and organ diminished in his ears, as though that too moved out beyond the Church, beyond the Monastery into the Guardarrama hills and was lost among the valleys.

Robin watched the coloured mist with a throbbing heart and an intense expectation of he knew not what. It began to thin, and he was suddenly aware of a complete silence about him, as though all the world down to the smallest stream was hushed. And in the midst of that silence, the mist parted. Altar, steps, priests, the low glass door, Philip of Spain, all had vanished and in their place rose a huge cross of brown wood on which hung the naked figure of Christ crucified. How long the silence lasted, and how long the vision remained before his eyes, Robin could not tell. But it vanished as swiftly as a shadow upon a mirror, and the music of a chant was soaring to the roof above his head.

There had been a message for his eyes, for his ears. Robin was sure of it, but he could not interpret the message. Some day and when it was needed the interpretation would be vouchsafed too. Robin had no less doubt of that. Meanwhile he stored it away in his memory with just this odd conviction in his mind, that the message was uttered for him by the Man upon the Cross, rather than by the God.

CHAPTER XXVII

THE BEGGAR ON THE CHURCH STEPS

IN the lodging of Giovanni Figliazzi Robin woke with the sunrise. He had come to the last day of his search. One way or another, on this day when it was already sunrise in Madrid, all the perplexities were to be resolved, the horrible torment in which he swung between hope and fear would come to an end. Either Richard Brymer was right and George Aubrey had died at the stake, or Walsingham was right and and George Aubrey starved in a squalid and miserable bondage ; or there was a little truth in both their stories, and he had died since.

" In two hours I shall know," Robin said to himself, and he dallied purposely as he dressed.

Beggars and cripples did not creep from their hovels till the sun was warm and the charitable were abroad in the streets ; and when he went out upon his errand he must not loiter. He made sure that his sword was loose in his scabbard and his dagger in his belt. He was dressed in a plain suit of grey velvet with a falling collar of white lace which, he hoped, would neither by any singularity of meanness or extravagance call any attention to himself. Giacomo Ferranti buttoned a short cloak—that too of grey velvet— upon his shoulders. He set upon his head a cap of dark blue satin without brooch or any ornament.

" It is time for me to start," he said with a prayer at his heart. " Yes, it is time."

For at this last moment his feet faltered and his knees were as water.

"God be with you, Signor," said Giacomo gravely.

He knew nothing of the search upon which Robin was set, but he was aware that Robin had gone to his first meeting with Santa Cruz with a greater valiance and a less troubled face than he took out with him into the streets of Madrid.

Outside the door Robin regained his courage. The day was still fresh, there was a balm in the air, the sun rode in an unclouded sky. It must end as serenely as it began.

"I shall find him," Robin thought. "By the time the roses are out at Abbot's Gap, he will be there amongst them, playing bowls with Cynthia on the lawn or taking his ease with his pipe in his arbour," and the picture so enheartened him that he stepped out and now had much ado not to run.

But he must saunter like any gentleman of leisure, gazing into the shop windows as he went, yet not stopping over long before any one of them. The streets were already full. Men of business in sober clothes hurrying on their affairs, poor people in rusty black, women of fashion clacking on their high wooden heels with their maids behind them, girls with mantillas on their heads and duennas at their sides, priests, hidalgos, horsemen. Robin hoped to slip through the throng unnoticed, but the modesty of his dress had rather enhanced than obscured the attractions of his person. His slim straight figure, his brown glossy hair under the blue satin cap, the beauty of his face, which had had its curiously spiritual quality increased by the loneliness and anxieties of his life, and above all his radiant youth caused many faces to turn to him and many a maiden's eyes to linger on him with a smile. Robin had been prudent enough to make

Giacomo Ferranti trace for him the route to the Church of the Virgin of Almudena, so that he was not forced to stop and make inquiries.

Of that old Madrid through which he passed not a trace remains to-day. It was a medley of squalor and magnificence. Small, mean houses jostled palaces, dirty runnels of water ran through the centre of the roadways and narrow streets of tall, blackened houses were dark as deep chasms even at noonday. It was into one of these that Robin turned. At the far end the sun blazed down upon an open square which, by contrast with the gloom and chill of this long cleft, glowed like molten metal. In that square stood the great Church of the Virgin of Almudena.

" In ten minutes I shall know," said Robin.

All his boyhood, all his early youth, had been a long preparation for the one minute which was to follow upon the ten. His heart beat with a suffocating force as a corner of the church came into view. He quickened his pace and emerged suddenly into a blinding sunlight.

The great building was surrounded by a wide and open space, and Robin skirted it until he came to the western end and saw a high flight of broad shallow steps rising to the great doors. So many people were climbing them, so many descending that Robin could get no clear view. Every now and then a lane opened and showed him nothing but the empty treads and closed again. Beggars there were in plenty at the foot of the steps, blind men led by children, women and children exposing their sores, but where he was told to look—no one. He walked with a sinking heart along the front of the steps and then he stopped. To the left of the three doors—on the edge of the river of people, he saw a faggot of old ragged clothes, a great bundle flung down there and left. But the bundle moved.

Robin's first reaction to that movement was a feeling

of physical sickness, a refusal to accept anything so shocking as the tale which it told. That was not George Aubrey, his good friend of the great laugh and the Purbeck Hills. No ! With a shiver of the shoulders, he turned away from the steps. Robin was still little more than a boy in years and such degradation as that crawling heap of rags implied was a horror which youth refused to contemplate. " Death, yes," cried youth, that had never had a taste of it in his bones, " but such shame—no. If it were possible—why then God was guilty."

So he turned away and having taken a few steps, his cheeks burned with his cowardice. Since it was not possible that that abject creature crouched upon the steps there was his father, why should he shrink from giving him alms—and condemn himself for the rest of his life to an aching fear, an embittering self-reproach ?

" What sort of life then for Cynthia and me with that worm of conscience gnawing at the roots of my heart ? "

He found himself on the steps mounting slowly in a sort of zig-zag course which at every tread brought him nearer to the figure of misery.

A hood was drawn over its head to shade it from the sun and the face hidden, but a skeleton's hand at the end of a wasted arm was thrust out and a quavering thin voice wailed :

" Alms for the love of the Virgin. Alms, young gentleman, for the poor and starving. Alms ! "

With a cry of joy, so great was his relief, Robin snatched his purse from the pouch at his belt. In that piping voice there was none of George Aubrey's heartiness.

" Alms you shall have, old man," he said.

He would have poured out the gold pieces into the old man's hand until his purse was empty, but a sense of prudence restrained him. Already one or two people had stopped and were gazing at him curiously. In a moment a crowd would be about him and after that —question would lead to question.

He dropped one piece of gold into the beggar's hand, and stooping as he did so, he said in a low voice :

" I will see you again, after nightfall."

The cripple on the steps looked up curiously, and for the first time Robin saw his face. It was hollow and discoloured and ravaged, the bleared eyes sunk in black caverns, the neck seamed and piteously thin. A white beard patched his jaws. Every furrow in it was incrusted with dirt. It was a face so shrunken, so squalid, that Robin had never seen the like of it. But it was his father's.

For a few seconds he was giddy. The church, the steps, the people, the beggar crouching at his feet whirled about him. He had to close his eyes and clench his hands in a terror lest he should fall. When he opened them again the old man was still peering at him curiously. The son might know the father, for after all he searched for him, but how should those dim eyes know the son whom he had last seen as a child, in this slim young gallant, speaking to him Spanish with the accent of Italy ?

" I must see you to-night," said Robin. " Where do you live ? "

" In a hut at the end of the Calle des Forcas."

" I shall find it. Expect me at eight."

The old man's head was lowered, and hidden again beneath the hood. But Robin heard his voice.

" I am alone and old. I am miserably poor, as your Excellency sees, but I am afraid."

" I shall not come to hurt you," said Robin very gently.

" I do not fear you, sir. But the place is unsafe. I must have a name before I open."

"Very well," Robin stooped a little lower. It would never do in this crowd of people to speak his own true name. He dreaded the effect it might have upon his father, the questions which would follow. "I shall speak my name to you through the door—but very quietly, as I do now." And the name followed faint as a breath :

"Carlo Manucci."

George Aubrey, since George Aubrey it was, remained with his face hidden under his hood, so that Robin wondered whether he had caught the name.

"You hear me ? " he asked.

The old man nodded.

"I heard you."

"And you will open your door to-night ? "

"I will open, young sir."

Robin went straight on up the steps, and as he mingled with the others he heard the thin quavering voice take up again its pitiful cry.

"Alms for the love of God ! Alms, kind people, for the poor."

He entered the Church, passed as quickly as he could without the appearance of hurry, along the aisles to a door on the south side, crossed the square and by streets different from those by which he had come returned to Figliazzi's house. There he sent for Giacomo Ferranti, and bade him buy a mule and a saddle for it, and an outfit of good clothes, such as would fit the shrunken form of George Aubrey.

With these and their own two horses and a day's food, he was to wait from half-past eight at the corner where the road to Segovia meets the street of Manzanares. Madrid was not a wailed town and Robin's plan was to ride southwards to Alcazar as quickly as his father's weakness allowed, make thence, with a greater comfort, for Alicante and take ship to Italy.

It would be slow travelling at the first, but as his father regained something of his old strength, the small party would move with a greater freedom.

While Robin made his plans, the beggar still crouched on the steps of the Church of Our Lady of Almudena and stretched out a skeleton's arm with a prayer for charity ; and just before noon a priest in a black robe stopped in front of him.

"Alms for the love of God," the beggar wailed. " I have news for you, Father. Alms for the love of the Virgin."

The priest looked down at him contemptuously.

" It is high time. Little good we have ever got for all our gentleness and pity."

" I have seen him, Father."

" Whom have you seen ? "

" Carlo Manucci."

The priest started and a light glittered in his eyes suddenly, a light of fierce joy.

" Point him out to me, my son ! "

The beggar shook his head.

" It was two hours ago when he stopped and gave me a gold piece. See it, Father, see it ! "

" Two hours ago and you raised no cry. You let him go ! " cried the priest angrily.

" Nay, Father," the beggar whined. " If I had cried out he would have gone in the instant. He is young, rich, a fine young gallant. I did better, Father," and the terror in his voice and his cowering pose were slavish and horrible—so dread a story it told of persecution and cruelty.

" Better ? Let me hear," and the man in the black cassock stirred him disdainfully with the toe of his buckled shoe.

" He is coming to my hovel to-night. At eight o'clock. Father ! Pity the poor cripple at the Altar's foot!" This to a compassionate passer-by who dropped a copper coin into his hand and passed on. "Be not too quick, Father! The place is open. If he sees you watching and a party of officers he won't come. You'll lose him. He seeks me out of pity, Father. My wounds and my poverty moved him. He is kind of heart, Father," and the old man tittered and giggled to insinuate himself into his master's good graces. "Be not in too great a hurry, Father. My sad story will hold him, I promise you."

The Father thrust out his lower lip.

"You are not deceiving me?"

"I dare not."

The Father smiled.

"No. For there's still a stake in the Quemadero, my son, which waits for a husband. He told you so easily his name?"

"Not easily, Father . . . For the love of Our Lady of Almudena, Senor pity! . . . I thought that it might be he, before he spoke his name."

"Why?"

"He spoke Spanish with the accent of Italy."

The other nodded his head.

"Yes. That was in the description."

"I pressed him for his name, Father. I dared not open without it," and again he giggled. "He whispered it . . . Carlo Manucci. I give him into your hands, Father . . . Carlo Manucci. To-night you shall have him, Father. Carlo Manucci," and again the thin arm went out and the piping voice quavered out:

"For the love of God, gentlemen. God will repay. God loves the charitable."

The priest turned down the steps again and mounted the hill to what is now the Square of San Domingo. But then it was the home of the Holy Inquisition.

CHAPTER XXVIII

GEORGE AUBREY

THE Calle des Forcas lay in the squalid and noisome quarter of the town to the south-east of the Church of Our Lady of Almudena. The houses were decayed, the gardens unkempt warrens with broken hedges where a few sickly vegetables provided food for vermin ; and even in the daytime the air had a damp unwholesome taint which smelt of fever and disease. At night mists from the river Manzanares at the back of the quarter crept and writhed into the alleys and dripped with the patter of rain from the branches of the stunted trees.

Robin had lived in a fever of impatience throughout the day and he reached the mouth of the lane half an hour before his time. He wore high closely-fitting boots on his legs and a dark cloak over his dress, and he carried a second cloak over his arm to protect and disguise his father upon their flight. Three tumble-down houses with shuttered windows and not a ray of light glimmering through any chink faced another three like to them at the narrow entrance. Even on a clear night like this night of April, when dirt is hidden and the ugliness of ruin smoothed, they had a daunting and sinister aspect. Robin stood still and listened. From far away cries the grating of wheels and the blended murmurs of a city reached his ears. But here a silence so complete enfolded him that a breath of wind rustling through the leaves was as startling as a pistol shot.

" At all events I have not been followed," he reflected and he stepped cautiously into the mouth of the alley.

But however lightly he walked, the ground was so littered with broken pots and fragments of iron that now and then he stumbled, now and then some old piece of earthenware cracked beneath his boots. Beyond the houses the lane widened a little. A few trees, broken remnants of wall and ragged hedges lined it on either side and added to the darkness. Robin blundered along it and came at last to a hut at the end which closed it in. He felt along the boards until he found the door and rapped gently upon it.

There was a sound within of someone moving clumsily, then a voice spoke low and anxiously—the old man's voice without the whine.

" Who is it ? "

Robin put his mouth against the panel.

" Carlo Manucci."

" Wait ! "

A heavy key was turned in a lock, a bar lifted from its socket. Robin could hear the straining breath, the rattle of the wood as the palsied hands lifted it. George Aubrey !

" Oh, be quick," he whispered and at the sound of that whisper, took a hold upon himself. There would be a time for pity afterwards. The door was drawn open inwards a little way, enough for a feeble light to show and for Robin to slip through.

It was a fetid kennel which he entered. One smoking candle stuck with its own tallow to a ledge lit it dimly, the flame wavering in the draughts of air. A filthy pallet of old straw in a tattered covering was stretched upon the boards ; a wooden stool stood beside it and by the side of the stool an earthenware platter with some broken food in it and a jug of water.

There was no other furniture in the room. High up in one of the walls a small unglazed window let in the rain when it fell and a twilight no doubt by day. And this bent creature before him with the wrecked body was his father. He lived here and had lived here these many years, he who had built and owned Abbot's Gap with all its dainty loveliness.

" Latch the door, good sir," he croaked, and Robin turned, latched it and locked it and set the bar again in its sockets. When he looked back the old man was whimpering in terror.

" Why do you lock the door ? No one will come. You have seen no one coming ? What harm do you mean me ? "

He had shrunk away with his arms uplifted to receive a blow. Robin let the cloaks which he carried fall to the floor and stood forward.

" None ! How could I mean you harm, my father ? " and he spoke slowly and very gently and in English.

The sound of the words affected the old man rather than their sense. He dropped his arms. He had the air of someone hearing again an old tune which had pleased him long ago.

" That's English," he said with a wandering smile and he beat time to it in the air with his finger.

" Yes, my father, your own tongue."

Old Aubrey's brows came down in a frown.

" You mustn't call me father," he said with a suppressed dull rancour in his voice. " I am no priest. I call no man my son."

" Except me," said Robin.

Suddenly the beggar was afraid of what he had said, of the hatred in his voice.

" No, not you. I dare not. Only the great ones speak of my son and torture him afterwards," and he

fell back upon his whine. " I am a poor beggar.
Alms for the love of God . . ."

Robin broke in upon him sick at heart, and unable
to endure the obsequious cringing prayer.

" Look at me ?   Who am I ? "

" Carlo Manucci," and he tittered very cunningly.
" Before you spoke your name I knew it."

" How so ? "

" You spoke Spanish with the accent of Italy."

Yes, yes—Robin did.   He knew it, he had said so,
he had written it.   But how did his father know ?
And then he understood—or thought he understood.

" Then of course you know me," he said with a
laugh.   " You are playing with me, father."

" You are Carlo Manucci."

" And I learnt Spanish with the accent of Italy
riding with you, my father, on the Purbeck Hills.
Up from Abbot's Gap to the Beacon—you remember
the Beacon always ready with dry brushwood and its
tar-barrel.   Up there, my father, with Warbarrow Bay
beneath us on the one side and Wareham on the plain
beneath us on the other, you taught me Spanish with
the accent of Italy."

Robin had dwelt upon the names and underlined
them with the accent of his voice for his own sake—
so distant and visionary did those places seem in the
sordid misery of this hut.   But on this old bemused
and broken man they worked more slowly.   The
names had a vague music for him—Abbot's Gap—
Warbarrow Bay—Wareham on the plain—faint melo-
dies heard in dreams, oh, so long ago.   The tears burst
from his eyes and rolled down his cheeks, before ever
he began to wonder how this youth had heard of them.
But he did begin to wonder.   He snatched up the
candle and, holding it with trembling fingers, he
approached Robin.

"You are Carlo Manucci," he said stubbornly, angrily.

"I am Robin Aubrey, your son."

"Robin!" The name broke from his lips in a cry. "No! No!" he screamed in a high thin voice. "It's a trick, a trick to save yourself. But it's played too late," and he chuckled, he actually chuckled with a malice which Robin understood no better than he understood his words.

Robin made no answer in speech. He unbuttoned his doublet and took from about his neck a fine gold chain on which a signet ring was threaded.

"You gave me this, sir, the night before you went away on your last travels with the Precepts of Cato in your baggage. I have carried it thus ever since."

He held out the chain to his father, who shrank from it and then snatched at it with the hand which was free and held it close to his dim eyes, turning it over between his fingers and his thumb—until at last he was sure.

"Yes," he said to himself rather than to his son, and for the first time he spoke in English. "My ring." Then he lifted the candle again to Robin's face.

"Robin!" he whispered. "Robin!"

He would have fallen but for Robin's arm about his waist. The boy took the candle from his father's hand and set his father on the stool and held him against his heart, comforting him as a mother might comfort a child.

"Robin," the old man's fingers crept upwards, touched his cheeks, his hair, flattened themselves against his chest, seemed for a moment to draw a strength from the strong young shoulders. "Robin!"

"Yes, Robin," said the boy, laughing. "Sit there, father, or we'll have the house on fire."

He stood up, melted again some tallow upon the ledge and held the candle in it till it set. He turned about again to see his father's face quivering with anguish and his eyes staring at him with a dreadful fear.

"You must go, Robin," he whispered with his fingers plucking at his lips, "at once! You must break through the gardens."

"We shall both go."

George Aubrey shook his head impatiently.

"I who must crawl on my body to the Cathedral!" and as he looked at his son, limber and supple and beautiful, a cry of agony broke from him. "Go, boy Robin, before they make you what they have made me."

Robin picked up the cloak which he had brought for his father.

"I shall carry you, sir. What Æneas could do, that can I," he said with a laugh. "And we have not so far to go."

"Too far, Robin! Wait! I'll see that the way is clear." He limped with a sideways wrench of his body as though, at each movement, he had to lift himself along. But Robin set his hand gently upon his father's shoulder and stayed him.

It was plain to him that his father was distraught by his unexpected coming.

"Both of us," he said. "Oh, I have been clever! I have made such fine plans for our escape. I have taken such care that none should suspect us," and suddenly George Aubrey was wringing his hands.

"Oh, Robin, why did you come?"

"I came for you! Walsingham had a letter years ago. Until I was grown up there was no one he could send on such an errand."

"Grown up!" the old man lamented with a protesting cackle. " You're a boy, Robin. But they shan't cripple and torment you and disfigure you as they did me. You shall go."

" Both of us," Robin repeated ; and seeing his father's face set in a kind of sullen obstinacy, he sat himself down on the stool. " Or neither."

He had not undergone his service in the employment of Santa Cruz to be baulked of its reward. He had not come at last to his father to leave him in his degradation and misery. The elder man had lived for such long years with fear to fill his waking thoughts and fear for the substance of his dreams, that he saw danger and torture even in the quiet of the night. What ! With Giacomo and the two horses and the mule for his father, waiting in the darkness by the river bank not half a mile away ! What ! With himself unknown, his father clothed, the road clear and money in his purse, give in, run away and let George Aubrey crawl back to-morrow to the Cathedral steps and crawl back again at nightfall to this hovel ?

" Or neither," he repeated.

A curious change came over George Aubrey. He straightened himself a little. There came a light in his eyes, a smile upon his lips. Robin saw a small spark suddenly kindled of that bright spirit which had once made his father his joyous companion.

" Both then," said George Aubrey eagerly. " But my way, Robin. You're my boy, aren't you ? You must do what I say. That's the law, isn't it ? That your days may be long in the land. Yes. You must kill me and go. But be quick, Robin," and he turned his head to listen.

Then he dropped upon his knees at Robin's side and prayed to him with folded hands :

" Take your sword from its sheath."

And he fumbled with his twisted fingers at the hilt

of the sword. " See how easily it slips upward from its scabbard. I shall die as easily, Robin. Through the heart here," and he bared his breast. " Feel ! It hardly beats even now. A touch, and it will stop."

Robin put his arm about his father's shoulders and, lifting him, placed him on the stool and stood before him.

" Nay, you shall never kneel to me."

Robin realised that he could no longer say the right word, so far had they who were wont to speak forthright to each other from the heart, drifted apart with the years of their separation. For his father's eyes dropped, he looked from side to side, there was shame—it could be nothing else—in the shrinking and contraction of his body.

" I should," he said in so low and husky a voice that Robin could hardly catch the words. " I should kneel to you, Robin," and, flinging out his arms in a gesture of despair : " There's a hue-and-cry for you, Robin."

Robin was startled for a moment. Then he smiled his disbelief. An excuse so that he might be persuaded to go without the burden of his father.

" For me ? Wouldn't that be strange ? "

" For Carlo Manucci, boy," and the old man shook Robin's sleeve with a petulance at his stupidity. " The youth who speaks Spanish with the accent of Italy. Did you never write those words, Robin ? "

Robin's smile died from his face. Had he so written ? Carlo Manucci who speaks Spanish with the accent of Italy? " Yes, once."

" I wrote to Walsingham."

" The letter was read, Robin."

" I sent it by a sure hand."

" Yet it was read. It was read in England."

" By whom ? "

" A neighbour. I know no more."

" No need to know more," said Robin.

He was very grave and quiet now. Bannet, of course. Father or son or father and son. Somehow—no matter how—they had seen the letter. George Aubrey was making no excuse, no distracted needless sacrifice of himself. But he was none the less premature in his calculations of danger. In a few days—even to-morrow—someone might get wind of Carlo Manucci ; there might be a risk of discovery. But for to-night they were safe, and to-morrow they would be amongst the mountains.

" You see, I only reached Madrid last night, my father. And I reached it without question, under another name. No one knows that Carlo Manucci is here, except three men who have held my life in their hands these many months."

Figliazzi, Andrea Ferranti, Giacomo Ferranti—those three. Not one of them had betrayed him.

" The Inquisition knows," said George Aubrey in a whisper ; and now for the first time some hint of the truth flashed upon Robin, blinding him like lightning and making him reel. How did this beggar, flung out on the steps of a church, know the hue-and-cry was out for Carlo Manucci ? Yet he did know. Was he set to look for him—to look for a youth who spoke Spanish with the accent of Italy ? Whence did he get that phrase ? With those questions forming themselves, asking themselves insistently, he saw his companion crouching in the most utter abasement and shame before him, not daring to look at him, shivering, abject.

" It was you, my father, who betrayed me," he said. There was a note of horror in his voice, not of

horror of the man, but of the fact that in this world
such a thing could have happened. And there was
more of wonder than horror.

"So you see, Robin, you must go. You must go
before they come for you, before they come here.
You must kill me first and go."

"No, no," Robin insisted. He could not go, not
understanding. If they were coming, they must
come. But he must understand. It was more
important than life that he should understand. For
what would life be worth unless he understood?

"Why? My father, why did you betray me and
betray us both?"

The old man would have sunk again upon his knees
before his son, had Robin allowed it. But he held
him so that he could not, and suddenly the father
clung to him piteously.

"You couldn't understand, Robin, what pain can
bring one to. Even a strong man, and I was strong
once—you know, you remember. See me now!
Pain brought me to this state, to this shame. I
didn't know, Robin, it was you they wanted. And
I didn't dare to face it again—oh!" and with a moan
he fell to whimpering like a broken child.

"Years underground in the dark, the iron collar
so that you could never bend your head, the rack,
the threat of fire and the rack again. They made me
walk with the penitents to the stake, and when I
steeled myself to endure it, made me watch the agony
—the slow, dreadful agony of the others as their feet
and their thighs and their loins were consumed and
they still lived, screaming. Such pain! Such pain!
God send you never understand it, Robin! They flung
me out on to the church steps in the end —to "—he
could hardly breathe the word, short enough though
it was, it was so full of shame—" to spy. A man on

the steps of a church—he sees much, he hears much, he can be useful, Robin. I lived on sufferance. The collar and the rack and the stake—day by day I was threatened with them. . . . And then Carlo Manucci came—the youth I was bidden to look for. . . . Perhaps I could gain release. God, if they had only let me die—as you must let me, Robin, before you go. I can't go back to the dungeon, Robin."

There was a yearning for a swift, clean death in George Aubrey's prayer which cut Robin to the heart, which almost persuaded him. But he could not yield to it. He did not argue, he was too certain that here was the one stroke forbidden him.

"There's someone in England to whom I couldn't go back and say, 'I killed my father. So I am here —safe.'"

A curious change came into the old man's manner, of furtiveness, which Robin did not understand. He lowered his face, and it seemed to Robin that a sly smile parted his lips, a little, sly, happy smile, as though he had found a way out of their desperate case. And he had. He could not hope to draw Robin's hanger from its scabbard before he was pre-vented. But something at Robin's belt sparkled in the candlelight—the jewelled cross-hilt of a dagger slung in a velvet sheath. But he must be clever— clever and cunning! Robin felt his father's hands suddenly grip the open edge of his doublet whence he had taken the ring and chain, and heard his father's voice in a startled whisper :

"Hush, Robin ! Listen ! "

It was the oldest trick in the world, but ninety times out of a hundred it succeeds.

Robin turned his head towards the door, and the old man snatched the dagger from its sheath. He flung Robin from him with a passionate violence. He stood up. For a second the hunched back straightened, the crippled limbs stood straight, the great laugh rang out. At the moment of his death, it was granted to his son that he should see George Aubrey again.

" Now you must go, Robin. I'm going first."

He drove the dagger into his heart and stumbled and fell.

Robin laid him out gently upon his pallet. No roses, then, were to bloom red for him in the garden of his pleasure-house of Abbot's Gap. Here in this hovel, amidst its squalor and dirt, his pain and misery had ended. But since death had come, what did the dirt and squalor matter ?

Robin knelt at his side and very reverently drew the dagger from his heart. The blade was wet and red, and Robin eased it gently into its sheath stained as it was. It came into his thoughts that there was a place waiting for that dagger, and that he must be quick and set it there. He had in the most unexpected way a vision of the Escorial and the lights and the ornaments fading and the huge crucifix looming up against darkness ; and again stirred within him the whisper of a message from the Man upon the Cross, a message still not understood. But it was not for nothing that at this sacred moment the mystery of that hour should again be vivid in his thoughts. There would surely come a time when its meaning would be made known to him.

" Good-bye, just for a little while," he said aloud, and bending kissed his father upon the forehead.

As he stood up there was a loud knocking upon the door, and a voice cried :

" Open ! "

CHAPTER XXIX

OLD TRICKS ARE GOOD TRICKS

ROBIN was cool now. Immediate danger had made him a creature of steel and ice once before in the high lodging of Santz Cruz. He had had time to plan then ; he did step by step what in those circumstances he had prepared to do. Now he must act on the instant ; but, to set against the want of preparation, he was in a cold and bitter rage. He drew his sword from its sheath and placed it standing against the wall by the door. He took the stool and placed it near the sword. Then, seizing the candle in his left hand, he shuffled noisily towards the door, and stood with his back against the outer wall of the hut. The door was just at his right hand and, as he remembered, it opened inwards. He reached out his hand and again the order came, harsh and violent :

" Open ! "

Robin laughed, not very loudly, not so loudly that he could be heard, but he laughed and all his body tingled. He reached across the door with his right hand and unlocked it. As the key grated in the lock, hands thrust against the panels. The stout bar bent in its socket, but it did not break.

" Open ! "

There were no oaths, no abuse. It was authority speaking, certain of itself.

" Aye, but I'll open too soon for you," Robin said to himself.

He dropped the candle on the floor and set his foot on it. The hovel was in darkness. Through the small, high window a star shone. Robin waved a hand to it. Who knew but what Cynthia at this moment was watching that same star from the window of her room at Winterborne Hyde. Robin grasped the wooden stool by one of its three legs with his left hand and raised it high. He felt for the hilt of his sword with his right. It stood ready by his right thigh, its point in a board of the floor. Then, leaning over again, he wrenched the bar from its socket, dropped it on the floor, and grasped the sword.

His father had played an old trick on him, and it had succeeded. He was going to play another on these officers of the Inquisition ; and that was going to succeed, too. As soon as the bar clattered on the ground, the door was pushed open and back upon Robin, sheltering him. Then entered in single file—there was no room for two to pass abreast—two men, cloaked and hooded in black. The first carried a torch in his left hand, a drawn sword in his right, the man behind him carried a pike.

" And that's how you keep your promise," said the first man grimly to the corpse upon the pallet, thinking that he slept. But he had not finished his words before the stool came thundering down upon his head and felled him to the ground. He rolled against the soldier with the pike as he fell, and thrust him against the side wall, twisting him round. That man had just time to see Robin by the light of the torch flaming upon the floor. He lowered his pike, but the butt of it knocked against the wall, so that the point still aimed above Robin's head. He was cramped in too narrow a space for so long a weapon. Moreover, he had not the time to use it. Even as the butt knocked Robin's sword flashed in the torchlight, cut through the soft flesh of his belly, and pinned him to the wall.

Robin let the sword go and slammed the door. A third man fell back from it, bruised and cursing, and a fourth cried :

" What has happened ? "

Robin picked up the torch. For a second he watched with a face of stone the soldier still clasping his pike in the agony of death, wriggling on the sword like a dancing doll, beating a tattoo on the floor with his feet, and praying with gasping breath for a reprieve from his pain.

" Yes, my good master of pain, you know now what pain is," said Robin.

He plucked the sword free and the soldier slid down the wall and the pike crashed upon the boards. Robin turned quickly to the door, but the two men outside were in doubt. Robin could hear them debating, and at times they stopped to listen. Robin kept very still.

" They mustn't go for help," he reflected. " Not one of them ! I must have to-night free, or as much of it as I can."

They would be waiting outside with their pikes levelled. Or perhaps one of them would wait and the other go for help.

" I must be quick," said Robin. He turned to the man who had carried the torch. He had not moved since he had fallen. Robin rolled him over. The stool had smashed his head in, and he was dead. Robin propped the torch against the broken fragment of the stool, tore the cloak from his body and put it on. Then he felt the dead man's belt and found in it a dirk. With a little smile of satisfaction he drew it out. His own, with his father's blood upon it, was dedicated to another service. For nothing in the world would he have stained it in the body of any of these. Why, his father's blood would shrink upon the blade from so vile a contact. He stood up, planning his next move.

He must take a desperate chance with those two men outside. There they were, standing outside the door, wondering what had happened and what was happening in that silent hut, whispering with hushed voices. He must make a little play upon their fears and superstitions, and then set all upon a quick surprise. His sword would hamper him, and it would be no match for a levelled halbert. He set it against the wall, driving the point into the floor again so that it should stand. Then he stubbed out the torch against the boards, and, but for that one gleaming star, the hut was now as dark as it was still.

Robin felt his spirits rising. It was another old trick that he was minded to use. If it succeeded ! Had there been a light in the hut and someone to see, he would have seen a smile of amusement on Robin's face.

Robin faced the door and unlatched it silently. Then very slowly, inch by inch, he drew it open. Against the glimmer of the night he could just make out the figures of the two men standing alert, their pikes presented.

But they would see nothing of him, shrouded as he was, even to his face, in the black, hooded cloak. Without a sound and slowly as though death itself held the handle and invited their entrance, he drew the door wide open. He heard one of the men gasp and draw back, and the other whisper a prayer to a saint. Then in the darkness Robin uttered a groan—just one—from the depths of the hut, and was silent again.

" We must go in," said one of the two guards.

" Certainly we must go in," returned the other.

But one voice shook a little, and there was doubt in both of them, and neither of the men moved except to draw back yet a step farther from that black, open doorway.

Robin reckoned that the time was ripe. He moved towards the door.

" *Madre de Dios*," he wailed, and in the doorway he stood and leaned his head against the jamb, like one overcome and spent.

" *Madre de Dios !* What a horror ! " he repeated, his voice muffled in his hood.

One of the pikemen stepped forward.

" Señor Capitan, what has happened ? " he asked, and his halberd was upright.

" This, man, this."

Robin whipped about as he spoke and drove his dagger into the man's breast. As he fell, his companion turned and fled. Robin flung off his cloak and followed. It would never do to let the man reach the houses in the mouth of the alley. But Robin was the younger and the fleeter of the two. In a few yards he was upon the fugitive's heels, and with a loud screech of despair the soldier turned. He let fall his pike and tugged at the short sword which he carried at his hip. But before he could draw it, Robin leaped upon him, and leaped high. He pinned his enemy's arms to his side with his legs, he seized his neck with his hands, and then, alas ! he behaved as no young Italian gentleman should have behaved, whether he spoke Spanish with the accent of Italy or not. He bent his head, and with the top of it he butted his enemy in the face. He butted him with the accent of primitive man, and he heard the bones of the nose smash with a primitive joy.

But the man must not live ; and as they fell to the

ground Robin thrust back his head and stabbed him in the throat.

He had, he judged, a few minutes to spare. The affray had caused some hubbub. There had been a clash of arms, a torch flashing, a loud scream, and officers of the Inquisition. If any were awake in the houses within earshot, the heads would be under the bedclothes. In a little while, when quietude had returned, the curious would steal out, a small crowd would gather. But not yet! Robin took the soldier with the gaping throat by the shoulders and, dragging him to the door of the hovel, flung him in. He treated the body of the soldier who had addressed him as Señor Capitan in the same way. He took the big key from the inside of the door. He was still primitive man, stripped of all the graces of youth and learning and courtesy. He stood listening savagely, his sword again in his hand, lest in the darkness a breath, a sign, a groan should show that one of them still lived. But all was still as the grave. He thought of them as some old Egyptian might have thought. There lay four slaves killed to serve his father on the last journey across the river of death. He shut the door, locked it from the outside, and removed the key.

He took a step or two away and was tempted sorely enough to stop. All through the years of his boyhood, he had dreamed of an *auto-da-fé* which, in vengeance for George Aubrey, should redden the sky from rim to rim. He was tempted to go back, light that half-burnt torch and set a funeral pyre blazing here, instead of in the far Atlantic, which should be remembered with awe for many a day.

One thing restrained him—the thought of a good friend, Giovanni Figliazzi, who had served him without question and taken perhaps some risk in the service. He made his way across the gardens to the corner of the road to Segovia. Giacomo Ferranti was awaiting him with the two horses and the mule.

" Our plans are changed, Giacomo," he said as he swung himself up into the saddle.

" We must go back, quickly, but not too quickly " ; and as they trotted along the river bank, Robin threw the key of the hovel far into the water. There were few people abroad and no one challenged them. But as they drew near to Figliazzi's lodging which stood in a street where now the Palace gardens run, they were aware of a great noise and flashing lights and a throng of people. For a moment Robin reined in with his heart in his mouth.

" It is his Excellency's arrival from Escorial," said Giacomo.

" To be sure."

It was impossible of course that the affray in the Calle des Forcas should be discovered so soon or measures taken to avenge it so quickly.

" Giacomo, you will take the horses to the stable, rub them down, and make sure there's not a sign they have been out to-night. Then bring the mule back with the baggage and the money."

He dismounted, and wrapping his cloak about him pressed through the throng to the door. Andrea, in the doorway, would have stopped him, but he moved his cloak aside from his face and passed in and up the stairs.

When Giacomo, having done his work, carried the baggage up to Robin's room he found not Carlo Manucci, but Guiseppe Marino awaiting him.

" The suit of clothes you bought, Giacomo, you will wear. Is that the money ? "

He opened the canvas bag and held it out. " Put in your hand, Giacomo, and fill it."

Giacomo however stepped back.

" I am going with you, Signor."

T

" No, Giacomo."

" Signor, I know very well that there have been
miseries this night. The more reason then that I
should go with you."

Robin was moved by the man's insistence, but he
shook his head.

" I am used to you, Giacomo. We have been
much together. We are good friends. Such loyalty as
you have shown me I shall remember all my life, did I
live till the Escorial is in ruins. Were it only danger
ahead of me, I would not have let you go. But alas,
Giacomo, in what I have to do now there is no room
for you. Take my hand in memory of our comrade-
ship. So! Now into the bag with it and fill it till it
will hold no more."

The tears were in Giacomo's eyes, as he drew his
handful of gold pieces from the bag.

" Now," continued Robin, " tell Andrea to ask his
Excellency whether he will receive Guiseppe Marino
for a minute. And you take the mule on to the
Toledo road and wait for me."

In a little while Andrea Ferranti knocked upon his
door. Robin filled he leather pouch at his belt with
gold, tied up the bag and following Andrea was ushered
into a bedroom where Giovanni Figliazzi sat in his
dressing-gown over a mulled drink.

Figliazzi looked up into Robin's face and his own
softened and grew kindly as he looked.

" Leave us, Andrea, and stand outside the door.
Let no one enter! "

When they were alone, Robin put the bag on to a table

" I may have brought some anxieties and troubles
upon your shoulders, sir, in return for your great
kindness to me."

" My shoulders are very broad, Robin. And it
would be odd if I had no kindness for a nameless

friend in London, and a much tormented boy who has found his way into the core of an old heart."

He rose and laid his hand upon Robin's shoulder, and the boy's face worked and he uttered a sob.

" Come, sit you down and share my drink with me."

He set Robin in a chair and poured out for him into a crystal cup a full glass of his mulled port. Then he resumed his seat and asked no questions.

" There is a hue and cry out for Carlo Manucci, sir," said Robin, and he added sombrely, " It will be louder to-morrow."

" Carlo Manucci ? Carlo Manucci ? Carlo Manucci ? "

Giovanni repeated the strange name in three different tones of bewilderment.

" An Italian, presumably."

" Enquiries might be made," said Robin.

" Of me ? "

Count Giovanni was in a fog.

" Really ? " he continued. " Were such enquiries made, I should have to ask my good friend King Philip whether in the midst of the extremely difficult work of persuading the Genoese bankers to lend him some money of which he stands desperately in need, I have to be distracted by enquiries about an insignificant Carlo Manucci. Do you know, Robin, I have my doubts whether the fellow exists. Let us dismiss him altogether from our minds."

" I have one care the less," said Robin gratefully. He had exaggerated the importance of Carlo Manucci in the troubled affairs of Spain. He added : " And since I bring you this money back, sir, you can let King Philip have a peep at it."

Figliazzi slapped his knee in delight, he loved a high spirit. Here was this youth who had plainly been passed through the fire that night, rising at the end of it with a jest. Then his face clouded.

" You don't want it ? "

" I have taken as much as Guiseppe Marino can afford to possess."

Figliazzi nodded and took a sip of his drink and then another. He looked into the fireplace where a great log of wood was burning.

" Robin," he said softly. " Do you want a father ? Here is one to your hand," and now he looked at Robin with so warm an invitation in his aspect that the tears burst from the boy's eyes. Under the stress of that unhappy night he told at last the story of George Aubrey, and himself. And since he would not wound this friend of his by too curt a refusal he must needs speak a little of himself ; a thing which he always found it difficult to do. At the end he said :

" I shall remember your words, sir, with a great pride and a heartfelt gratitude. But as you see, I am of my own country and must go back to it."

" I understand that," said Figliazzi gently.

" And I must go back by the quickest road," said Robin, and the Ambassador stared at him in bewilderment.

" By the quickest road," he repeated.

" Yes, sir."

" As Guiseppe Marino ? "

" Yes, sir."

" Without more than a few gold coins in your pocket ? "

" Yes, sir."

Giovanni Figliazzi thumped the table in an exasperation.

" Then how in God's name, are you going to do it ? "

" I shall sail with Oquendo on the *Lady of the Rose*," said Robin quietly. " Spain owes me a passage, but I hope to pay for it in our own currency."

CHAPTER XXX

ANTHONY SCARR

ROBIN ambled through the night on his mule, and put up in the early morning at an inn in the small village of Castillejo. He was careful to leave the priest-ridden city of Toledo upon his left-hand and travelling at the rate of forty miles a day came down over the Sierra de Guadalupe into Trujillo. There he had the good fortune to fall in with a strolling company of players who were making their way to Lisbon. Robin rode with them and found in their companionship an alleviation of his bitter memories and distress.

They were joyous and quarrelsome, good-natured and jealous, fierce in their disputes and emotional in their reconciliations and always with the noblest of phrases culled from the utterances of this or that heroic character, fitted to the littlest adventures of their wandering life. Robin lent a hand in setting up their scanty scenery and, since he was travelling light, carried some of their properties on his mule.

They sang their way down the roads, the tenants of a moving fairyland. Philip of Spain, the Invincible Armada, the wickedness of Elizabeth, the machinations of the Turk, the intrigues and convulsions of Europe never concerned them half as much as the intonation with which Alonzo cried " Mother, thou art avenged," or the miserable exhibition which the star of a rival troupe was in the habit of giving when the

presumptuous fool undertook the part of the blood-
thirsty Gomez of the Sierras. Robin was diverted
from the gloom of his own thoughts by the swift
reactions of their emotions. Their conversation never
flagged, they had a jest with which to whip misfortune,
and they were never so real as when they were false,
never so alive as when for an hour or two they struck
their attitudes in a village barn. Robin could not
but feel himself rising out of a hideous oppression of
his mind and senses, and when he bade them good-bye
at Estremoz and pushed on to Lisbon, it was with a
warm gratitude for their easy good-fellowship.

He reached Lisbon on the second day of May. The
Armada was at last ready for sea and Robin, waiting
on the quay for just this opportunity, thrust his way
through Oquendo's staff and dropped on his knees
before him.

" And who is this rascal," cried Oquendo, and
certainly Robin with the mud and dust upon his face
and his clothes, wanted some explaining. Already a
stick or two was raised.

" I am Guiseppe Marino, with your Excellency's
permission," said Robin humbly.

" And are you now ? " cried Oquendo. He had
just taken his dinner and was in an excellent humour,
" Yes, I certainly permit it. Just as I shall certainly
permit you to be thrown off the quay into the harbour
unless you give me a better reason for your insolence
than a name."

There was a small crowd now closing in upon Robin
and not a very friendly one. Oquendo was the young
protagonist of Spanish chivalry. Women might pester
him, but ragamuffins were not to burst into his Lord-
ship's presence. It was the Tagus for Robin unless
he spoke up sharply and quickly. Indeed it was only
Oquendo's easy mood which availed him up till now.

" Let the lad alone ! " he said. " What have you to say to me, Guiseppe Marino ? "

" Your Excellency, I was the bodyservant of the great Admiral," cried Robin, setting all upon the throw.

If the Inquisition in Madrid had traced back Carlo Manucci and discovered him in Guiseppe Marino, as by now it might well have done, his case was beyond all hope. The rack and the stake were as handy in Lisbon as in Madrid, and indeed for a moment he thought that he was lost. For there was a swift movement in the crowd at his side. A young man— Robin as he kneeled saw the fellow out of the tail of his eye—swiftly drew back. A ripple in the throng showed that he was forcing his way out. He had gone to inform, to claim his reward, to light another bonfire for another heretic.

Oquendo however came to his rescue.

" Eh, eh. What's that ? " he cried. " Stand you up straight, my lad ! " and as Robin got to his feet, " Guiseppe Marino ! Of Leghorn, eh ? "

" Your Excellency promised that I should haul a rope on your Excellency's ship," Robin reminded him.

" So I did ! Well, get you on board to the master and tell him I sent you. We have gunners, and pikemen and priests, but God knows we are short of sailors in the Grand Fleet. If he says aye, I'll not say no."

Robin did not wait. With a gabbled sentence of gratitude, he edged himself into the crowd, and was out of it again before a tenth of it knew that he had gone. The trouble was that that plaguey informer was hanging upon the outskirts. Robin knew very well where the *Lady of the Rose* was moored against the quay. He would not run, but he walked as quickly as his legs would carry him. Nevertheless the plaguey informer was close upon his heels. Robin mounted the gangway and found the master in the midst of such a confusion of sails, ropes, spars, blocks and cleats that it looked as if the ship could not put to sea for a fortnight.

He gave Oquendo's message and was put to work at once, and since he showed some knowledge of the seaman's trade was thereupon enrolled for the enterprise of England. But to his dismay, he saw that his pursuer had followed him ; Robin heard him talking and reckoned him to be a Catalonian from Marseilles. Was the fellow after all merely one of the crew like himself ? Or was he there to watch that Robin didn't get away, and to tap him on the shoulder, say an hour before the fleet sailed, and point to certain officers of the Inquisition waiting to arrest him ?

But nothing of the kind happened. And on May 14th of the memorable year 1588, after the blessing of innumerable banners, unending processions of priests and much chanting of choirs, the Invincible Armada sailed down the Tagus, its canvas billowing in the wind and its decks so crowded with a cheering multitude of soldiers that it was a wonder that the sailors ever got the ships to sea at all. As all the world knows, it was caught two days later in a gale and so violently dispersed that a fresh assembly of it must be made at Corunna. There it was found that in spite of all the prayers and blessings which had wafted it upon its way, the drinking water stank and the meat was alive with worms. It was therefore not until the morning of July 20th that Robin saw the black rocks of the Lizard like a shadow on the edge of the seas.

Medina-Sidonia's flagship, with a great new banner of the Virgin embroidered on white silk streaming from his masthead, led the centre of the Fleet and the flanks curved away to points, so that the whole stately formation had at a distance the look of a sickle with its convex edge advanced. Oquendo's Guipuscoan Squadron guarded the left flank and to Robin's delight the Admiral was posted on the extremity of the flank. As the Armada swept into the Channel more and more clearly the Lizard slid forward into the sea and in a little while he could distinguish, with a swelling of the heart which brought the tears into his eyes, on the uplands above the cliffs the chequer board of dark hedgerow and green field which is the true quartering of England. And here and there startlingly white little pyramids showed where the pits of china clay were dug.

All the while the wind was rising in the south-west, and the sky darkening.

" There will be a gale to-night," Robin predicted, his spirits rising with the wind. These clumsy galleons with their towering castles at bow and stern and their crowded soldiery would be sport for the gale and sport too for Lord Howard of Effingham and his great coadjutor Drake. Robin strained his eyes in his gaze towards the coast. Would he see a certain great ship, the *Expedition* of Poole—he was sure that he would recognise her amongst a thousand—or the *Sea Flower* and the *Grace of God*, the twins of Weymouth, or the *Lyon* of Fowey, or *The Golden Real*, which was built over there in Falmouth yard ? For Falmouth Bay was sliding past now. Pendennis Castle stood out upon its hill, the great teeth of the Manacle Rocks were abeam, and soon behind Dennis Head the lovely reach of the Helford river opened out between its woods. On a bluff at the mouth of the river, a big house half buried in trees shone in a gleam of sunshine like a jewel, and a glimpse was given of an ordered garden descending in terraces to the water's edge.

Robin heard at his elbow a little gasp of breath

and then a laugh of infinite pleasure and then three words spoken in English.

" Saint Mawnan's Chair.'

Robin turned very slowly and saw at his side a young man with a dirty stubble of beard and a face so begrimed that he had some difficulty in recognising the plaguey informer of the Lisbon quay. Robin, so near home, was not going to walk into any parlour but his own.

" Que dice usted ? " he asked as one mildly puzzled.

The other laughed again but with such a throb of elation in the note that no man could have doubted its sincerity. He touched Robin on the arm, he looked around to make sure that they were apart, and then he pointed towards St. Mawnan's Chair.

" My house," he said.

Robin remembered now some words which Sir Francis had spoken to him at Barn Elms. " You may meet a friend, you may not." He had been instructed, moreover, to pay no heed to Medina-Sidonia's squadron at Cadiz. Figliazzi the Ambassador had passed the instruction on to him. Here was the reason for the instruction at his elbow.

" You were with Medina-Sidonia ? " he asked.

" I had a nodding acquaintance with his secretary who happily was a very poor man," returned the other. " My name is Anthony Scarr."

" If I had known that," Robin returned, " I should have been spared some hours of anxiety. I saw you slip away out of the crowd at Lisbon. I was afraid that you had gone to lay an information. When you followed me on the ship I was certain that you were making sure I shouldn't give you the slip. Even when I lost sight of you, I was uneasy."

" I kept out of your way," said Anthony Scarr. " We should have talked in our own tongue."

It had been easy enough on that big ship since they were not in the same watch. Sailors were of little account in King Philip's ships, of hardly more indeed than the convicts pulling the oars in the galleasses. They slept where they could find a space, on the open decks, in the passages, on the companion stairs. No castles protected them, they were not paraded in divisions, or appointed places in the battle disposition.

"I knew there was a lad with Santa Cruz," said Anthony. "I guessed it was you when I heard you plead with Oquendo. I was in the same case as you. There was I at Lisbon, my work done, and no way of getting home. And you showed me the way, the perfect, satisfying, obvious way. Let the Don carry us! I hurried along at your heels for an excellent reason. I wanted the ship master to believe that Oquendo had sent us both to him, and that he very kindly did."

Whilst young Scarr had been talking, young Robin had been thinking.

"I am on the tiller to-night," he said. "I shall be relieved at midnight. I'll find you here, afterwards."

There were six in all of Walsingham's men who sailed on the Invincible Armada, but for the men who do their dangerous work secretly in the enemy's encampments no bugles are blown, no banners unrolled. Of these two alone is the story known.

In the battle of the Mewstone off Plymouth Sound, when the English Fleet sailing into the wind got to windward of the Armada, one great galleon was dismantled and carried into Dartmouth. Medina-Sidonia pressed on, in spite of signals of distress. He was not a sailor. To join with Parma's troops from the Lowlands at Calais, to escort them across the Straits in their flat-bottomed barges to the English shores, to land an army of trained soldiers and fight land battles, this was his strategy. The Armada for him was a transport, not a navy, and though Oquendo and De Leyva and Recalde might rave at him for his cowardice he held on before the gale, and the fate of England still trembled in the balance.

Robin, with three other sailors at the huge tiller high above the sea on the top of the stern castle, kept the plugging, rolling, unwieldy ship on her course, and behind them, short of powder and shot though they were, the hornets of the English Fleet raced up and fell back, and stung and stung again. Robin lived that night in a curious ecstasy. For as the darkness fell the beacons on the headlands blazed upon the night, and every now and then, through the wrack of hurrying clouds, a burst of moonlight made a white fire of the waves and of the country-side a vision of quiet peace.

There were pilots on the Armada who knew the Channel. Close in under Berry Head, where the ferns were growing thick and close as an animal's fur, into the steep, short seas and shallows of the West Bay, the Armada swept, and towards morning the wind fell. Robin had nursed a dream whilst he stood at the tiller that before his trick was done he would see the flare of his own beacon on the Purbeck Down. Dakcombe would be feeding it, his friends would be standing by. Cynthia, sitting on her horse with her eyes gazing out to sea and the flames of the beacon lighting them up and flinging waves of warm colour across her sweet and anxious face. The Bannets would be there—oh, for sure they would be there, the good loyal couple praying for the success of Her Majesty's arms and that the gracious tolerance of her reign might still endure. And not one of them would find a place in his wildest fancy for the extravagance that Robin

Aubrey was actually one of three holding the tiller of Spain's nearest galleon !

The roar of the wind through the rigging, the banging of blocks and sails, the lurch of the ship, the groaning of its timbers as though not for one moment longer could they hold together, the flash of guns out of the darkness, the crash of rending wood as the shot struck home, set Robin's blood racing and throbbing in his veins, and fired him to so high an exhilaration of his spirits, that he had much ado not to laugh aloud in the face of the ship's master.

But there was more to be done that night if God— not Philip's God, nor the Pope's God, nor Henri of Valois' God, if he had one, which was more than doubtful—but the God of Elizabeth and Drake and Protestant England would forward his endeavours. Below the high poop was the castle crowded with its soldiers, riflemen and pikemen and gunners. Below the castle Oquendo himself, with his staff, sat late in his great cabin over his wine. And below Oquendo's cabin lay the ammunition store, with its kegs of powder and its pyramids of shot. Robin was savouring the plan he had made—what a lad he was for plans ! Cynthia had cried half in mockery and half in admiration—when, to his dismay, the wind fell. It fell quickly and as quickly fell the sea, and strain his eyes as he might, Portland Rock was still lost in the darkness ahead.

Robin climbed down the ladder past the small minions of the castle, set there in their loopholes to clear the deck of boarders, past the passage leading back to Oquendo's cabin. A soldier with a loaded arquebus and a match stood on guard. But in the cabin the air was hot and Oquendo's door stood open. Robin could see him sitting at the table, a map out before him—a map of England—his glass at his elbow, his doublet unbuttoned, a smile upon his face.

" Hasta mañana, your Excellency," said Robin under his breath, " You must land me as close to my house as you can."

He found Anthony Scarr asleep on a mat under the bulwarks. He squatted beside him, covered his mouth with his hand and shook him gently till he woke. For a little while the two talked in whispers. The deck was strewn with men sleeping heavily. Every now and then one of them cried out in his dreams and turned over and continued to sleep. Every now and then the groans of a wounded man or the prayers of a priest broke the silence.

" To-morrow will be better," Robin whispered. " Another day's harrying and fighting, and they'll sleep so hard it'll take the Day of Judgment to waken them."

" All the more reason, then, that we should ourselves sleep now," said Anthony Scarr.

When they woke it was broad daylight, and the Invincible Armada was becalmed in the West Bay with Portland Rock dimly ahead like an island in the clouds.

CHAPTER XXXI

ROBIN PAYS HIS FARE

" **N**OW ? " Anthony asked impatiently.
" Not yet," Robin answered.

It was after midnight. All the day the calm had lasted. The soldiers had stood to their guns ; here and there a stray flaw of wind or a faster current had brought an English and a Spanish ship within gunshot of another. But the two fleets had lain apart, unable to manœuvre, the Spaniard heading up-Channel, the Englishman behind him, and, if only the south-west wind sprang up again, with the windward advantage. Medina-Sidonia had called his lieutenants to a conference on his flagship, and Oquendo had gone off in his barge.

The conference had been long, and all through it the fate of England trembled in the scales. The Great Armada was still a fleet in being ; a few ships had been shorn off, but the vast bulk of it still lay unbroken, keeping its formation orderly, and using this calm weather to plaster its wounds and repair its spars. Oquendo and De Leyva and Pedro de Valdes and the younger spirits wanted the bold policy—to run up the Solent, seize Southampton, land the fifteen thousand soldiers and march on London, raising their friends in the country as they marched. Parma would cross with what ships he had to protect him, and England would be caught between two fires. It was the dangerous plan for the realm. The Spaniards would have a base upon the sea and an unfortified country in front of them.

" It was Santa Cruz' plan," cried Oquendo.

But Medina-Sidonia was not a Santa Cruz. He had his master's orders, and he was too timid and too inexperienced a General to know the moment when he must be unable to read his instructions. He was bidden to join Parma, so he overruled the lieutenants and thus drove on outside the Isle of Wight to Calais and the fire ships, to the sands of Dunquerque and the gales of Cape Wrath, to the murderous coasts of Western Ireland and the homeward struggle of the remnant. Oquendo returned to his ship in a rage and shut himself up in his cabin. But with the fall of night the wind rose again and the battle was renewed. It was now past midnight. Robin had finished his trick at the tiller. He was crouching with Anthony Scarr under the bulwark.

" Now," said Anthony eagerly.

In the waist of the ship about the deck men were lying sunk in the deep sleep of exhaustion. There was a lull in the running battle, the English short of powder, the Spanish hurrying for Calais.

" No, not yet," answered Robin. With the time for action had come once more the cool spirit, the cessation of anxiety and doubt, the unity of fibre and mind.

A hundred yards ahead, the Bill of Portland with its shattered rocks stretched into the water under the lee of the *Lady of the Rose*. Above, the ridge of Portland Rock stood out against a wild moonlit sky.

" We must wait till we are through the Race," he said. " No swimmer could live in Portland Race on a night like this."

Already the ship was beginning the lurch and plunge in that welter of broken water. The Race was up that night and the clash of waves flung a sheet of spray over the deck. Oquendo's ship on the extremity of the flank got the worst of it. Medina-Sidonia in the centre hardly felt it at all. But here from every angle a short tempestuous sea shook and buffeted the *Lady of the Rose* till she dipped the muzzles of her broadside guns under the water and flooded her lower deck. Then, with an extraordinary abruptness, the strife and turmoil of the water ceased. The ship was through the Race and the Bay of Weymouth open.

" Now," whispered Robin.

He shook Anthony Scarr by the hand.

" There will be no time afterwards for a word. It'll be each one for himself. You know where to make for ? "

" Abbot's Gap."

" Yes. So it's God-speed for both of us now."

They crawled along the deck towards the companion. They were both stripped to the waist and with no shoes upon their feet. If a sleeper stirred they waited, holding their breath. If a man lifted his head they crouched. At the top of the companion Robin looked up. The passage to Oquendo's cabin was at the head of a few steps above him. The sentinel was leaning against the passage wall, asleep on his feet ; his arquebus had fallen across the doorway ; the match was out. When they had crawled to the companion they both looked down.

A sailor was seated on the third step, and his body was sprawled across the step above, his face resting upon his arms. He was snoring. But three steps below him the stairway turned upon itself. Robin listened, thrusting his head down. Beyond the turn the steps, he knew, led straight back to the door of the magazine. And there night and day a pikeman was on duty. Robin would have given one of his

U

fine ships to have heard that sentry snoring as heartily as the sailor on the stairs. But he heard nothing. He made a sign to Anthony Scarr and cautiously stepped down across the sailor. At the turn he squatted, and a few seconds afterwards Anthony was at his side. From their position they could not see what awaited them at the bottom of the companion. But a light shone up. Whatever they did must be done in the light and without a sound. Robin laid his face to the floor of the stair and peered round. At the bottom a soldier squatted on the ground, his back to the partition wall, his knees drawn up to his chin.

He was not asleep, for the butt of his pike was on the floor between his thighs and he was holding the weapon at the perpendicular with his hands. But he was not looking up the companion. Robin had that in his favour. He was staring at the wall in front of him, dreaming perhaps of some village in Castille, but most probably thinking of nothing at all. A horn lantern with a candle burning in it was hung upon a bracket on the wall facing him. He was looking up at it, and Robin could see his dark eyes glittering in the light and an open mouth between his beard and his moustache.

During the minute which followed, Anthony Scarr was the more tried of the two. At a gesture from Robin he crawled up the stairway to the side of the sleeping sailor. He knelt there with his dirk in his hand. He must hold the stairs, and his eyes moved from the sailor to the head of the companion, where a patch of moonlit sky showed silvery bright. If the sleeper beside him woke, if some dark figure blocked out that patch of sky, he must hold the stairway whilst Robin did his work. A few minutes and there would be one galleon the less on the left wing of the Armada.

He prayed that those few minutes would be given them with his heart beating as though it would burst.

At the turn of the companion Robin gathered himself up to his full height and sprang. The sentry saw the flash of a half-naked body. But his mind was slow. He was only aware of a swift movement, and before his brain could flash an order along his muscles, Robin had dropped upon him. One foot slid upon the steel corselet of the sentry, the other struck the side of his head. The pike clattered against the wall, and both sentry and sailor were in a heap upon the floor. But the sentry was stunned. Robin's hand sought his mouth and closed over it like a vice. He saw the man look up at him with the dark eyes whose glitter in the light had so alarmed him less than a minute ago. Now they gazed at him in bewilderment and with a sort of sheep-like fear, which made Robin hate himself. But the bewilderment would not last and fear would lend him strength, and this was Oquendo's ship in the Enterprise of England. Robin, with the dagger clutched in his right hand, felt under the soldier's armpit for the lace of his corselet, and finding it, drove the dagger in between steel and steel, and pressed upon the hilt with all his strength. The soldier's body arched up underneath him and almost threw him off ; he gasped, and in his agony his tongue came out horribly from his mouth. Then it was over.

Upon the higher part of the companion Anthony Scarr heard the rattle of the pike, the muffled crash of the bodies—and afterwards nothing more. Nothing more for an intolerable eternity. The sailor, sleeping with his head upon his arms, stirred, but only to smooth his face over on to the other and cooler sleeve. And no black form obscured the patch of sky.

But disaster had befallen Robin—Anthony Scarr had not a doubt of it. So long a procession of minutes had loitered by since that rattle of the pike. Robin had been caught upon it and tossed like a matador. And now ? Anthony's imaginings ran riot. He remained at his post, his eyes fixed upon the stairway above him ; that was his charge. But he had a conviction which made his blood run cold that behind him the sentry was quietly standing at the turn of the companion, and poising his pike for the thrust at his back. Anthony died a thousand deaths whilst he watched. He felt the chill of the steel against his skin, the grating of the point on bone, the snap of his spine. The soldier was playing with him, amusing himself. The sweat broke out upon his forehead and fell in beads upon his cheeks. Let him strike, he prayed, and have done with it ; and as he so prayed, a hand touched his shoulder.

Scarr turned his head with a gasp, and saw Robin's face ghostly white and dreadful to look upon. All its beauty, its very humanity, were gone. An evil grin disfigured his mouth, a savage exultation twisted his features and glittered in his eyes.

" Quick ! " he whispered.

Robin had broached a cask of powder and poured out its contents amongst the kegs, the matches, the pyramids of cannon balls ; he had laid a train to it and set up at the end of the train a long cannon match ; he had lit the match, and all the while he had heard through the planks above his head Oquendo laughing with his officers. He and Anthony had just the time before the match burned down to the powder.

They crawled quickly up the companion. It seemed to them both that so long a time had elapsed since they crept down it that the whole aspect of the deck must have changed. But it was still encumbered with men in every attitude of fatigue, and at the entrance of the passage-way to the great cabin the sentry still slept upon his feet, with his arquebus across the doorway. They separated as they had agreed to do. Robin crept forward, Anthony Scarr to the side of the ship nearest him. Both of them doubled a rope about a stanchion, crawled over the bulwarks and slid noiselessly down into the sea.

Robin dived and swam under the water till his lungs were bursting. When he came up he was astern of the *Lady of the Rose*. But he was still too near the ship for concealment. For though the sea was rising the moon was now bright as day, and a swimmer must leave a silver track behind him. He dived again, and rising on the crest of a wave, saw the lanterns of the Armada like a town at night. But the lights were diminishing. In a veritable agony of disappointment he watched them go. Had his match blown out ? Had an officer gone the round and discovered the dead sentry at the door of the magazine ? But the moment fear seized upon him it fled.

He lifted his body up with a cry of joy, which rang out above the noise of the wind and the water. The *Lady of the Rose* became a rose, a flaming rose with petals of fire scattered far and wide.

The great ship split with a roar of thunder, and with a rending of timber and a crashing of masts and spars she drifted in a hurricane of fire and smoke out of her line to leeward. From the ship next in the line boats were being lowered. Robin lay on his back and paddled with his hands. He could see men in the bows of the boats, searching the sea. A spar drifted to his side and he clung to it. It would hide as well as support him. But the boatmen were busy dragging the survivors into them, and, alas ! Anthony Scarr was one of those survivors.

Robin went shorewards with the tide, hiding behind his spar. The rescue boats were recalled by the boatswain's whistle. The cries died down. Away in the east the great fleet swept on, and the *Lady of the Rose* deserted by her comrades, tossed this way and that, the incandescent relic of a ship fighting her last battle against the moonlight.

Robin was under the lee of Portland now and less buffeted by the waves. Floating and swimming and resting upon his spar by turns, he reached the Chesil Beach towards morning, and felt with an inexpressible joy the shingle draw away beneath his feet. He climbed out of the sea and falling upon his knees, humbly thanked his Maker for his home-coming. Then, scooping out a little shelter amongst the pebbles, he lay down and, naked as he was, slept untroubled by a dream.

CHAPTER XXXII

NOW this was the morning of Thursday.

He slept for an hour and then, after labouring along that painful beach, he came in the grey of the dawn to the house of the shipwright who had built for him the *Grace of God*. He was pressed to stay and rest and eat and tell of his adventures and hear of the place his ships had taken in Lord Howard's battle-line, but he was in haste and would not. He was hungry and thirsty for his home and nothing must stay him. He borrowed money and clothes and a horse, and at ten o'clock in the morning, by the side of the still smouldering beacon on the Purbeck Hills, he gazed downwards at the woods of Abbot's Gap and the sea glittering in the sunlight. His heart was full and the tears in his eyes drew a mist across the scene. There should have been another riding with him at that moment—George Aubrey—but underneath his grief a sort of sober ecstasy possessed him. So many hours there had been when he had hardly dared to dream that he would ever see again this valley of enchantment.

It seemed to him that he was expected. For as the shoes of his horse sounded on the round of gravel before the gatehouse the door was thrown open, and Dakcombe, with a smile ready upon his face, stood in the doorway. But it was not he who was expected. For Dakcombe, after standing for a moment like a man turned into stone, uttered a loud whoop of joy, tugged at the bell as though the house was on fire and then rushed back into the courtyard shouting :

"Kate! Kate! 'Tis Master Robin home again."

Robin gave the horse to the groom and passed through the gate-house into the court. He had expected to see it a little neglected and dishevelled, as must be with an empty house, and he stood surprised. For never had he seen it so spick and span, so gay with flowers. Kate, his old nurse came running down the steps with the tears of joy coursing down her face. He kissed her, and one moment she thanked God and the next she lamented. He was thin and he was tired, and he was a dirty as a tramp. Robin was hustled up to his room and left to steam himself clean in a hot bath, whilst Kate hurried the cook in the kitchen and exchanged a good many secret whispers and cunning smiles with Dakcombe, and laid out such clothes and such linen in his dressing-room as Robin had not worn for many a day. When he came, shaved and trim, into the room in his dressing-robe, she was still at this work.

"Why, Kate," he exclaimed. "That's the best suit of clothes that ever I had. I bought it for the party at Hilbury Melcombe, and never wore it at all."

"And when should you be wearing your best clothes, Master Robin, except upon this blessed day ?" she said obstinately. "It's Thursday."

"Thursday ? What does that mean ? "

"It's not for me to say Master Robin. Put your clothes on at once."

He was being treated like a little boy whose perils and adventures had all happened in dreams, and it melted him.

"Very well, Kate," he said humbly. "You shall see such a coxcomb come down to his dinner as would set the Queen's Court on fire. But I shall need my long boots and a homelier dress afterwards."

Kate chuckled.

" So you'll be riding out Master Robin, after your dinner ? " said she.

" I certainly shall," said Robin.

" To be sure you will, Master Robin," and the notion that Robin was going to ride abroad after his dinner tickled her out of all reason.

" And Kate, will you send Dakcombe to me ? He shall tell me the news whilst I dress."

Dakcombe, I am afraid, was listening at the door, for he came at once into the room.

" Master Robin's riding out after his dinner," said Kate. " So he'll want his long boots and a riding dress."

And to Dakcombe the notion was as comical as it had been to Kate.

He grinned from ear to ear.

" Aye, surely woman ! Master Robin'll go ridin' this afternoon," said he.

" That he will, John Dakcombe," said Kate, nodding her head.

" We might ha' knowed it, we might," said Dakcombe.

He was a staid, elderly man, not given to laughter. Now he was convulsed with it.

" We might have and we do," said Kate.

" Here, you two," cried Robin, blushing furiously and hoping that the tan of his cheeks would hide the blushes. He was not going to be rallied because he chose to make a call at Winterborne Hyde. " That's quite enough. Stop it ! "

They stopped it and Robin, whilst he brushed his hair, asked Dakcombe for the news. There was no fear of the Spaniard in England. The Queen had reviewed her troops at Tilbury, and made a speech to them, so simple and so straight from the heart, she the mistress of intricate phrases and meaningless meanings, that all of wide England had been moved by the love and pride of it.

" My great bonfire was lit, Dakcombe ? "

" Aye, that it was, Master Robin.   'Twas the finest bonfire on the coast.   And who do you think, Master Robin, stood beside it and cheered the loudest."

" Tell me ! " said Robin, smiling.   He had not a doubt what name he was going to hear.   But he was wrong.

" Who but them papistical sycophanters, Sir Robert Bannet and his son, Humphrey."

Robin turned round in the act of pulling on his stockings.

" They were there ? "

" And singing very loud to keep their heads safe upon their shoulders, Master Robin."

" And Mr. Stafford, too, no doubt," said Robin.

" Oh no, sir.   Mr. Stafford's to be tried at the Assizes and hanged."

" What's that ? "

" Oh, all accordin' to law, Master Robin.   None of them Spanish tricks here.   Tried first and not hanged till afterwards—hanged and quartered.   Very particular they're goin' to be about the quarterin', I hear. People are sayin' the Queen's too kindly, and only hangs 'em as often as not, and people are wonderin' what the world's comin' to.   But 'tis all right with Mr. Stafford, Master Robin.   It'll all be done before Her Majesty can hear of it.   Tried accordin' to law and hanged and quartered afterwards."

Robin was very silent after that and sent Dakcombe from the room.   He dressed himself as Kate the housekeeper had bidden him, in a doublet and breeches of dark blue velvet, with gold buttons to fasten it, long white silk stockings and shoes of white velvet with white roses. He fixed a small white ruff of cambric about his throat and a gold chain upon his shoulders. Then he took up a sheathed dagger, which ever since his last night in Madrid he had carried under his shirt.

When he came out into the corridor he found Kate and Dakcombe awaiting his appearance, and Kate made her best curtsey and Dakcombe his best bow, and then they both clapped their hands. Certainly with his brown, shining hair, his sun-burnt face above his snowy ruff and his brave attire, the lad looked wholesome and gracious enough to enrapture a princess in a fairy tale. And there was besides something very moving in the gravity of his face and eyes.

" I shall not be long," he said gently. " But I have something to do, and I must do it before I break my fast."

He went into the library where the prie-Dieu stood from which he had taken an ivory crucifix that Cynthia might hold him in remembrance. It had been the crucifix of George Aubrey, his father. Robin closed the door gently, and drawing from its stained velvet sheath the dagger with his father's blood encrusted on the blade, he hung it reverently where the crucifix had hung. A memorial, but more than a memorial. A symbol that revenge and punishment were for God, not for him, a prayer lest he should sully his homecoming with resentments.

The two years of servitude and exile and endeavour had brought their benefit with their suffering. Imagination had come with them. As a boy in front of the lower school at Eton, when his great Mistress had deigned to call him forth, he had been able to stand outside himself, watch what he did and assess it. Since then he had learnt to stand behind others as separate from him as the poles, and see with their different eyes the strange and different shapes of the things which they beheld.   Santa Cruz, his father, the actors on the road from Badajoz, even the slow, joyless, priest-ridden Philip—he had learnt from them all something of the multiplication of points of view and the infinite variety of judgments.

Standing there before that dagger, now transfigured into a cross, he saw again the vision which had been revealed to him in the great Church of the Escorial— altar, priests, candles, steps, the church itself, melting away and leaving nothing but the gigantic figure of Christ Crucified, looming out of the darkness.   The message which had been hidden from him then was clear now in this room with its windows looking down the chine and over Warbarrow Bay.   The cry of the Man in the God triumphant over his man's anguish and crying aloud " Father, forgive them for they know not what they do."

Very humbly he sat down at his table and wrote a letter to Sir Francis Walsingham, praying him, that if he, Robin, had done anything to earn his favour, it might be shown in the remission of Stafford's crime. He wrote the letter with a great care to say all that he had to say in the fewest words—with so much care, indeed, that he did not notice a certain bustle and movement in the court, or even the opening of his door.

But when he looked up at the end of it, Cynthia was in the doorway watching him.

THE END